DIE Y~

AS ~~~

AS POSSIBLE

THE INCOMPLETE SHORT STORIES

ED MORONEY

outskirts
press

Outskirts Press, Inc.
http://www.outskirtspress.com

ISBN: 978-1-9772-1040-1

Cover Image by Ed Moroney

Outskirts Press and the "OP" logo are trademarks belonging to Outskirts Press, Inc.

PRINTED IN THE UNITED STATES OF AMERICA

"If, after I depart this vale, you ever remember me and have thought to please my ghost, forgive some sinner and wink your eye at some homely girl."

—H.L. Mencken

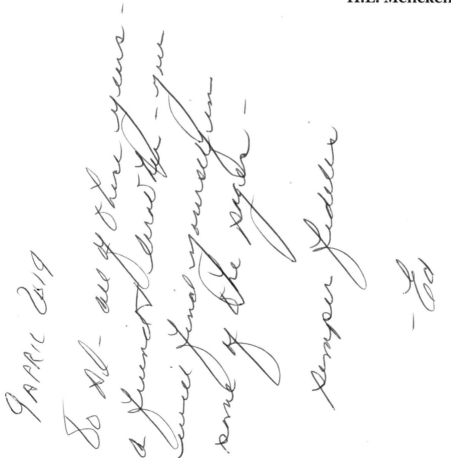

Sunta bona, sunt quaedeam mediocria, sunt plura mala, quae legis hic; aliter non fit, Avite, liber.

- Martial, Epigrammata, XV 16

(Here are some good things, some so-so, and some bad. There's no other way to make a book.)

Dedication

For Zane, Stella, Liam, Vera, Isabella, and Juno. Never has any one grandfather been so fortunate as to have each one of you in my life. Someday you may remember this book existed, and possibly you will read of your grandfather, and hopefully marvel at the man he once was.

Table of Contents

The Marine's Prayer

Almighty Father, whose command is over all and whose love never fails, make me aware of Thy presence and obedient to Thy will. Keep me true to my best self, guarding me against dishonesty in purpose and deed and helping me to live so that I can face my fellow Marines, my loved ones and Thee without shame or fear. Protect my family. Give me the will to do the work of a Marine and to accept my share of responsibilities with vigor and enthusiasm. Grant me the courage to be proficient in my daily performance. Keep me loyal and faithful to my superiors and to the duties my country and the Marine Corps have entrusted to me. Make me considerate of those committed to my leadership. Help me to wear my uniform with dignity, and let it remind me daily of the traditions which I must uphold. If I am inclined to doubt, steady my faith; if I am tempted, make me strong to resist; if I should miss the mark, give me courage to try again. Guide me with the light of truth and grant me wisdom by which I may understand the answer to my prayer. Amen.

...for Tom Bell, Faryl Fletcher, Harry Gill, Chris Jackson, John Kennerly, Ray Tucci, and Fred Kansik (KIA, 15 Jan 1969), Marines all, each a Vietnam Veteran, who sought adventure in their youth, service on behalf of their country, and along the way honed acquired Marine ideals that molded them into the men they are today.

Foreword

The short stories in this collection represent a compilation of some of my personal observations and experiences in my life as a career Marine, police officer, and human being. The title, "Die Young as Old as Possible," evokes an intent to plead with myself to pursue life to its fullest, and for others, to wit the reader, to reflect upon consequential decisions in life.

The title of the book conveys a thought of incomplete stories within its pages, and indeed in each story, I could have easily further entertained and expounded much more extensively than I have. Within the Marines and the police department, there were a limitless supply of characters and incidents from which to draw upon.

This book tells the stories of many persons I have encountered in this life, as all fiction is essentially written with some one person(s) or another in mind. Whomever I have interacted with in my time, should they ever pick up this book, they may think they are reading of themselves. It is possibly they are, and it is also possible they are not. Many of the characters in this book really do exist. Many of the characters are a combination of any number of friends, and, as kindly as I can write, many of who were not my friends.

In this regard, it is incumbent upon me to swear that any correlation to actual persons living or past events is entirely fictional, and the storybook product of my alleged fertile mind. However, I cannot write that without tongue in cheek, because just about everything the reader will absorb did occur to some extent. I trust the reader will be able to discern from the fictional characters and events to what is conceivably nothing more than my mind wandering off from many of my routinely and inattentive brain-walks.

However, there is one character in several of the short stories, who is as genuine as the character I have painted in words. George, "the Mad Munk," Munkelwitz is a real person and a police officer (retired), and who has kindly allowed me to use his real name and street persona within these stories. I consider him to be a good friend, who possessed a mischievous streak, and gleefully bedeviled management within the police department, on behalf of the rank and file police officers. Thank you my friend. Anyone who knew the "Mad Munk" would surely think, how could he not include such a character in any number of short stories he might write?

There is one other person who I need to highlight to some extent, and without revealing his identity. This friend and police officer confronted more incidents and events in his sole career that equaled the careers of fifty police officers. I do not exaggerate. He was every bit the legendary police officer. I purposely apply abstract language in this paragraph to help maintain his anonymity, and I fully confess to adjusting the story to accommodate my intended outcome, to apply some sense of mystery.

There are those who politely, kindly, and patiently reviewed my literary efforts in review for grammatical errors and innovative content. Especially my appreciation to my adjunct English instructors, who are remembered within the lines of some of my stories. Thank you.

I do not think I have done any disservice to friends, confidants, and colleagues. I would remind any reader I wrote entirely of fiction applying a concept of life as the primary requisite and story line. You may ask of me if I wrote about you, and likely I will not tell you if it was you. I like the idea of mystery surrounding some of my stories. However, if you are certain it is you that I write of, then thank you for being a part of my life, and for being you.

This book is my second effort and represents an intent to record memories while entertaining the reader (First Time Death is Still an Amateur). In pursuing this effort, I will receive an ISBN number that will allow me to be present long after my mortality has concluded. I hope my grandchildren enjoy my efforts well into their lives.

The Ghost in Cruiser 322

"I don't suppose you have to believe in ghosts to know that we are all haunted, all of us, by things we can see and feel and guess at, and many more things that we can't."

—Beth Gutcheon
More Than You Know

OFFICER GEORGE MUNKELWITZ hated the police department. Specifically, the Prince George's County Police Department. Oh sure, lots of policemen ending up hating the police department in the twilight of their careers. Pretty standard, but Officer Munkelwitz really hated the department. It was a spiritual and visceral thing with him. It's why he refused to retire.

On this particular occasion, the "Mad Munk," as he was known throughout the job, was working the midnight shift; eleven till eight. It was a Sunday night, and like a Sunday night on the street should be, it was proving to be one of those peaceful nights on duty where the calls were few and generally insignificant. Like barking dog complaints, bullshit burglar alarms, and the occasional domestic argument with scenarios like where the male half wanted to get laid but momma wanted affection instead, and so the whole neighborhood was invited to publicly observe their eternal love for each other.

It didn't matter much to Munk, he was parked behind a very dark and vacated warehouse located in a commercial area to rear of the Bowie/Upper Marlboro police station. As far as he was concerned, he had completed all of his police work for the night. Actually, when he thought about it, he had pretty much completed all of his police work in his career years ago. He just wasn't sure exactly when that crossing over point had occurred. If there were no more calls throughout the night - parked, was where he would stay until check off time.

The spring night air was mild, but thick with an intermittent light rain, causing the street lights to diffuse into huge misty globes, making it difficult to see. Munk enjoyed nights like these. With the window rolled down and a light pattering of mist on his face, he felt as calm as he possibly could these days. He would turn up the radio to that point to where it was just uncomfortable enough for his hearing, but still available in the event a call was dispatched, and then lay his head back on the headrest and would just drift in and out of consciousness. It was always a chance for reflection and the time when he most mourned the loss of his career - which more or less reflected the sense of failure in his life.

Munk had long ago evolved into the "armed report taker" status that so many burned out and embittered cops become. He hadn't made an arrest in three years - not since the incident, anyway. Sometimes it took more creativity and hard work avoiding an arrest situation then it took actually making one arrest. He hadn't written a citation during that time either. In fact, he always joked, that a citizen would have to flag him down, jump in the cruiser and beg for a citation, before he would limber out his pen and ticket book. Even then he would have to think about it real hard.

If the truth were to be known, he was ashamed of the type of police officer he had become. Oh, he knew he would save a life if he could, or chase down an armed robber if one was available. The problem was, that unlike television, such occurrences were few and far in between. However, there were plenty of theft, breaking and entering, and dog bite reports. Of course, there was the "cow in the middle of the road" call last week. Now that was real police work. His response was to ask the dispatcher if she thought he was "Heidi of the Swiss Alps?" The sergeant's response was a counseling form for improper radio procedures.

Munk laughed thinking about it. He stared up at the ceiling of the cruiser with his arms crossed in front of him. He was feeling dull and sleepy. So long ago, that one incident, he thought.

It had been a very messy accident scene on the beltway southbound just past Landover Road. He was the first police officer to arrive - even before rescue personnel. As he approached the turned over tractor-trailer, he was shocked to see that he wouldn't be able to get close without stepping in the blood that was steadily oozing from underneath the edge of the trailer. As he got closer, he could see what surprisingly turned out to be a portion of a squashed aluminum shed protruding from under the trailer. It looked to be about a six by eight, or ten, in size as he recalled. The beltway was total havoc; completely closed down with people screaming at him to do something. What the hell could he do? It took a few minutes, eventually he determined from a hysterical middle-aged black man that his two sons and a son-in-law were inside the shed. They had gone to the local Sears and bought an already assembled garden shed for a good price and tried to take it home on the back of their pickup truck. His two sons and son-in-law were the ballast inside the shed to keep it from blowing off. Only it did blow off - and a trucker in his rig following behind the pickup truck desperately tried to avoid hitting the tumbling shed. Combined with the screech of tortured air brakes and the sound of pavement peeling away tires by the inch, the trucker had skidded straight across the shed. He couldn't have done better if he had been aiming for it. As the rig's huge tires crushed the shed, the trucker still fighting with his rig and the laws of physics, incurred an abrupt tottering swerve, and the trailer came to rest square on top of the shed - and, the two brothers and a son-in-law.

Okay, that was bad enough. There just wasn't anything that could be done to help. However, it didn't stop there. While everyone was standing back and watching the cranes lift the trailer from off of the shed, one of the white firefighters chose just that moment to become stupid. The firefighter was a new hire to the fire department and was originally from Georgia. While observing the scene at hand, he had remarked in an aside to another fireman, "I guess you all can your niggers up here." Unfortunately, another firefighter - a black firefighter - a black firefighter in which two of his cousins, and one cousin by marriage, were inside the crumpled shed - overheard the exchange.

And the shit was on! It took every officer at the scene to break up the fight - in the middle of the beltway - with traffic backed up for miles - hundreds of bystanders watching - huge glaring lights illuminating the scene - and, with a reporter from every local newspaper and television station in the Washington DC area gleefully recording the outbreak.

In Prince George's County, a fight at the scene of an accident was a fairly common occurrence. However, the film at eleven wasn't well received by a police chief who was sensitive to racial politics and who was more interested in keeping his job. If you watched closely, or frame by frame courtesy of the networks, you could see Munk in the center of the melee trying to break up the fight, and where he was recorded striking a combatant with a nightstick, and subsequently arresting that combatant in a brief but obviously violent struggle. Which, as it turned out, unfortunately for Munk, was the offended black firefighter? It didn't play well in the public eye for the next few weeks. He didn't know who the person was and he certainly had no idea what started everything. All he knew was that this guy was hysterically whaling on some guy screaming, "YOU WHITE MOTHERFUCKER!" He was uncontrollable - and underneath him was somebody screeching for help.

Munk awoke with a start as the radio came to life. A call - but, not for him. The dispatcher had a soft voice and for a moment he wondered what she looked like? Probably best not to know, he thought. He laid his head back again, closed his eyes, and tucked his arms in tighter. The bitterness swelled within him like it had happened yesterday.

Onto the political sacrificial bonfire went Munk. And what a weenie roast it was. Every day in the newspapers and on TV at night. His whole career was on display for everyone to observe and comment upon. Even old complaints surfaced; basically the inevitable stuff in any cop's career, minor infractions actually, but all of which were supposed to be confidential investigations deep within the files of the internal affairs section. Munk often wondered how they were leaked to the press, but he could only guess. During all of it the Chief was his usual noncommittal self while hanging out the Mad Munk to dry.

It was only a matter of time before the department farmed him out to some station where he would not be heard from again.

Until the black firefighter appeared on a local talk show discussing racism and gave his side of the story. Amazingly, he admitted resisting the officer's attempts to break up the fight. He even said that he recalled striking the officer a few times while trying to break free to get back to his intended target. He was distraught with emotion due to the deaths of his cousins and just snapped when he overheard his supposed co-worker's comments. His anger was towards an insensitive and racist co-worker - not the police officer. Sure, everybody who wasn't a racist could understand his attitude.

The black firefighter eventually worked out a deal with the courts and received probation with a promise of a clean record in a year - and, kept his job. The co-worker was fired.

And Munk was eventually exonerated. Nobody ever apologized though. In fact, shortly thereafter he was transferred to his present station, which in a way was sort of a punitive action. Of course, he expected it, but he was never given any reason, other than it being management's prerogative to send him anywhere they pleased. However, it was intimated to him that due to his recent notoriety, it would be best if he were sent to a rear station where the pace was much slower. That way, it was more probable that he would be able to avoid any further complications in his career. So now he was assigned to a station with all the other burnouts, civil liabilities, and former lead stories on the six o'clock news.

In all that time the Chief never once publicly or privately offered him any support. Well, he's still the Chief, thought Munk, and I'm still a cop - well, sort of.

It's funny, mused Munk. Most people think that cops burn out from the stresses associated with the job. Nothing could be further from the truth. It was the politics, the maneuvering for power, and betrayals by the department's leaders that broke most cops.

Munk sighed, shifted his position in the seat to where he was slightly wedged into the corner with his head resting against the doorpost. He stretched his legs out for a second, tucked his hands under his arms, closed his eyes and let out a deep breath. Yeah, he wasn't going to retire anytime soon. He would see the Chief go first, and hopefully, if he was lucky, he would find some way to help the Chief on his way. He was looking. He had already collected some stuff, but not enough. Something would come up. Everybody was dirty. Then it was phone calls and faxes to the right sources. The Mad Munk chuckled to himself, it was only a matter of time, he thought, as he drifted off....

Munk's eyes suddenly flicked open. He stared! Fright surged through his body. He was momentarily paralyzed with fear. There was someone else in the cruiser with him. Eyes wide with terror, he let out a yelp. Trying to draw his gun from his right side, his other hand spasmodically clawed for the door handle. The door suddenly opened and he fell out backwards onto the pavement with his feet still in the car and a half-drawn gun pointing at the ceiling of the cruiser. Rolling to his right and scrambling to his feet he fled from his cruiser with his fully drawn gun pumping up and down with every fear driven stride. He looked over his shoulder to see if he was being chased. When he saw that he was alone, he stopped running and turned around to face his cruiser. Bent over, while trying to catch his breath, gun at the ready he peered at the cruiser with the driver's door wide open, now about sixty feet away.

"Ah, Jesus, Jesus, sweet Jesus!" he gasped. He stared at his cruiser. Police cruisers don't have interior lights, so it was dark inside. He could see a faint outline of.... somebody .... someone on the passenger's side. Vague outline of a head.... with lots of hair....it looked like a female!

"HEEEYYY! Who the hell are you!? Better yet, where did you come from?" Munk demanded.

A woman's voice responded in return. Yet, strangely soothing in its tone. It actually had a calming effect. "George, don't worry. Please, come back and get in and I'll try to explain. I didn't mean to startle you."

He started cautiously towards his cruiser. "You didn't startle me; you scared the shit out of me!" How did she get in there? He had locked all the doors. It was the first thing he always did when dozing off. He looked around expecting fellow police officers to come out of hiding from somewhere while simultaneously laughing hysterically because they had caught him asleep and vulnerable.

He walked back toward the cruiser, stopped by the open door, bent over and looked in.

"Hi," she said. "Come on, get in."

There was a smattering of reflected light derived from the street lights and the mist and he could see her a little clearer now. She appeared to be a police officer, or at least she was wearing what looked like a uniform similar to his own. He squatted down, reached in and turned on the dome light. He blinked. She was sitting in the corner with her back to the passenger's door, her left leg curled up on the seat, and her hands resting in her lap on top of each other. "Hello," she said. She was a police officer as best as he could tell from her uniform and badge.

His eyes searched around the interior of the cruiser for any other possible surprises that he could meet, then very slowly, while keeping his newly acquired passenger in full view, he carefully got back into his cruiser. "Hello," he said. "Now do you mind telling me who you are?" She looked familiar. "Do I know you?" He looked at her nameplate and it read "MCNULTY." McNulty, he thought, where, where, do I know that name? She had an attractive face, but it was the hair that he noticed. Thick dishwater blonde hair, every strand in place cut pageboy style, where the hair fell across her cheeks and the ends slightly curled under her chin. It just happened to be one of his favorite hair styles on women. A pleated skirt just above the knees would have completed the picture, he thought. The Mad Munk could never look at a female without considering her sexual worth. A slow smile crept across her face.

Then he noticed. Her badge was the department's old style. The one they used to call a cookie cutter because it was thin brass pressed into the shape of a standard "shield" style police badge. The department changed over from that style ten years ago. Odd. Her gun was a Smith and Wesson .38 with a six-inch barrel. Everyone now carried the new Baretta 9MM semiautomatics.

What the hell was it about her that was so familiar? "Don't I know you? I'll bet the fellows put you up to this to scare the shit out me, right?" Just like that time a few years back when he was dispatched to take a death report in the middle of the night. His fellow officers had a friend made up to appear deceased and when he bent over the corpse to conduct the required examination for any unexplained orifices - it came alive! As he was fleeing out the front door, he passed the whole squad convulsing with laughter. It was funny now - not so funny then.

"No, George, you don't know me."

The voice, so strange. Sort of musical.... like windchimes in a gentle breeze.

Then it struck him. No way! It couldn't be! His face drained of blood and he stared at her. He could feel the back of his neck begin to crawl. She's dead! Or supposed to be. "You're Officer Kathy McNulty...on the academy wall." He refused to believe it.

She smiled. Yes, George, that's right."

"Aw, Jesus! Now it's confirmed," he moaned. "The job has finally taken what's left of my sanity."

She laughed, and in that musical voice of hers, she said, "I'm really here George and you're alright. Please, believe me."

He just stared at her. It all came back to him now. He recalled that an academy instructor one day had discussed the mystery surrounding Kathy's in-the-line-of-duty-death as a result of a terrible accident after a long fast car chase into DC. She had died on impact, but in the coroner's final report, he had noted that the front of her uniform shirt had been soaked with tears, as if she had been crying throughout the whole chase. The instructor said that some hours prior to the chase she had cleared a call involving the death of a young boy. She had gone to an address to check on his welfare who had not been seen by the neighborhood children in the last few days. The neighborhood parents were worried because the mother was always acting strange and she didn't take very good care of the child. As a result, the police were always being called. When the mother answered the door, it was obvious that she was disoriented, but she refused to allow the officers to come inside. Suspecting something was wrong, based upon the demeanor of the mother, Kathy pushed her way into the apartment and immediately observed the child covered up and sleeping on the couch. The mother immediately began screeching and had to be restrained by another officer. Kathy went over to check on the child. The child appeared to be asleep but something didn't appear just quite right. She touched the child's cheek and found it to be very cold. Concerned for the child, she quickly pulled the blanket back and found the child to be nude - with his chest cavity fully eviscerated. The child's organs were later located in the freezer, where each organ had been placed in a separate zip lock baggie and stacked neatly on the freezer shelf.

Did she die that night from inattention to survival skills

during the chase? Distraction due to the emotional trauma of seeing the eviscerated child? Or did she die by her own hand? Maybe her sergeant should have sent her home that night. Who knows?

"Are you a ghost?" he asked. What the hell else would explain this?

She smiled. "I don't know. Maybe. I'm just here to help you."

"Can I touch you?" He tentatively extended a finger.

"Sure, go ahead, it won't pass through."

He looked at his finger, brought his arm in, and said, "I think I'll pass." She just smiled. Always the smiles.

"Can you do one of those fading acts, where you disappear in layers, like, uummm, first the skin, then the circulatory system, and eventually down to your skeleton? You know, like in the movies?"

"I don't know, I've never tried. I don't think so. That would really scare hell out of you then, wouldn't it?" she asked.

Munk laughed. Thought about it for a second. "Yeah, I guess. Well, what about a God? Does one really exist? And did you come from heaven?" The Mad Munk was going to get out of this all he possibly could while he had the chance.

She smiled at George and said, "I'm sorry George, I'm not trying to avoid your questions. It's just that I could never adequately explain the complexities associated with where I came from."

"Oh, I see, it's back to the faith thing again." George sighed, "Well, exactly why are you here? Can you tell me that much?"

"Yes, of course. That's no problem. I'm here to help you in a fast chase that you're about to become involved in."

Munk stared at her disbelieving. Then he started laughing. "I'm sorry, but you don't understand. I don't do police work anymore. I'm retired - retired on the job. I just write a report when I'm called to a scene, and submit it at the end of my shift. Somebody else does the police work. Real simple.

In between calls I read books. I don't want to be bothered by anyone."

She smiled. "I know that George. However, tonight is different. You wouldn't allow a fellow police officer to be unnecessarily hurt, would you?"

He looked at her quizzically. "Well no, of course not. But what the hell's going to happen while we're sitting here? There isn't a cop around for miles."

"I didn't think so. You're right; there aren't any cops around for miles." She hesitated and looked down at her hands and was very still. Softly she said, "A Maryland State Trooper was just shot three times a few minutes ago. He was on a traffic stop at Route 301 North and Croom Road. He's alive, and is in fact, right now, chasing the suspects in their vehicle on Route 301 northbound. His vest stopped two of the rounds, but a shoulder wound is bleeding profusely. He will only be able to maintain consciousness for a few more minutes." She looked at him expectantly.

His eyes were wide. "How can that possible be? How do you know that?" But even as he asked - very faintly.... a siren, way off, was but becoming louder.

Just then the radio split the moment, "Any cars in the area of Route 301 North and Pennsylvania Avenue, State is chasing on 301 north a dark blue 88 Chevy Cavalier with Maryland registration Adam-Baker-Charlie four-seven-one in which the suspects are wanted for a shooting. The information that we are getting from state is a little confusing but apparently the chasing trooper may have been wounded during a traffic stop with the suspects. The last State heard was that their trooper was passing Pennsylvania Avenue."

Even before the dispatcher had completed her transmission, he had shot out of the parking lot and skidded onto Trade Zone Ave and sped towards Route 301, where he was now poised on the median crossover.

Tense hands gripping the steering wheel, Munk was

hunched over the wheel looking past his passenger, stretching his sight south down the northbound lane of 301. He was practically bouncing up and down in his seat, "Come on you sons of bitches, I'm waiting for you!"

She was calmly gazing out the passenger window. Jesus she's laid back. He noticed she wasn't wearing her seatbelt. "Quickly, put your seatbelt on!" he ordered. She turned towards him and just smiled, "Sure, George." and then she added, "I appreciate your concern."

He never heard her. The siren was getting louder, the sound always traveling further at night. Then...in the distance, just below the horizon, creeping into view, were what had to be the trooper's red and blue emergency lights. Spinning crazily into the night and surrounded by a brighter glow of moving headlights, a car with its hi-beams on crested the hill at a high rate of speed. Barely a second behind was the trooper.

"Jesus Christ, they're moving!" Munk snatched the microphone, and while consciously instructing himself to sound calm (so that afterwards, everyone would remark how cool under fire he sounded, after all, situations like this was how reputations were made), casually announced, "Radio, I have the trooper north on 301 approaching Trade Zone Avenue. And they're moving! I'm in pursuit!" Munk flung the microphone on the seat beside him and stabbed at the button that turned on his red and blue emergency lights. "Let the bastards see me as they're coming!" he said to no one in particular.

The fleeing car came flying past with the trooper keeping a safe distance behind, both vehicles cutting through Munk's cruiser's hi-beams, and for an instant he could see two people in the suspect's car. Munk mashed the accelerator and fishtailed onto 301, then floored it as the engine screamed in protest as he tried to get up to speed. Caught by surprise as his cruiser skidded on the pavement, he exclaimed, "Jesus, I've got to remember the streets are wet!" He glanced over at his passenger. She was calmly looking ahead and he noticed that she was holding the microphone.

He turned his attention back to the pursuit. In what seemed like minutes, Munk was quickly behind the trooper who was in the left lane. He flicked a glance at the speedometer - they were pushing the 100 MPH mark. Something was wrong. The trooper's cruiser would begin to drift off of the road onto the shoulder, and just when the trooper seemed to realize the danger, he would jerk the cruiser back onto the road. Not a smooth maneuver by any means.

"He's beginning to lose consciousness because of the loss of blood, George. He needs help. He probably doesn't even know we're with him."

"Well then do something!" he yelled. "You're the omniscient one!"

"I'm sorry George; you'll have to do it alone. I'm here to help you - not him."

"Well this isn't helping me!" That pissed him off. He flung the cruiser into the right lane and sped up beside the trooper. Carefully watching the trooper, beginning to drift to his left, he switched the spotlight on and lighted up the interior of the trooper's cruiser. Holy shit! The trooper's right side from the neck down was dark from blood. His facial muscles were strained so tight that his face appeared to be preparing to assume rigor. He looked like a dead man driving and probably soon would be if he didn't get help immediately. By now, the trooper's driving was becoming very erratic and Munk had to keep jockeying his cruiser position in order to keep the spotlight on the cruiser. He could see that they were falling behind the suspects. He flicked the spotlight on and off a few times into the trooper's face. The trooper blinked - and his cruiser began to slow down.

Munk jammed the accelerator down and he shot forward. In the rear-view mirror, he saw the trooper stop partially off the road, left wheels on the shoulder. He felt around on the seat for the mike, found the cord and yanked on it, but his passenger said, "I've got it George; I'll let the dispatcher know where to send help."

Munk grinned. He would like to see the dispatcher's face when that transmission was being made. He was going to have a lot of explaining to do when this was over. He was gaining and his hi-beams outlined the rear of the vehicle. The passenger was constantly turning around looking back at him. The driver was hunched over the wheel intent on his driving. Munk punched a button and the take down lights flicked on bathing the fleeing car in bright light. He could see inside now. He adjusted his cruiser to where whenever they looked in any of their mirrors, all they would see is police cruiser. The passenger turned towards him and he could see his face fully. He was terrified and he was yelling something at the driver. In the next moment he spun completely around and reached out the window with his left arm and pointed a gun, firing it three times!

Munk yanked the wheel hard to the right, and then swerved back to the left. Three flashes. A round struck the roof line over the passenger's side. Aw, Christ! I hope Kathy doesn't get hit. Then he laughed out loud - what difference would it make. Two bullets passed through the windshield, one went between the two of them, and out the rear window. Shit! The window was starred and wind was whistling through the hole, but it was still intact. It sounded eerie. Appropriate, thought Munk.

Route 50 was coming up. Bridge construction over Route 301 for the past three months had whittled the northern route down to only one lane. The fleeing car began to slow a little. Trying to make a decision which way to go, I'll bet. The driver chose straight ahead and fled for the construction area. The car swerved into a funneled lane outlined by orange traffic cones that caught Munk by surprise. Before he knew it, he was speeding over a string of orange cones that were being spit out from underneath his cruiser, and in his rear-view mirror, he could see a huge roostertail of cones flying into the air and crazily bouncing on the ground spinning off into every direction. "HaHaaaa!" He had always wanted to do that.

They were approaching the Bowie exit now. The fleeing car started to slow and began edging to the left. What the hell are they doing? Giving up? Suddenly, without warning, it veered to the right and onto the exit into Bowie. Once again, the maneuver caught Munk by surprise. He snapped the wheel to the right trying to follow. Tires screeched and the cruiser started skidding to the left. He had been too far right to make such an abrupt maneuver. He was losing it. Shit! He jerked hard on the wheel trying to turn left into the skid that was less than a second away from crashing into a barrier. As hard as he tried, the steering wheel wouldn't turn. But it was turning - turning in his hands, only slightly though. Confusion pummeled his senses - wait, the cruiser had straightened, and was under control again. It occurred to him that maybe it wasn't him who had been driving his cruiser through those last few seconds. God, that was close. He pushed the thought away. He was speeding down the exit now and behind the suspects again. "Aw shit! They're going into a housing area. They're going to try and lose me on the side streets." The suspects turned their car a hard left onto Belair Drive, the back end swerved right, struck a curb blowing the right rear tire, the rim scraping concrete erupting into a shower of sparks for a few feet. Now their car disabled, they couldn't go as fast, but they were trying. Even wobbling down the road, throwing off pieces of tread, they were trying to get their speed up. The Mad Munk was on their ass now.

Munk knew what was coming. They were going to turn on a side street and bail out at the first opportune moment. It would be hell trying to capture both of them among all of these houses. So far, he was still the only police officer in the chase. Many others were coming he was sure, but when? "I don't want to get in a foot chase," Munk wailed.

"George, they're going to turn onto Knowledge Lane," she said suddenly.

He chanced a quick glance at her. That's three blocks away. They could turn onto any number of streets before then. She was smiling. Not even hanging onto anything for stability. Just as casual as you please. She could at least show some excitement. The term "demure" clicked into his thoughts.

It was then he saw a cruiser approaching fast from the opposite direction. That cruiser is going to force them to turn, there's more behind him, and they know it, he thought. Even as he realized what was coming, the suspects turned violently onto Knowledge Lane, and Munk could hear the car's engine protesting as the driver mashed the gas pedal down.

"Awww, fuck it! I'm through playing." Munk impulsively swung the cruiser to the left - up, over the curb, onto the sidewalk, and with the rear end swaying from left to right, desperately trying to regain traction, shot across the lawn of the corner house. He floored it - and aimed for the side of the suspect's vehicle - right for where the driver's door is located. The tires were gouging the lawn and spewing trails of grass and dirt as the cruiser fought for traction. Somebody's going to be pissed. He stretched his arms to full length on the wheel and braced himself for impact. "Hang on!" he screamed. "YeeeeeeHaaaaahhhaa!"

The cruiser smashed into the side of the suspect's car. The cruiser's front end bowed in, the hood flew up, and the radiator exploded, engulfing both cars in a fog of white hissing steam. Munk grabbed for his gun, fumbled for a second with the seat belt, and bolted out of the cruiser. He ran around to the passenger's side, because nobody was coming out the driver's side, and pointed his gun through the open window. It was unnecessary. Both suspects were alive, but the driver was bleeding from a head injury and his right arm appeared to be broken. The passenger was just simply crying.

It was all over. Munk stood off from the wrecked cars and surveyed the scene. There were at least a dozen police cruisers at the scene now, and both suspects were safely secured and under arrest. There would be plenty of charges. In total - it amounted to about ten to fifteen minutes worth of excitement. Enough to last most people a lifetime. The paperwork would take hours.

Munk looked over at the yard he had driven through. The sergeant was standing talking to the owner, who was dressed in pajamas and a robe, and evidently very angry as determined by the waving arms and worked up expression on his face. There were only a couple of deep furrows running diagonally across the yard. It wasn't really that much to get upset over, thought the Munk, the county would pay for the repairs - hopefully.

Munk chuckled to himself. Then it hit him. Oh shit! Kathy. He had forgotten about her. He ran over to the passenger's side of the cruiser. Gone. Of course, she's gone. Well, what the hell did he expect - stay around and meet the fellows? He opened the door and looked in. The seat belt was still hooked up. On the seat, a badge - he could see immediately, due to its old style that it was her badge. He bent down, picked it up, and rubbed his thumb across the face. Her ID number, number 869, in blackened numbers, was engraved into a scroll above the county seal. He looked back down at the seat. Then he saw it. It was about twelve inches below the headrest - a neat, clean bullet hole. It must have struck somewhere around her heart. He looked in the back. It had also gone through the back seat too. Probably in the trunk somewhere.

"George!" he looked up. A fellow squad member, Doug Lileks, was walking towards him. "You okay? Man, that was something! You should have heard yourself on the radio. You sounded some kind of laid back. Every time you gave out your location, you would've thought you were carrying on a simple conversation. I'm impressed." He slapped George on the shoulder.

"Yeah, I'm alright. Thanks. I could use some help with all of the paperwork though. By the way, what's the status on the trooper?"

"No problem with the paperwork. The sarge already assigned two of us to help. The dispatcher came across a few minutes ago and said that fireboard says he's stable and should make it. Fortunately, where he ended up at was only half of a mile from a fire station. He's being air-evaced to Baltimore." Another slap on the shoulder. "I'm telling you, that was out-fucking-standing!" He turned and started to walk away, and over his shoulder, "See you at the station."

Munk looked down at the badge in his hand. It was shiny, as if it had been recently polished. Weird. A ghost...something...Kathy, had given him what originally seemed like an intangible object that he now held in his hand. He never did give out any locations during the chase. He was too excited to remember that simple requirement. He closed his hand about the badge and slipped it into his pocket. He smiled to himself. No one would ever believe him. He looked about him. Time to go back to work.

It was soft across his cheek. An airy sensation - but real. It was a feeling as if....as if, he had been kissed. There was a slight feeling of being touched, then warmth, with a lingering sensation of moisture on his cheek. Puzzled, he reached up - and his cheek was wet. He heard her then, barely a whisper - "Stay safe, George. Whether you realize it or not, you're a fine police officer. Goodbye."

The Mad Munk felt for the badge in his pocket. It was gone. Maybe he had dropped it onto the ground by accident. No, it wasn't there either. He was still standing in the same position he had been when he was examining the badge in his hand, and then had slipped it into his pocket. He experienced a fleeting sense of melancholy. Yet, he knew he had done well, and that was cause for some good feelings. He laughed out loud. Yeah, he was the police again. It didn't feel so bad either. "Goodbye, Kathy," he said out loud. He turned away and looked for Doug. Spying him standing by his cruiser he yelled, "Yohhhh Doug! Need a ride back to the station."

1XD (1 Chicken Dinner)

"And believe me, a good piece of chicken can make any-body believe in the existence of God."

—Sherman Alexie
The Absolutely True Diary of a Part-Time Indian

HE WAS JUST an old man. Another amongst many we all come across in our lives. They are there, we just don't see them. He was to touch my life though and his loss would become more acute as my years passed as I was also being absorbed into that transparent aspect of our population.

There was nothing especially remarkable about him. He was of average height, slightly stooped, a fringe of white hair at the outer edges of a bald pate, and always wore the same black horn-rimmed glasses ever since I knew him. He could be cantankerous and often times he was just plain grouchy. Other times he just seemed to be lost in thought. He smoked too much.

I worked for him for many years as a store clerk in his private chicken "take home" restaurant business called Mister Chicken. He was Mister Chicken. I worked for him while I was in high school and when I came home from the Marines after a tour in Vietnam. The government told him that he had to give me my old job back of a dollar and a quarter an hour. He served broasted...not fried... chicken. It was a "take home" restaurant and not a "carry out" restaurant. He often emphasized to me this distinct characteristic of his business. I didn't see any difference, but neither did I understand many such subtle distinctions while my personality was still forming.

His real name was John, but went by Jack. Why...I have no idea. I and the other clerks just called him "Boss" and would do so all of our lives.

I do remember that chicken though. It did not taste like "fried" chicken. Fresh from the broaster it was crispy and had a golden color and it was moist to the bone. It was delicious and I would eat way too much of it over the years. He said the taste was because the chicken was cooked under pressure and not just dropped into a fryer. Oh yeah, there was a secret recipe too. All I knew was that I took boxes and boxes of chicken, threw some sort of special flour all over the pieces, and put everything into a manually cranked device to ensure the chicken pieces were thoroughly dusted. When people order a dinner, or called in a "take home" order, I would enter the order as "1XD" on the ticket, the "X" representing the chicken part of the order. That was the only shorthand we had for any item on the menu. I always thought the "X" was a reference to the poor chicken no longer being of this world.

He was often short and temperamental with customers. He did not accept complaints well. When a customer would come in and ask for all white meat or dark meat, or they did not want any wings, I would just stand back and watch occur the subtle humiliation of the customer. You see, God made chickens a certain way and each has two breasts, thighs, legs, and wings. A four-piece dinner comes with a breast, thigh, leg and wing. That is the way he served his meals and he was not going to change it based upon a customer's request. Of course, we served three-piece dinners too but he never explained to me how he decided what pieces went into that meal. Well, regardless, his product was just so good that he could get away with upsetting the occasional customer. In town they talked about what a contrary bastard he was but that his chicken was some kind of good. I had seen some customers depart the store muttering about how they were going to come back and burn the place down.

To me he was a contrary sonofabitch at times! He was also one of the great men I would admire in my life. I learned much from him and although it took a while, I also learned he had a great sense of humor and liked to play practical jokes. I and other clerks liked to occasionally call the store, or another clerk, and when he, or the other clerk answered, "Mister Chicken!" we always asked is this "Mister Chicken?" Invariably the answer was always a subtly irritated response of "yes," which set up the moment and we responded, "Well, this is Mrs. Chicken get your ass home!" and hang up. Okay, so you had to be there. We thought it was funny. Still do now that I think about it.

One time, when he had expanded his menu to include hamburgers, he liked to slip a plastic cup cover under the patty and then studiously watch you take your first bite. He loved the puzzled expression that would invariably appear on your face while questioningly looking at your hamburger. It would be many years before I could trust a cheeseburger again.

When business was slow, we would talk about many things. He would sit in the back of the store, invariably smoking, while telling me about his youth. He grew up in Michigan and in his first business he owned a drive-in hamburger restaurant, which he lost to his first wife in a divorce. He never had a kind word for that woman. In my limited and developing cognition abilities I could tell he had been deeply hurt. During World War II he worked in a bomber aircraft factory. He was a critical skilled laborer and therefore was exempt from the draft. He moved to Maryland to start his chicken restaurant but mostly to escape his ex-wife. He was married again by the time he moved to Maryland but she was twenty years his junior in age, which I thought was pretty cool and gave me great hope for my old age someday. She was Italian and he said they were the best women to marry. So later I married an Italian too, but I am not so sure his advice was as insightful on that occasion.

Once when I was in the car with him when he was backing his Buick out of his driveway he stopped suddenly and said, "Look at that rock." There was a large rock about the size of a football at the edge of the curb next to his driveway. It was multifaceted and reflected earthy pink and beige hues in the sunlight. He said it was a rock whose consistency was of quartz. He thought it was interesting, and remarked the way the sun played across the varied surfaces. I thought it was just a rock and never gave it another thought. Why would anyone take out time to look at a rock?

Many years later I would remember such a seemingly irrelevant event in any one person's life while in Colorado exploring an old gold mining site. I found a large gray rock, about half the size of a football, and it was completely freckled with gold flecks. Gold...maybe? The one last remaining piece that some miner had overlooked? In my hands it was heavy and dense and in the sunlight it sparkled magnificently. My brother who was with me at the time was thoroughly impressed with my find. Yet, in those few seconds my memory forced to the forefront of my thoughts, so many years ago, of an old man admiring a quartz rock. In that minor and inconsequential epiphany, I had become a little bit wiser as inadvertently induced by that old man from so many years ago.

He would live to the ripe old age of eighty-eight. I would go over to his house to visit him in my encroaching old age. Although I never visited him as often as I should have before he died. He always appreciated my visits and we would sit together in the living room, he invariably smoking, with an oxygen machine beside his chair to assist him in breathing as a result of a diagnosis of emphysema. I would chide him for his smoking habit and he would just laugh and ask me if I really thought stopping would make a difference in his life now. I have to confess he really did have a valid argument.

I used to take him for walks in the neighborhood. Not far for he did not have much energy. I watched him closely as he shuffled along ready for any moment in which he might stumble and fall, while wondering how much longer it would be before I needed someone to similarly watch me. It was one of those occasions when he suddenly said to me that he felt very lucky to have me for a friend. I was slightly taken aback because I had never had anyone say that to me before. I just patted him on that shoulder and said thanks. I should have told him that he was one of the great men in my life. I did not.

He died suddenly shortly after that time. In the middle of the night he had awakened and gotten up to use the bathroom.

An urge in my encroaching old age I know so very well. I assumed through a combination of old age and grogginess and the discomfort of a treacherous and likely only partially filled bladder, which would surely require a concentration and an exertion to void the small amount of pressing urine, he had lost his balance and struck his head. He survived in a coma for only two days.

I presented the eulogy the day of his funeral. He was cremated. I wrote a poem entitled "1XD" and told everyone it was written by a famous poet. Of course, I was not famous, maybe not even a poet either. It was a febrile attempt at humor at the time. Nobody asked who the famous poet was. I have been to many funerals and I have heard many eulogies, as has each of us. I do not think eulogies ever do credit to a person. I do not think I did well that day in my ten or so minutes of the summation of my friend's life. I told of how cranky he could get and of the occasions when he was mad at me, because it was humorous. One should always bring a little levity to death. I also told of how he never held his anger against me or any other clerk. That he was one of the hardest of working men I had ever known, and who continued to work long days in his restaurant well into his eighties. I did not adequately convey, whether due to an inability to do so, or I just forgot, or did not see it at the time, a realization of this man's influence in my life. I am sorry.

I think of the Boss on occasions and always when there is something to do with chicken. I and fellow clerks all readily agree that we have never had chicken since that was as good as when we worked at Mister Chicken. Oddly I sometimes think of him too when I have the urge in the middle of the night. Thanks to my friend I take those few extra seconds to insure I have my balance before I confront both my treacherous bladder and my just before ripe old age...every night.

A Cancer So Venomous

"If I had terminal cancer, I had a few weeks to live, I was in a tremendous amount of pain - if they just effectively wanted to turn off the switch and legalize that by legalizing euthanasia, I'd want that."

—**John Key**

THE OLD MAN was dying.

He lay in a hospice bed, in which the upper third of the bed was partially raised. To an onlooker he seemed almost lifeless and inert. Whenever he was awake and seemingly alert, albeit essentially in a state of half consciousness, his view was limited to the confines of his hospice room. A room painted a pastel blue color likely intended to aid in easing the anxieties of the dying person. There was a window off to his right that caught the morning sun. Early in the mornings he would awake to brilliant sunshine pouring through the window and splattering across the floor. He would stare at the sunlight as it slowly eroded by the hour as the sun traveled across the roof of the building, usually gone by the noon hour. He would laugh inwardly and tell himself by concentrating on the sunlight in his room he was practicing for when he saw that bright light everyone talks about as you die. He liked that he still retained some sense of humor. Every day he had a different hospice volunteer in his room trying to keep him comfortable, and they would to a person pull the curtains shut thinking the sunlight was too bright for him in his condition. With mammoth effort he would feebly raise his hands, slowly turn his head left and right, and hoarsely complain that he wanted the curtains left open.

He was half conscious most of the day, but during the remainder of time he slept. For the first time in his life he did not appreciate the extensive hours of sleep. Yet, his failing body demanded he sleep in some vain effort to try and defend against the monster eating his body. He was fully aware he was dying and although he did not especially feel any great concern or anxiety, he was angry that his body was under attack by a cancer and that biology was choosing his manner of death and not he. After 84 years of life, and after all that he had done, and all of the times he had almost died from previous illnesses, or accidents, or wars, or his time as a police officer, he now had to lay recumbent while wearing a diaper and waiting for the one cancer cell leading the pack to climb the hill and plant the flag and declare victory. He did not want to die this way, and really, who does? And there wasn't anything he could do about it.

It was during one of his few remaining days when he awoke in the afternoon that he saw the snake. In addition to a room window in his hospice room there was a sliding glass door that opened onto a pinkish-reddish flagstone patio into the backyard. The hospice workers would usually keep the curtain closed in the morning, thinking that would be too much sunlight for him also. Usually about early afternoon, at that time of day when the sun having passed well overhead above the hospice, which routinely extinguished the blinding glare that daily invaded his room, they would pull the curtains back allowing him to see markedly into the backyard, where with his glasses on he would stare outside by the hours, immobile, contemplative, dying. This afternoon he could see clearly outside into the yard allowing him on this occasion to see the snake, who was coiled and motionless and about six feet from the door. He immediately recognized the brown, black and tan markings as a copperhead... poisonous, looked to be about four feet in length. Although the snake's head was facing directly toward the sliding glass door its eyes were closed and there was no movement. The snake appeared quite content. Unlike how he felt. He continued to stare at the snake and wondered where in the surrounding woods that it lived.

He did not like snakes, and didn't know anyone who did. He remembered a time in the Marines when he was down in French Guiana training with the French Foreign Legion, who were the instructors for a jungle commando course. He hated the fucking jungle ever since his time in Vietnam. There were insects and diseases and animals in the jungle that scientists were still discovering to this day. The Legionnaires had a large boa constrictor locked up in a large wooden hut. That damned snake had better living conditions than the Marines and Legionnaires. The idea was for each of the Marines in attendance to pin the boa down with a tree branch and then grab it behind its head and pick it up. What the Legionnaires referred to as an exercise in snake familiarization. After twenty-five plus Marines had engaged in this familiarization exercise it was his turn. By this time the boa was quite angry and was hissing and striking out at anything within close proximity in protest. Fortunately for him he was the ranking officer in the hut and no one could order him to pick up that fucking snake. Later in the week some French military high-ranking officers came through the encampment, and in their honor the boa was killed, skinned, cooked, and fed to the Marines and visitors. Ironically enough it actually tasted like chicken, although with a somewhat tougher consistency.

He thought he should tell the hospice worker about the snake, who was not present at the moment, and who likely stepped out to get something to eat or go to the bathroom. Wasn't there a danger for anyone walking around the yard, especially if they should come upon it by surprise? After a few moments of intently observing the snake he thought that it was indeed an awesome creature. Ruefully he admitted to himself, if he wasn't dying, and was healthy, he would be looking for a shovel to cut its head off. The warm and bright sunlight highlighted his markings. He knew persons who had been bitten by copperheads and of course they had become very ill. The venom could do everything from paralyze a victim to making you believe you had been set on fire, with all of the associated illness, vomiting, and diarrhea. Probably a few other physiological miseries too. Ironically, even without the anti-venom serum most persons survived an attack, unless prior to the bite there was something frail about the person, like already having a debilitating disease, or an allergy, or a woman who is pregnant. Or, he thought, like an aging and feeble man with cancer who is days away from dying.

When he awoke the next day, he immediately looked for the snake. He knew it had to be close by in the yard somewhere. He knew that snakes hung around the area until they were hungry enough to go off looking for food somewhere else. It was likely hiding along the tree line. The hospice volunteer in the room asked if he was comfortable or if there was anything he needed. He really just wanted to be left alone. He was hoping that the snake would come back into the yard to prove his theory...and it did. He could see it crawling across the grass back toward the patio. It likely wanted to rest on the flagstone patio and absorb the sun warmth from the stones into its body like it had done the day before.

However, this time the hospice volunteer, a woman, saw it too, shrieked and went running from the room. A few moments later he saw three hospice volunteers in the yard, not including his volunteer, throwing rocks at the snake, one volunteer was armed with a straw broom. A lot of good that was going to do. The snake would likely not take kindly to being swept across the lawn. He could see that the snake immediately engaged a hasty retreat from the back yard and quickly disappeared into the tree line. They could really move very fast when frightened, he thought. It was the most excitement he had experienced since he arrived at the hospice a week ago. The rest of the day he slept.

He awoke in the night, disoriented, his mind and remaining sight sought a large illuminated clock that he knew was located on a dresser across from the foot of his bed. Slowly focusing on the light, the fur receding from his weakening mind, he ascertained that it was about 1:30 AM. A hospice volunteer had told him the clock was to help hospice residents to maintain a sense of equilibrium when awaking for any sudden reasons, whether in the night or even in the day. Assuming they were lucid and had some remaining vestiges of cognitive

◆ 36 ◆

ability. Although it was night time there was a three-quarters phase moon. The hospice volunteer had not pulled close the curtains to the sliding glass door after he had fallen asleep that afternoon. The door was partially open, about twelve inches, and a cooling breeze passed through the screen mesh door and wandered into the room. It felt wonderful. He could see through the sliding glass door that the back yard was bathed in silver moonlight and shone like a lightly tarnished silver coin. He marveled at the sight and thought it was quite beautiful outside and that this would be a good night to die if he had to choose a night.

His hospice volunteer was not in the room. He did not know which one it was, who likely assumed duties while he was sleeping earlier. He could hear voices further off in the building and he thought probably it would be some time before the volunteer returned to his room. He was tired but not sleepy.

He knew how physically weak he was and what he had in mind was not likely going to go well. He remembered the large amounts of weights he used to lift in his younger days, and how he could run for miles and never seemed to tire. He couldn't even wipe his ass now because it takes too much effort. Who would have ever thought it takes a lot of strength to wipe your ass. Regardless, he was going to do this. Dying was going to be on his terms.

He pushed his bed covers away from his body, off to the left side and onto the floor. Christ...that took a lot of effort, he thought. The breeze wafting into the room and brushing past his bare legs protruding from under his hospital gown felt invigorating and sensual. The sensation gave him a false surge of satisfaction that he knew wasn't going to do shit for his body. He slowly pivoted his body to the right dangling his legs over the edge of the bed until they touched the floor. He was breathing hard. He pushed himself up to a standing position, grasping the side of the bed, while trying to steady himself. Pain tore up his backside and he stifled a gasp by biting into his hand. He steadied himself and listened carefully for the possible return of his hospice volunteer. He could still hear voices engaged in conversation, not loud or obnoxious, but the building had high ceilings and sound carried far. He tore out the intravenous lines from his arm and flung them onto the bed.

With a sense of determination entwined with a concern that the hospice volunteer could return at any time, he willed himself to take a step forward toward the sliding glass door. Looking down he observed he had managed to achieve all of a few inches with one foot, whereas in his mind it seemed like he had accomplished one large step for mankind. This was not going to work. It occurred to him that maybe he could do better if he were on his hands and knees. Grasping the bedframe, he lowered his right knee to the floor, while leaning slightly forward, extending his right arm out and catching himself before he could fall flat on the floor. This seemed to work better for him. He started out resolutely crawling across the tile floor. Every movement...bring his knee forward, extend the arm ahead, push forward, demanded a level of exertion and effort that he could not ever remember having previously experienced. He wondered if his ass was exposed from under his hospital gown. It didn't matter, he was doing it, and he would be at the sliding glass door in minutes.

He arrived. The top of his head slipped in between the wood frame and the open sliding glass door. He was breathing hard and needed to catch his breath, his partially balding head rested against the screen mesh. He smiled, still some life in the old boy...not much maybe, but enough at the moment. With his right hand, he reached out and grabbed the frame of the sliding glass door and pushed to the quick limits of his strength trying to open the door further. Fortunately, the sliding glass door rolled on a smooth track and it opened easily enough emitting a low-level sound of a "whoosh." That was good, he thought, but if the screen door is latched, he was fucked and his efforts would all be for nothing. His fingers fumbled along the aluminum frame where he tried to dig his fingers into and between the screen door and the frame. It was unlocked...he pulled at it and the screen door slid open a few inches but it had made a scratching sound that caused him to freeze in place. No one came to investigate. He pushed the screen door further open, which provided him an opening sufficient to allow him to slowly and painfully and resolutely continue his quest and crawl out onto the flagstone patio. In a moment, truly exhausted, his head sagged, hung from his shoulders, and in a slow jerky motion his body floated downward to the ground, forehead striking the stones first, body now sprawled across the patio, his right cheek rested on the patio stones. The pain pulsing from his groin area to his jaw was staggering and caused him to involuntarily catch his breath. Stunned from the pain, his face and breathing absorbed the cool air of the night. The life sensation was wonderful but brief and he became sad knowing it would be short-lived. For that split second it felt like a soft caress. He willed himself to recover from the exertion of crawling over the door frame from his hospice room to the patio. But it had been too much for his rotting body and he passed into unconsciousness by degrees, all in a matter of seconds, while clinging to a vague thought that he was very impressed with his deed.

The snake had been curiously watching the old man from the tree line as he crawled from his room outside to the patio. It didn't know the old man was dying. It didn't even know that it was an old man. It didn't care one way or another. For that matter, it didn't know how to care and it didn't even know what dying was. It was a reptile animal that was imbued with basic survival instincts and throughout its complete life it only wanted to continually eat something and keep comfortable. The old man was probably one of those creatures he should stay away from. Still, it was hungry, which was really most of the time anyway, and it was very cold out tonight. It did not know it but the weather had been unseasonable, and the nights had suddenly cooled off causing undue amounts of chilled dew in the mornings. Not exactly the ideal nesting conditions for a snake of its stature. He continued to watch the old man lying on the patio, watching to see if he would move...or not.

The old man had not moved for whatever amount of time the snake had been watching him. The snake was not counting minutes, did not know time, it only was aware of one moment to another. It was cold and wanted warmth. It started toward the old man, very wary of its surroundings, very concerned the old man might suddenly get up and try to hurt him. Within inches of the old man it stopped and watched intensely for any sign of movement. Seeing none it slithered next to the old man and curled up alongside of the old man's back where it quickly found warmth and settled in finding contentment.

The snake was startled, quickly realized that the old man he was resting up against had moved. In a lightning sense of self-preservation, the snake reared back and struck the old man in his back below the shoulder. The fangs easily penetrating the hospital gown, parchment like skin, and the thin layer of remaining muscle. Its fangs sank deep, inward, and one struck bone breaking off from its mouth. He could feel the old man shudder as it pumped its venom into his body. The snake snapped its head back, and pulled back and was stunned at the loss of one its fangs. It saw that the old man remained still and was not turning toward it to attack. However, there was now another fear, a woman had appeared in the door and was screaming. The snake reared up, evaluating the new threat from the hysterical woman, who had since fled back into the building. The snake realizing there was no further threat quickly turned aside and withdrew back toward the tree line.

The old man was aroused to semi-consciousness by the sound of a woman screaming. He was not sure where it was coming from but it was close. He felt a burning sensation at his shoulder and a fiery feeling spreading across his back. The snake! He had found it. For a few seconds amidst the few moments he had remaining in his life his mind slipped back again to his memories of when he trained with the Legionnaires. He remembered the small zoo of captured snakes from the surrounding jungle, some poisonous and some non-poisonous, that the Legionnaires used for jungle training purposes. One of the Legionnaires had instructed one of the Marines to reach into one of the cages that contained a non-poisonous snake and try to catch it. The Marine did so and the snake promptly bit him. The Marine was stunned and kept muttering to everyone within ear's reach that the damned snake had bitten him. Later on, after he had calmed down, he said it felt no worse than an intense cat bite. The Legionnaires had a good laugh at the Marine's expense.

The old man knew it would not be long now, and he was satisfied. Maybe he was happy too. His mind was fading and beginning to close down. He wanted to retain as much equilibrium and cognitive ability as possible before he died. Likely minutes away now. He wanted to bask in the triumph of winning against life. He had chosen to die, and when, and how, and not by someone or something else deciding for him. He knew in his condition he had accomplished a physical task of mammoth undertaking and had known what the consequences could possibly be. He felt he had a right to be impressed with himself.

Hospice personnel were gently lifting him off the ground now and taking him back to his bed. He knew he would be gone by the time they got to his bed. His thoughts were fuzzy now, but he was thinking they probably think he is dead now because he was staring straight ahead with no biological responses.

He wasn't dead though, or maybe he was. He was intently staring ahead because he was looking for the white light that the dying always insist they see.

It Was Just War

"A helicopter is close enough to be brought down with small arms fire when you can no longer completely cover it with your thumb held at arm's length."

—Vietnamese Rule of Thumb

I FIRST MET Lance Corporal Frederick Kansik, the Third, United States Marine Corps, forty-three years ago when he and I first checked into our new unit, the Radio Section at Headquarters Company, 3rd Marine Regiment at Camp Carroll, in South Vietnam. He was in company with a friend, Lance Corporal Tom Bell, who would become a lifelong friend to me and who would transition over the years from an amiable personality into a cantankerous son of a bitch (but that is another story for another time).

Fred and Tom were both from Michigan and had met each other for the first time when they responded to their draft notices to appear at the local military processing center. There, some official had gathered all of that day's draftees in attendance into one group, and with one sweep of his arm, had split the group in half and instructed those to the right, which contained Fred and Tom, to gather on the opposite side of the room. The official then congratulated their group for being selected to be United States Marines. As Fred told the story he said that he experienced in that moment two disturbing sensations: an icy cold spasm of fear that shot through his body that caused his extremities to tingle, because he had heard all of the stories about Marine boot camp at Parris Island in South Carolina, and a mind numbing realization in which he knew he was going to Vietnam for sure at some point in the near future.

Fred, Tom and I were school trained radio operators. In one sense the good news was that we had been assigned to a command element. Therefore, we would not likely be out in the jungle humping from one location to another and engaged in combat operations up close and personal. However, Camp Carroll was the armpit of Vietnam located on a hilltop a few miles south of the demilitarized zone (DMZ) – a type of no man's land and geographical designation separating

South Vietnam from North Vietnam). It was a poorly planned and laid out array of sandbagged bunkers and tents seemingly plopped down amid squalor and mud and decorated with varying earthy hues of browns, greens and grays. It rained all of the time and everything was either wet, or soon would be wet, with dampness being a temporary condition.

We were assigned to our living spaces in a tent with a mud floor and a narrow and bubbling stream bisecting the center of the tent. I admit that at night I liked listening to the patter of the falling rain on the canvas tent roof as I would drift off to sleep. However, that experience was for other nights. No sooner had we dropped our equipment onto our cots, which were partially sunk into the mud, the Duty Staff Noncommissioned Officer (SNCO) unceremoniously flung the canvas door flap open, and leaning forward with his head protruding into our tent announced that as newbies we were on sentry duty that night and to report to the guard shack at 1730 (5:30 PM).

That night I was assigned to a foxhole with a Marine I did not know, but as I recall he had already been in country for some time. Fred and Tom were put together in an adjoining foxhole to my left, maybe about 20 meters away. We were assigned to 12-hour tours and the Marines in each foxhole were allowed to work out a schedule as to who would stand watch while the other Marine was sleeping. I took the first six-hour watch in my foxhole. There was no way in hell I was going to sleep. It was dark, very dark, and very frightening. It was raining off and on and there was water in the foxhole just enough to cover the tops of my boots. There were rows and rows and coils of concertina wire laid out in front of our foxhole defining the perimeter of the base. Every once in a while, somewhere on the base some section or another would intermittently pop off flares, preceded by a hollow thunk, then a fizzy hissing sound, the area would be temporarily illuminated as small parachutes floated downward allowing the area to be lit up and exposed for about a minute. Each time a flare popped, the illumination contrasted and reflected back against the rain and mist. It was very surreal, a word that I had no concept about at that time in my life, and a scene I would see in future movies about Vietnam. When you heard that hollow sound you had to close one eye so that you could retain some partial night vision and hunker down in the foxhole and stay very still so as not to bring attention to your position. Sometimes I would peek out of the corner of my eye looking over at Fred and Tom, but all I could see was the just the bare tops of their helmets. I had three hand grenades laid out along the edge of my foxhole in front of me, I had my K-Bar combat knife sticking in the mud for quick retrieval, and I spent most of the night peering down the sights of my rifle into the dark. I was 19, I was cold, I was wet, I was homesick, and I did not even have a girlfriend back home to write to. Yet, I was prepared to kill anything that came at me that night.

I don't recall the name of the Marine who was in the foxhole with me. I can barely remember what he looked like. I woke him up when it was his turn and then I tried to sleep myself. I had calmed down considerably by that time but I was still apprehensive. It was a restless effort and I would awaken every few minutes. On one occasion I saw my fellow Marine resting his head against the edge of the foxhole and it was evident he was asleep. Of all of the mistakes that a Marine could make, falling asleep on sentry duty was the ultimate mortal sin! I woke him up and told him to stay awake. He was not happy with me disturbing his slumber and combined with a few "Motherfuckers" told me to leave him alone. He retorted that Charlie (officially known as the "Viet Cong" who were South Vietnamese Communists and who were enemy guerillas drawn from the local populace) had not attacked the base in over a year and that the last time they did they had used flashlights to find their way up the hill during the attack. That was small comfort to me who thought there was an enemy soldier likely lurking everywhere in front of me. A few moments later he fell asleep again. I was angry. I took my K-Bar knife, and turned it to the dull side, I slipped it under his jaw while grabbing his left arm and twisting it behind his back and upward. I whispered in his ear that if he did not stay awake the enemy was the least that he had to worry about. At first, he froze and then when he realized it was me, he began struggling. This was all being done quietly within the confines of the limited space in the foxhole. Some groans and gasps, water splashing about, and the intermittent whispered and emphatic obscenities, but not enough to have the sergeant of the guard to come out and see what was going on. A few moments later Fred appeared alongside of the foxhole with a pistol in hand. While speaking in a low voice he wanted to know what the hell was going on. The struggle had alerted him to a problem and he had low crawled over to my foxhole to investigate. By this time, I and the other Marine, both breathing hard, we were facing each other. I told Fred what had happened and he started giggling and said he had it coming. He turned around and low crawled back to his foxhole. The rest of the night that Marine stayed awake, as did I. I now had the problems of Charlie somewhere out in the dark combined with an angry Marine in my foxhole.

After that night Fred and I became good friends, and in company with Tom, we would spend a lot of time together during our tours. With the passing of the years I mostly remember Fred now in an image of a photograph that I had personally taken one afternoon. It is a small snapshot with Fred as the primary focus. What few colors there were originally in the photograph were derived from the stark background of the base have long faded to a dull and washed out print. Fred is standing next to a jeep on the driver's side with his right arm propped on the canvas roof, his right leg poised on the jeep's running board. He is looking directly into the camera and he has a cigarette dangling from the left side of his mouth. He was a tall man with a slender build, a light complexion and light brown hair with a Marine style buzz haircut. He was a handsome man and would have been ideal for a Marine recruiting poster. He is wearing the standard issued olive drab jungle utility uniform at the time, but within a few weeks we would receive the first issue of the camouflage jungle utility uniforms. A person looking at the photograph would see a confident young man who was proud of being a Marine and believed he was doing the right thing by being in Vietnam. For an enlisted Marine he possessed a very rare attribute at the time. He had a college degree. After graduating he had lost his draft deferment and that was the beginning of his journey to his final and present destination in the Nam. He was also newly married and would quickly show photos of his wife to anyone who was interested. Since we were all female deprived at the time, we were all interested in seeing photos of any women.

Within a couple of weeks of our arrival Fred was assigned as the personal radio operator for the regimental commanding officer. I wanted that job. His job was to follow the colonel everywhere and ensure that he had communications with the regimental combat operations center (COC). So, when the colonel flew out in choppers to visit his various subordinate units, which was just about every day, and there were a lot of units, Fred was dutifully following a few paces behind the colonel while humping a radio on his back. When the colonel was being driven around the unit's area of responsibility visiting those units that were accessible via roads, Fred was right there as a passenger in the jeep seated directly behind the colonel, ready to pass the radio's handset to him if he wanted to talk to his watch officers. Whereas I was confined to the base standing 12-hour radio watches every day in the COC, assigned to work parties when off watch, I was behind the wire, occasionally dodging haphazardly launched rockets and mortars that Charlie would direct toward the base, Fred was out seeing the war and compiling adventures. It was frustrating enough to make a grown and aggressive Marine weep and maybe request a transfer to a front-line unit. I never did make such a request.

Some evenings when the three of us had time off and were relaxing, Fred would tell us about his experiences. He easily spent a couple of hours flying around the area of operations (AO) almost every day in various types of helicopters. He lived in separate quarters set aside for the colonel's staff and was not required to support innumerable work parties, like burning shitters, of which I was quite accomplished. I was very envious of his adventures. In Huey choppers he used to sit just forward of the machine gunner by the open door, always on the left side so he could comfortably lay his rifle on his lap pointing outboard. The only thing between him and the ground below was a seatbelt. The problem with helicopters was that you never knew you were being shot at until the aircraft was struck. One time the machine gunner was pounding away at something or somebody on the ground and kept yelling at Fred to shoot also. Fred said he couldn't see anything or anybody but just fired away in the general direction of where the machine gunner was aiming, all the while ensuring he did not accidentally fire into the helicopter's rotors as it banked hard during evasive maneuvers. Another time he was on a fire base in the jungle which was being probed by Charlie, while the colonel casually discussed operational plans with a company commander. Bullets were flying all around but the colonel and company commander just continued on with the business at hand and they never flinched. Fred said he was sitting in a foxhole with his knees up to his chin. On one occasion the colonel's command group had to sprint for their incoming chopper, which was trying to pick them up in a hot landing zone (LZ). They would have to scramble aboard during the few seconds it hovered over the ground and then the chopper would quickly depart the firebase. Fred was the last Marine in the party and had just stepped up onto the skid in an effort to climb into the cabin when the chopper started to lift off...

banking hard to the left. Unfortunately, the abrupt maneuver, in combination with the weight of the radio on his back, flung Fred backward from off of the skid and he tumbled to the ground about eight feet down. He was not hurt but he remembered while lying on his back and watching the chopper depart, seeing the colonel's head protruding from the chopper's cabin looking back and down at him, all the while yelling something to the aircrew. There were many other stories and I would go back to my hootch and lie in my rack and nurse my frustration like a sore tooth. I wanted to be doing what he was doing, instead of burning shitters every other day.

Late one morning I was awakened by Tom after having completed a 12 hour midnight radio watch in the COC. I was groggy and disoriented from being aroused from a deep sleep, so it took me a few moments to understand what Tom was trying to tell me. Fred's chopper had been shot down departing from one of the unit's location on a firebase. Accompanying both Fred and the colonel on this trip was the regimental sergeant major and the commanding officer of 1st Battalion 12th Marines, which was an artillery unit. Nobody knew exactly what had happened, if everybody, if anyone, had survived, but Tom said additional information was coming into the COC as we were talking. I quickly dressed and followed Tom back to the COC. I knew the senior watch officer on duty, a first lieutenant who was spending the last part of his tour in the COC before going back to the world. It was standard practice to rotate Marine officers out of the field after six months to a position behind the wire, if they survived that long. This lieutenant was one of the largest of men I would ever see in my lifetime. We called him "Man-o-Mount" because he was a huge as a mountain. Easily six feet and six inches he weighed three-hundred pounds plus and sported a full and unauthorized large bristly moustache. How it is that Charlie had not succeeded in shooting him when he was in the field was a mystery to all of us. He told me that preliminary reports indicated that the crew and all passengers aboard the chopper were killed, either from the initial ground fire, or from the impact of the crash. When he told me this I noticed he looked away when he was telling me of the death toll and at the time I did not take much notice. Tom and I departed the COC together both disheartened and mourning for our friend and fellow Marine.

That night when I reported for my scheduled radio watch at the COC the lieutenant was just completing his watch tour. He saw me and beckoned me over and told me to follow him back to the watch officer's office, which was basically a small cubby hole with maps all over the walls, a makeshift desk constructed from discarded ammunition boxes and a coffee pot in the corner. He had to turn his massive body at a 45-degree angle and waddle his way through the door. He said he knew I was close friends with Fred and that he wanted to tell me what had happened that day. He also asked me not to pass the information around within the headquarters' unit and swore me to silence. He then went on to tell me that late that afternoon he had personally debriefed the infantry squad (grunts) that arrived first at the crash site, and actually literally within a minute of impact. As it turned out the grunts were from a platoon that he had commanded while in the field. The squad sergeant had previously been under his command and was on his second tour of combat duty for which he had volunteered. He said the sergeant was a hard case but an exceptional combat Marine and that he had witnessed the complete event from the chopper being struck by ground fire to impact into the ground. The sergeant said it looked like the chopper was hit by a rocket propelled grenade (RPG) combined with small arms fire. The enemy had been waiting for it to take off; basically, waiting for it when it was most vulnerable. The rocket struck the pilot's hatch and immediately the chopper nose-dived and impacted about 50 yards away from where the sergeant's squad had been emplaced the previous day providing perimeter security to the firebase. An explosion occurred which resulted in the chopper catching on fire and also setting the surrounding jungle on fire (a common threat in the jungle when the prevailing climate consisted of high temperatures combined with dry conditions). The sergeant and six Marines went running down the hillside in an effort to hopefully rescue personnel. They did not know that the regimental commanding officer was aboard along with other unit representatives. When they arrived at the scene, they could not get very close to the downed chopper. The heat was intense and there was the added apprehension of whatever kind of ordnance that was in the chopper might cook off. The sergeant said the destroyed chopper made him think of a crushed tomato soup can. The pilot and copilot were slumped over the dashboard but they were both on fire. Due to the heat, flames, and angle of the impacted chopper they could not see clearly into the cabin of the chopper. However, they could hear someone screaming; someone...a Marine, who was screaming, and who was being burned alive.

The lieutenant was telling me all of this, and at this point he hesitated in his description of events, and looked away from me, just like he did earlier that day when he conveyed to me what initial information the COC had managed to obtain. He looked back at me and then told me what happened. The sergeant was immobilized when he first heard the screams; in a daze almost, as he and the other grunts described the event. The lieutenant hesitated for a moment and told me that maybe the sergeant was remembering some other event at that moment; the loss of a Marine in combat, or maybe he had a similar experience in his earlier tour. He did not have those answers. The Marines were yelling at him, "What do we do Sergeant?" What was really only a matter of seconds in time from arrival at the scene to hearing the screams of the trapped Marine inside the burning chopper; he brought his M-16 rifle up to his shoulder, clicked the safety lever to "automatic" and began firing through the flames into the downed chopper. He did not order or instruct his fellow Marines to follow his lead; but, they did. In a matter of seconds each of the Marines had unloaded a full magazine into the burning wreck. The screaming stopped. One Marine aghast with just what had happened kept asking himself and repeating to himself, "What have we done?" All of the debriefed Marines said the sergeant turned toward them, showing no emotion, but with an expression that suggested he was somewhere else and told them, "We just killed dead men...that's all." The lieutenant said there was an ongoing investigation but if it had been him in that chopper that is what he would have wanted done. He said those grunts were heroes and they would have to live the rest of their lives with those images in their memories.

I departed the lieutenant's office totally immersed in thoughts and conjuring up pictures in my mind of what it must have been like at the crash-site for the deceased, the dying, and those grunts. In my youth there was much I did not understand about life. Everything then was basically black and white in my thinking. We were in Vietnam to thwart Communism and we had to kill them before they killed us and took over the world. The lieutenant said it was just war. Over the years I would hear that explanation applied to every event and atrocity in warfare since the beginning of time. Yet, I would also eventually comprehend the intricacies of that simple statement. I thought what those Marines did was likely the most difficult thing they would ever have to do in their lives. I remember thinking that I was glad I did not have to make such a decision. Later that night I also realized if it had been me in that downed chopper suffering the agony of such death, I would have wanted them to do what they did. Many years have passed now and I can't even remember if we had a memorial service for Fred. I can't even remember what was the tone and sensibilities of the command in the ensuing days after all of those deaths. Time does have a way of erasing many aspects of our lives that we do not like to think about. I do know that as Marines, within that command and regiment, we had no choice but to recover and continue the mission.

The next day I was assigned as the personal radio operator to the new commanding officer.

A Bite Out of Crime

"my eyes are your eyes to watch and protect, my ears are your ears to hear and detect evil minds in the dark, my nose is your nose to scent the invader of your domain, and so you may live"

—**K9 Rebel – Prince George's County Police**
End of Watch 26 October 1984

A CHILL SWEPT through the cemetery and across the hill-side where the Prince George's County police officers, wearing their dress blue uniforms and white gloves, stood in formation surrounding the gravesite. An iron gray sky threatened rain and enveloped the funeral party below. It was appropriate funeral weather and invoked a sense of heavy loneliness. Corporal Joey Wingo, with his arm around his softly crying wife, stood staring forlornly at the grave as the last notes of Taps sounded across the now very still hillside. A man in a suit stood by the gravesite prepared to push the button that would lower the casket into the grave when he was given the nod. Wingo looked around and noticed that many of the cops were looking at him closely. To a cop, the looks were all expression-less, and Wingo wondered if they blamed him for what had happened. In his grief his mind slipped back to that night and he wondered why, why...

The huge German shepherd lunged forward and his leath-er lead snapped taut, where it was tied to the police cruiser's spotlight. Up on his back legs, the dog strained viciously against the lead, snarling with yellow teeth bared. The dog was fully a hundred and fifty pounds, with thick luxurious fur splotched beige and black, and massive paws that slapped the ground. Two more inches and he could bury his teeth into the man's crotch.

The man was standing between two Prince George's County police officers who had a firm hold on each arm and were pushing the terrified man toward the police dog. Sometimes just enough to where the dog's wet nose would smack against the man's crotch, leaving a snotty imprint of his snout. Ropey threads of the dog's saliva were splattered across the front of his trousers. A hairbreadth before the Shepherd's jaws could close on the man's groin, the officers would barely - but, just enough - pull him back out of harm's way. It was enough to anger any police canine into a legitimate frenzy when experiencing the frustrations associated with his job.

They were behind the Market Plaza shopping center in an alleyway where overhead backdoor lights glistened in puddled areas of the asphalt from an earlier rain. Only moments before the man had been caught inside the clothing store where he and a friend had broken in through the rear door. A silent alarm had summoned police, and when the officers on the scene had located the entry point, they had called for a canine officer and his dog to respond and search the premises.

No cop with any degree of common sense was going to go into a darkened store looking for some person who could be hiding anywhere, armed with anything. That's what police canine dogs were for - they were expendable. Human cops weren't! That's why they got paid with extra dog biscuits and a scientifically balanced nutritional canine diet.

That's when Corporal Joey Wingo and his departmentally issued dog "Confederate" hooked the call. When the dispatcher put out the request asking for any canine in the area to respond to a breaking and entering with a suspect still possibly inside, Wingo knew in his gut that it was a good B&E. And when Wingo was excited - Confederate became downright agitated. Every time Wingo keyed the mike to ask for directions to the scene, Confederate could be heard howling in the background and jumping around in his cage. Another bad guy was going to get eaten before the night was out. To Confederate that meant afterwards a pat on the head from Wingo and a trip to McDonalds.

When Wingo skidded into the scene with his red and blue lights pounding the night, he immediately got on the loudspeaker and announced, "COUNTY POLICE! COME ON OUT

OR I'LL LET THE DOG IN!" Now that the general orders were adhered to and not waiting to see if anyone was going to come out, he flung the mike down, swiftly exited from the cruiser, opened the back door, and smoothly hooked Confederate to a long leather lead as the dog gracefully slid from the interior into the alley. Confederate immediately lunged forward practically dragging Wingo to the rear entrance of the store. Confederate was pulling so hard on the lead that he was gasping for air. The cops, who had been tactically poised watching the back door subconsciously stepped back. Many a cop had been bitten accidentally by an agitated canine dog. You could point at your badge all day long, but a canine dog answered to only one master - his handler. Wingo asked if anyone wanted to go in with him. One of the police officers stepped forward and said he would.

Once inside the door, guns drawn, Wingo let the dog loose. The only light available came from street lights that shone through the front display windows. Immediately, Wingo knew that either someone was inside the store, or there had been someone inside very recently. Confederate had his nose on the ground and was sniffing hard. Agitated, whimpering, he kept shaking his shaggy head back and forth searching for the strongest scent. Wingo looked back over his shoulder for the other officer and saw him frantically motioning toward a circular display rack of suits. The officer quickly walked over to Wingo and whispered in his ear that there was someone curled up on his knees under the rack. Wingo grabbed Confederate's lead off the floor and jerked Confederate toward the clothing rack. Confederate approached the rack, froze, and started pawing the floor. With a snarl he leaped into the clothing and the man under the rack started screaming. Confederate, his hind end poised up in the air protruding out from in between the suits hanging from the rack, tail madly whipping back and forth, and his paws furiously pedaling on the slippery linoleum floor, desperately tried to drag the man out from his hiding place. Wingo reached into the clothes and grabbed the man by his shirt collar, dragged him out into the open, and started yelling to let go of the dog. The man by no means had control of the dog. The dog definitely had control of the man. Nevertheless, Wingo struck the man on his shoulder with a blackjack. By now the man was screaming and sobbing, "GET HIM OFF ME! Sob - sob! GET HIM OFF ME! Sob - sob! AAAAAHHHHHHHHHAAARRGGGGGHHH! Oh, God please!" Confederate had his teeth buried into the man's forearm and was shaking his head back and forth and jerking backwards with all of his might. The man would later say the pain felt as if his arm had been closed in a car door and the door couldn't be opened.

Wingo and Confederate followed the other officer out of the store as the officer dragged the now handcuffed and sobbing suspect out into the alleyway. Blood soaked the front of his shirt and was dripping from his hands cuffed behind his back. A few moments earlier Confederate had refused to release the man's arm on command. Wingo had straddled Confederate, wrapped his arm around his neck, and pulling back until Confederate began to choke, he had pried his teeth from out of the man's forearm. Once outside and feeling safe now, the man began swearing and cussing at both officers and Confederate. In the alleyway, realizing he would soon be transported away from the scene, he became even bolder and started threatening Confederate and the other officers on the scene. When asked if there had been anyone else with him, he had told the officers, and specifically, "YOU ALL...ESPECIALLY THAT MUTT DOG, CAN GO FUCK YOURSELVES AND I AIN'T TELLING ANYBODY SHIT!"

Wingo had smiled at the man. He led Confederate over to the nearest cruiser and tied the lead securely to the spotlight. Grabbing Confederate by the collar he led him away from the cruiser to the length of the lead and gave him the command, "Sit!" The officers restraining the prisoner knew what was coming next. The man wasn't sure what was going to happen, but he knew he was in trouble when the officers started shoving him toward the dog. He started protesting and began struggling with the officers. Confederate cocked his head curiously - and suddenly lunged forward, when Wingo commanded, "Attack!" The man began screeching, and in between his screams, began apologizing for his attitude. Every time Confederate's snout smacked into his crotch, the man's buttocks would flick backwards desperately trying to avoid the teeth that were right under Confederate's nose. After a few moments, Wingo ordered Confederate to, "Heel!" Confederate promptly plopped on his haunches, breathing hard, and awaiting instructions.

Wingo asked again, "Was there anyone else with you tonight?"

The prisoner, now reduced to tears, shook his head yes and sobbed out a name. Suddenly Wingo grabbed the man by his shirt and yanked him to within an inch of his face. Barely able to suppress his fury, he searched the man's eyes for a moment and then spoke into the man's fear, "I don't give a shit about myself, mister, but don't you ever threaten my dog again! Do you fucking understand me?"

The man stuttered a, "Ye...ye...yes S...s...sir," and started sobbing again. Wingo flung him back toward the waiting officers. He turned away, went over to Confederate, patted him on the head, and untied the lead. In a matter of moments, he was on the road again. The street cops would do all of the paperwork and take the suspect to the hospital. His job was done.

After making sure that a dog was not needed anywhere else in the county, Wingo drove out to College Park to a McDonalds a block away from the University of Maryland that was open all night. He ordered a Big Mac and a large order of fries for Confederate, and a large vanilla milkshake for himself. He drove into the back-parking lot and parked his cruiser in the corner and let Confederate out and gave him his share of the food.

At that moment another police cruiser pulled into the parking lot and Wingo recognized the officer as George "Mad Munk" Munkelwitz. Munk pulled up alongside and started laughing when he saw Confederate with a complete Big Mac in his mouth trying to juggle it in between bites.

"I take it he got another bite tonight," Munk said.

"Yeah, over in Landover. The Richman's Clothing Store was broken into and Confederate caught one hiding under a clothes rack. There were two suspects, but one of them boogied out the back when he saw the police coming through the parking lot. He didn't even tell his partner. Just bolted and left him." Wingo laughed thinking about it.

The Mad Munk got out, stretched, and walked over to where Wingo was sitting on the curb. He sat down beside Wingo and watched Confederate eat the hamburger. He had worked with Wingo and Confederate on many occasions and he had a healthy respect for Confederate, although he wasn't afraid of the dog. Unless Wingo gave a command that instructed Confederate to become aggressive, he was as gentle and friendly as any dog he had ever known. Wingo and Confederate often went into the grade schools to give safety lectures, where Confederate would be surrounded by dozens of kids who were struggling among themselves to get next to him and pet him. Confederate would just sit there and take it all in while basking in the attention. He had all the right moves; paw the air, whimper, and pant with his long pink tongue hanging out. The kids loved it. If Confederate had been a human being, he would have been the consummate politician.

A car coming through the parking lot slowed down and then stopped by the officers. It was occupied by four girls, who were obviously students at the University of Maryland. The passenger up front, an attractive blonde with hair cascading across her shoulders was leaning out the window. The driver was leaning across her lap trying to see out the window.

"Is that your dog?" the blonde asked. "He's really pretty." By now the back window was open and both of the girls in the back seat were pressed cheek to cheek gripping the edge of the door trying to look out the window simultaneously.

Wingo smiled and said, "Yes he is. His name's Confederate."

Munk smiled to himself. Having a dog around the university was a real female magnet. A lot of the canine officers met many of the coeds that way.

Wingo turned toward Munk and winked, then turned back toward the girls and went on to explain, "However, he is a trained attack dog, so it's not a good idea to get too close to him."

One of the girls in the back squealed. The blonde passenger smiled and said "really cool" and they drove away. Confederate had barely noticed the girls. After he had determined that there was no danger he had turned back toward Wingo and was more intent on watching his master drink his milkshake.

Munk watched Wingo with fascination. Wingo would eat a spoonful of the milkshake, and then feed Confederate a spoonful – with the same spoon! Confederate would engulf the spoon with a snap of his jaws, work it around in his mouth until he had gotten most of the ice cream, let it go, examine it carefully, then wrap his huge floppy pink tongue around it until what dregs remained was all gone. Wingo would take another spoonful for himself and then feed Confederate another spoonful. He kept this up until the cup was practically empty.

Munk shook his head. No doubt about it, Wingo was nuts! He had known him for years and the man had always been a study in contrasts. The man could quote Shakespeare and had season tickets to a drama theater in downtown Washington, D.C. Yet he loved the viciousness and excitement associated with police work. He was a man who was wound up, which was evident in the way he walked with his arms bowed out from his sides and his hands clenched into fists all of the time. Tall, slender, dark, and slightly balding, it was his eyes that a person always noticed about him. They were light blue in color; suspicious eyes, which never betrayed emotion, and were always flickering about the area, as if he knew something was going to happen soon but didn't know just when. Some cops were more afraid of Wingo than they were of his dog. Still, he was the best canine cop on the street, and the Munk always felt secure when he and Confederate were on the scene.

Wingo had the milk shake cup extended out toward Confederate, who had his nose inside the cup with his huge tongue thumping the insides of the cup as he tried to slurp up the last drops.

"You're nuts, Joey! How can you feed Confederate with the same spoon that you're eating from?" The Mad Munk asked.

Wingo gave a side glance toward the Mad Munk. He looked back at Confederate and reached up and patted the dog on the head. "His mouth is cleaner than yours Munk."

"Jesus Joey, how the hell can you say that? He was probably licking his balls a half hour before you got here. Who knows what other portion of his anatomy he's been licking too?"

Wingo started laughing and started to answer when he was interrupted by the radio. A female voice, evidently bored with her shift for the night intoned, "Time 141, respond to Kettering Middle School in Edward Three beat for five intrusion alarms off. Officers have secured the building and have located a possible point of entry through a broken window."

Wingo grabbed his radio from his gunbelt and responded that he was on his way. "I'm out of here Munk. Sounds like another good one. Maybe Confederate will get a second Big Mac before the night is out."

"Yeah, take care Joey. Bye Confederate. Stay safe."

Wingo was on the road, red and blue lights sweeping into

the night, and well on his way to the call in a matter of minutes. Confederate knew they were going to work again. In the back of the cruiser, which had been altered to allow for a platform and a large roomy cage, he paced back and forth, whimpering in anticipation. He could tell by the way his master was driving that they were probably going to another good B&E call. If lucky, he might get his second bite of the night - and another pat on the head and another hamburger.

Wingo rolled quietly into the parking lot with his emergency and vehicle lights off. Another police officer in the lot approached him and quickly briefed him on what they had. Two of the officers on the perimeter had been pretty close to the school when the call went out and had gotten on the scene within a minute of the call being dispatched. So, if somebody was inside the school, it was likely that they had gotten here in time to successfully contain the suspect, or suspects inside.

Wingo quickly put Confederate on a lead and went around to the door that opened into the school's boiler room. All of the canine officers had keys for every school's boiler room in the county, which was the primary point of access to the schools after they had been closed at the end of the school day. Just before inserting the key, he stopped and yelled as loud as he could, "COUNTY POLICE! COME OUT OR I'LL LET THE DOG LOOSE!" Now that the general orders had been adhered to, and not waiting to see if anyone was going to come out, he unlocked the door and yanked it open. The ever-eager Confederate shot through the door dragging him into the boiler room. He had done this a hundred times and knew that they had to go through the boiler room to get into the school. He pulled Wingo across an iron grate, down the stairs and through a door that brought them into an auditorium. Except for Confederate's nails clicking on the linoleum floor, it was spooky quiet and dark. Some weak shafts of light from the hallway leaked in through the small windows set in the doors that separated the auditorium from the hallway. Wingo felt a tingle of excitement race up his spine. He smiled and he knew! There was somebody inside.

It occurred to Wingo that he had forgotten to ask if any of the officers wanted to come in with him. Well, no big deal. He had done this hundreds of times by himself. He shrugged it off and directed his attention back to the search.

Confederate knew it too. He was pulling so hard on the lead that it took both of his hands to control him. Wingo held Confederate in place and unhooked the lead from his collar and let him run loose.

"FIND!" Wingo commanded. In a moment they were in the hallway where Confederate would stop before each door. He would sniff at the bottom of the door, and finding nothing, would lope down the hallway to the next door.

It was the next door!

Confederate stopped, sniffed at the bottom of the door, yelped, and started trying to dig under the door. Wingo grabbed Confederate's collar, pulled him back, and in a low voice, said, "Good boy! Good boy!" He opened the door, flinging it back against the hallway wall, and Confederate leaped through the doorway into a darkened classroom. There was some light spilling in through the windows from an outside security light attached to the side of the building. The classroom was cluttered with many desks, and there was a small room in the back, probably a bathroom, and a large cabinet beside the door.

Confederate started sniffing the carpet, zigzagging through the room, frantically trying to find the scent. Wingo started to direct him toward the bathroom when Confederate suddenly looked up and bounded toward the cabinet. He rose up on his hind legs, slammed his paws against the wooden door and barked twice. He began snarling and raking his nails across the wooden door.

Wingo drew his handgun from its holster, a semiautomatic Beretta, and yelled, "COUNTY POLICE! COME ON OUT AND

YOU WON'T GET HURT!" Then he commanded Confederate, "HEEL! CONFEDERATE! HEEL!" Confederate immediately backed off and came down on his haunches, watching the cabinet closely - a low rolling snarl in his throat.

The door cracked open - and then was flung viciously open, striking Confederate in the side of the head. Confederate yelped once and tumbled over on his side. A man inside the cabinet, in a blur of movement, leaped clumsily from his crouched position in the cabinet to the floor, stumbled to his knees, and landed beside the prostrate form of Confederate. Confederate, although dazed snarled at him while still trying to get to his feet. In his upraised arm, weak light glinted off metal, as his hand plunged down toward Confederate.

Initially taken by surprise, Wingo screamed, "NOOOOOOO!" and started running toward the fallen dog. Confederate howled and writhed in pain, his hind legs convulsively batting the air.

The intruder jumped to his feet, backed up against the cabinet, and seeing Wingo's gun pointing at him, flung the knife to the floor.

Wingo pointed his gun at what he could see now was a young white male - maybe sixteen - with long greasy hair, a dirty T-shirt, and torn jeans. He looked at the knife lying on the floor, barely evident in the dark. He could see that it was a cheap imitation of a World War I trench knife; a very large style knife with a brass hilt that enclosed around the handle to protect the bearer's hand. Short spikes protruded from the flat edge of the brass hilt. It was the cheap kind of knife you could pick up in any surplus store, or order from dozens of different magazines.

He looked down at Confederate, and could see a large black puddle creeping from under the dog, growing ever larger, and larger. He had to get help quickly!

Wingo turned back toward the youth. Fear for Confederate, and rage for the suspect, struggled for domination of his mind. He looked at the youth, searching his eyes. The youth, with his back pressed against the cabinet, and his hands spasmodically clutching the edges stared back at Wingo. It was Wingo's eyes that frightened him. In the muddled light it seemed as if everything around him had ceased to exist except the pure hatred that spewed forth from the cop's eyes. He started to speak – maybe it would help if he tried to apologize.

Wingo's grip tightened on the gun butt. Very quietly, just enough for the intruder to hear, he said, "Freeze! Drop the knife!"

The medic driving the ambulance cut off his siren, leaving the red lights on, and turned into the school parking lot. A cop waved him down and ran up to his window.

"Hold up!" the cop said, "We're bringing him out to you now. Get ready to get moving."

The ambulance driver looking confused, "Who are you bringing out? I understand you got a cop down and a suspect who has been shot. We've got to try and stabilize him first before we go anywhere. You're not supposed to be moving anybody until I say so." He was pissed now. These cops know better.

"Which of these guys is injured the most? Another medic unit will be here in a minute and they can take the one who's hurt the least."

The cop started to answer when a door to the school slammed open. The cop looked over and quickly turned back to the driver. "Jesus, let's go man! They're bringing him out now! Let's go!"

"Aw shit man. I'm not taking any responsibility for this fuck up!" The driver jumped from the ambulance, followed by his fellow medic, he ran around to the back and quickly opened the doors. He jumped up into the cabin and turned around to assist the cops with their load.

"Whhaaat the hell!" exclaimed the driver.

Wingo stood between the open doors cradling a bloody Confederate in his arms. His uniform was barely visible for all of the blood that covered him. A cop stood on each side of Wingo and grabbed him under his armpits and helped hoist him into the ambulance. He lowered his head, shimmied forward a couple of steps and sat down on the bench seat. Blood was beginning to drip on the floor, even as Wingo pressed a bloody T-shirt against Confederate's wound. Confederate's head rolled loosely in his master's arms and his thick wide tongue hung lifeless from his mouth.

The driver was incredulous. He flopped down on the opposite seat. "That's a dog! I'm not here to take a dog to the hospital," he said.

Wingo slowly raised his head and looked at the driver. In an even voice with an undertone of menace, "Yes - Yes you are! Now let's go!" The driver looked out of the back of the ambulance into the night. It was a madhouse. There were police cruisers parked everywhere. The school was lit up with headlights and spotlights, and red and blue lights kept arcing through the night. There were at least a dozen cops now standing around the rear of the ambulance looking in. Some of them he even knew. They were watching him very closely.

The driver looked around. Nobody said anything. He shook his head. Aw sweet Jesus, he thought. My ass will be hung out to dry - but, I'm not about to piss off half the police department tonight. He quickly exited the vehicle, secured the doors, and ran around to the front of the ambulance, where both he and his fellow medic jumped up into the cab.

He muttered to himself, "Man, I don't ever want to look into those eyes again." As he put the vehicle in drive and flipped on the emergency lights and siren - a thought emerged - I hope that other ambulance gets here in time to help whoever that other person is that needs assistance.

The first rifle volley snapped him out of his reverie. A light rain had begun to fall. He hadn't even noticed. Two more volleys were fired by the honor guard. He watched the man in the suit push the button, there was a low whirring sound, and the casket started to lower slowly into the grave. In a few moments it disappeared from his sight.

He felt a hand on his shoulder, turned, and looked into the eyes of the Mad Munk.

"Let's go Joey," he said. He suddenly realized, except for the man who pushed the button, he and the Mad Munk were the only ones left remaining by the gravesite.

"Yeah, I'm coming." He glanced one more time at the grave, flipped a lazy salute off the brim of his hat - and turned away.

Anything Blue
Is Where You Will Find God

"The sky grew darker, painted blue on blue, one stroke at a time, into deeper and deeper shades of night."

- Haruki Murakami
Dance Dance Dance

THE RAIN WAS relentless, and it had been raining on and off all day, and Terri Reilly was tired. Right now, it was raining again, late at night, where with her husband Ted, they were both on their way home from a cocktail party hosted by Ted's boss from work. He was driving on Croom Station Road to their home in the rural part of the county. It was Fall and the long familiar and well-traveled road was blanketed in Autumn's falling and fallen leaves. The vehicle's headlights stabbing into the night blackness of a road, without streetlights, illuminated splotches of asphalt passing beneath the vehicle. The road was bordered by shoulders that were a mixture of stones and dirt, now muddy and leaf covered, that edged over into gullies and a densely wooded countryside. An experienced driver knew to engage in caution while driving on rain soaked and leaf covered roads, because it could be like driving on ice in a winter storm, especially when going into a sharp curve.

However, Terri knew Ted to be a good and careful driver and she harbored no worries of an incident on the way home. The wind slapped the car and splattered the falling rain against the windshield, the windshield wipers furiously whipped back and forth just barely maintaining a clear view of what lay ahead. It was strange to see the rain sluicing sideways across the road in the headlights' beams. She laid her head back against the seat's headrest and felt the fatigue rush down her neck and across her shoulders. She did not want to go to the party tonight, but knew it was necessary for her to make an appearance with Ted, and say hello to those persons who were instrumental in his career to date, and who were also considering him for a promotion as a director of operations for his company. She did not have much to drink, two glasses of wine, but she knew that restrained amount was contributing to her sensation of fatigue.

If truth had been known she would like to have had more

glasses of wine. It wasn't that she disliked the idea of attending the cocktail party; it was that she was depressed and sorrowful and wanted to be left alone at this time in her life. In that second, combined with the weight of fatigue and the sadness in her heart, she could feel the tears welling up in her eyes as images of her sister spontaneously slipped from her memory into her reality.

She willed herself to control the tears. She did not want Ted to see her crying some more, although he would do what he had been doing for the past two months since her sister's death, which was to take her into his arms until she had cried herself out. She couldn't help it though and her mind slipped back in time and aroused again the livid pain that had sped across her heart when she learned of her sister's death in a car accident.

Her sister, Staci, had been her closest friend throughout her life and for her to be senselessly killed by another person, who was texting while driving, had been more than she could bear. Staci was only a year younger than she. They were what are referred to as Irish Twins. For eleven days of the year she and Staci were the same age. The term refers to Catholic parents who quickly have another baby before the first child is one year old. Hence, her birthday is on 28 March, and Staci's birthday is on 17 March.

But to die at age the age of 43 is a travesty, and so unfair, and why did God have to take her, she thought. They had shared all of their life events together; drivers licenses, sports, school pranks, boyfriends, loss of virginity, college, careers, marriage, and children. They knew each other's darkest secrets and would stand united and firm against their parents when both were in trouble. Yet, Staci was more religious than she was and they often had theological discussions. Staci was a devout Catholic, but she was a seemingly good Catholic in practice only, and attended services and rituals out of habit and indoctrination, or at least that is how she explained it in their conversations. Besides, she told Staci that she was very uncomfortable confessing intimate sins to a male priest on the other side of the curtain in the confessional box. She argued that nuns should be allowed to hear the sins committed by females and give absolution. Staci thought that was actually a good idea, but it was not Catholic doctrine, and therefore unacceptable as a proposal.

Staci was a beautiful woman and had brown eyes that always projected warmth, and she always had a smile for everyone she met. There was standing room only at the funeral. The most striking aspect of her beauty was a luxurious mane of chestnut colored hair that reached halfway down her back. She always kept it tidied up into a loose ponytail style, and always wore a blue ribbon just below the nape of her neck, which cinched everything together. Throughout any day, her hair on both sides of her face would eventually work loose and attractively framed her features further enhancing her charm and beauty, much like an Andie McDowell from the movies. Staci's favorite color was blue and she always said that you can find God in anything blue. Terri would always respond, "It depends upon how you see it." Staci would smile and say, "That is exactly right." The sense of loss, emptiness, and pain, resided as a stone in her heart.

They had made a pact from when they were young girls in high school. In addition to incessant catechism lessons that always touched on death in some extreme or another, each promised the other, whichever one of them died first, she would return somehow and visit the other one and let her know she was OK. No matter how desperately she prayed that Staci would come to visit her in whatever form she so chooses, it had not happened, and of course likely would not. A really stupid idea when she thought about it. Fragile human beings trying to rationalize death or trying to ease the torment reference something that awaits all of us. Now remembering their promise to each other, despair stitched across her heart as a thick sob tried to surface in her throat, and for a moment she lost her breath.

Through sleepy half lidded eyes, Terri stared ahead dully listening to the rhythmic clicks and swooshes of the windshield wipers. The car's hi-beams cleared the darkness aside in the road ahead. The light fought with the lashing rain; oddly every raindrop was fully visible and now falling in slow motion, and radiated brilliance projected into the passing landscape. In her mind she was startled, the moment seemed out of sync, disassociated, and aroused an eerie sensation within her breast.

The car slowed as Ted skillfully negotiated a particularly sharp curve to the right. As he smoothly accelerated into a straighter portion of the road, she idly watched the headlights follow the curve of the road and shoot off into the wet darkness as the car came around. Then she saw it...something...no, someone...a woman...a woman who was naked curled up in a fetal position, with her back toward the passing vehicle, on the shoulder along the left side of the road. She sat upright in her seat looking back over her shoulder, straining to see what she thought she might have seen...did she really see such a thing? It had only been for a split second.

Ted was looking at her questioningly. She exclaimed, "I saw something back there on the left side of the road as we came into the curve. I think it was a woman. She was naked. Didn't you see her?"

"No," he responded.

"Ted, stop the car we have to go back now, please, I know I saw someone. She needs help, I am sure of it."

Ted wasn't sure what to do and seemed confused. "Okay, Honey," as he reached over, placing his hand on his wife's knee as he brought the car to a stop. Quickly applying a three-point turn he started back toward the curve. He drove slowly, cautiously, searching now the right side of the road. Terri had removed her seat belt, both hands were gripping the edge of the dashboard, where she was leaning forward intently peering out through the windshield, willing the windshield wipers to give her a clearer view of the road and shoulder.

"Ted! Right there! – See it?" She was pointing right where the curve in the road was most extreme. "I saw a woman lying there...and look, the shoulder and mud looks disturbed compared to the surrounding area." Ted was staring ahead desperately trying to see what she had seen. Indeed, he could see that the shoulder showed signs of a disturbance. The furrows of mud trails easily revealed something had gone off the road, scraped the shoulder clear of stones and leaves, successfully tearing through the mud and debris, and likely went over the side down into the woods.

He pulled off to the side of the road, put his hazard lights on, reached over Terri's lap and retrieved a flashlight from the glovebox. "OK, let's go take a look. Button up your raincoat tight," he said.

Pulling the collar of his coat up high over his neck, he quickly exited the car and was immediately drenched by the rain and wind flung water from the surrounding trees. Turning on the flashlight, he leaned forward into the rain and started toward the spot that Terri had pointed out. Looking back over his shoulder he could see she was following him, even though he had told her to stay by the car. Reaching the site where Terri had pointed to he could see that something had happened. She stood beside him now and said, "This is where I saw the woman. She was naked and her back was toward me, and she was curled up into a fetal position. I could just see over her and could tell her arms were across her breasts, and her knees were drawn up toward her chin. She had long brown hair that was lying in the mud."

Squinting his eyes while trying to avoid the stinging rain, he played the flashlight's beam around the shoulder area following the muddy furrows to the shoulder's edge, where he directed the flashlight beam down into the gully, into the woods, and into the inky blackness. The flashlight played across something that winked red back at him. Flipping the flashlight back he fully caught a red reflection, held the flashlight steady and realized he was lighting up the reflective brake light to a car.

He turned to Terri and said, "Honey, I think there is a car down there at the bottom of the gully. Call 911 and report an accident. I will go down and see if anyone is injured."

"Oh my God!" she exclaimed. "Please be careful Ted," she said, as she turned back toward the car to retrieve her phone and call for help.

He was already trying to negotiate the steep side of the gully. He grabbed a tree as an anchor and took a step over the side, slipped in the mud and fell flat onto the ground. He wasn't hurt but the front of him was covered in mud. Nevertheless, he continued to work his way down to the vehicle, continually slipping and sliding in the slick and muddy terrain. It was evident that a vehicle had careened over the side and hurtled down into the gully. Many trees had been torn from the roots, or cut in two, or damaged to some degree. It seemed longer to him but it was really a matter of a minute by the time he arrived alongside of the car. Terri was calling to him and he yelled up to her that he was alright. She yelled back, "The police and fire department are on their way." She could see his flashlight flicking about in the darkness.

He was beside the vehicle now, a dark colored Ford Focus. He was stunned at what he saw! He couldn't believe his eyes. The flashlight's batteries were beginning to die on him and the flashlight's beam had taken on a yellowish pallor. Still, he had enough light remaining to mostly see what he had unfortunately found. The driver of the car was a woman, obviously dead, directly due to the antlers of a large deer impaled into her throat, her throat having been fully ripped open. She must have struck the deer as she was coming around the curve. Due to the force of the impact the deer was flung up and over the hood, smashed through the windshield and pierced her in her throat severing the jugular vein. My God there was blood everywhere! Obviously, she had lost control of the car and must have careened across the road, out of control and onto the shoulder, sliding through the mud, over the edge and down into the gully, all the while with the carcass of a large deer across the hood of her car, with its antlers buried in her throat. Absolutely amazing he thought, and absolutely tragic. In a moment he was overcome with a swelling sadness as he realized the horror this poor woman had encountered. Yelling up at Terri he told her he had found a car with a woman driver who was dead. He didn't hear a response.

The woman must have seen it all, likely alive throughout the extent of the horrific event. Through the door's open window, the glass having shattered at some point during the accident, her eyes were still wide open and surprise and horror were deeply etched into her features. Blood had spurted all over the interior of the car and partially onto the deer that killed her. He observed that the deer was huge with a very large rack. Ted had friends who were hunters and they always talked about how the amount of points from a deer's set of antlers helped determine age. The more the points to the antlers the older the deer. Deer in the area did not have natural predators, and as a result the area was swarming with them, their only natural predators being the American car industry. This deer was a fully grown male and whereas Ted could not hazard a guess as to how many points it possessed, maybe ten, simply put from what he had seen in the past it was essentially a very large deer. Anyone who lived in a rural area of the county could relate tales of either almost striking a deer, or actually having struck a deer. The animals were so stupid; sometimes they would run directly into a stopped vehicle. Not a day goes by that there isn't a deer carcass by the roadside somewhere in the area.

As all of this was passing through Ted's thoughts, he was suddenly startled by a low whimpering sound. Was the woman still alive? My God! He quickly focused the flashlight beam on the woman's face, but there was no movement and no indication she was still alive. She still had that sightless stare that only death could confer. But he heard it again, and realized it was coming from inside the car. The batteries to the flashlight were almost dead. It occurred to him to use the flashlight from his cellphone. Pulling his IPhone from his pocket, the bright screen allowed him to quickly locate the flashlight application. He tapped the flashlight app and chose the brightest setting. He tried opening the rear door on the driver's side but it was jammed and would not yield. He flashed the light through the window. It took him a few moments before he realized he was looking at a child in a children's car safety seat strapped into the back seat behind the passenger's seat. The child's face was covered in blood and he could only see the whites of the child's eyes. Good God, the child was drenched with blood and was just staring at him, although more likely just staring at the light. When the child blinked or closed its eyes its face was absorbed back into the gloom.

How did the child get so much blood on it? He could only surmise that the mother had been able to partially turn sideways while dying and had drenched the child with the blood gushing from her throat wound. It was likely the deer may have also contributed to the child's bloody soaking. Ted quickly scrambled through the mud and vegetation to the other side of the vehicle. He was able to get the door open and after fumbling with the restraints to the safety seat, he carefully removed the child from the vehicle while simultaneously protecting it by cradling the child in his arms. In the light of his IPhone he thought maybe it was a boy. The child appeared to be about a year old. In his arms the child was silent, except for an occasional murmur like whimper, but mostly the child just stared up at him through the blood on its face. He tried to wipe some of the blood from the child's face, holding his hand into the rain to cleanse the blood from it. There was no way he could carry that child up the side of the gully. He would have to wait for the rescue personnel to arrive on the scene. He could hear sirens in the distance. In the interim he covered up the child with his coat. It was cold but it was too late to worry about trying to keep dry. The child took priority now. He yelled up at Terri that he had found a child who did not appear to be injured. However, it was likely she could not hear him over the wail of the approaching sirens.

The rescue personnel had actually arrived fairly quickly. A police officer was the first to arrive and had been only a few miles away when he was dispatched to the scene. After quickly closing off the road with flares, he positioned his cruiser perpendicular to the road and aimed his take down lights down into the woods where Ted was located. The area was now brightly lit up and she could see Ted alongside the left side of the car. He had taken off his coat and it was wrapped around something that he was holding to his chest with both arms. She knew he could not see her on the shoulder looking down toward him.

When the first responders arrived on the scene, based on information that the police officer had been passing to the dispatcher, they knew what they would encounter. There efficient movements seemed choreographed and no movement was wasted. In moments they threw ropes over the shoulder of the road and into the gully and two personnel quickly worked their way down to the car. The police officer standing next to her told her the persons were emergency medical technicians and would control the scene once they got to the car.

Suddenly, she felt the burden of being depressed, because she already knew the woman driver was dead. In a moment if she did not gain control of her feelings the tears would begin. She could not help thinking about the woman she had seen coming around the curve. Was that the woman in the car? How is that possible? Did she even see what she thought she saw? They would not be here now if she hadn't seen the woman lying in the mud on the shoulder of the road. Ted did not see the woman. The image of the woman in extremis was permanently imprinted onto her mind. She knows what she saw, as she continued to try and convince herself. How could he have missed seeing her? It could have been days before anybody would have found the car and the driver. As her mind and confusion pondered the mystery of this incident, for some odd and inexplicable reason, her memory of her fleeting glimpse of the woman lying in the mud made her think of Staci. There was something that she could not quite fathom that seemed related to her sister. She would think about it later. The rescue people were bringing up the patient transfer boards.

Ted had managed to make it back to the shoulder of the road and was walking toward her. My God he was a mess! Soaked to the bone and covered in mud and without his coat. The wind was flipping his hair about his forehead and droplets of moisture would flick off into the air. He looked somber.

"I think we saved a life today. There was a baby in the back seat of the car who appears to be safe and not harmed," he said

"Oh my God! Really? He nodded. "Look," he pointed. She turned to where he was pointing. They could both see a female emergency medical technician in the back of an ambulance holding the baby in her arms. She was gently rocking the baby back and forth, while in a low tone she sang to him. "They are getting ready to transport the baby to the hospital, go over and look at him," he said.

They both started toward the ambulance. At that moment rescue personnel pulled the patient transfer board from the gully onto the roadway, which partially blocked their path toward the ambulance. The deceased woman driver was secured to the board and covered. One of the rescue personnel quickly detached the lines and with the assistance of another person, both persons now positioned alongside of the board, prepared to lift the board into the rear of another ambulance.

It was at that moment a gust of wind fled across the road-way flinging rain about and pushed up against Ted and Terri. Terri's hair flew parallel to the ground. The strong gust of wind adroitly slipped past each of them and scooped up the blanket covering the deceased woman with a resounding snap. The blanket was haphazardly flung back toward the first body re-straining strap of the board, fully revealing the face and upper torso of the deceased woman.

Terri gasped! The wound to the woman's throat was ter-rible. She had never seen anything like it. Ted noted that her eyes were closed now. But the wind that had flung back the blanket seemed to be playing about the deceased woman's face and ruffling her hair about her forehead. Terri thought it seemed as if the wind was caressing the woman's face. Then in a second the woman's hair, which had been scrunched up along the right side of her face, previously hidden from them, suddenly blew straight up and quickly fell to the ground. The gust of wind became a gentle wind playfully teasing at the ends of the woman's hair. Anyone could tell that she had a beautiful head of hair. It was very long, thick and dark col-ored, appeared to be very soft, and even now it shined with highlights and reflections from all of the lighting on the scene. It was fashioned into a loose ponytail style, similar to her sis-ter's style.

Then she saw it and she gripped Ted's arm. "My God, Ted! Look! She has her hair in a ponytail with a blue ribbon holding her hair together....Just like Staci did." She was incredulous. How was it possible that so much of her sister was here at this moment? "Ted, we saved a life today...that little baby," she said. "I know Staci was helping us find the accident and the baby. I know it! That was because of the woman I saw on the side of the road. I don't know if that was the deceased woman or if it was Staci lying on the shoulder. Oh my God, Ted, it is a miracle!"

Ted thought about that for a moment. Maybe. Everything

that has happened required a lot of thought to begin to even believe all of the circumstances at play today. He held his gently weeping wife in his arms as they watched the rescue personnel place the deceased woman into the back of the ambulance. He knew there was going to be sorrow in someone's home tonight, but the child was alive, and maybe this "miracle" would help Terri get past the death of her sister. He turned her aside from the ambulance and started walking her back to their car. Time to go home.

"Freeze! PC Police!"

"I know that even now, having watched enough television, you probably won't even refer to them as lepers so as to spare their feelings. You probably call them 'parts-dropping-off challenged' or something."

— **Christopher Moore**
Lamb: The Gospel According to Biff, Christ's Childhood Pal

TWO MALE FRIENDS are in a restaurant engaged in conversation about recent newsworthy events:

"I am pleased that the racist bastard is banned from owning a basketball team for life," said the one friend. He was referring to recent events in which the aging owner of a professional basketball team offered disparaging comments about race in the confines of his private home. The comments were illegally recorded by a girlfriend during a phone call and which she subsequently released to the media some months later.

"I agree," said the other friend, "but you can't use the word 'bastard' to describe him."

"How come?"

"It is a derogatory term and demeans one's dignity," he said

"Well, yes, I can see what you mean, but who cares here in this restaurant?"

"Whoever overhears us and takes offense, that's who."

"What do you mean? It's a private conversation. It might sound rude but it's none of their business," he retorted.

He leaned in, looking around, nervous, in a low voice said, "It doesn't matter, if we are overheard, someone records us, and it is sent out via social media, you know Facebook, Twitter, the like. Even now someone could be taking a video of us. We would become instantly infamous. We could lose our jobs, our friends might turn away from us, and we would be subject to national humiliation."

His friend taken aback, "Really, you think that?"

"You bet I do, happens to cops all the time."

"Jesus Christ! I hadn't thought of that!" he exclaimed"

His friend looking horrified, "You can't say things like Jesus Christ!"

"What?"

"Yeah, that is a religious reference and completely unacceptable in this country, either as an exclamation or a topic of public conversation. You can use words like "s*t, f*k, and other vanilla emphatic expressions. Movie stars and rock stars do it all the time, some politicians too, but you cannot invoke religious images."

"For Christ's sake! You can't be serious?"

"Shit! You said it again," his friend moaned while his eyes flicked left and right to see who might be listening.

"This is a free country, we are allowed to say what we like," he argued indignantly.

"Of course, it is," his friend countered. Then hesitatingly, "Sort of is and sort of isn't."

Leaning back, hands grasping the edge of the table, "What do you mean?"

"Of course, you can say what you want, anytime, anywhere, and not worry about the government, but there are other consequences to be considered."

"What other consequences?"

"Well, what about the politically correct police?" he suggested. "The PC police," he emphasized.

His friend started laughing. "There is no such thing...that is just something mythical at the government level, although I guess some politicians perpetuate the myth."

"No, my friend, it is true. They do exist. Although nobody can really say who they are. They operate in the shadows of our government and they can reach into anyone's private lives at any time."

His friend, now incredulous, "You mean like an organization with uniforms and weapons and patrol cars? They go around looking for people who make inappropriate statements they don't like, and think other people don't like them either?"

"Yes, exactly...well, not exactly like police departments as you know them. Only one establishment can identify the PC police and who they are, and they are all around us assisting the PC police as enthusiastic supporters."

His friend, rolling his eyes, "Who might that be?"

Looking around again, he leaned in and in a low voice, "The media...they are everywhere, ever on the alert for anything they can apply as a news topic and wring dry for their viewers, or readers. They know...they know exactly who the PC police are." He winked, "And another thing, the PC police are also all Democrats."

With that statement, his friend burst out laughing. "You can't be serious! All Democrats? No Republicans?"

His friend looking hurt, "Well...tell me one Republican who attacks someone for public statements they may have made?" Tell me one Democrat who is publicly pilloried with the same level of animosity as a Republican. Better yet tell me one Democrat who allows a Republican to express his or her views without a media supported blistering attack in return?" He leaned back in his chair, feeling smug, knowing full well his friend could not answer his questions.

"Well, I guess I can't...I see your point," he said.

"You betcha!" He went on, "I know this is not like Nazi Germany or Stalinist Russia, anything like that...where everyone watches their neighbors and children turn in their parents for statements they may have overheard. He paused, "Come to think of it that does happen sometimes, like when kids tell their teachers, or even call the police, and tell on their parents who are using drugs. I have heard of that before."

"Me too, but I don't think such repressive regimes can happen here. Can it?"

"Well, I guess it has to start somewhere, I suppose. Must have started out in Germany and Russia similar to what is going on our country today. But," he insisted, "That is way too extreme, not here!"

"Yeah, but the government, the police, can listen to you any time they like. Everybody has smartphone recording devices, although I guess only the police and college professors have to worry about that tech ability today."

"What worries me is that everyone has said or says something that can be defined as stupid, raunchy, racist, sexist, or taken out of context, whether it was said in private or in public. In no time these statements and photos are made public and the whole country is reviling your existence. A classic PC police tactic."

His friend was quiet and was looking away. His face was flushed and he seemed embarrassed. He turned to look back at him...in a moment he spoke. "I am sorry, but I have to be concerned about myself and my family and my job."

Questioningly, "What do you mean?"

He explained, "You have said some things here tonight that could get us in hot water if someone had overheard us, and maybe someone has."

He responded, "Your point being?"

"Well...I was getting nervous with some of your views and I recorded portions of our conversation and I have posted it on my Facebook page."

"What! You did what!?"

"I am sorry, but I have to protect myself. Nowadays you just don't know what people are going to do or say. I sent out a Twitter post too, disavowing any association with some of your comments," he said.

He sat there stunned...speechless...staring at his friend. Finally, he managed to speak, "I have heard you say and declare many inappropriate statements before, especially when you have had too much to drink. Come to think of it you are the one who made most of the controversial statements tonight."

"I know." He looked miserable. "I am sorry but since I managed to get it out first it will seem as if I am clean and that I don't associate with some of the views you have espoused."

"You espoused the views. All I did was ask questions," he explained.

"Yes, that is true, but depends upon how one interprets those portions of our conversation that I recorded and posted on Facebook. Regardless, I am good with the PC police now."

The friend did not have a response to that statement and sat there feeling betrayed in combination with a smoldering sense of anger.

"I have to go now. Again, I am sorry, but I am sure you understand." With that final statement he pushed his chair back, stood up and left the restaurant.

He sat there for a few minutes staring straight ahead, still feeling numb from his exchange. He looked around the restaurant, ideally searching for the server. Then he noticed it. Many of the diners were now looking at him, some with disapproving expressions on their faces.

Not possible. That soon?

Requiem for a Cop

"It takes two people to make you, and one people to die. That's how the world is going to end."

—William Faulkner

THE SHOVEL BIT savagely into the hard dirt. Officer George "The Mad Munk" Munkelwitz, of the Prince George's County Police Department, worked the handle back and forth, reached down and grabbed the base, and swung the shovel up and over the edge of the grave, throwing the shovelful of dirt onto a growing pile. He speared the shovel into the grave, now about two feet deep, sat back on the edge, wiped a sleeve across his face, and remarked to the three other cops slouched in various positions against the hallway wall, "That's enough for me. One of you guys take over."

One of the cops, Bill "Big Jake" Richards, stood up and said, "I got it Munk. It's my turn."

Bill walked over and jumped down into the grave as Munk was climbing out. He grabbed the shovel handle, worked it loose and started digging.

Munk walked over to where the other two cops were sitting, turned around placing his back against the wall and slid down into a crouched position. Munk tilted his head back against the wall and let the coolness from the wall seep through his sweat soaked shirt.

He looked over at Connie Marshall in the dim light. "Hey Connie, give me some water, please," Munk asked.

She reached into a cooler alongside of her, rummaged around stirring half melted ice, and produced a plastic bottle of water which she handed over to him.

"Thanks."

"Anytime," she said. "But I still think we should have brought some beer."

Doug Lileks who was sitting to her left snickered, "Yeah, this Buds for all you gravediggers." They laughed.

Munk retorted, "That's all I need for one of us to get drunk while we're laying the Sarge to rest. Besides, it's crazy enough that we're doing this sober."

"You got that shit right," said Doug, as he sprawled out on the floor, folding his arms across his chest, and placing a county police ball cap across his eyes. "Wake me when it's my turn. It's way past my bedtime anyway."

Munk glanced at his watch: the luminescent dial read one-thirty in the morning. One-thirty on a Sunday morning on a Memorial Day Holiday weekend, he thought. That would make it past all of our bedtimes.

He looked over at Connie, whose features were barely perceptible in the poor lighting. She was seated with her back against the wall with her long legs pulled up under her arms, and her chin resting on her knees. She was glumly staring at Bill digging in the grave. It was obvious she wasn't thinking about the work he was doing.

It was pretty gloomy in the hallway where they were sitting. Actually, it was pretty spooky, he thought. He had felt that two Coleman lanterns; one lantern placed at each end of the grave would be sufficient. Outside the glow from the hissing lanterns, he couldn't see anything else in the building. The rest of the hallway and the remainder of the building, which was somewhere in the mid phase of construction, were enshrouded in darkness. The growing pile of dirt at the edge of the grave, which was next to a pile of broken concrete chunks, flowed together as dark amorphous mounds barely visible next to the stack of equipment and bags of concrete that they had brought with them.

He looked over at the casket alongside the hallway wall - the reason why they were there. The Sarge was in there - deceased for a week now, and buried three days ago. Light from the lanterns glowed dully on the brass handles where fresh smears of dirt were evident along the length of the casket.

Munk rubbed his face and stared at Bill steadily digging in the grave. What the hell were they doing here? The cool dank air in the hallway weighed heavily on his sadness. The Sarge, their street supervisor, had shot and killed himself a week ago after being diagnosed with a baseball sized tumor in his stomach that tripled in size in a matter of a couple of weeks.

He remembered back to that day when a friend from communications had called him and told him what had happened. While off duty, the Sarge came over the air with his issued personal radio, and after identifying himself by his ID number, had nonchalantly requested that the dispatcher send beat officers and homicide investigators to his address for a suicide. When the dispatcher asked him what he had, he replied that he had a suicide victim with a gunshot wound to the head. Within minutes the first beat officer arrived at the Sarge's home. The officer found the Sarge sprawled face down in his driveway - with his head and shoulders inside of a large black trashbag; the heavy-duty kind. The Sarge's right arm was up inside the bag where he had shot himself through the roof of his mouth with his departmentally issued 9MM Baretta sidearm. The beat officer had remarked that a trail of thick viscous cranial blood had leaked from the bag and puddled around the Sarge's feet. A note pinned to the bag asked the responding officer to have the mess cleaned up before his family came home that evening.

Munk shook his head - a hell of a way to go, he thought. Lots of cops did it that way though, and for lots of other reasons than disease. Sarge wasn't the first of his friends to die that way. Munk often wondered what he would do if he were faced with a similar situation.

Munk could see that Bill was beginning to tire. He said," Jake, take a break and let Doug take over."

"Okay by me. Hey Doug! Get your ass in here! It's your turn." Doug groaned and sat up. Dutifully he got up and walked over and took the shovel from Bill.

Munk watched Bill as he slowly walked over and sat down. He looked tired, thought Munk, but then they were all tired. Yet, we're all here because there isn't a one of us who doesn't owe the Sarge for something.

He looked over at Bill who was slumped down against the wall wiping his face with a towel, and remembered that Bill owed his job to the Sarge.

Fifteen years of Bill's life almost went down the drain because he couldn't control his drinking. It was probably a combination of the job and the destruction of his second marriage that started him drinking heavily. Just like most alcoholics, he hid it well for a while. Yet, as the bouts increased, he started showing up to roll call looking like hell and smelling of alcoholic beverages. Everyone thought it was funny at first, because Big Jake was a funny man when he had been drinking. That was when he liked to tell his "Big Jake" jokes, which, were of course responsible for his nickname. Simply put, "Big Jake," was a euphemistic reference to a specific, significant, and dominant portion of his anatomy. As Big Jake liked to tell it, whenever he was driving around the beltway that encircled Washington, D.C., and had to take a piss all he had to do was pull over to the side, disguise "Big Jake" as a tractor-trailer, and no passing motorist was ever the wiser. Munk smiled thinking about the old joke. Jake had a hundred of them.

When Jake's problems first started, the squad tried to cover for him hoping it was only temporary. Connie seemed to care for him the most and would stay with him all through the shift, while the other officers would volunteer to take all of his calls. The Sarge caught on really quick. During roll call one morning the Sarge suddenly ordered him to take a breathalyzer test, and then Jake was in the shithouse. Any other sergeant would have charged Jake and it would have meant the end of his career. The Sarge took him home that day, covered him on the books for the next few weeks, and during his off-duty time, helped dry him out with the help of the departmental psychologist. A wonderfully empathetic woman who loved cops and delighted in working with cops who had personal problems without the upper echelon's knowledge. The Sarge even introduced him to his present wife, which precipitated his third marriage, now into its second year and going strong. Yeah, he owed the Sarge alright, and it was one of the reasons why he was here.

Munk watched Doug steadily throwing dirt out of the grave and thought about the reason why he was here. When he first pulled everyone together and told them what they had to do because it was the Sarge's final wish, to his surprise, not a one of them balked. They just wanted to plan it down to the most minor detail to make sure that they could pull it off. He thought he would have to argue with one or two of them, but he figured he could get them to do it in the end. He had prepared an argument that he never even got to use. Later, when he thought about why he was instigating this event, he could never arrive at any one specific reason.

He had worked for the Sarge as his Senior Corporal for the past four years. A lot of cops wanted to transfer to the Sarge's squad. He was a very popular and highly respected supervisor - amongst the street troops that is. Management hated him and he had been around long enough that he had something on just about everyone at the top. He had worked beside most of them at one time or another when they were just peons trying to get off the street and onto a career track that would take them to the top. And as the Sarge would tell it, in addition to making their own mistakes as young police officers, it also meant they fucked someone, somewhere, along the way.

The Sarge was always taking up for some cop who had screwed up. More often than not, he often managed to save the cop's ass and it pissed off the higher-ups royally. He had been offered many times the opportunity to get out of patrol and to transfer to more prestigious jobs such as vice or special operations. He could have gone pretty much wherever he wanted to in the department.

Munk remembered one night, when the squad was having a shift party into the early hours; he asked him why he didn't take advantage of the opportunity to get the hell off the street.

The Sarge had keys to a local water park and the squad often went there after an evening shift, where they were far away from the public eye and could act as "cop stupid" as only police officers can who have been drinking. The Sarge and he would always climb up to the top of the park's roller coaster, a nine-ty-foot ascent, with a six-pack in each hand. They would sit on the tracks with their feet dangling over the edge, with only a two-by-four railing in between them and a quick one-time thrill ride. After he had asked his question, the Sarge became quiet and didn't answer him. In fact, Munk recalled, he didn't think he would answer, as if he had offended him when he asked the question. They had completed about a six-pack be-tween the two of them, when the Sarge suddenly said, "I don't want to leave the squad, and wanting to stay on the street has nothing to do with it. Any sergeant can transfer...eventually. If I left who would take care of you guys? Who would take care of the poor smuck cop who gets into trouble while trying to be a cop? You cannot do this job out here, and do it properly, with-out eventually getting into some kind of trouble. I'm the buf-fer between you guys and the assholes above us who will serve you up in order to save their cowardly asses." He had been taken aback. The Sarge's answer had virtually hissed hatred for the department's managers. There was something more there, but he elected not to pursue it.

"Hey Munk," called Doug, arousing Munk from his rev-erie, "One of the lanterns is dying." The lamp closest to the Munk was sputtering and he reached out and pulled it to him. Doug went back to his task at hand. Munk removed the fuel cap and started pouring fuel into the tank. Replacing the cap, he pumped some air into the chamber and the light immedi-ately brightened. He pushed it back towards the grave. Doug halted for a second and said, "Thanks," and resumed digging.

Munk stared at the light. It was hypnotic and tugged at his sight. It helped his mind to wander.

It was on one of those nights up on the roller coaster when

he first had an inkling that something was bothering the Sarge. Many times, after a few beers, combined with the intoxicating feel of a warm summer night and a magnificent view of the surrounding area that on star strewn nights stretched clear into Washington D.C., they would enter into deep philosophical discussions. On that particular night they had talked about dying, as they did on many nights, and if they had a choice, how they would like to go. It was a ludicrous subject, but dear to most cop's thoughts when they were drunk and in a reflective mood. The Sarge had confided to him that if he were to die anytime soon, what he wanted was to be...

At which exact moment, Jake, who was ninety feet below under the roller coaster, rolling around in the grass with some girl who had come along for the party that night. She was suddenly heard to exclaim, in a voice crystal clear in the still night, and tinged with breathless excitement, "My God! And it's all for me!"

They had almost fallen off the roller coaster they were laughing so hard. From that night forward "Big Jake's" reputation was intact. But most important, Munk remembered, he never thought that the Sarge's request that night would ever conceivably become his assumed duty.

Suddenly, "Munk! Wake up, I've had enough for now, it's Connie's turn now."

Munk rubbed his eyes and looked over at Connie's sleeping form, curled up on her side with her hands under her head. She would be angry if she was passed up. But he didn't have the heart to wake her. "I'll take the next tour. How far down are we?"

Doug peered down into the grave. "Considering that I'm six-foot-tall, and my noggin is just peeking over the edge, I'd guess about five now. Figure another two feet, and the foot of concrete over the dirt, and the Sarge should stay buried for eternity. At least in our lifetimes, anyway."

Munk could just see the grin on Doug's face. As Doug

started to climb out, he sat on the edge, and slid into the grave and grabbed the shovel. Doug went over to where Munk had been sitting and took up his spot.

Over his shoulder, Munk said, "Get some rest Doug, I'll try and finish this off. Hopefully, before Connie wakes up."

"Okay, see you then." He laid his head back and pulled his cap down over his eyes. In moments he was out.

Munk stabbed the shovel into the dirt and began the tedious and back breaking task of digging the grave deeper. Doug had done quite a bit of work during his turn. Still, it was getting harder to heave shovelfuls of dirt over the edge.

Doug Lileks, he thought, what a character. Munk believed that the eccentric cops always made the best cops. Doug had only been with the squad for the past year, but had quickly ingratiated himself with the squad members. He was built like a gymnast, and was proud of his physical condition. He had a perpetual scowl that hid a likable personality, and a shock of blonde hair that refused to accept a comb. He had joined the police department right out of the Navy, but that could never be discerned from any military conversation that a person might have with him. He had been a Navy corpsman assigned to a Marine reconnaissance unit, and that was how he identified his military experience - Recon! During one of their late-night parties after a tour of duty, a lively discussion had ensued about surviving under the direst of conditions. Doug had flatly declared that if a person was desperate for water in order to survive, they could drink their own urine in its place. This quickly became a hotly disputed subject in which some members of the squad refused to believe that anyone would drink their own piss. One disbelieving fellow cop offered to pay Doug twenty bucks if he would do it on a bet. Soon, the whole squad thought that was a capitol idea, not to mention a safe bet. In moments a total of one-hundred and eighty dollars was riding on the bet. Doug quickly agreed, but demanded that it had to be his own urine. Everyone thought that was fair, but, with the additional proviso, that he had to pee in a readily available glass beer mug, in front of the squad for verification purposes. Connie was excepted if she so chose, which she did not so choose. Then he had to drink it immediately afterwards; all of it. Doug readily agreed all the while with a grin on his face. Since they had been drinking for some time, Doug was able to accomplish an impressive piss effort. A full mug, and then some, to include a frothy head, which he immediately quaffed down in one effort. To fling added insult towards his squad members, he wiped his mouth with his sleeve, belched, and expressed a satisfying "Aahhhhhhhhhhhh!"

Munk started laughing to himself just remembering the event. He shook his head. Everyone had been so shocked that it was seconds before anyone could say anything. They just stood there mute. Connie later told Munk that she thought he would just sip it, or something, never actually believing that he would drink it all. Doug walked away a hundred and eighty dollars richer that night. It wasn't long before his fame spread throughout the department. Munk looked over at Doug partially tilted over in his sleep. A hell of a cop though.

Munk stopped for a moment, stretched backwards, and then resumed his digging. He was getting there. Another hour maybe. He should probably wake up Connie and let her finish the rest. She would be angry if she thought she was being given less work than the others. Especially, if she thought it was because she was a female. She needn't have worried about that female status crap. She was well liked and respected on the squad. After the Sarge had killed himself, she had been very distraught and had walked around in a daze for days. In fact, he had been so worried about her inattention to her duties, that he had removed her from the street for a few days and assigned her to desk duties. The Munk thought that she and the Sarge may have had something going at one time. But so what, it was none of his business.

Munk couldn't help but smile whenever he thought about

Connie. She had recently assumed minor national media notoriety after an incident in which she received negative attention
from some local animal rights groups. She had been dispatched
to a house to check on the welfare of a resident who hadn't been
heard from in days. The mail was overflowing from its box and
there were newspapers all over the front porch. After a quick investigation, and talking with some neighbors, she had contact-
ed the Sarge by radio and he had given her permission to force
entry into the house. She had found the male owner in a dimly
lit back room - deceased - partially consumed by a twelve-foot
boa constrictor that had been resting peacefully in a far corner of the room. Now disturbed from its somnolence by Officer
Connie Marshall. Connie, upon hearing the rustling sound, had
flipped on the light, screeched, and promptly emptied sixteen
9MM rounds into what animal rights advocates later defined as
a "harmless snake." When Connie later explained to the Sarge
what had taken place, she said that she had taken one look at
the snake, who had taken a longer look at her, all the while licking its chops - at which point the Sarge pointed out that snakes
don't have "chops," - and Connie responded, "Something was
licking something" - and all she knew is that it wanted her. So,
as she later wrote in her "Discharge of Firearms" report - "she
aced the fucker!" Everyone thought that was pretty funny, because Connie would have let the report go through channels.
She was that kind of cop. However, the Sarge insisted she re-
write the report. For weeks she would come to work and find
little rubber snakes peeking out of her mailbox. She was a media cult hero for about a week, and she took it all in with grace
and humor.

Munk had a warm spot for Connie. He couldn't help it. If
more female officers were like her, there would be a lot less
conflict in the ranks.

Munk stopped and examined his work so far. It looked
deep enough. He couldn't see over the edge any more. A quick
measurement gave him a rough seven feet from the center.

"Hey, fellows...wake up! We're finished. Come on over here and take a look." In a moment they were standing around the edge looking down into the grave at Munk.

"Help me out of here," he asked.

Jake and Doug reached into the grave and pulled him out. Brushing the dirt off of his clothes, he walked over to the casket.

"Alright, this is what we have to do next," instructed Munk. "Someone grab the straps and run them under the casket and up through the handles. We'll carry it over together, hanging onto the straps and handles, and then lower it down into the grave. Should be simple enough. Not like when we lifted it out of its original grave." They all started laughing.

Munk watched them go over to the casket and start working the straps under the Sarge's casket. When they had first gone to the Sarge's original grave site at the Veteran's cemetery, it had taken them only a few hours to dig up the fresh dirt. After that it was havoc. They were trying to figure out some way to get the straps under the casket, when Doug, who had been leaning over the edge peering into the grave with a flashlight examining the placement of the casket, slipped over the edge head first when the side of the grave he was leaning over partially crumbled. He landed with a resounding thump when he struck the casket. On the way down he lost his flashlight and was enclosed in complete darkness, deep inside a freshly dug grave, inhabited by a recently deceased person, who was only separated from him by a mere half inch of oak. It didn't matter that it was the Sarge, the Sarge was dead! And that fact alone was sufficient enough for Doug to panic. Doug began yelling, while desperately trying to claw his way up the side, which only further served to pull more dirt down on top of him. Failing in that method to get out of the grave, he started bouncing up and down, which made him look like a jack-in-the-box to the others ringed around the grave. They were laughing so hard at Doug's demise, that it was minutes before they tried to calm him down and help him out.

They finally did get Doug and the casket out. Munk had gone down into the grave and wrestled with the casket for an hour trying to get the straps under it. Doug refused to go back into the grave to help. However, the worst part was pulling it up. Munk thought he would have a hernia. It had occurred to him that while they were tugging and pulling at the casket trying to get it out, they would have a lot of explaining to do if they were caught now. But they got it out, and put it in the back of Jake's pickup truck which had a camper top. The plan was to have Jake drive the Sarge to his house, hide the pickup and Sarge in the garage for the remainder of the night and all of the next day. The following night they would get back together and re-inter him.

However, prior to filling in the Sarge's old grave, they removed an exact replica of the same coffin from the back of the pickup and prepared to bury it in place of the Sarge's coffin. Connie and Jake had driven up to Elizabeth City, New Jersey, the day before dressed in baseball caps, sunglasses, and nondescript clothing. They had purchased the new coffin from a funeral home director, who was quite pleased to have conducted a cash transaction, and who barely gave them a second glance. Between the four of them the coffin had cost some big bucks. Dying was expensive business.

Prior to lowering the new coffin down into the grave, Doug had opened the lid and placed an eight-by-ten glossy picture of the Chief inside. Munk thought it was a nice touch. God forbid their sarcastic humor should ever be discovered; though he would like to be present it if ever occurred. It didn't take them long to fill in the grave, tamp it down, and clean everything up after themselves.

Munk recalled that Jake picked him up first the following night as instructed, and that by the time they got around to picking up Doug, Connie was sitting in the front seat with

Jake and Munk, which meant that Doug would have to ride in the back with the Sarge. Doug had flat out refused, and in the interests of expediency, he allowed Doug to get in the front while he and Connie got in the back with the Sarge.

Much to their mutual frustration, Munk recalled, he had insisted that they surveil the building, and monitor their portable police radios for at least an hour before they went in. When he felt that it was safe, they had driven around to the rear with the pickup's lights out. The pickup truck was backed up to a door that he had selected a few days earlier when he had surveyed the building and the surrounding area. Quickly he unlocked the door with some picks and they unloaded the Sarge's casket, equipment, and supplies. Then while he, Doug and Connie were inside, Jake had driven the truck to a shopping center two blocks away, parked it and jogged back to the new grave site.

Now they were ready to move the casket into the new grave. Munk said, "Alright, let's try to do this as smooth as possible. Everyone grab a corner, hold the strap ends in your hands as you grab a handle so we don't lose them, and when we position it over the grave, shift your hold to where you are only holding it by the straps. Then we'll lower it down a little at a time." Looking at each of his friends, "Got it?" They nodded simultaneously. "Okay, let's do it!"

Together they bent over, secured a firm hold, and while looking at each other to see if everyone was ready, they slowly lifted the coffin until they were all standing upright. When Munk nodded, they shuffled over to the grave and poised the coffin over the hole. Carefully, each cop grasped the straps, while simultaneously letting go of the brass handles, and when Munk nodded again, and said "Okay," they started lowering the coffin into the grave a few inches at time in controlled, jerky movements. In a matter of moments, the Sarge was safely down in the grave.

"Alright!" said Munk excitedly, "Good job!"

"Jesus! I don't remember the Sarge weighing so much," exclaimed Jake.

Munk pointed, "Okay...Jake, you and Connie start mixing the concrete, while Doug and I start filling in the grave."

Connie and Jake started over to where the bags of concrete were stacked against the wall next to a much-used mixing pan that they had found earlier. Munk and Doug both grabbed shovels and began scooping dirt from the dirt pile into the grave. The first few shovelfuls made hollow whooshing sounds as each shovelful splattered across the casket.

Munk kept thinking to himself over and over, he couldn't believe that they had actually gotten this far. He had forgotten all about the Sarge's request that night up on the roller coaster when they had been interrupted by Jake and his happily astonished girlfriend.

Cops always came up with weird and different ways to finish their lives out. It was a big macabre joke amongst all of them. A gallows humor sort of approach to subconsciously counter the vague concept of death that was so pervasive in one form or another in their lives. He hadn't ever given the Sarge's idea a second thought. So, when he received a letter in the mail two days after the Sarge's death, reminding him about that night and his request, he had been stupefied with surprise. He felt as if the Sarge had actually reached out to him from the grave. Well, maybe not from the grave, but certainly from somewhere. Surprisingly enough, when he put it to the other three, the only other members of the squad that he even trusted to do something like this, they had quickly agreed, especially Connie, who had been ecstatic, and for the first time that week seemed alive again. There only question to him, was how were they going to pull off something like that? He had told them to stand by; he would come up with something. And now here they were. Christ, just when you think you've heard it all. Go figure.

Filling in the grave was certainly easier than the digging

part, he thought. In a moment, they were all jumping up and down on the mound in effort to thoroughly tamp it down. With much grunting and a few obscure curses, Jake and Doug dragged the mixing pan full of concrete over to the edge and started pouring concrete into the floor opening. Two more pans were required in order to completely fill in the hole and cover the grave. Once the concrete had been poured in, Jake, who had worked as a laborer with a concrete company during his summer vacations between semesters in college, smoothed off the surface with a two-by-four, and then began working the surface. As the concrete began to dry a little it became even easier to work with, and Jake was able to blend the surface sufficiently well enough with the surrounding concrete floor. Hopefully, so as not to be noticeable in the dim light when the workmen returned to their job on Tuesday. Once the new concrete was totally dry, and some dirt and dust had been spread over the spot and ground into it, it would take some focused attention and intentional scrutiny to notice anything out of the ordinary.

When Munk had first examined the hallway floor, he had noticed varying shades of concrete throughout its length, and there were sporadic areas where the workmen had done some patch work for whatever reasons. By the time the workmen laid the linoleum down, which, judging by the extent of the construction on the building, could be any time now, there would be no evidence of any tampering, or of their presence. Hopefully. Munk checked his watch. It was now about twelve-thirty. The warmth of the May afternoon was already seeping into the building.

"Alright, stack the equipment by the door and make ready to go. When night comes around twenty-one hundred hours this evening, Jake will get the truck, back it up to the door and we'll load the equipment back on. That includes all the concrete chunks and whatever else that we dug up. Then you guys are out of here. I'm going to stay for a little while longer, make sure we didn't leave any evidence of our presence, and try to make the Sarge's final resting place look a little more worn." He looked at each of his fellow police officers one at a time. "Any questions? None? Okay, everybody go off and lie down until we can get out of here."

After staging all of their equipment and accumulated debris by the door, everyone, exhausted after a night of back breaking labor, quickly fell asleep.

When nightfall had come, Munk awoke Jake and sent him after the pickup. An impatient Connie and Doug were ready and waiting when he returned, and even before Jake had completed backing his pickup up to the door, they had started slinging equipment and chunks of concrete into the truck's bed.

After they had quickly loaded the pickup, Munk insisted on a quick sweep of the work area. Finding nothing, he told them to get the hell out of the area and he would see them on daywork. He reminded Jake to pick him up around midnight at the corner of Barlow Road and Landover Road. Watching them leave, Munk closed the door, and walked back to examine the grave site. He flicked on the streamlite flashlight and played it around the site and the surrounding hallway looking for evidence of their presence. Not finding anything, he dropped his gaze to the Sarge's grave. He felt strange. Tingly all over and his stomach was doing flip-flops. It felt very eerie, all alone, and standing by the Sarge's new grave.

Pleased, he muttered to himself, "Not bad, not bad at all." Then he smiled, and said, "Well, this is what you wanted Sarge. I just hope you approve." He turned away and took a few steps over to the wall, put his back flat against it and slid down into a sitting position, drew his knees partly up, and draped the arm with the flashlight over one knee.

He just needed a few minutes to say goodbye, and then he would leave and go meet Jake.

You were the best, he thought. I hope if I ever become a

sergeant that I can do half as well as you did. He marveled at the ability and leadership of one man, who was able to subtly inspire such devotion from his officers, that even after he was dead, he was able to get them to do something for him. Munk shook his head.

His thoughts slipped back to that night when he and Sarge were up on the roller coaster. The Sarge had confided in him that he was dying with a type of cancer. He asked if Munk would be able to assist him with a last request. He had told Sarge if it was in his power then it was guaranteed. Sarge told him that a year ago when he had visited England on a vacation, he was struck by how many persons of royal stature, military heroes, government officials, clergy, writers and musicians were entombed in the floors and walls of historic churches. All across the country in every village, town and city. He thought he would like to be entombed in one of the department's many buildings after he died in the near future. He did not say or hint he was going to take his life. Well, how the hell was he going to do that, he had countered? A sly smile had come across the Sarge's face. He said, think...the new police academy has just broken ground, and that would be the perfect receptacle, if you think you could pull it off. Incredulous, Munk told him that would be quite an undertaking, but he would think about it, while also thinking at that moment there was still plenty of time to consider this unconventional request. The Sarge would die in a matter of a few weeks by his own hand. Although Munk had not expected such a tragic ending, he understood it.

Regardless, it had now been done. He stood up and involuntarily groaned. He was going to be some kind of sore in the next few days. He flicked on the streamlite, walked over to grave and took one last look. "So long Sarge, stay safe," he said. He flipped a half casual salute, swung the streamlite around the area, making one final security sweep. Satisfied, he started walking down the hallway working his way towards the front of the building. He passed rooms of varying dimensions intermittently spaced throughout the building, and occasionally out of curiosity, he flicked the streamlite's beam into each one, idly wondering what they would look like when they're finally finished.

Finding a door to the front of the building, he cracked it open a few inches and listened and watched. Sensing no problems, he quickly stepped outside onto a sidewalk that bordered a partially completed parking lot cluttered with construction equipment and materials.

Munk stood still for a few minutes alert to any danger. Then very casually, with his hands in his pockets, he strolled across the parking lot towards a large sign facing the sidewalk that ran the length of Barlow Road. He wanted to take one more look at the sign before he went to meet Jake.

Munk stood on the sidewalk looking up at the sign. It was partially lit from a streetlight nearby, and although it had been in the weather the last few months, it still retained some of its slick appearance with the colorful Prince George's County heraldic seal dominating the left half of the sign. The writing on the right side of the sign was a combination of lower- and upper-case lettering professionally inscribed in dark blue paint. It read:

Scheduled to Open in July 2002
The New Prince George's County Police Academy
Nicholas Valltos - County Executive
Chief of Police – Darvan Mitchum

The Mad Munk laughed out loud, turned away, and started walking down the sidewalk towards Landover Road to meet Jake. Whistling softly, he thought to himself - all that remained now was to start the rumors.

Love Is a Many Splendored Thing

God assigned full moons as a satellite,
To stand sentinel over sad lovers
The cold pale blue is a secret delight
Tunnels to flee over whom it hovers."

—Ed Moroney
Poem, Orion, First Time Death Is Still an Amateur

SHE WAS COMING tonight!

She always came on one of the nights during the cycle of a full moon. In their past it was when they had loved each other the most, when her passion overflowed into his life in gasps, and she had hungered for what he brought into her life.

He never knew how he knew. He just did this late afternoon. He couldn't say to himself that he "sensed" her pending arrival. He couldn't sense much of anything. He didn't know when he was hungry, or if he had to shit or piss, or if he even had a hard-on, unless he happened to look down and see the bulge. He wouldn't know if a rat were chewing on his leg.

In his mind he felt the excitement of her coming. If he were able to move, he would pace the floor in anticipation and excitement. It was maddening to feel her in his mind, thoughts whirling in a storm, with no possibility of physical release. Maybe he could chew his next meal with a vengeance - the next time he was fed. He wanted to do something to be ready for her, to do anything in appreciation. Yet, he had no physical ability to do much of anything, much less clean or straighten out the apartment to be readied for her presence.

The cleaning of his apartment was done by a white-haired and diminutive shrunken elderly Japanese woman, who always knocked lightly, entered the apartment and bowed to him before she started cleaning. There really wasn't very much for her to do, after all it wasn't like he peed all over the toilet bowl. She would move from room to room, clucking quietly to herself in her own language, sometime singing low, and applied an Asian efficiency which seemed acceptable to him for some reason. Before she would leave, she would stop in front of him, where confined to his wheelchair he would look at her with a blank stare that even he could feel. She would touch his cheek for a brief moment, there was sadness in her eyes - he consumed every drop of her sentiment - she would bow slowly and quietly leave.

He was able to move his wheelchair, barely, with a minimum of movement from his left hand, spasmodically jerking a small lever in various directions. Which was fortunate, he often thought, since a minimum of movement in that side of his body was all that he had anymore that was remotely close to his resembling a human.

Without his visiting nurse every other day, to bathe him and change his clothes, and occasionally feed him, he would be completely alienated from the rest of life. She was an odd woman; there was no compassion in her ministrations. Neither mean nor abrupt, she was all business, brusquely applying her necessary duties, for which she was well compensated as a result of the settlement. He assumed he was just one more broken human being she had encountered throughout her career. He never bothered to ask, he didn't want to know, there was no interest. Prior to leaving she always asked him if there was anything she could do for him? His thoughts always pleaded for her to dispose of his body on the way out. Maybe place him in one of those heavy-duty trash bags, cinch it tight, drag him out the door, down the stairs with a heavy thump on each downward step, and then heave his carcass into the dumpster where he belonged. If he were found, for sure no one would remark that someone had thrown away a perfectly good handicapped human being. But he never answered, for what purpose? He just stared back at her. He allowed her to continue to attend to him because he just wasn't quite where he was willing to call it quits. He was close, but not just yet.

His wheelchair was positioned in the living room about six feet in front of a large cloth covered couch. The huge soft kind with full cushions that absorbed the body. This is where she wanted him to be when she arrived. She had made that conditionally clear the first time she had visited. He could hear the wall clock in the kitchen ticking all the way into the living room. He stared at the front door and waited and remembered. He was good at this...there wasn't much else to do.

There were many ways to remember Anne. The first time he had seen her was at a dance with her husband, all chestnut hair, green eyes, and long legs, wearing a black dress that rose just above her knees, and high heels that accentuated a sensuous gliding style of walk. All of which served to define her lovely form. It would be years of stolen glances and a compilation of accumulated sighs before events would bring her irrevocably into his life.

In this modern age the affair had begun innocently enough with a daily exchange of e-mail. Initially it was all jokes and discussions of day to day events. But then subtle thoughts, feelings, and wishes began to creep into the exchanges. It wasn't long before he was aware of the overwhelming sadness in her life, of her failing marriage, and the mounting frustrations that served to abruptly cause her to enter into funks, often and erratically becoming morose, distant and very sad. While simultaneously frustrating, it had been fascinating to watch her emotions at play.

Yet, he wasn't much happier either, also with a damaged marriage, a loss of spirit, and a sense of shame and disgust toward himself for past indiscretions. As far as he knew he was the only person he ever knew who had completely lost his soul. They were perfect for each other, but they were also the binary chemical ingredients that would result in inevitable conflicts and hurt toward each other.

A thinly veiled suggestion had resulted in an afternoon of clumsy lovemaking and her tears. For him it had been the beginning of something beautiful until it began to erode into endless antagonism and his resultant pain today. For her it had been the beginning of further alienation from her spirit, and any joy for life. Still, the following months had been wonderful. Weekend trips away from everything and everyone, passion filled nights and playful mornings. She was a magnificent lover, wild and demanding, every time impatiently asking to be on top. In her rhythmic movement and rising passion, she spewed gasped exclamations of undying love, sometimes with tears, every time climaxing in tremors of ecstasy, seemingly in pain, her fingernails dug deep into his chest leaving angry red weals. Unfortunately, as the months passed it was the only time, she would illustrate any passion. Whenever he reflected back on their affair, outside of their lovemaking, he could not remember one occasion when she exhibited any enthusiasm or genuine happiness.

Still, there was that one night that would be unforgettable in any man's life. It was during a weekend trip where they had gone to the mountains in West Virginia to visit some property he owned. He wanted to take her to the top of the mountain to see the view in the moonlight. They had carefully traversed downhill along an old logger's trail, and had emerged onto the ledge of the mountain that revealed a view that was bathed in the bright white light of the full moon. In the mountain air the moon had been huge, clean white, every detail of its surface fully exposed in the earthly atmosphere. It was if they had been spectators in a museum examining some detailed model of the surrounding countryside...seemingly removed as if they were observers from another world. Every sound from within the valley was clearly heard - the sole car driving along the mountain roads, livestock softly mooing into the night. It was a wonderful and memorable and magnificent spectacle - a moment as perfect as could be for two lovers.

She had sought his arms and warmth. He had bent to kiss her, but her hands and intentions signaled otherwise. In moments he was sitting on his jacket spread out on the ground, his trousers and underwear down and about his ankles. She was sitting on him, he deep inside of her, his hands under her blouse caressing her breasts, soon fully exposed in the moonlight. She rocked rhythmically against his hips and again declared her love for him. He had loved her in total wonder, the full moon positioned behind her outlining every feature, applying a silver halo about her features, suggesting to him the presence of an angel. In that moment, he knew he was beyond return and he loved this woman with everything he was able to muster within the mere limitations of his human status. God was a full moon that night, and the only God that he had ever believed in.

Yet, it wasn't long after that, short days later, even for brief periods during that weekend and after that night, before he sensed a change emanating from her. It was mostly Anne, always Anne it seemed. She would become quiet for long periods of time, not responding to his touches, nor touching him in the spontaneous ways that lovers do. Some days she never called or responded to his e-mail, offering excuses for missed time between the two of them; her work demands or she was exhausted, or there was no one to watch her daughter after school. His heart sunk and he knew the initial stages of the end of a relationship. Try as hard as he could, he could never get her to talk to him and explain her feelings. In her mind his hurt and futile efforts to try and honestly explain his feelings were always hateful words to her. She had that way about her, to select only those passages from any letter or e-mail that angered her, and turn it around and fling it back into his face, blaming him as the cause of their deteriorating affair. When she became angry, every time, he knew he had hit home. It only made him sadder. She never could see the love the passion, and concern in anything he said to her or wrote to her. Only her own anguish in life. As she moved further away from him, and as he continued to delude himself, it became a matter of trying to confront the inevitable and obtain some closure, than continue to forlornly hope. This, as he shamefully knew, was the way the loser in every relationship always acted.

He knew in his heart what had happened, what she was going to do. The sense of guilt had creeped into their relationship, pushing her further away from him. She would try and save her marriage. Maybe one night dress up provocatively for her husband, pursue a second honeymoon, and embark on a cruise somewhere. It didn't really matter though, the end result would be the same, and the sorrow in her life would take on a new and even fiercer pain in the future. Of course, he could not tell her that and expect her to understand. Her vulnerability and naiveté had been traits that had endeared her to him.

But his whole life and the nature of their relationship changed that one Saturday afternoon...

His thoughts were suddenly interrupted by the scratching sound of the key in the lock. With a rush of anticipation his eyes realized that early evening had arrived. He often floated away in travels of thought, without regard for time, an acquired skill since the accident which allowed him to successfully negotiate another day. There were no lights on in the room yet. No matter he often sat in the dark room hours upon end. The night outside was brilliant with the light of the full moon which spilled into the living room through an open window. Intermittently a slight breeze followed causing sheer white half-curtains to gently billow outward for a brief moment and then flow back toward the wall.

She was here!

He watched the door handle twist downward ...the door opening part way, and Anne slipped quietly into the room, her back to the door, pushing the door gently closed behind her. She stood for a moment with her arms behind her still grasping the doorknob, her back resting lightly against door frame, allowing her eyes to adjust to the room's gloomy conditions.

His eyes took her in, willing himself to look something like the man she once knew. She was wearing a dark colored skirt, maybe black maybe dark blue in the dim light, which came above her knees. Her short-sleeved blouse was of white linen that buttoned up the front. She wore white stockings and black high heels. Her long chestnut brown hair fell about her face and shoulders, where she watched him with a cautious expression and shining eyes. Beautiful green eyes, slender but wide, where the green assumed various shades and levels of moisture, dependent upon her surroundings. The kind of eyes that were the seed of all men's fantasies and dreams about women. With her gaze she was able to make many men experience a sense of brief giddiness.

She walked slowly across the room toward him. She would not touch him just yet, she never did at first. She stopped in front of the couch and watched him for a moment, her posture relaxed, her hands loosely by her side.

And he waited...

With one hand she slowly reached up toward her blouse, freeing a button from restraint. In moments her hands quickly undid the remainder, her blouse falling open and exposing her white bra stark and vivid in the moonlight and highlighted against a recent tan. Her nipples were evident in the sheer fabric. Although her breasts were not large, they filled the cups to a round and full softness.

He could not feel his heart beating faster, but he knew it to be so from the warmth of sensation about his temples and cheeks.

She put her arms behind her, downward, and the blouse slid to the floor. Leaning to one side she pulled on the zipper to her skirt causing it to loosen and partially slip down her hips, then releasing it, where it fell to the floor enshrouding her ankles and heels. She was wearing a white garter belt with thigh-high stockings - and no panties. She always wore a garter belt and stockings. It was the one aspect of their relationship, and developed fantasy, they had planned to do one evening - but it never happened.

In that brief moment, he absorbed her body and image into his soul. The anger and sheer frustration at his helplessness arose in his throat. Inwardly he cursed his body and some God somewhere - wondering why him? He remained motionless, not daring to show emotion. If he were to disturb this moment she may leave. She had done so in the past. Whenever she came to him she always seemed remotely detached, sometimes as if she were in a trance. He had learned in the past to the discomfort of his heart, it was always thus.

She stared at him, seemingly detached, possibly defiant, but willing to allow him to possess her with his eyes. He watched hungrily and reminiscent of the passion and sensations he once so readily knew. Her body was recently tanned from the last time he had seen her, displaying erotically defining tan lines he had always enjoyed on any woman. She was possessed of wonderful curves, firm and supple flesh, and muscle in all those areas that mostly define a woman. She always complained of the extra pounds that had settled in her stomach after the birth of her only child...Liz. To him it was the epitome of her womanhood, a badge of motherhood, a gentle feminine swell that only enhanced her beauty where he most loved to stroke her body and to rest his head. In fact, she showed very few signs of motherhood on her body, but consistently complained of physical imperfections and her weight. He had suspected her of mild bulimia. She had muscular legs, not well defined, but with perfect form and smooth lines, and a slight bowleggedness derived from riding horses since she was a child. She had been a champion performer winning a closet full of ribbons and trophies, which she never looked at any more (he had always wondered why that was?). Her pubic area was thick with dark curly hair hiding secrets and his memories. But he knew how hot wet she could become there, often ruining her panties for the rest of the day. This ability of passion often caused him to marvel at her in wonderment. To him, though, she was all women and every woman he had ever met or ever dreamed about. But it wasn't enough for her - there wasn't anything that was enough for her. She was only capable of understanding herself, and even then, she did not do that well.

By now she had removed her bra allowing her breasts to fall forward. He immediately recalled the wonderful softness and firmness within his hands, of kisses lovingly searching for her nipples. The sadness rose up within his heart and the pain was staggering. He felt as if he might choke.

He watched her sit on the edge of the couch, slowly turn and bring her legs up, and stretch supine across its length. His mind was screaming with fury that he could not get up and go over and touch her. He often thought this is what it must feel like to be in a straightjacket, hung from the ceiling on a meathook.

In a flash the turmoil in his mind unexpectantly savaged his view with vivid remembrances of that day.

It had been a fun day even though she had been more de-tached from him than usual. With Anne and her 8-year-old daughter, Liz, they had gone to a civil war reconstruction re-plete with troops, cannons, weaponry, and horses recreating civil war era lifestyles and battles. It was after one of the re-enacted battles, while they were watching some "Northern" cavalry officers prancing around on their horses. Anne had wandered closer to examine the horses. Liz had stayed back watching her mother; she was apprehensive of horses at her age. One of the horses refused to respond to its rider's com-mands. Another "cavalry officer" had taken his saber and laid it hard across the rump of the defiant horse. The horse sud-denly bolted in surprise and shock. It was later learned the horse's rump had incurred a severe laceration from the sa-ber. The horse fled directly toward where Liz was standing, the rider unable to control his mount and yelling at people to get out of the way! In those few swift seconds, and actions that were later difficult to recall, he had yelled at Liz to watch out, grabbed and pulled her to him out of the way. In doing so, they both stumbled falling to the ground where he had re-flexively covered her small body with his. The out of control animal had passed over the both of them, but struck him in his back and spine area in two separate places, crushing two vertebrae. The blows had succeeded in knocking the breath out of Liz. It was enough to paralyze him almost completely from the neck on down. Not entirely though, there was some limited erratic motion remaining in one arm - but not enough to turn the pages of a book, wash himself, feed himself - or jerk off. And certainly no longer any ability to make love to Anne, or any woman - ever again.

The sequence of flashing images dissolved in his mind... her low soft moans emanating from across the room interrupting his recalled anguish, this moment's pain now substituting for the past. Her legs were drawn slightly up, wide apart, her hands in between. The splattered moonlight throughout the room accentuated the non-tanned areas of her hips and breasts, bathing the length of her body in a loving caress. It seemed as if the moonlight was participating in her efforts, softly enfolded about her body, cuddling her flesh into ecstasy. The sheer white and moon-bright illuminated nylon of her stockings failed to conceal the muscles of her legs, which gently rippled with the movement of fingers and passion. She was a symphony of movement and beauty and eroticism. Her right hand moved rapidly in furious motions, then slow to a gentle tempo. Her body arched upward and her head slowly rolled back, the intensity evident from her wide-open mouth soundlessly gasping for air. He knew she was on the edge. In their past she always came quickly. He had taught her with loving and erotic patience to hold her breath and float along in that nether region just before final release. He loved to watch her face in those moments. Her hair wild and unkept and forming a frame around her face. Her eyes squeezed tightly shut, her mouth slightly parted. In moments she would gush an exclamation she was coming. It was a vision only a lover's memory could possess, and no painter or photographer could ever render such an image onto canvas or paper.

As he stared, transfixed, her breasts rose and fell repeatedly in the throes of a body demanding air, fingers wildly probing her sex. She couldn't wait much longer he knew. In that moment...she abruptly turned her head toward him, eyes wide and round, glistening wet in the half-light, seemingly a look of surprise on her face. He remembered and imagined the icy tendrils of sensation along his spine - wishing hard now for such a miracle. Her head tilted backward, her mouth opened wide as her body erupted into a contorted heave, arching upward where she froze in position, the only movement her fingers stabbing downward in between her legs. In one convulsive inwardly drawn breath she consumed his sorrow and agony into her body - holding for a brief moment the pitiful remainder of his life in her heart. She collapsed onto the couch, spending brief moments trying to control her breathing.

He knew what was next as he watched her with all the inner pain his heart could produce. Turning toward him, she sat up and curled up into a tight ball, her knees against her breasts with her arms tightly wound about her. She began to cry softly to herself, burying her face into her arms. She never let him see her cry - anymore. In the past he had always been there to hold her. He had often wondered what it felt like to cry and be held by someone you loved. He guessed maybe she was the fortunate one.

He waited for her as long as she wanted. There was nothing else he could do. She did not want him to say anything, admonishing him in the past when he tried and threatening to leave. She did not want his pity either. Indeed, as he inadvertently recalled, at one time, about the time of the accident, did she even want him anymore.

She slowly unfolded her body, wiped her face of tears, and stood. She watched him for a second and then started toward him. The moisture from her body was smeared across her inner thighs, the moonlight skating across the wetness. He pressed closed his eyes in fury at his inability to reach out toward her.

Anne stood in front of him now. He could smell her orgasm and moisture. Her scent was never one of an "odor," it was a sensation of cleanliness and damp warmth. He opened his eyes and hungrily took in her presence. She stared straight into his eyes. He could see, even in the poor light, the widely dilated pupils of her eyes, which could not fully suffocate the green of her eyes. Oh God, how he had loved those eyes! Always searching for her gaze, falling into the green, amazed at such beauty.

He watched in awe as one hand slowly sought her femininity, her fingers slowly disappearing, lingering deep inside of her body. In a moment removing her fingers, shining slick with the juices and moisture of her orgasm, she swiftly placed the back of her fingers against his mouth.

In a moment he took the fingers into his mouth, his tongue darting all about, sucking, fully exploring their length and texture, the smooth surface of her nails, his head moving in small erratic convulsive circles. He could not control the small whimpers that escaped from his mind. No food, wine, candy or water had ever tasted better, or could have slaked this thirst. The odd taste of her body was delicious and for a fleeting moment he felt alive again - but only for a moment.

She slid her fingers from his mouth, even as his head tried to stay with her motion. She touched his cheek with the wet fingers and traced a path of moisture down one side. She grasped a breast, staring at it momentarily, and pinched the nipple to hardness. Leaning forward she placed her breast against his mouth, where he pressed his face hard. He began kissing the soft wonderful surface and flesh, luxuriating in the sensation. In his mind he imagined his hands roaming the extent of her body, exploring, probing, lingering, and seeking out each breast. His mouth hungrily sought her nipple, clumsy in his efforts like some newborn infant; she helped him, guiding the nipple to his mouth. He greedily consumed her, remembering love and past, and pulling her being into his body seeking to grasp somehow, and extract forever, a newly born lease on his life which she now, if only fleetingly, offered to him. He sucked eagerly, reveling in the wonder of the swollen and hard nipple against his tongue. Idly stroking the back of his head, she pressed his head harder into her breast. She never spoke to him when she did this, but he knew she was crying again. Sometimes the tears would fall onto her breast and trickle down into his mouth. She would let him suck until his mouth ached, never complaining of discomfort, sometimes switching him to her other breast.

It was time again...he knew. She removed her breast from his mouth, leaned down and kissed him full, hard, her tongue probing into his aching mouth. He sucked gently, then hard, and scoured her tongue with his. He was all too aware of the lack of sensation in his body. She pulled apart - too quickly he thought. She held his face in her hands, their warmth an all too familiar memory. She looked into his eyes, holding him still... mesmerized, she was that beautiful. He waited, knowing what she was going to say. She spoke for the first and last time that evening, as she did on every visit. As during all of her visits she said, "I love you Ed. I always have. Thank you for saving Liz's life!"

She never said anything else. Just those few words. He wanted to know about her life. About Liz...even her husband. When she departed, he would hate her for days to come. But with the oncoming of each new full moon he knew he would hunger for her presence again.

She turned from him, maybe reluctantly. He could never tell. She went back to the couch and slowly dressed - daring not to look at him. He understood that, he could not tolerate to look at himself either. In moments she was walking across the room, and quietly departed. Not once looking back at him - she never did. It was as if she had never been there. The only evidence of her presence was a slight scent of her body on his face, and the ache in his heart. Neither of which he could even touch.

The tears streamed down his face. He always cried after she left. Not loud sobs, nor body wracking bawling, just tears that fled from his body, as he wished what remained of his life and soul would do so. He could never cry when he had his body, in his previous life, even when he was the most hurt in his life - even when she hurt him the most. His display of discipline and inner strength had been his one victory over her. Of those few occasions when he felt he needed a sense of release, he would go out and rent a sad movie. Sometimes it worked - most times it did not.

He sat there watching the curtains rustle with the breeze... replaying the events over in his mind. And he wondered how it was that he was supposed to make it through another minute of this life? Someday she would not come and he could finally die. But then he knew that she knew that. For some reason he suddenly remembered the time when she told him that she did not love him anymore - when it all came to an end. In the same breath she had responded that she was sorry for all that had happened but that she genuinely liked him. He could have mouthed that line before she even completed her sentence. His heart had constricted and his breath had been expulsed in short gasps. In his mind had flashed a response he had never uttered...that he loved her beyond the extent of his life, and would willingly proclaim it to all about him. But time, her complexity, indecisiveness and unhappiness had scoured his psyche.

He thought about her crying each time she came. Her tears were for herself and the agony of her betrayal to a dead husband. She had wanted me, and took me, or maybe she just wanted the excitement of a forbidden relationship, but all in conflict with everything she knew between right and wrong that became stark reality after the death of her husband. There would have been lesser sorrow and pain if she had just kept emotions out of the relationship, and simply wanted to fuck. All of those tears now were really for nothing and were not going to change anything.

He knew all of this because he knew his tears were only for himself.

His head slumped forward. He prayed! For her and himself, fervently, and that she would not return during the next full moon!

Anguish Gladly Disposed

"Time is the substance from which I am made. Times is a river which carries me along, but I am the river; it is a tiger that devours me, but I am the tiger; it is a fire that consumes me, but I am the fire"

—Jorge Luis Borges

IT WAS THE kind of night that sought out lovers. Lovers, who strolled beneath a star strewn sky, and felt together the surrounding warmth of summer about their faces. Where the delight of being in each other's company unconsciously slowed their stride in such a way as to disparage time and adjust it to their timetable. Such lovers blissfully unaware of others about them and location and tomorrows, and fully unaware of the magic of the night that conferred a privilege of escape into their dreamy world.

It was also the kind of night when Charlie, back in 69, would probe the lines looking for weaknesses in the perimeter. All night, silently, crawling through the bush attempting to locate claymore mines, trip flares, where the Marines were located in their fighting holes. Wearing black pajamas style uniforms, faces painted in black, in their disciplined patience they could creep through thick foliage and vegetation without ever giving an indication of their presence. Lovely and balmy nights in Vietnam were harbingers of death.

All of these thoughts, and more, were on the mind of Major Eric Stockey this night as he cautiously and furtively, picked his way between the headstones of America's military dead at Arlington National Cemetery. On this night the intimacy of the late-night sky spread across the cemetery as if providing a protective overlay of warmth over America's war dead. Security lighting from the Pentagon and the Navy Annex, located along the northern and western boundaries of the cemetery, respectively, provided ambient light that bathed many areas of the seemingly endless rows and multitudes of granite gravestones with a dull light, effectively bringing into relief every grave marker to the casual onlooker. It was like looking at a negative of a photo of the cemetery. Although, due in part to limitations in lighting, combined with the inky velvet darkness of the night sky, the sprawling grounds appeared

mystical and displaced in relation to its surrounding city envi-
rons of Washington, D.C. and Arlington. Although technically
known as Arlington Cemetery, everyone one in the D.C. area
simply referred to the cemetery as Arlington.

The easiest way to access the cemetery was by jumping the
stone wall alongside of the parking lot at Fort Myers, which
was located along the southern perimeter of the cemetery.
The base's primary mission was to provide support for the
ceremonial internment of America's Veterans. The wall was
constructed of large stones and was raised to a height of about
four feet. Not an easy obstacle to overcome while wearing a
Marine dress uniform. Once over the wall he had almost two
miles to go to reach the gravesite he was seeking. That is two
miles if he were traversing the cemetery via the streets. Where
he was going to, he would walk right by the Tomb of the
Unknown Soldier, where a ceremonial soldier was on sentry
duty twenty-four hours a day guarding the tomb. He would be
seen for sure if he went that way. On this occasion, he swung
far right to avoid the tomb, staying off the road, which would
add another half mile to his journey, maybe more. He knew
where he was going and had visited his friend's gravesite
many times since his death. Walking amidst the gravesites
and negotiating the headstones could be an arduous effort in
the dark of night. In addition to possibly turning an ankle, he
mostly did not want to fall and get his uniform dirty.

He had to be careful. The cemetery was closed to visitors
at dusk, and there was a roving security patrol that he definitely wanted to avoid encountering. If he had his Rolex on
he would know the exact time but knew it would be close to
midnight. He had left the Rolex with his wife, along with a
long letter. It would be very awkward trying to explain to security personnel his presence this evening. Especially since he
was wearing his Marine dress blue uniform, oft referred to as
simply "blues," which was normally worn for official and aus-
picious formal occasions, such as parades, birthday balls, and

funerals. Tonight, was a special occasion, he thought to himself, and therefore he was wearing the appropriate uniform for his pending ceremony.

The present-day dress uniform for Marine officers, patterned from historic uniforms going back to the Revolutionary War, consisted of a midnight blue blouse (almost black) and dark sky-blue trousers with a red stripe down each side (representing the blood shed by the officers and staff noncommissioned officers at the battle of Chapultepec during the Mexican War). The left side of his uniform above the pocket was adorned with three rows of full size medals, topped by a set of gold jump wings, and fastened to the face of the pocket, a Joint Chiefs of Staff service badge. What little light there was danced across the many anodized gold medallions. A gold oak leaf attached to each epaulette indicated his rank of major. Three rows of assorted ribbons, four ribbons in each row, for milestones in his career, and various other awards, for which there was no designated medal, were displayed on the right side of his uniform above the blouse's pocket.

He stopped in his stride for a moment, looking about the cemetery, acutely listening for vehicles that might indicate security close by. He looked down at his feet where he could see the dim dusky light reflected on the tips of his black corfam dress shoes, whose surface was as shiny as glass. In full light one would be able to see their face reflected in the tips of the shoes. About his waist, he wore a Sam Brown belt, again of corfam materials, which the shiny surface sometimes and erratically, caught the diffused lighting spilling into the cemetery from the adjoining cities. A shoulder strap affixed to a brass clasp at the left side of his belt was threaded across his chest, through his blouse's right epaulette, and down the left side of his back to reattach to the belt via a similar brass clasp. The Sam Browne belt's sole purpose was to support the weight of a weapon, pistol or sword, and was worn in such a way as to ease the heft of the weapon being carried on the Marine's side. It was the only military uniform that consisted of all of the colors of the US flag.

He was not wearing his barrack's cover, more readily referred to as a "hat" by the uninitiated. The barrack's cover is constructed of a bright white material, with gold filigree across the shiny black corfam visor, further indicating his rank of major. The top of all Marine officer's covers was adorned with an embroidered quatrefoil (historically to aid sharpshooters in the ship's crow's nest in identifying Marines amidst enemy boarders way down below on the ship's deck). Wearing his cover would have been the same as telling the security personnel that he was present and available for apprehension. It was that bright of white. It would have outlined his person against the stark gloom of the night sky. Security personnel would have seen a polka dot carefully and slowly moving across the expanse of the cemetery. Presently, it was stuffed into a small black backpack that he was carrying in his right hand. There were other items in the backpack that he knew for certain would cause apprehending security personnel great agitation and consternation if he were confronted.

He had a long walk to his intended location. He was a man of average height with a slender and muscular build, offset by a high and tight military style haircut. He moved with the gait and alacrity of an accomplished athlete. Indeed, he was a dedicated runner and rarely did a day pass that he did not put in some miles, but those long and lonely street miles no longer padded his pain anymore. He had strong tanned features, outlined by a cut jaw line, enhancing piercing brown eyes. The expression locked onto his face conveyed a stern intention and grim determination only known to him at that moment. People who met him and learned of his career often remarked that he was what one would think a Marine officer would look like.

He arrived at his intended destination without being discovered by security. Only once did he observe a security vehicle leisurely patrolling throughout the grounds. Its head-lights illuminated the seemingly vast rows of geometrically set headstones, light beams sweeping across the grounds, as the driver slowly negotiated curves and turns. Yet, it was far off from where he stood behind a tree as he cautiously watched the vehicle, determining there was no threat to his presence, as the vehicle slowly receded off into the distance. For a few more moments he remained in place, feeling the darkness, trying to commune with the numerous souls entombed within the vast grounds before him. He wondered what it was like to continually wander throughout Arlington all night long. Many people were nervous and often frightened around cemeteries. Their supernatural fears working overtime in their thoughts. Oddly enough, he thought to himself, Arlington was the one cemetery where no person should ever feel apprehension or fear. The deceased here were all persons, all Veterans, who with the precious expenditure of their lives, wanted to ensure no one person, no family member, no loved one, would ever succumb to fears of the unknown, whether divine, evil, or a visible entity. He had been here many times over the years visiting those he had served alongside of and who had fallen in distant war zones. Not all had died in combat. Many had just died for whatever unfair reasons, and had chosen to be interred at Arlington, as was their deserved right and well-earned privilege. Whom he was going to visit this night, was one such friend, and another who had also been unfairly killed by God.

He stood before the gray weathered headstone at a loose posture of attention. By habit his heels were locked together, arms straight by his side, showing the deceased the respect, he deserved. As in all of the times before, the ache of sadness crushed his heart making it difficult for him to breathe. Staring down, he strained to read the familiar information etched onto its face, information he had reviewed countless times previously in his many prior visits. His friend and the grave's resident were identified as Captain Edward Padraic Chasseur, United States Marine Corps. Additional information indicated his date of birth as 17 March, 1969, and his date of death as 30 May, 2000.

His close friend had died of an aortic embolism. One moment he was flipping hamburgers at a picnic, and the next moment he was on the ground dead. That quickly! Doctors had told him that Paddy, he went by his middle name, had been a ticking health time bomb for years. It was a congenital affliction and the doctors were surprised he had lived as long as he did. His friend who routinely participated in marathon races, whose superb athletic ability combined with his super human endurance, was felled by a physiological disorder lying in wait. Where was the fairness in that?

They had known each other for twenty years. Both had begun their careers as enlisted Marines. Paddy had started his career in the infantry, whereas he had started his career in communications. Previous to entering the Marine Corps Paddy had earned an Associate in Arts degree in criminal justice. Once he had graduated from boot camp and had been assigned to his first unit, in his every waking moments he devoted his total time to completing his college degree. He applied for and was proudly commissioned as a second lieutenant. Due to Paddy's superb academic and practical performance at the Basic School, follow on training after the officer's candidate school, he was able to choose the counterintelligence field as his military occupational specialty. Eric first met Paddy as a student counterintelligence officer at the school house in Virginia Beach. Again, Paddy's academic performance established him as one to watch in the field. He had that much sought-after natural leadership ability that allowed him to be able to fuse common sense with tactical proficiency. Paddy oozed Marine Corps. Less than average in height, his many hours in the gym packed muscle on his frame that strained the seams of his uniform. Almost daily five to ten-mile punishing runs were practice for the many challenging races and marathons he continually competed in. He had thick black hair that had to be cut every two weeks in order to meet Marine Corps grooming standards. He could tan in an afternoon in the sun, coloring his face to a light chestnut brown. Dark brown eyes under thick eyebrows peered beyond a prominent nose that questioned his Irish heredity. His mind was much to be admired. He remembered everything. He could put forth a suggested resolution to a problem in a matter of moments.

Eric was an instructor at the school house and was already a newly promoted captain when they first encountered each other. However, he had been a staff sergeant when he applied for a commission as a second lieutenant. By the time he met Paddy he had already been in the Marine Corps thirteen years, about ten more than Paddy. Other than professional interaction with Paddy while he was a student, he never really got to know him at that time. It would be in the later years, when they would encounter each other while assigned to the same units or encountering each other while on similar missions around the world. The counterintelligence field in the Marine Corps was a restricted specialty with limited staffing. It was common for everyone in the field to know each other; if not personally then certainly by reputation. Both had deployed around the world, each served in the Gulf War, Bosnia, and Kosovo, sometimes together. They eventually became the best of friends. They would each serve as the best man at the other's wedding. For Eric it would be for his second marriage. However, it would not be to a woman he truly loved.

Thoughts cascaded through his mind and the pain of his impending duty clutched at his heart; his breathing became shallow and strained. Within all of these memories pushing outward, she was always at the forefront. Paddy's wife, his lover. Lark. Even now she was clear in his vision. The green eyes slightly angled upward, her luxurious chestnut brown hair that swept across her shoulders. She was a lover who was hungry for attention, both to her heart and to her body. He was just an unhappy man whose marriage had long ago collapsed into ruin but continued to exist. He blamed himself mostly for that state of affairs, but he just did not know how to repair the marriage, or maybe he just didn't want to. In moments of reflection he was never sure of which.

It took some years before they succumbed to participating in their forbidden relationship. Oddly enough it took shape via e-mails, in which subtle ideas were broached and reading in between the lines. There were many social occasions where they interacted with each other, but it was the exercise of writing to each other, initially casual exchanges, ultimately exposing each other's soul to the other. Dinner one night and a frenzied exchange of kisses in a parked car resulted in a passionate evening in a hotel room. It would be the first night of many occasions of intimacy, to include weekends away together. Yet, she had a part of her that she never allowed him to know about. Lark could become moody and distant and incommunicative, but always coming back to him with tears, heat, and a promise to love him even more.

He thought it was maybe the guilt of the affair. Bone crushing guilt, combined with a fatalistic sense of despair, of which neither suffocating emotion ever seemed sufficient enough for either one of them to consider stopping their affair. When he was in company with Paddy in any given situation, he found that he could not look him in the eye and kept his contact to a minimum, always making excuses for not being around so much anymore. In time he realized Lark went to remote places in her head and heart where no one was allowed. He suspected she was suffering from depression. She denied it. He loved her and she always declared she loved him. The only moralistic thing he ever did within the extent of the affair was that he never asked her to leave Paddy and marry him. Hardly sufficient to ease or neutralize his sins.

Then Paddy died suddenly. A Marine who was in a superb

state of physical condition, a competitor, suddenly dies. The irony of the situation was staggering. Witnesses who saw him collapse said there was no look of anguish, or yelp of pain, no words; he just crumpled to the ground. Doctors said it was a brain embolism basically just waiting to occur.

He had rushed to the hospital. He saw Lark with her father, crying and shaking. He felt utterly helpless and overcome. He did not know what to do. He could have gone over to her and put his arm around her, but the hypocrisy of such a movement would have been evident in his mind. Maybe she wanted him to do something, maybe she didn't. He opted for holding her hand and feeling miserable. However, after a few moments she snatched her hand away and pressed both hands against her face and began sobbing. In all of his life he had never felt so helpless. Was it because he was her lover and the guilt was staggering for her? Did she believe God was punishing her, both of them? Or was she genuinely sorry that her husband had died? He did not know and he would never know.

At the funeral he was selected to present her with the flag from a grateful nation. He did not want the task. However, he could not conceivably offer a reasonable explanation why he couldn't do it when considering the level of his friendship with Paddy. He rationalized it from the perspective of his relationship both with Paddy and Lark, as twisted as it might have been viewed by most others. In reflection never had he ever participated in a more prevalent act and display of hypocrisy. Never had he committed a larger sin in his life. Possible Lark felt the same way. He wanted to reach out to her and thought about waylaying her somewhere at some point or another. They needed to talk. Yet, he was as sorry as she was, and they both had their pain and sins to confront and resolve. As lovelorn and silly as it sounded in his mind, if she genuinely loved him, he would hear from her. He never did. It had been two years since Paddy died.

Even up to this evening here at Arlington, he did not know

where Lark was now. After the funeral she had divested herself of any association with the Marines she had known. Most notably with him. He was not even able to collect any rumors about her. The despair was a stone in his heart and he believed his sin would be a shadow over his life to the end. In time he suspected he would need to confront the pain and his disgrace. That time was tonight.

He stared up at the night sky and slowly began a review of his life. Memories were pushed aside as his mind insisted on taking him back to an event in Vietnam. On that occasion, as a radio operator, he was assigned to the headquarters section of an infantry company. He had been in the field for over three weeks participating in a search and destroy operation. They were due to be rotated out of the field and back to the rear in order to recover. They were filthy dirty, hungry that day, and very thirsty. The company had run out of food and water two days ago. They had encountered some heavy fighting, and Marines, and some his friends had been killed. They could not be resupplied by helicopter due to the thick triple canopy depth of the jungle and lack of cleared spaces for a chopper to land.

The company had maneuvered to a hilltop where they had spent the better part of the day clearing trees and brush to allow choppers to provide resupplies and begin lifting Marines out back to the rear. It was blazing hot and the humidity was as high as he had ever experienced in his life. The Marines were exhausted and dangerously dehydrated. When the first chopper arrived, an attempt to land resulted in trees and brush being chopped down by the blades, and the pilot had to abort until the top of the hill was further cleared of hazards. The problem was the chopper trying to land was basically a beacon telling the enemy where there were Marines located. In a matter of minutes after the chopper pilot departed from the area, incoming mortar rounds began to impact around the company perimeter. Fortunately, there were no immediate injuries or fatalities, but in combination with the heat and the dry vegetation, small fires erupted throughout the area that quickly began to burn out of control and seek and connect with other initially set fires. The fire pushed the Marines back into the partially cleared landing zone. Even then cut down trees and piles of brush began to ignite and the atmosphere became thick with smoke, and a wall of flames seemed to have completely surrounded the Marines. They quickly scrambled to stop the fire from spreading. They took off their utility blouses, filthy and shredded after weeks in the bush, and began to beat back the flames. Other Marines dragged away debris from the landing zone and threw it down the hillside. The firestorm was barely being held at bay. After a few minutes of fighting the fire Marines began to collapse from dehydration, incurring heat stroke and exhaustion, and other Marines had to pull those who had succumbed to the heat and smoke back to safety, taking away manpower from the fire defense.

No one died that day but many of the Marines had to be treated on an emergency medevac basis and received priority transport back to the base. He had spent considerable time contemplating his near escape from the inferno. One Marine who was a fervent Christian explained that fire is a cleansing agent from God. The fire had been a warning. For whom, he had asked the Marine? "For all us," answered the Marine. He went on to argue that it was about this war, the leadership, the politics, and the innocent who are the real victims. Well, biblically, he supposed he could kind of comprehend that idea, but mostly he just thought it was an accident as a result of impacting mortar rounds.

He often thought about those ideas and whereas they had seemed so blatantly skewed then, in thought his tortured soul began to accept the idea of fire as an instrument of wrath and an opportunity to cleanse his soul. Maybe someday in his next life he would meet up with Paddy. He knew he would ask for forgiveness but he wasn't so sure that Paddy would forgive him. Traipsing through eternity with Paddy angry at him was a very disconcerting thought. Maybe he did not need the forgiveness, only for Paddy to know he was sorry. He knew deep in his heart his sorrow was a combination of Lark's rejection of him after Paddy's death, and his betrayal to his friend. It was not his desire to possess her after Paddy's death, but it had been his desire for her to understand his emotions, his feelings, and his sense of loss as a human being. He wanted to be there for her. In the end the stark realization was clear; he had never meant to her what she had meant to him. This sudden realization was embarrassing for both his sanity and for his soul.

He tried the counseling route. He had visited a counselor over a period of a few weeks and finally got tired of seemingly not accomplishing anything. The male counselor, never really resolved any of his issues; his treachery, humiliation, his broken heart, as lovesick stupid as it sounded in his own mind. He was looking for a comprehension knowing full well he had betrayed a friend and there was no simpler explanation. It was like a persistent sensitive tooth that you knew verged on a toothache and vicious pain, but chose to hope it would go away if you continually massaged it with your tongue. The counselor never made any declarative observations, he just kept asking questions, such as, "How did that make you feel?" or "What do you think you could have done?" The reason he was there was because he didn't have any of those fucking answers!

Next, he tried religion. He was a Catholic, not a practicing one, but maybe there was refuge in confession. The priest heard his sin that he dragged into the confessional box with him and offered absolution in the form of a requirement to complete prayers spaced out on a rosary. It was that easy, and afterwards he was now supposed to be clear of his unfaithfulness and betrayal. He was back enroute to Heaven, some day, and Paddy, roosting in the ether and eternity somewhere, likely had overheard the confession, and had forgiven him. Yeah, that was bullshit too!

Alcohol had been in the mix during the entire time after Paddy's death. His consumption increased to such levels that he began to put himself to sleep every night via a drunken stupor. He had received counseling from superior officers for smelling of alcoholic beverages while in uniform and in the office. He didn't care and the amount of alcohol he poured into his body increased. Soon he was isolated, and he felt isolated, from his peers and friends. His fault and he knew it. He had tried to push the guilt away into the corner of his mind. It was a wound that he had self-incurred and he knew a medevac was not inbound for him.

Nevertheless, in any decent person with such sadness and loss in their daily thoughts something had to break. That occasion had occurred this night, before where he now stood, and he had not had anything to drink either. His depression enveloped him as if it were a suit of armor similar to what was worn by medieval knights. His eyes began to swell up and form tears. In a split second he was ashamed of himself for his weakness and willed his mind to control his emotions. He brought his hands together, bowed his head, and slowly recited the Lord's Prayer. He pleaded with whomever was listening to forgive him for his past betrayal of a close friend and fellow Marine, and for what he was about to do.

Opening the backpack he had brought with him, he extracted his barracks cover. He looked across the expanse of the cemetery one more time searching for security patrols. Seeing no movement, he set his cover upon his head, ensuring it was correctly placed, with the bill positioned two fingers above the top of the nose. Satisfied it would not fall off while he bent over and retrieved other items from the backpack, he reached down and removed a gallon milk carton filled with gas, a Colt 1911 45 caliber semi-automatic handgun, and a role of duct tape, each of which he laid out on the ground in front of him between Paddy's headstone and himself. From within his pocket he produced a Zippo stainless steel lighter, engraved with "Bastards from the Sea," a reference to the 3rd Marine Regiment with whom he had served with in Vietnam. The lighter was scratched and nicked and the engraving was worn down. Any person examining the lighter would be required to squint and turn the lighter to just the right angle to ensure there was enough light highlighting the metallic surface for the engraving to be read.

Staring down at the items for a moment he reached down with his right hand and grabbed the pistol. It felt familiar and comforting in his hand. An old friend he had carried with him in Vietnam. He had mailed it home just prior to rotating home from Vietnam. In those days you could mail a jeep home if you were willing to be patient and do it part by part. Both his hand and fingers comfortably curled around the grip, and by habit his index finger, the trigger finger, extended along the frame of the weapon just above the trigger well. He thumbed the magazine release and the magazine slid out of the grip into his left hand. A quick examination verified six 45 caliber rounds already inserted into the magazine. At full capacity it could hold seven rounds in a magazine and an extra round in the chamber for a full eight available rounds. However, tonight six rounds were more than he was likely to need. He put the magazine back into the base of the grip, pushing it up into the pistol. With the heel of his left hand he tapped the magazine tight into the weapon and heard it click into place. It sounded loud in the still air and unconsciously he looked around him to see if anyone had heard him. Feeling somewhat silly and paranoid, he turned his attention back to the pistol. With his left hand, he snapped the slide back, racking a round into the chamber.

He grabbed the duct tape and peeled off a long and lengthy piece. With his finger now lightly curled around the trigger he wrapped the duct tape a few times around his wrist and hand ensuring the pistol was firmly held in place. He flexed his hand and fingers to test the tape but the weapon was well pressed against and restrained within his grip.

With the weight of weapon in his hand now resting idly by his right side lightly pressed up and against along the scarlet stripe to his trousers, he stared off into the distance looking out across the gentle rolling hillsides of the cemetery replete with its thousands of granite markers. He wondered if any of the dead were watching him at the moment. Standing beside their gravestones in their dress uniforms watching him with sadness in their hearts. He wondered if any of them would try to stop him. He wondered if Paddy was watching. He wondered if what he was about to do would be enough for Paddy. He wondered if she would care when she heard.

A deep sigh emanated from whence a place he knew well, and within the space of a few seconds, pain followed in succession.

He reached down with his left hand, grabbed the gallon size plastic milk container filled with gas, popped off the cap with his thumb, unhesitatingly, swung the plastic jug upwards above his head and pouring the contents over his head and body. The gas splattered across his cover, draining downward in slender rivulets from the brim onto his shoulders and back, thoroughly soaking his uniform and exposed areas of his body. It felt cold and seemed to seep into his pores. His face stung from his having recently shaved. He couldn't help but breath the smell in. The hairs within his nostrils vibrated in protest. He opened his eyes and immediately they began to sting.

It was time.

Reaching into his left trouser pocket he pulled out the Zippo lighter. For a brief moment, examining the lighter in his hand, rubbing his thumb across the time worn metal, he tried to feel the words engraved on its surface.

With a practiced and smooth movement, no less than a person snapping their fingers, he flicked open the Zippo, thumbed the igniter, which sparked blue-yellow skipping into a flickering orange-yellow flame, resolutely reaching outward toward the fumes saturated air.

He didn't hear the explosion as the gas ignited. Involuntarily, the pressure from the ignition forced him to squeeze his eyes shut. The initial pain screeched across his body via searing heat. In that split second, in his mind, he reminded himself to wait until the pain was gone, when the nerves had been incinerated. Falling to his knees, tumbling to his left side, his total body ablaze, he tried to transfer his mind and suffering back into his past. For a moment he could see his fellow Marines again in the LZ. The face of the Marine who told him he could be cleansed in a fire flashed before his mind's eye. Paddy quickly came and went. He tried to remember Lark's face but only heard laughing instead. For a moment he thought he was happy. All thoughts and sensations and horrors and pain and sadness, all arrived within a matter of a few seconds. Seconds maybe the length of one deep breath. A blink of the eyes. A mere few heartbeats. Still the agony would not lessen or cease. He could hear his flesh burning, or was he screaming?

In his now addled brain, he tried to reach out to his body's nerves. He was not near enough to reaching his goal. Within all of that pain, he felt sorrow for failing in his contrition. He quickly brought the pistol up placing it against his temple, pulling the trigger, the bullet passing through the width of his head, originating and expanding a gaping hole, violently shoving his flesh, memories, sorrow, and pain out the left side of his head where in a microsecond it all slapped into the grass. If one were able to hear the dying sound separate from the sound of the self-inflicted gunshot, difficult to occur due to the parallel immediacy of the action, in the still night air of Arlington National Cemetery that night, it would have sounded as if he had heaved a huge sigh of relief.

He was free.

The Cat Cop

"The purity of a person's heart can be quickly measured by how they regard cats."

—**Unknown**

CORPORAL GEORGE "MAD Munk" Munkelwitz, of the Prince George's County Police Department, was seated on the curb facing across the driveway that led up to the front entrance of Patuxent Elementary School. The night was quiet and cool in the early hours of the morning, and a slight breeze occasionally ruffled his hair hanging limp across his forehead. His knees were drawn up and he was leaning slightly forward with his chin resting on his arms that were folded across his knees. Every few seconds the same breeze tugging at his hair would snap the rope to the school's flagpole against the mast and a hollow aluminum sound would tinkle in the breeze. Every time he heard the sound, his eyes flicked toward the flagpole. Each time it happened, he wondered if he should just get it over and go insane now. Or maybe he should drive straight to the department's personnel office, wait for it to open in the morning, and put in his retirement papers before Internal Affairs could get him before a departmental trialboard.

I can't figure out how I get involved in this shit, he thought.

His gaze shifted from the flagpole to a trash dumpster in a small area just off from the main driveway. In the half-light vainly tumbling from the one of the school's security lights, haphazardly suspended from one worn screw and twisting in the breeze causing the beam to skew off in every direction but its intended one, he could see all of the dead cats lying around the dumpster. He figured they were dead about six to ten hours now. They appeared in varying sizes as shadowy clumps and amorphous mounds. There was at least a dozen of them. A few tabby cats, a white one, one black Persian cat, a silky-smooth grey one, and the rest just mixed breeds. One of the tabbies had long ago lost its tail. All feral street cats. Maybe some of them belonged to people who lived close by. Who knew? Every one of them poisoned.

Munk's gaze switched back to the entrance to the school. Every once in a while, the breeze would nudge the security light, and a splash of light would flick across the edge of the alcove where one had to walk through to enter through the school's front doors. For brief seconds, Officer John Farrell, the Cat Cop, as he was known to his fellow officers, could be seen sitting on a wooden bench that the school left outside for parents waiting to pick up their kids at the end of the school day. He was slumped down on the bench with his arms hanging loosely by his sides and his chin lay resting on his chest. Standing in front of him, leaning slightly over him, with a hand resting on Farrell's shoulder, a concerned Officer Joe Frolich quietly spoke with his fellow officer and best friend.

The Munk watched the two of them in humorous wonder and shook his head. He had known both of them for years. They were known as the "Tobacco Brothers" to drug dealers and users in the sector. To the black drug dealers and users in the sector, they were known as the "Tobacco Bros." It was an incongruent label because Farrell didn't smoke or chew tobacco. Although Frohlich didn't smoke either, he chewed tobacco all of the time.

Farrell, the Cat Cop, was well known to all of the police officers in the district. He was considered something of an eccentric by fellow officers. When they were on the evening and midnight shifts, every evening he would go up to the school and feed all of the stray cats. It was strange because the cats were always waiting for him, sometimes lined up in formation on the edge of the dumpster impatiently awaiting his arrival. A couple of them would be on the ground pacing back and forth, their tails switching to and fro to the tune of some unheard cadence. They knew him on sight and would leap from the dumpster, flow in one huge mottled furry mass toward him, surround him and start rubbing up against his legs mewing in chorus. He had been feeding them for years. Everyone - citizen, criminal, and cop, knew him as the Cat Cop.

On one occasion that Munk recalled, he had watched fascinated while at least two dozen cats converged on Farrell. Each vied for his attention; they rubbed against his legs, or stretched up the side of his leg meowing loudly. Most were actually purring, sounding like some out of synch noisy air conditioner. He had asked Farrell if he wasn't afraid of catching fleas and ticks from all of those alley cats. Farrell just shrugged his shoulders and had said that he hadn't given it much thought. A week later, Munk had gone back to the school with Farrell to observe the ritual again. All of the cats were waiting for Farrell as usual, but this time they were all sporting brand new flea and tick collars. Who would have believed it?

Yet, Munk considered him one of the finest officers he had ever worked alongside. Munk had long ago defined a personal theory that eccentric officers often made the best cops. They were always loners and preferred to police on their own. All of them were trying to cover up some level of pain. Munk knew that Farrell was hurting, but there wasn't much anybody could do for a cop's pain. It was an individual thing that had to be worked out by the cop. His last marriage had fallen apart after fifteen years. His wife had up and left one day, moving out of the state, and refusing to allow him to see their son. He missed his son very badly. As his wife later told a very sympathetic judge during the divorce proceedings, she had enough when one day her husband and their son had come screaming into the kitchen - both stark naked. Well, not quite naked, they had on police gunbelts and were wearing departmental baseball caps backwards in the fashion of the day, brandishing Beretta 9MM handguns, unloaded of course, all the while demanding that the imaginary bad guy that they were chasing, "FREEZE MOTHERFUCKER! OR WE'LL MAKE YOU LOOK LIKE SWISS CHEESE! It was enough for the liberal oriented, prowomen's judge, who failed to understand the complex masculine ritual associated with male bonding, to rule the divorce in her favor, and suggest that Farrell seek psychological help. It was enough to break Farrell's heart. As he remarked later, he could understand why she didn't want to stay married to him, hell, for that matter, he could understand why any women wouldn't want to stay married to him. But at least she could have let him see his son occasionally.

In a matter of weeks after the divorce Farrell became another worthless cop. He came to work, took his calls, and backed up other officers when they needed assistance - and that was it. He had evolved into an armed report taker. It wasn't long after that when Munk found him one night up at the school feeding the cats and petting them while they ate. He told Munk that his son liked cats. Munk had just shrugged it off. He remembered thinking that we all had to have some sort of an outlet. God knows he had his share of domestic strife in his career. Sometimes it was just best to leave a cop like Farrell alone. And everybody did.

Until Joe Frohlich was transferred to the squad. In a matter of weeks Farrell underwent some kind of mysterious transformation. Between the two of them, they made more drug arrests than all of the cops in the district combined. It was astounding. One-night Munk took Frohlich aside and asked him what he did to fire up Farrell? Frohlich, with his cheek bulging with Redman chewing tobacco, just smiled and said that he had given Farrell a new lease on life. Munk left it at that. Farrell was policing again and seemed to have a new lease on life, and a fellow cop couldn't ask for more than that.

Come to think of it, thought Munk, in fact, he couldn't remember a time he hadn't seen Frohlich with his cheek pushed out like some squirrel gathering nuts, and intermittently spitting out long streams of phlegm and off-yellow tobacco juice. Six-foot-tall, slender at the shoulders, and always with a fresh crew cut, he presented a professional cop image in his uniform. His uniform shirts were starched crisp and displayed a freshly shined gleaming badge and nameplate, and both a shooting badge and a small flag pin, each of which the department had recently ordered removed from the shirts. It was his one act of defiance to wear the additional pins. He was respected and was often sought out by the younger officers for his advice. During rollcalls, he sat in the rear of the room and in the same seat without deviation, where he would spit tobacco juice into some type of container; coffee cup, coke can, the trash can if it was close by. He once told Munk that his craving for nicotine was so strong, that when he was out of chewing tobacco, he would dip a napkin into his spit cup and suck on the napkin. Munk watched Frohlich talking to Farrell. He wondered what he was saying to him. Even in the half-light he could still see Frohlich's bulging cheek occasionally. He was gesturing with his hands and would bend over trying to look into Farrell's eyes. He would straighten up for moment, spew a stream of tobacco juice into the grass, gather his thoughts, and return to his conversation with renewed vigor. The gently swinging security lamp gave the whole scene a surrealistic and very un-real appearance. Once in a while, depending upon how the light fell, for just a fleeting moment, their features looming larger than life, including Frohlich's apple sized cheek in pro-file, were pasted briefly across the dark glass front doors of the school.

They were two of the most feared police officers in the sec-tor. Frohlich was the calm one; always polite and never dis-played a temper, unless you lied to him. Munk smiled to himself thinking about the occasion one night when he had gone look-ing for the two of them. He was approaching a brick archway leading into an apartment courtyard when a black male came running through the archway with his arms wrapped around his head and screaming, "I'M SORRY OFFICER FROHLICH! I'M SORRY. I DIDN'T MEANS TO LIES TO YOU, SIR." And hot on his heels, Frolich came tearing through the archway, waving in the air his departmentally unauthorized Baltimore blaster style nightstick of thick machine lathed walnut, screeching at the fleeing man, "DON'T EVER FUCKING LIE

TO ME AGAIN! And directly behind Frohlich, came Farrell, his Baltimore blaster also in hand. With every step the leather thong snapped against the back of his hand. He had a smile on his face, prepared to provide backup if necessary.

A foot chase with a cheek full of Redman chewing tobacco. Munk shivered. How can anyone chew that crap, he wondered? God, that stuff is nasty!

Yet, in contrast, Farrell was a different story. Sometimes Munk wound himself into knots trying to understand those two. Farrell always looked like he had just gotten out of bed. Slightly shorter than Frohlich, he had a slender build, and a tendency to walk slightly stooped over. His hair was ruler straight, stiff and punctuated with cowlicks. His uniform was always in disarray, and sometimes the shirttail would be partially hanging out of his trousers. He was forever tucking it in. The badge was never polished and he had three different kinds of pens protruding from his shirt pocket. Munk sometimes thought that when Farrell took his uniforms to the cleaners, he must have the wrinkles put in them. But, God, was he funny!

For a moment, Munk's thoughts flipped back to that night when he responded to the rear of the Lasalle Apartments to back up the both of them with two suspected drug dealers. When he arrived, two black males were spreadeagled on the wall with Frohlich patiently attempting to question one of them. One of the suspects was known to Farrell and Frohlich, but the other was new to the area. The new suspect had a mouth and it was working hard.

"Fuck you! You ain't got no motherfuckin' right to be hasslin' us!"

The mouthy suspect's friend was being very quiet. Frohlich, very calmly asked the man again why he was in the area at this time of night?

The response was predictable. "Kiss my black ass! I ain't telling you shit!"

It was at that moment the other suspect suddenly spoke up, and his voice was quivering with fear, "Oh man, Rofer, don't be talking to these poh-leece like that. Man, these are the "Tobacco Bros! Please, man! You don't know, man!"

"Fuck them and their tobacco. I ain't taking any of their shit!"

The other suspect, while peering over his shoulder, suddenly wailed, "Aw shit! Sweet Mother of God! Look what you gone and dun now!"

The mouthy suspect spun his head toward the officers. His eyes widened in disbelief and his mouth dropped open. Officer Farrell's head was twitching violently and his mouth hung slack. He had begun moaning and his arm holding his Baltimore blaster was spasmodically dancing at his side. The leather thong had begun snapping against the back of his hand in rhythm to the spasms.

The respectful suspect began moaning, "Aw sweet Jesus. It's happening. Aw shit! Aw shit! Officer Farrell don't mean it none! He don't wants to hurt nobody. He can't help himself when it comes over him. Oh Goddamned! Rofer, look what you gone and fucking dun!"

Frohlich had quickly leaped toward his fellow officer and wrapped his arms around Farrell. By now Farrell's eyes had rolled back into his head and he was foaming at the mouth.

Frohlich yelled at the mouthy suspect. "Jesus, man! I can't hold him much longer! He gets like this when he's mad! You had better start shittin' some answers."

The mouthy suspect looked wildly around. His friend was shaking his head and trembling hard. He looked like he was going to cry. He kept whining, "Please! Please, Rofer, man, you gotta talk to 'em."

"Okay, Okay," he gasped. "I didn't mean to start no shit, man! Just please keep your buddy away from me!"

Always upon meek compliance, an amazing transformation would occur. Farrell would begin to calm down. He would apologize, weakly declare that he was okay, and walk off into the dark and bend over and pretend he was puking.

Munk shook his head ruefully. Unbelievable! Yet, it worked. Eccentric cops, he thought.

However, it was this night's work that had brought them to this school and this point in time. Earlier Munk had responded to Frohlich's urgent request to come quickly up to the school. When he arrived, he had found a frantic Frohlich trying to calm a very angry and vocal Farrell. "Look what the fuck he did!" Farrell screamed, pointing over toward the dumpster. Munk had gone over to the dumpster to see for himself. That was when he discovered the dead cats. There was a plastic bowl of partially consumed cat food protruding out from under the bottom edge of the dumpster. When he looked back over his shoulder, he could see Farrell walking around in circles, arms flailing wildly in the air, rubbing his eyes, and muttering unintelligible curses into the night.

Frohlich came up to him and told him that they knew who did it. When he asked who? Frohlich asked him if he remembered that night when they locked up that asshole from the cemetery.

He remembered alright. How could he forget? The dispatcher had put out a call from the night watchman at the Saint Edward's Cemetery complaining about trespassers. Frohlich and Farrell were close by and had volunteered for the call. Generally a routine call. Locate them and chase them out of the cemetery. Before they arrived on the scene, the night watchman, who was watching the trespassers from inside the sales office, had called back and said that there were four white males, and they had just broken into one of the mausoleums. As a result, more officers were dispatched and even Munk had started to ride toward the cemetery.

Frohlich and Farrell both parked their cruisers well away from the area. Already knowing the layout of the cemetery, they approached the sales office looking for the mausoleum that the night watchman had described. It didn't take them long to find it. They could hear laughter and a lot of scuffling noises. Since other officers also riding on the call were close behind, they elected to confront the subjects before they realized the police were on their way and a foot chase ensued.

Farrell took one side of the mausoleum, Frohlich the other side, and together they converged on the front. When they came around the sides and flashed their flashlights, they immediately located two of the suspects and the source of the scuffling noise. Both of the suspects had been playing soccer with a still decomposing head, recently entombed within the last month. Pieces of the skull, a few teeth, and shreds of desiccated flesh littered the concrete pavilion in front of the mausoleum. The two suspects, along with their other two friends, who were subsequently caught inside the mausoleum, had opened three of the crypts and dumped the contents of the caskets out onto the floor. All the suspects were drunk, and, or high on drugs. At the station in the processing area, three of the suspects quickly turned on the remaining suspect. They claimed it was all his idea, and gave written statements to that effect. The very angry remaining suspect was identified as Nick Santos, a nineteen-year-old white male with an extensive record of misdemeanors and minor drug violations. He was also very drunk and had been arrested by Farrell on a previous breaking and entering charge, and didn't appreciate the way he was handled on that occasion. He didn't like Farrell, and claimed Farrell had beaten him while Farrell was having some kind of a seizure. So, when Farrell wasn't looking, he blindsided him with a punch to the temple. When Farrell went down, Frohlich and all the other officers in the processing room promptly applied the modern day "swarm" tactical method of policing. By application of this departmentally sanctioned procedure, it was put forth that a violent suspect, and the officers who were attempting to subdue him, were less likely to be injured. As Munk later explained to the Captain, the "swarm" method worked beautifully. No police officers were injured, and the Santos subject only had to spend a week in the county hospital, instead of the month he probably would have incurred, during the earlier days of the department's existence.

However, while Santos was being placed into the back of the ambulance by Frohlich, and assisted by the now revived Farrell, Santos had begun spitting at everyone through his swollen mouth. He screamed at Farrell that he knew he was the 'Cat Cop,' and that he knew where all of his cats were and that he would kill them all. They saw it as just another drunken loudmouth punkdog, flinging threats to be stacked with the rest of the threats any real working cop receives during his career. No cop ever took such threats seriously.

That is until tonight.

Munk knew Frohlich was concerned for Farrell. Frohlich had argued that they had no choice but to do the one thing that would help Farrell deal with what happened. When Frohlich outlined his plan, Munk had looked at him incredulously. When he looked over at Farrell pacing back and forth, wringing his hands, with a wild-eyed stare spewing anger and frustration, he knew then, he was about to cross the line once again.

Munk sighed. No one else ever took care of us out here, he thought. So they had done it. Munk only insisted that they do this 'vengeance' thing after they got off at one-thirty in the morning, and that only the three of them were to be involved. If they got in trouble over this, at least it wasn't on company time. Frohlich had quickly agreed. Farrell was absolutely ecstatic over his partner's plan.

They had waited the better part of an hour for Santos to come out of The Lucky Snooker Bar. He was a regular there and they had often seen him stagger out of the bar after closing on many other nights. A quick 'tavern check' earlier by Munk had located Santos drinking and playing pool in the backroom. The only fear had been that he might leave with a friend. He usually walked home since his driver's license had been revoked a year ago for a hit and run accident and drunken driving. He only lived a couple of blocks from the bar in the Severn Apartments that bordered the commercial area.

At two thirty in the morning, in that area, exterior apartment lighting relied upon the maintenance personnel to replace all of the smashed lights from the night before. So, the time and area were ideal for their plan. Thinking back now, Munk realized that it had been very quickly done. Frohlich and Farrell slipped quietly up behind a drunken Santos, placed a hand across his mouth, punched a knee into the back of his leg, and down he went. They grabbed him from both sides and he was dragged off into the shadows and quickly handcuffed.

Munk could only guess what Santos had been thinking when he was first snatched. Up to that point where he had been handcuffed, he had probably been very scared. But when the handcuffs were expertly and quickly applied, he probably figured right away it was cops. He had been around the system enough, he knew the feeling. At worst, he probably thought the cops were going to slap him around and lay some bullshit charge on him that wouldn't stand up in court. He probably was going to yell when the hand was removed from his mouth. But when he was suddenly slapped across the side of the head, the blow must have stunned him for a few seconds. Enough so, that he didn't realize that the hand had been removed from his mouth. Frohlich told him later they had gotten duct tape across his mouth before he had time to cry out. So nobody had heard anything. At that moment, Santos had to be terrified. Surely, he was thinking, cops didn't do this shit!

Farrell and Frohlich had quickly lifted Santos to his feet and dragged him to the waiting cruiser where the Munk had been waiting impatiently at the wheel. They flung Santos into the back seat on his stomach and Farrell had leaped in on top of him. After Frohlich quickly looked around, and was satisfied, e made his way around to the passenger's side and quickly scrambled inside. After Munk had snatched a quick look into the back, he had calmly driven away and started back toward the school.

While Munk had watched through the rear-view mirror, more in an effort to make sure that Farrell didn't go too far, Farrell had wrestled with Santos' arms and had finally turned him over onto his back. Santos' sudden full weight on his handcuffed wrists must have hurt. While on his back, Farrell none too gently yanked the duct tape from Santos's mouth. He yelped more from surprise than from the pain. Santos had tried squirming to bring himself in an upright position, but Farrell had grabbed him by his shirt and had jerked him partially up. Santos's eyes had become the size of saucers. Mere inches from his face, Officer Farrell's eyes were flickering back and forth, and drool leaked from the corner of his mouth. His head was twitching violently and he was trying to speak. Santos knew from experience what was coming next. The Cat Cop was having one of his seizures!

Santos had screamed. In between his sobs, he had begun pleading. "Please! Please! Oh God, Please! I didn't mean to hurt them. Honest! I just wanted to make them sick for a while. I didn't know they would die. Oh God, don't hurt me! Please!"

Farrell had begun making choking sounds and his head started bouncing back and forth. Santos was crying by then and his legs had started bicycling furiously as he tried to back away from Farrell and slide into the corner of the back seat. Farrell had jerked hard on Santos' shirt, and it had partially torn away with a loud ripping sound. As he flung his head forward to get closer to Santos' face, spittle had flicked off onto Santo's face. "GET AWAY!" he screamed. "I'll tell you anything you want to know," he sobbed. His head kept turning from left to right. "I'll tell you who all of the drug dealers are. Please! Just please let me go!" he begged.

Munk remembered that while watching the whole performance in the rear-view mirror, it was all he could do not to bust out laughing. When he looked over at Frohlich, he could see that he was trying to contain himself also. He was chomping hard down on the wad of tobacco in his cheek, and his shoulders were shaking. Trying to divert his attention and maintain his composure, he had rolled the window down and had spewed a long stream of tobacco juice into the street. By then, Farrell had flung Santos down in disgust and had quietly backed off into the darkness in the corner of the cruiser making retching sounds.

A breeze tugged at the flagpole's rope. A snaplink, used to connect the flag to the rope, smacked against the aluminum flagpole and emitted a sharp metallic sound which fled through the night.

The sound penetrated Munk's musings, and he shook himself out of his reverie. He gazed up at the flagpole. Even now he couldn't believe what they had done.

Santos, his hands and arms, and legs and ankles, were bound together with duct tape. Duct tape had also been wound around his head and across his mouth a few times assuring his silence. He was hanging upside down by his ankles from the tip of the flagpole, securely fastened to the snaplinks and rope that attached to the flagpole. An orange tabby cat with no tail was tied to Santos's belt so that the dead cat hung right at face level. His torn shirt was hanging below his head and gently flapping in the breeze. Santos was staying perfectly still. An old bed box spring and a partially ripped and stained mattress, which they had found by a dumpster close by, was stacked against the base of the flagpole, just in case the rope should break.

Munk looked over at Farrell and Frohlich and saw that they had left the alcove. They were slowly walking away toward their cruisers, side by side deep in conversation.

Munk took one last look, turned and started toward his

cruiser. He didn't think Santos would make a complaint. He was too scared. The only one that he had seen was Farrell, and he truly believed that Farrell was psychotic. If Santos did make a complaint, Munk knew that Farrell would never give him or Frolich up to Internal Affairs. Anyway, Internal Affairs would have a difficult time proving they were responsible - since he, and Frohlich and Farrell, were all over at his house right now playing cards after a long evening shift. Or so the alibi would be played out if necessary.

Munk took one last look in his side view mirror. He would give anything to see the faces of the school's staff in the morning. He twisted the ignition on, placed the cruiser in gear, and slowly departed from the scene.

He laughed aloud. Sure, he thought - all those dead cats, I would think that the Cat Cop was involved too. But that's just an investigative lead. It barely amounts to circumstantial evidence. Internal Affairs would have to prove it. And after all, he mused, circumstantial evidence is how cops become legendary.

Clonskeagh

"Some ghosts are so quiet you would hardly know they were there."

—Bernie McGill
The Butterfly Cabinet

I CAN ONLY tell the story as it happened to me.

I plead with the reader to be patient with my explanation of events and to hear me out before you decide to discard my story or pass judgment on my sanity.

I do not suggest that I am different or distinctively singular in outlook from that of most people around me; only to offer that possibly...maybe, I approach certain aspects of my life with a higher level of intensity than most people could comprehend. I am often accused of being forgetful or off somewhere in another dimension. When I take my brain walks, it is not uncommon for me to bump into objects or walk out into traffic without thinking. I bless the man who invented the car horn. I had a widow's walk constructed on the roof of my house just so as I could have a place to retreat to and review the night sky and full moons and be in sole attendance to my private contemplations.

I have long concluded that I have been confronting a sense of depression for quite some years.

For your see...if you are able to understand, I had lost my faith, my faith in a God, some years ago, as does happen with many people. Not my soul, mind you, if such an elusive item does indeed exist. I am not an evil person or a lawbreaker. There is no specific reason or event that I can point to as cause for this realized and discouraged state of loss. I can only write that in my indifferent and neutral state of consciousness I have long accepted that my sense of emptiness was derived from a combination of events in my life, and without going into great details, suffice to write my experiences in wars, the loss of true love, the failure of friendship, both on my part and on the part of others, family disappointments, and I could likely go on and on. I need but to point to the state of the world as it exists today and all of the wars, conflicts, riots, corruption, and suffering humanity to bolster a claim that there exists no God, no afterlife, nor any eternal respite from prevailing misery, loss, and sorrow.

I dare write for the reader you are likely wondering at this point why I think I am so different from others. I again inquire of your patience.

It was about two years ago, while sitting perched atop my house on my widow's walk; the summer night sky a cloak about my thoughts, a shallow breeze softly slipping across my upturned face, when intuition, indeed, an epiphany I think, struggled to the surface of my thoughts. What initially seemed a haphazard musing soon became a dominant idea and ultimately a lengthy and expensive journey.

It was really a simple concept and I wondered why it had taken me all of these years to develop this idea.

I would seek out and find myself a ghost! Yes, a ghost... a spirit, a banshee, or a soul caught between dimensions. Whatever movie image you wish to apply, I was going to find one. Any ghost would suffice...good or evil, but most assuredly one that I could see with my believing eyes and fully accept that it existed. That would be genuine proof of a God and an afterlife. It was so simple in concept that even I could admire the genius of my idea.

Surely the reader agrees with me?

That very night, much energized by my idea, combined with a prevalent sense of quest, I began my research online. That same night I found on Amazon a huge reference book on ghosts, which I immediately ordered. I even paid extra for an extradited delivery...2 days. In the interim I continued my research and began to compile a list of places that I could possibly visit and achieve my goal of coming face to face with a former human being. When the book arrived, I spent considerable hours reviewing the book from cover to cover. I continued to expand my list of applicable locations of where ghosts had been alleged to have been seen and where my best chance seemed to be of meeting or confronting a ghost.

Please understand, clearly at this point in my story I am not explaining to you that I believed in ghosts. Actually, if the truth were to be revealed, quite to the contrary. I believed I was engaged in a silly and likely, more than likely, probability of encountering nothing. It is difficult to explain but at the time I was so desolated in my own thoughts, wrapped up in my sense of depression and feeling of abandonment, that some perceived goal, regardless of how ludicrous it sounded in conversation, gave me a reason for life.

I started to visit the destinations on my list. For some reason or another I could not grasp why a large number of ghost sightings always involved castles, or the moors, or battlefields. Why not my back yard or the den in my house? France seemed to be a leading region for alleged sightings. Also, old mansion style homes in England from the Victorian era. Although, there never seemed to be any claims of ghosts being sighted in English castles. I would have thought there was one of King Henry the VIII's wives haunting a castle, or the Tower of London. I wondered how come there were never any sightings of ghosts in public bathrooms. A ghostly sense of decency on their part, I suppose.

As my travels progressed, I developed many questions about ghosts. Mostly, I wanted to know whether or not it was a good to be a ghost? Why are you a ghost? How long does one have to be a ghost? Does someone, or something, keep an eye on you when you are a ghost? Do you ever get sick? Do you have something to look forward to at the end of being ghost? Do ghosts watch people get undressed or go to the bathroom? Do ghosts socialize with other ghosts? Do ghosts need to sleep? How come there are no Jewish ghosts? I had plenty of other questions too. As the reader can readily ascertain I had given a lot of thought to the status and requirements of being a ghost.

It would serve no purpose to itemize each of the places that I visited in my search. Some places I stayed overnight in a castle, or a mansion, or in a hotel in a village. I often spoke with the local residents about the legends and stories of ghosts in their areas. Most persons would just smile and say it was true although they themselves had never seen any ghosts. In one small village in France a bookseller confided to me that the stories of ghosts were really intended to attract tourists to the area and boost the economy. This was evidently a successful marketing ploy as in evidence by my presence and a purchase of a book discussing the eyewitness accounts of the presence of ghosts within the province. He further suggested I might want to take the Normandy battlefield tour. He wasn't aware of any specific stories about ghosts, but surely there had to be some ghosts available where thousands of American soldiers died on D-Day. He was polite and gracious but I am sure he was laughing at me on the inside. I did not find any ghosts in Normandy.

After a month in England I did not find any ghosts there either.

I had told myself after three months of travel that this effort was for naught, although I was enjoying the actual sightseeing part of my quest. I had traveled to places that the large majority of tourists never make an effort to visit. Still, I had become disheartened and had further sunken into a funk that deprived me of the full value and enjoyment of being a tourist. I was not the friendliest tourist by the time I arrived in Ireland.

I had read in my ghost reference book, the one I had ordered from Amazon, about the village of Clonskeagh. It was a small village poetically nestled in a shallow valley just a few miles shy of the northwest coast of Ireland. Authors always describe a location by its geographical features of forests, and meadows, and hills, and mountains. In the description of Clonskeagh in the ghost reference book the writer (who was not identified) wrote about varying shades of green enveloping the village, and he especially highlighted the ferocity of a constant and blowing wind that was bitterly resented by the villagers. According to the legend, the village was supposed to be inhabited by those who are deceased and awaiting ascension into heaven. However, no one could depart the village due to the intensity of the wind which pinned their souls to the earth after their deaths. This constant wind emanated from the Irish Sea, striking the cliffs and traveling up and over the edge, and spreads out across the countryside with Clonskeagh directly in its path. The wind approaches a large hill that is located a mile outside the northern edge of the village, which flows over the top of the hill, and swiftly, while clinging to the terrain, follows the contours of the valley downward and uniquely rushes through the center of the village.

I hired a taxi to drive me to Clonskeagh. The driver was a talkative sort and said that he had heard stories surrounding the village, but then again, he had heard lots of stories about any number of villages in Ireland. He was a man of just about everything average, about 45 years old, with trimmed and graying brown hair and wearing a cap like the one John Wayne sported in the movie, "The Quiet Man." He had that thick Irish brogue that is prevalent in movies about the Irish Republican Army (IRA). He said there were better places that he could take me to than the village of Clonskeagh.

It was a small village and in a matter of seconds we found the one pub in the town, the One Leg of Lamb, which had a small and faded painted sign next to the entrance that read rooms were available for stay. The village was quaint in an Irish way, and was obviously an older village in need of community attention. A lot of wear and tear was evident and many of the buildings could have used some new paint. However, that was fairly common amongst the many Irish villages that dotted the countryside. There were only a few stores; a small grocery shop, a bakery, and a drug store whose hanging sign was being batted around erratically against the wall by the wind. I guessed the remaining buildings were residences.

The wind! As the book explained it was a strong wind but not so much so that it was uncomfortable to stand in. At the moment, after I had exited the taxi and grabbed the one suitcase I possessed from the trunk, or the boot, as he called it, and while paying the driver I remarked that I thought it felt refreshing.

I told the driver to come back tomorrow about this same time to pick me up and I would meet him outside of the pub. He looked at me funny, then looked around, back at me, and asked if I was sure that I wanted to stay here. He said there is nothing here and that the town was desolate. He was not far off in his view, but the pub looked busy to me and there was a woman pushing a baby carriage on the sidewalk who was going to pass me by in a few seconds. She was staring straight ahead the whole time, almost glassy eyed, and seemed very resolute in her efforts to get wherever she was going. When she passed me, I could see from her clothes that she was probably impoverished, and she smelled of urine. If she had asked for money, I would have given it to her. The wind was whipping her dress about her pale white legs in a reckless manner. I saw another woman further down the street - the wind was whipping her long brown hair about her head while she continually tried to push it away from her face - crossing from one side of the road to the other. She was looking at me very intently.

The taxi driver shrugged his shoulders and told me to be careful and he would see me tomorrow. He said there was another village about 2 miles further up the road where there was a pub and lodging was available. I thought that was an odd statement because I would think it would have been evident I was staying at the Clonskeagh pub which had a sign offering a vacancy.

I waved goodbye to the driver as he was driving off, picked up my suitcase and entered the One Leg of Lamb. The light was dim but what I could see showed me a very pleasant establishment of dark colored and worn wood with thick beams protruding from the white plaster ceiling extending from wall to wall. There were two patrons in attendance sitting at a corner table with partially consumed pints of a dark beer in front of each man. They took note of my entrance, looked my way, and then turned back toward each other, likely remarking something or another. I did not sense any animosity or unpleasantness, just a casual observation of a newcomer entering the pub. I took a seat at the bar and was greeted by the bartender who I would learn later was the owner. It was strange when I think back, because he was friendly enough but just somehow seemed detached, like someone who purposely keeps you at arm's length to avoid getting to know you very well. He did have a smile on his face and served me a Guinness at my request, which was the first of about two more I would have into the evening. Or was it three more?

I engaged the bartender in a running conversation all of that afternoon. With his Irish brogue, combined with friendly features, his florid complexion, but always breaking out in friendly smiles, I thought the village was indeed a nice place. Somewhere around the third Guinness I confided to him my reason for visiting his village. I remember how quiet he became, for about ten seconds, while studiously examining my features, then breaking into another of his smiles, this time followed by a laugh; he said he knew of what I spoke of. He explained that it was all Irish lore; a combination of religion and ancient stories passed from one generation to another. He emphasized there were no Irish little people either...and winked.

So I had another Guinness and essentially I was enjoying the interaction with the bartender, the pub atmosphere, and fully accepting that my journey was coming to an end. A little while later he suggested to me that while I was here in the village that I should take a stroll to the top of the hill. He told me that I would enjoy the view. At that point I was feeling a combination of sad disappointment and maybe the effects of one Guinness too many. Mind you, I wasn't drunk...there was only a low-level whirring sound in my head, and if I was careful, I was able to walk with some dignity.

I took my time and eventually reached the top of the hill just shy of dusk. The village was at least a mile away and I could see another village a few miles away on the other side of the hill. I could also see a flock of sheep being tended by a sheepherder in a rolling meadow about a half a mile away. I looked for lights in Clonskeagh, but maybe it was still too early because I did not see any. The top of the hill was flat with some large rocks the size of small cars strewn about and the ground was covered in a thick green carpet of grass and intermittent plugs of purple thistles. The grass and thistles were bent away from the wind, like people who were turned away against a driving rain. It was very peaceful.

Thoughts rushed into my head. For whatever reason, I suddenly thought about a Victorian era medical experiment from a time when doctors tried anything in an effort to learn something about the human body. In this instance doctors would place a person who was dying, naked and dying, on a weight scale, with the intent to measure the deceased's weight immediately upon declaration of death by the august body of medical experts in observance. The idea was to observe if there was any change in the deceased's weight immediately after giving up the ghost (heh, heh...I had to write that), with the thought being that any abrupt change of weight was proof positive that the soul had departed the human form. Some doctors insisted that a variance did occur, in that the deceased was suddenly lighter by 21 grams, about three ounces, which theorists therefore postulated was the weight of a person's soul. Laughable, I know. I would think any God would be quite amused.

Maybe I had too many beers...maybe I was just tired from traveling...maybe I was coming to the realization my trip was ending and I had not even come close to my goal. I realized...

finally, an epiphany...and it was all about my really ludicrous and stupid journey. I wondered how many people I met who must have laughed at me. I thought the pub owner from the village must be laughing at me that very moment, sharing his story with his regulars...those two men sitting in the corner. I realized I was crying. The wind blowing against my face was trying to dry my tears. I am embarrassed to confess what happened next, but I found myself on my knees sobbing uncontrollably. I looked toward the sky and cried, "I am just trying to understand!!"

I remember falling to my side and turning over onto my back and staring into the night sky. The wind swept across my body tugging at my clothes and pushing my hair back from my forehead. I held a hand up and let it whip through my spread fingers. It felt good. I don't remember very much from that moment onward. I must have fallen asleep.

I was awakened the next morning by someone calling my name. It was my cab driver from the day before who was gently jostling me and asking me if I was alright. I awoke to bright sunshine and a dry mouth which caused me to keep smacking my lips, certainly because of too much drink the night before, as I had recalled from my past experiences similar to this one. The driver, while helping me to my feet, told me he had climbed to the top of the hill to see if he could see me on the road, since he did not see me anywhere in the vicinity of the pub waiting for him. He knew he was early but it had been a slow morning and he thought he would come out to see if I wanted to leave early. He thought maybe he would see me walking back from the adjoining village, and that is when he found me lying on the ground asleep. I looked around, for what I was looking for I do not know, but all I saw was bright sunshine and a whole lot of green. I kept thinking something was odd and out of synch. I shrugged it off as likely just my hung-over status. We started back toward the village and the parked cab.

When we were approaching the town, it was odd, but something seemed different. I didn't see anyone on the streets or any of the small stores open. I thought maybe it was just too early in the morning. When we arrived back beside his cab, I told the driver I needed to go into the pub and get my suitcase. I do remember a strange look from him, similar to the look he had given me the day before just before he departed, but he did not say anything, just as he did not say anything the previous day.

The One Leg of Lamb was closed. The door was locked and no one answered my knocks. I needed my suitcase. I resigned myself to having to wait for the pub to open, but, for whatever reason compelled me, I tried the door again...and it opened. When I stepped in, I had to remain in place for a minute to allow my vision to adjust to the lack of light.

As my eyes adjusted to the interior, I experienced a sensation I had not confronted since I was in Vietnam as a young Marine. I was totally frozen in place from stark naked fear! I can only assume I must have looked like a fish out of water gasping for air. My suitcase was sitting on the floor next to the bar where I had set it down late yesterday afternoon when I first came in and ordered a Guinness. The pub was in total disarray! The bar had partially collapsed, a few tables and chairs, all broken, were haphazardly strewn about and lying on their sides, a large mirror behind the bar was smashed with a few shards remaining in the frame, there was dirt and grime a half inch thick covering the windows, there was trash all about the place, and when I looked down I saw that I was standing in thick dust that now partially covered my shoes, and looking behind me I could see my few footprints that I had imprinted into the dust when I first entered the pub.

I don't know how long I remained in place. I am sure it was only for minutes. I think I ventured deeper into the pub and looked around further, but really, everything is only a vague memory after that initial confrontation with my sanity. I know

I grabbed my suitcase because it is home with me now. Yet, I seem to remember that when I picked it up from off of the floor, I noticed the floor was clean underneath, and the outline and exposed floor in the dust matched exactly the dimensions of my suitcase.

In my whirling state of confusion, I recall being suddenly aware that I was standing beside the cab. The driver sensing some disorientation, even as I tried mightily to mask my emotions, he asked me if I was OK. I don't recall my answer...if I even answered him. I know he grabbed my suitcase from my hand and stored it in the boot while I stood by and watched him.

It was then I realized what had been nagging at me all morning; what had subtly caused my sensations of consternation and unease, and whose point of origin I had been unable to fathom. The wind had stopped! I mean, there was not a wisp of air moving; no wind, no breeze. Absolutely nothing! You could hear and feel the silence, as crazy as that may sound. I looked around the village in awe and I saw no persons and I heard nothing. I pointed out to the cabdriver the desolate atmosphere that seemed especially attuned to the village. His casual response shocked me and further confounded and heightened my prevailing sense of disquiet at that moment. He said that nothing seemed that much different from yesterday when he first brought me to the village. He went on to tell me except for the wind the place was as empty and as desolate as the day before. I peppered him with more questions and each subsequent answer seemingly further intensified my sense of encroaching delusion. He said he had not seen any other persons when he dropped me off in front of the pub. As he understood it the village had been abandoned many years ago due to the loss of industry that was once prevalent in the county. He had been apprehensive about leaving me there alone, but just assumed I wanted to walk the remaining distance to the next village in order to take in the countryside views.

I did not tell him what I thought I might have experienced. I was too worried that he might bypass the airport and take me straight to the hospital. When we drove off from the village, I kept staring out the rear window hoping I would see something, or someone, that would dispel or neutralize the experience I think I had encountered. I remember thinking that it was ironic I might have found what I was searching for, but simultaneously attempted to counter my experience with rational thought. Of course, there was just no rational reason to explain the pub.

So, dear reader...I have told you exactly as everything happened to me. Your thoughts, if I may so request? I have spun this event around in my head by the hours and I have long ago concluded that something happened. I am just not sure what happened. I do have a different perception of much of what life represents to me now...and, I am no longer afraid of dying. When I think back, as I often do when seated atop my widow's walk while examining the night sky, I am most frustrated that I never got to ask any of my questions I had prepared. Most notably I still do not know why there are not any Jewish ghosts.

Maybe I will go back. I am thinking about it.

Tensile Strength

"*Did you really want to die?*"
"*No one commits suicide because they want to die.*"
"*Then why do they do it?*"
"*Because they want to stop the pain.*"

—Tiffanie Debartolo
How to Kill a Rock Star

WHEN I THINK back all of these years, I cannot recall her face so much as I can remember her form.

I and my rookie police officer that I was training at the time were in a basement staring upward stunned by what we had found. An elderly white woman, maybe in her eighties, her facial features partially obscured in the shadows of the eaves. Her posture suggested a woman who had demurely turned her face away to her left, slightly downward, and stopped in mid-blush as if shying away from a compliment. I could not fully see her features due in large part to the light in the basement being diminished in increments as one looked up toward the ceiling. Plus we had just come in from the daylight, late morning, and our eyes had not yet adjusted to the gloom of basement lighting. Her right cheek was glaringly white. I was reminded of observing a phase of a moon through a thin layer of clouds that obscured portions of the surface, but allowed for a clear view of other areas. Her hair was fully gray, shot through with wide streaks of white, short, and seemed to caress the side of her face. The dim light reflected the earpiece and frame and a lens of her glasses. She had a thin mouth, her lips tightly closed. I would have thought the pain would have caused her to cry out in anguish sealing a surprise to her features.

I had seen many things in my career to date. This was a first, and oddly I remember being quite detached in my observation of this horror. My rookie, on the other hand, a young lady who had just graduated from the academy a few weeks ago, was quite excited at our find. She was an intelligent young lady, small in stature, with a short bob hairstyle, dark brown color. She looked just like the Campbell soup girl, and would wear that description her whole career. She had a lot of energy too. Probably like what I possessed when I started.

When we arrived at the scene a family member was waiting

for us. He told us he had found his mother in the basement of her house where she had killed herself by hanging. I asked the obviously distraught man if she were still as he had found her. He had indicated an affirmative, and my rookie and I started toward the house. Out of the family member's hearing I casually told my rookie to have the dispatcher request homicide to respond, which she dutifully obeyed. In a second sentence, casually over my shoulder, conversationally, I indicated because she was still hanging. Without a missing a beat, my rookie then announced to the dispatcher, which was overheard by any one of a couple of hundred police officers and citizens who may have been monitoring the police radio for the district, "...because she was still hanging." Yeow! Funny in retrospect, all these years later, but I knew my sergeant was going to tear me a new one later that day for instigating that breach of radio protocol.

When we entered the house and started toward the basement my rookie wanted to go first, which I allowed. She had to learn sometime. We only had to go to the bottom of the stairs to locate the woman. I had seen many deaths and many suicides, but this was a disturbing sight, and an icy sensation spread from my brow to my feet. Later my rookie told me she experienced something similar but found the incident really interesting.

You would think as long as we stared up at her I could remember her face to this day. I don't understand it. I can certainly remember everything else about her. No shoes, her feet pointed downwards, dangled around about my chest high. I remember thinking how perfectly still her body was, her arms limp by her sides. The noose about her neck seated deep into her flesh had been formed from a course light brown colored coil of rope. It was a thin piece of rope but it had enough strength to hold her body in place. Her neck did not appear to be broken; I thought she must have suffered terribly before she had found what she had sought. She had stood on a stool, kicked it out from under her, and it now lay haphaz-ardly across the bottom step of the basement stairs. She was wearing a one-piece summer style cotton shift, a washed out decolored yellow dotted with faded daisies. It reminded me of a favorite piece of clothing everyone has, a t-shirt, pants, dress, that a person washes out until the fabric is thin and faded. Most notably, curiously, there was a streamer of gray-green mucous, snot, expelled from her nostrils that extended the length of her body and then some, and stopped, approxi-mately twelve inches before the concrete floor. It reminded me of a huge piece of gum that had been stretched to its limits.

There were energized ants in seemingly uncoordinated armies running about on the floor. They were beside them-selves trying to determine some way to get to the body. I found a can of insect spray and gleefully exterminated the hundreds as if I were some would-be South American dictator. Not this day was anything else going to harm this woman any further.

We remained in the presence of the dead woman until de-tectives arrived, although there was no reason to believe it was anything other than a suicide. At one point my rookie reached down to pick up the stool the women had kicked out from un-der her with an intent to set it upright. I quickly stopped that action yelling "Don't!" She froze. "Leave it for homicide to do." We found a letter in the kitchen from the deceased woman ad-dressed to her family. In it she explained how sorry she was for what she was about to do, but she knew she was very ill and was dying, and did not want to be a burden to her family.

After my initial reaction upon finding her body, which was likely caused by some deep-seated fear we all possess, I felt myself transitioning to a detached and cold state of mind. While we waited for the detectives to arrive, I do remember just staring at her, wondering, stupidly, if she really was dead. Like most dead people I had seen in my career, she appeared to be asleep. She looked like anyone's slender version of a grandmother. Probably could bake a mean cookie, and loved her grandchildren. I couldn't feel anything though. I tried to muster a sense of compassion, any emotion. This woman deserved someone's tear, a lone tear at a minimum, a feeling on the part of someone of having lost a loved one. She deserved a prayer, but from someone with sincere beliefs in their heart. This moment and not later. Yet, I could not arouse myself to reach such heights. The coldness inside of me was a stone and I could not expel it from my mind. I yearned for a sense of humanity.

When I and my rookie returned to our duties, there was a silence between us for a while, mostly while she was writing the mandatory report. Later on, we would talk about it more in depth, but mostly from the perspective as a learning opportunity for her. In my reflections I would remember something that Ernest Hemingway once wrote about; that it took courage to take one's life. I guess he would know. Was she therefore deserving of admiration due her motive in taking her life? I only knew that she was dead, but I did not know that I was dying. That would not arrive until some years later.

Regardless, she deserved to be remembered if only in a short story in a book that will likely be read by only a few.

The Anti-War Protester

Legal observers said the new drive to hunt down Vietnam deserters is designed as a deterrent for soldiers being sent to Iraq. "They're really hardcore about this," Ms Abney said. "I think there have been a lot of these young guys now trying to get refuge in Canada, and they decided they were going to set an example."

—Julian Borger
Guardian Newspaper – Article – 13 March 2006

ENTERING INTO THE twilight years of my life, I had long ago acquired a practice that I routinely enjoy a few times each week. In my widowed and retired status, I now reside in a small town along the Chesapeake Bay in Maryland, where on each occasion that I am referring to I enjoy an isolated and languid lunch at the same restaurant each time. The restaurant is more along the lines of a diner style eating establishment located along the docks in the town's center. I enjoy the solitary occasions and it is an opportunity for me to read the newspaper from the front page to the closing page, while intermittently looking out the window and appreciating a view of water and boats and sunlight. Sunlight was a by-product of my town but even when the weather was gray, or chilly, or even cold outside, I always felt fortunate to be sitting in the middle of a setting that I considered to be taken from a Norman Rockwell painting. The staff was friendly and always made me feel welcome.

I mostly liked to read the Washington Post newspaper. I thought it to be a newsworthy and informative daily publication, although forthrightly some of its content and much of its editorials leaned somewhat far to the left of my own personal politics. I have written the previous sentence as politely as I possibly can. However, I had learned long ago to simply stop reading anything that I felt offended me and proceed on to the next item of possible interest in the newspaper. Yet, the newspaper did occasionally publish an opinion or an editorial piece that was more balanced in content.

It was on such a day, only a few patrons in attendance for lunch, where outside the warmth of the day was evident in the brilliant sunshine competing with slight and erratic breezes teasing the water across the harbor, I had become engrossed in reading an article about Vietnam. I was doing so mostly out of casual interest since I am a Vietnam Veteran. The news article was about a Marine who showed up unannounced at the US Embassy in Vietnam and wanted to turn himself in as a deserter from the Vietnam war. There was an accompanying black and white photo with the news story. The photo depicted an elderly man standing next to an unidentified official from the embassy. The elderly man was string bean tall, almost emaciated, his cheeks pushed inward. His hair was long, parted in the center and touched his shoulders, but obviously white in color from age, and a short beard, gray-white in color. He was wearing a casual light-colored shirt that hung from his boney shoulders and outside of his trousers. The trousers had no form and showed signs of extensive wear. They were too long for even his tall frame, where excess cuffs gathered at his feet, shod with standard native sandals, partially covering them up. There was no expression on his face. He was just simply looking into the lens of the camera when the photo was taken. The article went on to explain that the man had been married to a Vietnamese woman who had recently died. A name of Michael Bloodsworth was given.

I studied the photo intently. I began to experience a tingling to the back of my neck. I realized in the next few seconds that my respiratory rate had increased.

I knew this man! I had only known him as "Michael" and I never did know his last name. I sat back into my chair, idly fingering the edges of the newspaper, and wondered to myself if this was possible after all of these years...after almost fifty years! I stared out the window of the restaurant. I did not see the tourists, or the harbor, or the pleasant weather that prevailed through the window. Instead, in my memory I had flashbacked back to Vietnam and the war. Of all the memories that I had from that time in my life that had long ago slipped into the dim recesses of my mind, there is the one occasion in the jungle that I was never able to forget. If this is the same man from all of those years ago, deserter or not, I and the others in my patrol...we owed him big time.

My unit, an infantry squad with a company of the 3rd Battalion, 3rd Marine Regiment, was atop Firebase Heidi in the middle of the jungle just east of An Hoa combat base, where the regimental headquarters was located. A fire base was a hill higher in elevation than most others in an area of combat operations. Engineers would be choppered (helicoptered) onto the selected hill, and via explosives and heavy equipment, they would clear the crest and fortify the position. Artillery units would be assigned to the new fire base with the sole mission of providing artillery support to combat maneuver units in the field. By the occasion of this story we had been at Heidi for a month. Our job was to provide perimeter defense to the battalion's command element deployed at the firebase. We were tired, filthy; our clothes were rotting off our bodies. It was mid-October and the monsoon season was in full swing, which was further making life miserable for everyone. During the annual monsoon season, which lasts for roughly four months or so, the rain is off and on and intermittent in intensity. If you were living in a foxhole (fighting position) then you were living in a bathtub. The foxhole was emptied of rainwater when a Marine felt he had the energy to do so by using empty C-ration cans to bail out the water. Many an exhausted Marine would fall asleep in a foxhole with a foot of water covering his boots. In the mountains the temperatures were just shy of being really cold, especially at night. There was plenty of mud to go around, and the constant fog and mist cancelled helicopter flights and air operations. Therefore, by extension, we were unable to receive routinely scheduled resupplies of food and ammunition. The humidity was an extra layer of clothing, and when awakening in the early morning the Marines were always soaked and cold. Twice in that month we had been unable to be resupplied for almost a week on each occasion. Fear and hunger and filth were constant companions. All the while, Charlie, a slang term for North Vietnamese and insurgent forces, was continually probing our perimeter, mostly at night, but primarily to antagonize us, while simultaneously trying to map our defensive positions. However, even though it sounds like it was an uncomfortable assignment; it was actually a break from the war. The alternative was much less appealing, which was to hump daily through the jungle looking to make contact with Charlie. A hump is a march to a designated point, usually an exercise in human endurance, where during which, hopefully, you did not encounter the enemy.

I was a corporal in rank at the time and I was also the assigned squad leader. Normally there are thirteen Marines in a squad (three fire teams with four Marines each and a sergeant), but we were down to seven Marines due to combat deaths and wounds. Usually a Marine squad is led by a sergeant, but he had been killed a week ago during a mortar attack, and he was presently wrapped up tightly in a couple of ponchos, secured in an underground bunker until he could be choppered out and back to An Hoa for processing. There needed to be a break in the weather so that flight operations could resume for that to occur.

We had been socked in for about two days when I was summoned to the platoon leader's bunker. Our platoon was commanded by a gunnery sergeant, a rank which by Marine tradition is often referred to as a "gunny," who was on his second tour in Vietnam. Normally a platoon is commanded by a second lieutenant, but he had been medevaced from Heidi two weeks ago after having succumbed to malaria. He had been found passed out with his face in the mud outside of the entrance to the bunker to the combat operations center (usually referred to as the COC). Although inexperienced he had been a good officer who was willing to learn. Infantry units in Vietnam learned not to become too attached to their officers and senior enlisted Marines because they were constantly being moved around, transferred, wounded or killed. Continuity of leadership was an elusive quality in that war. However, the gunny was a good Marine and was close to his retirement age and mostly he cared about the Marines he was responsible for. He had seen a lot of war in his lifetime to include having served in Korea as a machine gunner. To have someone of his expertise in our chain of command, who was cool headed and composed, was a real plus.

When I went to see the gunny, he was waiting for me with a grim look on his face. I sat down on an upended empty ammo box and waited expectantly to hear why I had been called to his bunker. It was dim in the bunker, the misty filtered gray light from outside not getting much further than the entrance. A gas lantern was sitting on his makeshift desk, which had been constructed from discarded ammo boxes, and was providing the only light in his bunker, this light quickly dissipating into the dank and heavy air a few feet from the lantern's base. About every other minute the lantern would begin to sputter in protest then ease into a satisfied low hiss. The floor to the bunker was all mud but I hardly noticed it at the time.

I remember him leaning forward across his desk, clasping his hands together, an intense look stitched across his craggy features, the light from the lantern accentuating age lines around his eyes and highlighting the iron gray in his high and tight haircut. If ever there were an image of what a Marine Corps gunnery sergeant should look like, it was this man. "Battalion intel wants to know what is going on in the area of the firebase. They are concerned there might be a buildup of enemy forces in the area in preparation to try and take this firebase and our sister firebases. The other firebases are also experiencing more intensive probes within the last week, similar to what we've been dealing with over the past few weeks," he said.

Hesitatingly, I asked him what it is he wanted me to do. I did not have a good feeling about why he wanted me there after conveying to me the command's apprehensions.

He looked at me intently, and taking a deep breath, he said," I know you are not going to be happy with this, but I

need you take a recon team out, do a little snooping and poop-
ing and see what you can find. You have the most experience
in this company and you have done reconnaissance missions
before."

He was right, I was not happy. Yes, I had done a number
of previous recon missions, but not during monsoon season
when visibility during the daytime was sometimes limited to a
few feet in front of your eyes. This kind of weather, combined
with a triple canopy jungle, visibility could be at its worst, and
a Marine recon team could wander into, through, and out of an
enemy encampment before they knew where they had been. It
had happened. It sucked and I wanted no part of it. However,
my feelings on the matter were of no concern to the Marines
Corps. I basically had no choice. I simply told the gunny, "Aye
aye, gunny, I will take care of it." He told me I could take other
Marines from other squads if I wanted to, and that it was up
to me as to how many Marines I took with me on the mission.

I did not want any other Marines from another squad, and
I decided only four Marines were going outside the wire on
this mission. If I was going to go on a mission this dangerous,
I wanted persons beside me whom I knew I could trust in a
firefight. When I went back to the squad and I explained what
the gunny had instructed me to do, I asked for three volunteers to go with me. I knew which three Marines I wanted and
hoped they would volunteer, and they did. In fact all of the
squad members volunteered.

I needed a machine gunner. The M60 was a heavy weapon to lug around in the jungle, but if we were cornered, and
we were fighting for our lives, we could not ask for a better
weapon to provide defensive support. That is where "Chief"
was a valuable asset. In the Marine Corps, all Indians were
called Chief. He was a Cherokee Indian from the reservation,
and he had joined the Marine Corps to escape the poverty
and restrictions the reservation imposed in his life. I knew his
last name to be Smith, and I am not lying. He said there was

actually a large family of Smiths on the reservation, whose descendants were settlers who came west and intermarried with Indians. He was a tall man with broad shoulders and thick arms that contained the strength needed to handle a weapon that the Marines had nicknamed "pig." He could handle that machine gun like no other Marine I had ever seen. The machine gun weighed almost 24 pounds without ammo, but he could shoot from the hip with his right hand, while holding outward an extended belt of rounds in his left hand. One time I had seen him in a firefight stand up and clear a ridge line of enemy soldiers. He coolly directed fire down range and vectored in tracer rounds until he could see bullets impacting against human flesh. His sole effort resulted in breaking up the attack. We don't know how many of the enemy he killed, because by the time we cleared the ridge, Charlie had dragged off the dead bodies. The ground was soaked with blood and body parts littered the assault site. Charlie dragged the bodies away because they knew the Marines conducted body counts after each firefight. When there were only body parts remaining, the Marines would piece as many parts together as possible to construct one enemy soldier, and claim a statistic. Grisly business for sure, but that was the nature of that war. Chief received a Silver Star medal for that action.

I chose Ray Tucci to go with us too. Ray had been in country for the past 10 months and had been in more firefights than the squad combined. He had grown up on the mean streets of Detroit city and had been given a choice between going to prison for an armed robbery of a convenience store, or joining the Marine Corps where he would likely end up in Vietnam. During his time in Vietnam he had grown a thick and full moustache that he continually cultivated. He was often seen running a comb through it and examining it in a field mirror. His particular skill was his proficiency with a "blooper" grenade launcher. Think of a short barreled and very fat shotgun that fires a very large bullet. In actuality the blooper fires a 40 mm round, really a grenade, which could travel as far as 350 meters. In a firefight Ray would find his target, and with a detached sense of nonchalance, close his eyes, calculate the distance to the intended target, and send a grenade down range. A round discharged from the blooper always projected a hollow thumping sound, so you always knew where Ray was located in a firefight. Most Marines would carry the blooper and a 45-caliber pistol on patrol. Between the blooper itself and the number of rounds that had to be carried, Ray could end up humping a lot of weight on patrol. If he ever needed a rifle, it was theorized he could always pick one up on the battlefield.

A capable point man for this mission was critical. The point Marine was responsible for leading the patrol safely through the jungle, and whose responsibility it was to see the enemy before they saw him, or us, find booby traps, and essentially warn of any kind of danger. A lot of responsibility. I chose Faryl Fletcher who was likely the only Marine in the platoon who actually enjoyed being in Vietnam. Fletcher was all of five foot and two inches, but he was built like a fire plug. With sandy colored hair cut into a crewcut he chewed on multiple vitamins all day, and when the unit was in the rear back at home base, he would lift weights religiously. He had an easy-going personality and an uncanny second sight when it came to protecting his fellow Marines. Many occasions he had brought the squad to a standstill and called me forward, where he showed me a trip wire or a punji pit. On two occasions he had discovered tunnel complexes just by a sense of smell, and while observing foliage that was a different shade of hue than the surrounding area. He consistently volunteered to be the point man every time the unit conducted a hump. He never boasted about his abilities. He explained his skills by simply telling everyone who asked that he had grown up hunting and fishing in the bayous of Louisiana. In many ways the bayous were more dangerous than the jungles in Vietnam.

One night in the rear and while he was drunk, he revealed that he was a virgin, and the only sex he ever had to this point in life occurred one night when a girl he knew from high school let him play with her "tits." He being a Catholic thought for sure he was going to Hell as a result of an impure act. On the other hand, we thought it was hilarious, and told him detailed stories of our "numerous" conquests just to tease him, and to give him an idea what to do for when he ultimately encountered "the mythical golden fleece." He proclaimed many times in drunken fervor that his whole intent in Vietnam was to survive his tour in Vietnam and go home and lose his cherry. After that, come what may.

I scheduled departure for midnight. About an hour before our departure I met with my three Marines in the gunny's bunker, where I briefed them on the mission requirements and checked their equipment. In practice a recon mission is a relatively simple undertaking. The idea is to find the enemy and get back to the base with the intelligence, and without anyone ever knowing you were out and about. The primary requirement was to avoid contact with the enemy! We were to be out for twenty-four hours and back. Headquarters wanted an idea of what was out there, although sarcastically, I could have told them the answer was there were people out there who wanted to kill me and my Marines in the worst way. Of course, they understood my concern, but more urgently they wanted to know how coordinated and organized this effort was to try and kill us all. Although reluctantly in my heart, that was a tactical consideration I understood.

A light drizzle was falling, but fortuitously fog and mist had not yet formed, as we departed from the firebase through a prepared opening in the concertina wire. We had relatively good visibility although one was basically staring into blackness. We were each about ten feet apart from the Marine in front. Faryl was on point, followed by Chief, then myself and then Ray behind me. I was pleased, I could not hear any noise of us moving through the jungle, or of any equipment clinking identifying humans moving through the jungle. Cautiously, and slowly, descending the side of the hill down onto the flat surface of the jungle required meticulous attention and exertion. We were about halfway down the hill when I lost my footing, plopped on my ass, and starting sliding downhill. I recall purposely trying not to call out. In an instance I was sliding past Chief, while trying not to lose my rifle or any equipment, all the while my downward speed and inability to catch myself was aided by the slick mud enhanced by days of rainfall.

In another second, I went sliding by Faryl who had just turned his head back to see what the commotion was. I remember seeing the whites of his eyes enlarge, highlighted by the camouflage paint on his face. I was desperately trying to slow my descent, my arms flailing wildly about as I searched for anything to grasp, a root, a branch, vegetation...anything! I started to slip sideways and struck an unyielding object with my hip, I don't know what it was, but I flipped hard over onto my chest, as mud splattered into my face and into my mouth. My body was covered in mud and accumulating more by the seconds. A few seconds later I came to rest at the bottom of the hill. I lay there for a few moments trying to regain my perspective and catch my breath, knowing full well how much danger I and the team was in at that moment. In an instance my Marines were with me, propped me up and were checking me for injuries. All accomplished without a sound and a word between us. I quickly gestured to them that I was OK, for them to back away and take defensive positions, wait and see if we had been discovered. I wasn't moving until I was sure we were safe. If necessary, we would go hauling back up the hill to the firebase if need be. If Charlie was close by, at least we had immediate fire support if we needed it.

We sat in position for an hour. Black darkness. All the while, with hands and fingers and by feel, I was scraping mud from my face and person, and wiping mud from my rifle and equipment. I knew from our point of departure from the firebase we were pointed north. We were expected to have humped to our first checkpoint by dawn, which was about a thousand meters out. All within the next twenty-four hours, after having arrived at the checkpoint, we were supposed to turn ninety degrees, basically a turn to the right, and complete one-hundred and eighty degrees to the southern base of the firebase. We had a lot of humping to do. We were supposed to be back in the gunny's bunker by midnight and with intelligence.

We had five hours until dawn. Faryl moved slowly, taking us around various obstacles, I did not even see until I passed them. About two hours into the hump, Chief raised his right hand indicating for us to stop, a gesture each one of us did in order for the Marine directly behind to know what was happening. The stop requirement would have come from Faryl. Chief came back to me and told me that Faryl wanted me to come up front. When I say he told me that Faryl wanted me up front, his mouth was almost touching my ear, I could feel his body heat in his breath, and he very lightly whispered what Faryl required. Sound travels in the jungle.

When I had made my way forward and I was beside Faryl, he simply pointed to his left side and mouthed "booby trap." Leaning over I could see it was a standard punji pit, the stakes likely tipped with human shit, with intent to cause infection. If this hadn't been a recon mission, we would have dropped a grenade into the pit. That was not an option. The other problem was now we had found evidence that Charlie was likely close by, which meant there were probably other traps in the area also, and not necessarily all were punji pits. Some were likely rigged with hand grenades, or varying types of munitions. Regardless, our presence had become very dangerous for us.

I had been counting steps, with one of my steps about equal to a meter, and estimated we had gone about six-hundred meters, a little over halfway to our checkpoint. Yet, now that we knew Charlie was close by, and I had a screeching fear of booby traps, I elected to set in place and contemplate our next move. There was no way I was going to take myself and my Marines another four-hundred meters through terrain that was likely dotted with booby traps. Who knows how many we had passed already?

After the Marines had set up a loose defensive perimeter, I sat next to a tree and unrolled a poncho and put it over my head, effectively constructing a makeshift confined area where I could examine a map in my lap with a red light. It is hard to navigate by terrain with three layers of jungle vegetation over your head, although I could read a map fairly well. In review of the topographical features prevalent in the area, and considering the booby trap we just found, it occurred to me enemy forces were likely encamped in the area which had been originally designated as our first checkpoint. I shuddered thinking about what we may have walked into. I pulled a compass out from a side pocket full of mud. When I opened the compass, I immediately saw the glass shield was shattered, damage which must have occurred while I was sliding down the hill, and from when I struck the obstacle. I experienced a sinking feeling that momentarily created a sense of despair. I only had a general idea where we were. We were essentially fucked!

I wouldn't say we were lost...yet. Our options were few and restricted. We could retrace our steps back to the firebase, but we would have to wait for daylight for us to be able to do that. That is assuming we had left any kind of a trail while we had been moving cautiously forward. If we went back at daylight, we would not have much information to pass to the intelligence people, other than we found a punji pit trap. Not exactly a significant product for our efforts. The other option was to continue with the mission toward the south entrance to the firebase, as instructed, and navigate via the map and terrain features, of which there were few and far in between. There was a stream somewhere close by, and the map showed down-hill slopes, some hilly terrain, and large gullies, but you could never be sure how accurate these maps were.

The Marine Corps is hardly a democratic organization relying on the majority votes of its membership. However, I gestured toward the Marines to gather about and I explained very quietly via hand signals and mouthing certain words our situation and what our options were. It was easy by sign language explaining that we were "fucked." I pointed at each one, then made a circle with my left index finger and thumb, and with the social finger to my right hand, I thrust it up and in an out of the circle. I remember seeing Faryl's white teeth through his grin. I told them majority rules and we go back and just explain we were lost and the compass had been destroyed in an accident. Or we continue with the mission. To a Marine they agreed to continue the mission. It sounds hokey after fifty years to say so, but I could not have been prouder of them at that moment. They understood the importance of the mission and the necessity to continue onward, even at the risk of their own lives. Who could ask for better friends?

I conveyed to them that while there was still darkness I wanted to continue to move toward the southern entrance to the firebase. The humidity was thick and dense and fog was already beginning to materialize. We were soaking wet and our weapons and equipment were becoming heavier and cumbersome, the usual ordeal associated with any lengthy hump.

We started out again. We continued to move in a direction I could only guesstimate was toward our intended goal. We would stop every hundred meters, or so, to allow me to throw a poncho over my head and examine the map. Some terrain features matched, or seemed to match. Sometimes where I thought I was did not correspond with the contour lines and elevation figures on the map. Dawn appeared via a lighter darkness, and in the encroaching morning hours, slowly transferred into a pearl-gray fog. A combination of mist and haze overburdened with suspended moisture that dripped in rivulets from our faces and soaked our clothes and equipment.

Visibility was sorely restricted in the early morning, but expanded outward by the passing hours. At some point I could see Faryl about twenty meters ahead. Although our forms were pretty much absorbed by the surrounding vegetation, there were other ways to tell if persons were moving about in the jungle, other than actually seeing them. That is if such persons were not cautious as to how they moved and not alert to the perils in their environment. We moved at a pace that was under the tempo of a casual walk, but slightly faster than a baby crawling. Come to think of it, maybe a baby could have crawled faster. I could see Faryl's head fixed directly ahead of him, and occasionally he would slowly look from left to right. One was not enjoying a casual saunter for pleasure; one was trying to stay alive. Each of us was our own lookout and responsible for that area in our view. We did not just look about and ahead of us. We projected our vision...examining intently that area ahead and to our flanks within our sight. We didn't just look; we peered into the underbrush, our eyes seeing in between the trees, past the foliage, our minds matching any scene that might be out of sync with what we knew to be normal. We forced ourselves to believe we had x-ray vision and could see in time whatever could kill us first.

I saw Faryl raise his arm to bring us to a halt. He looked back toward me, and with a slight gesture of his head indicated for me to come forward. As I was crawling forward, I knew that both Chief and Ray were already on their bellies with their weapons pointed outboard targeting anything that seemed out of place. I crawled up beside Faryl, who pointed forward, spread the palm of his upraised hand a few inches from my face, indicating five meters, and with his index finger drew a long line in the mud. He had found a trail. I told him I would wait for him and to go check it out. Unhesitatingly he started crawling toward the trail. I watched him start to disappear into the greenery, he hesitated and held in place for about thirty seconds, and then he was gone. I lost track of time waiting for Faryl to return, and then suddenly he was back. He abruptly appeared like some wraith from the jungle as he slowly wiggled his way past foliage he did not want to disturb, thereby avoiding leaving traces of his presence for Charlie to find. He told me the muddy trail bore evidence of a large body of soldiers passing by, likely within the past few hours. How many soldiers, he could only guess at, but indicated you could not see the original trail for the number of footprints in the mud. I told him to get us across the trail without leaving any indications of our presence, and we would set in on the other side and see if any more soldiers came down the trail. The boot print of a US Marine is easily recognizable, and we had to be sure one of us did not inadvertently leave imprints while crossing over the trail.

About twenty meters from the trail we found an area that was sparsely covered in foliage and leafage, but well concealed by the surrounding jungle. It was just far enough away from the trail that a casual observer would not notice its location. We would take turns crawling forward, which would put each of us in a position where we could observe the trail, while simultaneously being well concealed. Faryl volunteered to go first. He quickly shed his person of most of his gear and crawled off toward the trail. I told Chief he was up next, but for now he and Ray needed to get some rest. I also told them to put a t-shirt in their mouths to suppress the possibility of snoring. Without hesitation they were down in the mud, on their sides, heads propped up on their packs, legs drawn up to their chests for warmth, their arms hugging their weapons closely, as if they were snuggling up against happy girlfriends who did not want to leave. When I think back now the images of them lying in the mud with t-shirts protruding from their mouths is pretty funny, even though it was deadly business at the time.

I had propped myself up next to a tree and I was under the poncho again studiously examining the map. The map did not show any trail in the area, but that did not mean anything. The trail could be overgrown in a few weeks and cease to exist. With enough persons transiting through the jungle, such as enemy soldiers, another trail can just as easily be temporarily established as this one had been. Trying to read the map, I had the uneasy feeling that we had actually been drifting north as opposed to an eastern trajectory back to the firebase. Without a compass I was sure we were floundering about and likely surrounded by enemy soldiers, who did not yet know we were close by. With the enveloping fog and layers of jungle over our heads, I didn't even have the sun as a reference aid.

I remember sighing to myself, removing the poncho from over my head, rolling it up, and shoving it back into my pack. I laid my head back against the tree in despair. I was soaking wet and my shoulders were chafed raw from the pack's shoulder straps. Of course, I was tired but I had to stay awake and provide security. I felt discouraged because I had let my Marines down, and it might yet cost us our lives. I sat there, dull, listless, pondering alternatives. Staring off into the bush, I saw the shrubbery across from me undulating, which was odd because the air was very still. From across my lap I quickly brought my rifle to bear, simultaneously and quietly slipping the selection lever from safe mode to automatic fire. The huge majestic head of a large tiger suddenly appeared from the foliage. It stared at me, looked about, and in a second casually sauntered into the hide!

I was fucking terrified! I could have killed it easily with my M16A1 rifle with an automatic burst of eighteen rounds, and notified every enemy soldier for miles around there were Americans in the area. An M16A1 rifle has a distinctive report separate from the enemy's AK47 rifle. Once Charlie knew we were in the area our life expectancy was likely reduced to thirty minutes or less.

I had not even been that scared in combat! I could hear the blood pounding in my ears. I could feel myself wanting to take deep breaths. I was frozen in place. The tiger continued to stare at me, as I stared at it, and I wondered if he was sizing me up for a meal. His gaze held me transfixed, and every few seconds glistening orange-green eyes would slide from my face to the two sleeping Marines. It occurred to me if either one of them stirred the tiger would surely pounce. The tiger raised its head and sniffed the air, and then simply walked across the width of the hide, right past me, about two feet away, and went back into the jungle. I remember taking note of huge fur padded paws, the fluid motion of his body stalking across the hide, noticing the thick muscle across his shoulders that effortlessly bore his weight. When he had walked past, he smelled pungent to me, but it was not an unpleasant scent. I immediately thought of Faryl, but quickly realized the tiger had gone off in the opposite direction from where he was likely set up.

I was shaking so hard that I had difficulty putting my rifle back on safe mode. What could have happened made me tremble with fear. I doubt if Chief or Ray would even believe I was telling the truth when I told them what happened. Fortunately, there were huge footprints in the mud that I would show them later as evidence to bolster the validity of my story.

When Faryl came back and reported that he had not seen anything, I told him to wake up Chief, have him stand overwatch, and for him to get some rest. I pointed at the tiger's foot prints in the mud and told him to remember that he had seen them. I would explain later. I was too wide awake to want to get some rest myself; I was still shaken by my confrontation with the tiger, so I took the next watch on the trail. I reminded Faryl to put a t-shirt in his mouth because I knew he snored.

I had been in place for about fifteen minutes, on my belly, hiding about five meters from the trail when I saw a lone enemy soldier, cautiously negotiating the trail. He was slightly bent over in a defensive stance, his AK47 rifle at the ready extended in front of him. Slowly, tortoise like, his head routinely swiveling from left to right in search of danger. It was almost ghostlike how he had materialized from out of the fog into view. In a moment more soldiers appeared behind him, slowly emerging into view, all in single file and spread out with about one meter between each one. Most were armed with an AK47 rifle and all of them humped backpacks. Some were armed with SKS semi-automatic carbines with the folding bayonet. They all had hand grenades stuffed in their pockets and attached to their packs. About every tenth soldier was carrying an RPG 7, a rocked propelled grenade launcher. A few soldiers were humping RPK light machineguns. I saw some soldiers carrying tripods for weapons systems I was unfamiliar with, likely mounted machine guns. I understand that most readers will not be familiar with the weapons that I have pointed out. Suffice to explain these soldiers were well armed with a variety of weaponry that suggested an assault of the various firebases was being prepared, or was imminent. The soldiers did not look like hardened and experienced combat troops. They appeared well fed, their uniforms were new, and had not been subjected to the harsh destructive elements of the jungle. There was energy in their steps, and they strode along as if they were on a casual hike, and did not display the sullen and resentful shell that becomes of combat experienced and hardened soldiers. I counted one-hundred and three soldiers, sufficient manpower to comprise almost two infantry companies. There were likely many more behind them.

When I returned to the hide, everyone was awake and awaiting my return. They had heard Charlie passing by. This was not a good situation for us to be in and we had to get back to the firebase quickly. I was honest with them and I told them that I thought we were lost, but I had a general idea in which way to proceed. I definitely knew which way I did not want to go.

Ray had been humping a PRC25 radio in addition to his

blooper and ammo. It was a good radio, cumbersome, but could be cantankerous, and definitely did not handle monsoon weather well. We were required to report in every six hours. I am sure the gunny was standing behind the radio operator back at the firebase, anxiously looking over his shoulder, as he copied each of one of our situation reports. I had passed to headquarters about what we had seen so far, and that we found a booby trap. I also passed our compass was damaged, and we were lost, and unable to determine a heading due to fog and restricted visibility. The gunny came back and said the artillery Marines would fire a round every hour, in which the discharge and report sounds should give us an idea which way it was back to the firebase. We did hear the artillery discharges. Unfortunately, due to a combination of terrain and weather, the reports could not be isolated from any one direction, but instead reverberated throughout the entire area of operations. After a few rounds had been fired, and the effort was proving to be futile, I asked the gunny to stop firing off artillery. Since the firebase had a general idea where we were, they were not firing any of the locator rounds in our direction for obvious reasons. I was afraid Charlie would figure this out and come to the realization there was a Marine recon team in their back-yard. I passed to him we were going to hump for a few more hours, possibly collect more information, set in for the night, and try to get back to the firebase tomorrow sometime. We would continue to check in with him at the prescribed times.

Faryl did find another booby trap. This time a "popper" type grenade trap, which when activated by an unsuspecting Marine stepping on a pressure plate, generally camouflaged with dirt and vegetation, would cause a grenade to "pop" up to about hip high and explode. We could not destroy it due to the noise factor. Faryl wanted to try and dismantle it but I nixed that idea. Too dangerous. The best we could do was re-move the camouflage hiding the pressure plate, and hopefully someone would see it well before it could be activated. After the find I told Faryl to find us a hide for the night and we could set in and get some rest. I did not want to be moving about the jungle in the dark with the potential for finding other booby traps. If you have found one booby trap, that means there are plenty of others around. When we set in for the night, each of us was responsible for security overwatch for two hours each. I reminded them to put t-shirts in their mouths. I would take the first watch. I remember idly wondering if there were any tigers close by.

When dawn arrived, Faryl, who had the final overwatch shift, awoke us. I was stiff, sore, and still wet and cold. I was no more miserable than the rest of my friends. The morning was just as humid and fog bound as the days before. Fucking monsoon season! I told my Marines that the map showed a stream a little bit north of where we were, or so I thought. The stream meandered eastward through the valley and around the hills, continuing around a sister hill just next to and west of the firebase. The problem was locating the stream and using it as a navigation tool placed us in great peril. Anywhere there is water out here, there may be villages close by with indigenous persons wandering about the jungle, or enemy encampments which use the water for hygienic and cooking purposes. The bottom line was where there is water, there is life, and that translated to danger. We had no choice, finding the stream offered the only opportunity to possibly determine our location and a way back. We sent in a situation report to the gunny and I explained what my intentions were. He advised good luck and he said he would be waiting for us.

We started off in the same marching order we had been using. For the next two hours, other than occasionally stopping so I could look at the map, we steadily humped toward where I believed the stream should be located. We followed contour lines and terrain features from the map that seemed to line up with where we were in the jungle, but I wasn't sure, and I was becoming more disheartened as the morning wore on.

It was at this point I saw Faryl raise his hand for us to stop. He slowly crouched down, his rifle at the ready. Without moving his head, intently continuing to search forward, he pointed to his left ear. He had heard something! I saw him go down into a prone position. By this time we were all in a prone position, our weapons trained forward. In seconds I crawled through the vegetation toward him until I was beside him on his right side. I looked at him questioningly. He mouthed very slowly there is someone out there. Immediately I thought we might be close to the stream and we had come across a villager in the jungle. If it had been Charlie there would have been more noise. When I looked back over my shoulder, both Chief and Ray were on the ground with their weapons pointed outboard. I gestured for them to stay put.

Astonishingly...from forward, I heard a low disembodied voice eerily emanating from out of the mist, maybe about ten to twenty meters ahead. "Hey Marines, do not shoot! I am not armed. I want to talk to you. I know you are a recon team." I immediately assumed we had been discovered and it was an enemy soldier playing with our minds. I quickly realized there was no Vietnamese stilted accent, and oddly the voice sounded American.

We were frozen in place, expecting any moment a firefight was going to erupt, and we were sure to be the losers.

Again, the voice, American sounding, "Marines, I am one of you; I want to talk with you. This is not a trick. I can help you get back home." We couldn't quite tell where the voice was coming from because sound is often distorted in the jungle. Generally, somewhere out in front of us. Faryl had produced a grenade and was ready to pull the pin. I shook my head and whispered not yet. I wanted to know who we were dealing with.

My mind was in a whirl as what to do! If we had been found out, and it was the enemy, we were dead anyway. If it was not the enemy, then who was this person? We had nothing to lose.

I called out to him, trying to keep my voice low, "Who are you? Come forward so we can see you."

Immediately he answered, "My name is Michael and I am coming out now."

"Hands up!" I responded.

At this point we were all staring intently forward, weapons at the ready. A man came out of the mist, hands up, and a big grin on his face. "Hello," he said.

"Far enough," I ordered. "Are you alone?" I asked. He nodded his head yes.

He was quite tall, easily a few inches over six feet. A very slender frame, long blonde hair haphazardly parted in the middle, but in dire need of a comb. He had a reddish dirty blonde beard of medium length. There was a splattering of jungle rot along the left side of his face, which is a malady of sores and scabs, and a common infection for those who spent extensive time in the jungle. I became most disconcerted when I realized he was wearing the remnants of a Marine camouflage utility uniform, which was partially rotted from off of his body. He appeared to be unarmed. My level of astonishment was stupefying. I quickly glanced at Faryl, whose mouth was hanging partially open, and seemed as if he could not take his eyes off of the stranger.

We had our weapons trained on him as I instructed him to walk toward us. A quick search by me verified he did not have any weapons on him. The other Marines kept a cautious distance from him but I instructed him to sit down on the ground. I had lots of questions for him.

He did not give a last name. He confessed that he was a deserter from the Marines. He had fled his unit one night while he was blind drunk. His unit had just come back from an operation where six Marines from his squad had been killed taking a hill, a hill they had taken six months previously. It didn't make any sense to waste those lives, just up and depart the conquered objective, knowing Charlie would repopulate the hill in a matter of days. He had gone out onto the perimeter for the solitude, just to sit and drink and stare at the night sky. That was when he decided he was going to leave...desert. He was going to make a statement. The Marines were definitely not going to send him home because he was tired of the war. He decided he would just walk out the front gate to the compound, keep walking and see what happened. He really did not care. He had no family back in the "world," a slang term for anyplace outside of Vietnam. He knew he could be killed but he didn't care about that either. At least that is what he told us.

Of course, I did not know what to believe. We did not know about post-traumatic stress disorder during that war. If you refused to go out and kill the enemy you were accused of cowardice and assigned to a federal correctional institution somewhere.

He actually managed to walk a long distance before he was captured the following night by Charlie. While walking down the road during daylight hours, hungry and suffering from a hangover, to where he had no idea, convoys of troops and vehicles would pass by, the soldiers would yell out at him and wave. None questioned him why he was outside the wire with no weapon and war gear on. Later that night around midnight, when he stopped to rest, he was grabbed by enemy soldiers, tied up, and dragged off into the jungle. They interrogated him for days, but other than being slapped around a bit, they did not really hurt him. He was just a Marine groundpounding grunt, lower than whale shit, what information could he possibly have they would want? The weeks and then months passed in captivity, but after a while they took no notice of him. One night they came to him and told him he was going with them on a mission. He refused and told them he was not going to kill Marines or Americans. Initially, they were angry at his refusal, ultimately deciding that he was going to come along anyway, but they offered a compromise saying they would give him an unloaded AK47 rifle. He agreed. He knew if he were seen with Charlie, he would be branded a traitor, even if he was carrying an unloaded weapon. Who would know it was unloaded? He had resigned himself to the idea that he could never return back to America.

I had heard from many others before all of the arguments and rationale why the war was so fucked up. When Marines are alone and passing a bottle around, they inevitably engage in philosophical and political conversations, trying to determine the justification for why they were in the Nam. None of them ever thought deserting was a remedial resolution. At least not in Vietnam. Maybe back in the world, if home was close by. I listened to Michael's story, and hard as I tried, I could not generate much sympathy for his plight. There had been sightings of a blonde headed American fighting alongside enemy soldiers. It was obvious Michael was that person. We were going to take him back to the firebase with us, except we were lost and didn't even know which direction to proceed.

Michael told us how he discovered us. He said another hundred meters we would have found the stream depicted on the map. However, it did not lead back to their firebase, having long ago been rerouted by the whims of the jungle. He confirmed there were enemy encampments along the banks of the river. He said he had been hunting in the jungle. Charlie did not feed him and he had to fend for himself. He was armed when he first confronted us, but left the rifle behind when he walked out of the fog toward us. He could retrieve it later. While hunting, tired, he sat down next to a tree to rest; he was half asleep when he was alerted to our presence. We had passed within two meters from where he was resting. That is not an odd experience in such an environment. It all depends upon the amount of vegetation and foliage, of which there is an overabundance in the jungle. You could urinate on a man's head by the side of a trail, and not see him through the underbrush and shrubbery. He knew right away from the direction we were heading, we were going to walk right into a hornet's nest. We were likely dead men for sure.

But Michael knew where we were, and he knew how to get back to the firebase. I told him that my compass had been smashed when I fell down the hill to the firebase. He told us when he saw the direction we were going, he knew we were lost. He also told us the closer we got to the stream; we would have encountered more booby traps. I shuddered when he told us this. He did not want to see us get killed. He hated the war, not his fellow Marines. He told us we could try to take him back, but he knew where he was in the jungle. He could likely escape while they were trudging around looking for the firebase. Most importantly, he said we were guaranteed to eventually run into the enemy. If it had not been for him, we would all likely be dead now. I knew we could put up a good fight, but we would all be killed. I knew that. I couldn't even call for air or fire support if we got into a firefight. I didn't know where we were. Or, he could show us the way back to the firebase, and we let him go afterwards.

I had only minutes in which to make a decision. I empathized with Michael. I did understand where he was coming from and why he did not want to go back to America. The country was falling apart with anti-war demonstrations and race issues. The effect was being felt in Vietnam by the military, and unit disciplinary issues were increasing in multitude. There was a sense of sullen futility and tactical frustration on the part of the troops as to why we were still in Vietnam. Or at least in regards to the way the war was being managed. With a constant stream of change in leadership and personalities, unit cohesion was a term from World War II, and did not apply anymore to my generation. Watching a famous movie star on the news cavorting with members of the North Vietnamese government and military was very disheartening and difficult for me and my friends to comprehend.

I took my Marines aside, without great detail, I explained

I was going to accept Michael's offer, and I would let him go once we arrived at the firebase. No one said anything. Each of my friends just stared at me. I didn't expect any resistance, and I got none.

We started out with Michael leading us through the fog. He told me we were about three hours out from the firebase. He instructed us to keep a tight formation and follow his lead. There were booby traps everywhere. Although there were large numbers of enemy troops about, they would not be in the area we would be humping through on our way back to the firebase. We moved at a pace equal to a fast walk, which was counter to my instincts, but it was the least of my concerns. We were making some noise, but not overwhelmingly loud. Mostly the sounds were similar to the swish whispers of foliage sliding across clothes, on the level of an animal moving through the bush. Michael would look back and grin. When we stopped for a break he would reassure me it was safe. I could hear the tension in my body screaming in my ears. If this was a trap, I promised myself that Michael would be the first to die.

During one rest moment he told me there was going to be a major push by Charlie to take out the firebases. I did not tell him about the troops I had previously seen. Company size elements, with supporting mortars and machine guns, would be assigned to attack each firebase simultaneously. This was going to occur in two nights. I asked him more questions but he refused to say anymore.

Michael's estimation was close and it took us just a bit more than three hours to arrive in the vicinity of the firebase. I was well familiar with the terrain surrounding the firebase. When we were first assigned to the headquarters element at the firebase a month ago, we conducted numerous security patrols throughout our area of operations. I knew when we were close to the southern approach, we would come to the edge of the jungle that we had been tromping around in the past few days. We continued to hide in the foliage while we listened and surveilled the area. Normally we would be looking out across an open area of tall, chest high, green razor grass, sometime even taller than Marines of average height. From atop the firebase the Marines could easily watch the area for enemy activity. Although on this occasion between the fog and incessant drizzle they would not be able to see much. An elephant could cross through the grass and they wouldn't see it. Such terrain was a perfect place for Charlie to ambush an unsuspecting Marine recon team. Again, I wondered if Michael was leading us to an ambush. One also had to be careful humping through and across such an obstacle, because you were sure to incur fine razor cuts across exposed flesh, such as hands faces, which often became infected and festered into jungle rot. However, across the field was our goal and the firebase, and food and rest and safety. I knew the razor grass thinned out at its base. If anything, that side of the firebase always looked exposed. However, I knew that not to be the case. There were more than sufficient defensive procedures and obstacles in place, if needed. Charlie wasn't the only one with a few catastrophic tricks up their sleeves. Up the side of the hill to the firebase the Marines had cleared vegetation, and cut down trees preparing fields of fire in the event of a ground attack.

"Well, here you are," Michael said in a low voice.

I remember looking at him...looking into his eyes, blue eyes, although I had to look up at him somewhat, because he was considerably taller than me. I was considering if I should let him go as agreed, or take him in with us, whether he wanted to go or not. There was not much at this point that he could do about it if I decided to take him with us. I guess I must have locked eyes with him for about thirty seconds, and I know that he knew I was thinking about not letting him go. A lot of thoughts passed through my mind in those few seconds. I had been in Nam almost ten months by then, and every argument he had put forth for why he deserted actually made sense to me. I understood his frustration about going back to the same objective months later, and seeing Marines die for the same real estate they had taken in a previous battle. The required body counts and inventory of captured weapons firmly illustrated the desperation of the leadership to validate their presence in country. Except, I was not willing to discard my sense of morals and have the US military searching for me for however long it took for them to capture me. Spurned women and the US military have long memories. As fucked up as the war was, I still firmly believed in the values and ideals that had led me to enlist in the Marines in the first place. I remember thinking, "Fuck it!" and decided to let him go.

I told him I would honor our agreement, although I tried to convince him to come back with us. He said he appreciated my concern and thanked me for keeping my word. None of the Marines raised an objection. He told me that this area was clear of the enemy and that they were presently in staging areas preparing for an assault in two days' time.

Prior to his departure he took me aside and gave me more information involving the attack he had told me about. I realized that he purposely held back the additional information in case I did not let him go. He would have used the information as a negotiating item, if needed. He told me, reference my firebase, at midnight two nights hence, the enemy would conduct an assault on this side of the firebase, from right where we were standing. However, it was intended as a feint. It was hoped the Marines would consider the south side of the firebase to be the most vulnerable approach, due to the open terrain, and concentrate most of their defense and Marines in this area. By approximately twelve thirty, the main thrust will occur to the north side of the firebase. While the attack is ongoing on the south side, the enemy would probe the perimeter on the north side, positioning sappers in place, who would blow the barbed wire back at the sound of a whistle, about thirty minutes later. A mortar barrage would be initiated in concert with the sapper's efforts to destroy the barbed wire emplacements. The explosions initiated by the sappers would be a signal to the enemy poised at the base of the firebase, and concealed in the jungle, to proceed with a full-scale assault. That enemy on the south side, who participated in the initial assault, would retreat back to the edge of the jungle, where they were hiding now. Using the jungle for concealment, they would follow its boundary around to the north approach to the firebase to assist the other attackers. Excluding the sappers and those of the enemy conducting the mortar attack, a full company with rocket propelled grenades and heavy machine gun support will be attacking the firebase.

There was no handshake or wishes of good luck. Michael just turned aside and within five steps he disappeared into the mist and the jungle. I had everyone gather around and asked each man to keep what happened between us. Not so much about being lost and floundering our way back to the base, but about having encountered Michael. Every man agreed and there were no harsh words between us. We knew we were lucky to be back safely and we owed it to Michael. Our real problem was how we were going to be able to explain how we managed to accumulate so much intelligence about the pending attack? The kind of information I now possessed was not obtained by surveillance on enemy troops who spoke a different language. With this weighing on my mind, I instructed Ray to radio the gunny and notify him we were safe, concealed at the jungle's edge, and we were coming in. I knew he would go out to the perimeter security and personally make sure no Marine on watch got trigger nervous seeing us emerge out of the mist.

We were safely back to the firebase within an hour. As I knew he would be, the gunny was waiting for us. I told him that I had a lot to report. I cut the Marines loose and told them to get some chow and rest. The gunny and I went to his bunker where I could make my report. I still had no idea what I was going to say to him. I had information that could save lives, and I had information about a Marine who had deserted, but in all likelihood saved my life and the lives of my fellow Marines. If everyone were to find out about Michael, headquarters would want to know why I did not bring him back, either alive or dead.

When I sat down in front of the gunny, in front of the same gas lantern intermittently coughing and hissing in an effort to stay lit, which in my mind I sourly noted I thought it was a worthless piece of equipment, I had made up my mind to be fully honest with him. I asked the gunny if I could request of him his confidence, and if some of what I was about to tell him could be kept between us. He looked at me closely, examining the earnest look I must have had pasted onto my face. I can't even remember if his eyes blinked. I know I looked away at some point. He told me that he could not promise that to me. I sighed, and said I understood. I remember rubbing my face and pushing my hair back, probably I was stalling for time. In combination with the clammy humidity in the bunker and my filthy physical presence, I felt tired and overcome. I took a deep breath and for the next half hour I told him everything that had happened, and what was about to happen two nights from now. He listened carefully, while occasionally taking notes. He sat straight up and pulled back into his chair, his face disappearing into the gloom, when I came to the part about Michael. After moments of sustained silence, he did not say anything, just gestured for me to continue with my report. When I had finished telling him everything, including the contact with the tiger, he was quite astounded, almost speechless. Except he told me that it was all "fucking" amazing! He said he wasn't sure how all of this was going to unfold, but he would get back to me, and for to me clean up and get some much-deserved rest.

Later that night, a few hours after nightfall, the gunny

passed word for me to come to his bunker. He told me that he had written up a report that he had already submitted to battalion headquarters. The report included all of the information I had passed to him, except for the contact with Michael. Instead, he had indicated in the report that an enemy solider had been captured, captured by my recon team during our mission, and while during his interrogation, advised of a pending attack by his unit, to include intended tactics. Further, according to the gunny's report, the unfortunate soldier had never experienced combat before and was very afraid of the Marines. He had tried to escape but was killed while crawling under the barbed wire. I remember the gunny winking at me. He told me if the attack came off as planned, there would be plenty of dead soldiers to identify as the one who gave up all of the tactical information, and who then tried to escape. However, he said I was not completely off the hook. He had passed the information about Michael to an intelligence officer who he knew well, and who he could trust. The intelligence officer would report the information, but indicate the information was obtained from confidential sources. He may make a helicopter trip out to Heidi to interview me. The intelligence people had a lot of leeway when it came to writing reports.

I was about to depart when the gunny stopped me, and told me he had one more thing for me. The commanding officer for the battalion had put me in for a Bronze Star medal with a "Valor" device. I immediately began to protest. I started to argue that I did not deserve an award for what I considered a failure of leadership and skill on my part. He laughed and said, "That is not the way the CO sees it." I told him if anyone deserves the award it was Faryl. He was the one who led us around booby troops, found the trail the enemy was using, and one could argue he also found Michael. The gunny thought on that for a moment and then said he would see what he could do.

After my meeting with the gunny, I went looking for my

friends. I told them about the report the gunny had written and its contents. I told them about the medal too, and I was embarrassed, but I told them the gunny was looking at the same award for Faryl too. They were good with it, and again we renewed our collective vow to keep what happened out there between us. I also told them about the tiger, and to a Marine they did not believe me. I asked Faryl if he remembered when I told him to take note of the large animal footprints in the mud. His jaw dropped open, and Chief and Ray suddenly had shocked looks on their faces, aghast, both with their mouths hanging open. I swore to them it was true, and asked them if they ever knew me to make up stories. Then we all started laughing.

We were attacked two nights later, just like Michael said we would be. The weather had stabilized and the fog had lifted; it seemed as if it were cooperating with Charlie for the night's pending events. A month of continuous rain and fog, and the atmosphere suddenly clears the night of an attack? One could not help but wonder whose side God was on? The enemy conducted their assault exactly as Michael had laid it out for me. We were prepared and had artillery, and gunships, and air support standing by. Just as the gunny promised, he found one corpse with identity papers, and used that identity to support his initial report reference our recon mission.

Sadly, Ray was killed during the attack. He was found shot in the chest, slumped over in a foxhole with an M16A1 rifle cradled in his arms, his blooper lying in the mud beside him, his ammunition depleted. He had shaved off his moustache the night before the attack. When he had been laid out on the landing zone awaiting chopper transport back to the rear, I noticed how glaringly white his upper lip looked against the rest of his face, while he lay dead. My heart ached for my friend, and I had to turn aside. He would be missed and is to this day.

I am not sure how long I had been reflecting on my past in Vietnam. The waitress was standing by my table apparently trying to get my attention to see if I wanted anything else. I apologized for my wandering off into my past, quickly paid my bill, and then went outside to stand by the docks looking out across the water.

Like me, Chief and Faryl also survived Vietnam. When Chief went home, restless, he wandered about the country for a number of years, working where he could find it. He was married for a short while, but his wife divorced him due to his excessive drinking. He eventually entered college on the GI Bill and studied computer engineering. He opened a computer repair shop just outside of his home reservation; retiring a few years ago. He remarried and had two sons, who both joined the Marine Corps, against his wishes, and each did tours in Afghanistan. One son was mildly wounded in the leg, if there is such a thing as being mildly wounded.

Faryl, on the other hand, became a police officer in Los Angeles. He was married three times, but never had any children. He said before he ever became married, he had sex with every "none charging" and willing female he could find, and would sheepishly admit, also a few women while he was married. He knew now he was definitely going to Hell. He eventually became a captain on the department and was a commander in the communications division of the department. He was involved in two shootings, killing both bad guys. One occasion occurred off duty while he was shopping in a liquor store. The Marines did ultimately award him a Bronze Star with the "Valor" device, but not until ten years later when it showed up in his mailbox with a letter apologizing for losing his paperwork all those years ago.

We keep in touch, and about every five years, or so, we try to get together for a reunion. We never did tell anybody about what happened on that mission, although we often talk about it among ourselves. The intelligence officer never did come out to Heidi to interview me. Just as well, I suppose. I was not sure if I was required to tell him the truth, or maintain the deception the gunny had cunningly and successfully con-trived. None of us know whatever happened to the gunny. I assumed after he rotated home he retired from the Marine Corps and started a second career. I guess he is likely deceased now, but he will always be one of my heroes.

I knew I needed to call Chief and Faryl. I wanted to know if they were aware that Michael had surfaced in Vietnam after all of these years? I also wanted to know if they were willing to help Michael, such as write a letter on his behalf, relating how he had saved our lives? Or maybe appear at his court martial on his behalf? I doubted they would have any issues with the idea. The likelihood is that Michael would stand before a court martial, probably offer a plea, and then be released from the Marine Corps with a Dishonorable Discharge. What would he do after that? After almost fifty years America cared even less-er about those who served in Vietnam. The country wanted Vietnam to go away and stay buried in history. Besides, there had been more recent wars that now attracted the fickle atten-tion and the public eye of America.

I heaved a sigh and turned to walk away and head back home. I thought to myself, I was sick of people telling me, "Thank you for your service." It was an unapologetic asser-tion that had morphed into a politically correct statement in our uncertain times. It had evolved into an everyday common expression; a tip of the tongue explanation for a failure to support America's military when it was unpopular to do so. It was more so a passing verbal gesture than an actual and fervent thought of appreciation. I thought if America really wanted to thank someone for their service, then they should thank Michael, a Marine, who had fought hard and lost many friends, soon followed by the loss of his heart and mind.

I would call Chief and Faryl this evening.

A Dish Best Eaten Cold

"I don't like it, but my hands are tied. I just want you to know this: if ever I get the chance to betray you, I will. If the opportunity arises to pay you back, I'll take it. You'll never be able to trust me"

—Darren Shane
A Living Nightmare

"When someone is mean to me, I just make them a victim in my next book"

—Mary Higgins Clark

THE CHIEF OF Police for Prince George's County, Colonel Darvan Mitchum, stood before the picture window to his office looking out over the parking lot to his police headquarters and police academy. He was in a contemplative mood this afternoon and was feeling particularly pleased with himself. With his arms folded across his chest, and his legs slightly apart, his stance bespoke arrogance and confidence while watching his police officers in the parking lot going to and from their business.

The Chief was a slender man of average height who took great pride in his trim, clean cut, athletic appearance. His uniform white shirt, with the silver eagles pinned to the crisp starched collars, and his sharply creased French blue colored trousers with the black stripes down the sides, were tailored and form fitting. His face was a long oval with deep set small brown eyes. But it was his hair that was his most noticeable feature. Thick and dark brown and every hair in place, and meticulously parted on the left side with a slight streak of gray sprayed across the front. It was inevitable that cartoons in the police union's newsletter depicted him with a huge head of painstakingly combed hair and a long perfectly coiffured forelock extending out over his forehead. When the first cartoon appeared, it was accompanied by a sarcastic newsletter article that intimated the Chief had entered into a business agreement with Mister Sal's Hairweave Company. The story alleged the Chief had opted for a free "Awning" haircut in exchange for allowing his photo to be used in any commercial venture the company may choose to pursue. The Chief had been outraged when he saw the cartoon - in private. He went on a rage for hours, throwing and slamming office furniture around and eventually breaking his telephone. In public he shrugged it off, showing everybody what a good sport he was. Shortly after the article, everyone noticed that the Chief was cutting his hair much shorter in the front.

A long day, he thought. It had been the usual day of endless paperwork, staff meetings, citizen meetings, and of course, more paperwork. Never ending. Yet, nothing out of the ordinary. One final appointment with Major Jefferson Simpson in about fifteen minutes and he could call it a day. He smiled to himself, he was looking forward to this meeting. Finally, he was about to get the Black Police Officer's Association, or, as it was known departmentally wide, the 'BPOA' - off his back.

Even with that thought in mind, he was looking more forward to later on tonight when he could meet his new girlfriend of the past few months - Lieutenant Elizabeth Mary Francis Paul, or just plain Betty, who was assigned to the Public Information Office.

He knew what Major Simpson wanted; exactly what every Major on the department wanted - the promotion to the Lieutenant Colonel's position that now stood vacant. He smiled to himself. Major Simpson was wasting his time. He had somebody else in mind.

He shifted his weight and swung his arms behind him, locking his hands together. He loved this job. Nothing gave him greater satisfaction. Except maybe Lieutenant Paul, but even then, that was still a far second place.

It was all about power. It was amazing what was available to him. Private vehicle, social status, and travel. When he thought about it, the police department in some ways represented a private army. It was really very simple - they responded directly to his bidding - or else! He even had his own secret police - an internal affairs section that answered only to him. And the perks! He had a brand-new police headquarters and academy under his command, a huge newly decorated spacious office which even had a bed that folded out of the closet for those late nights. And, there had been quite a few of those late nights lately since he had begun seeing Betty. Late nights which consistently angered his wife. Yet, overall, he thought, his position probably wasn't that much different from any other police chief who commanded a large department.

His gaze shifted over to the flagpoles with the American flag, Maryland State flag, and the County flag flapping in the sunlit spring breeze. The County flag may represent Prince George's County, but as far as he was concerned, it was his symbol of office. Whenever he was present at the headquarters, the Public Service Aide assigned to his office, known as 'PSA's', who was usually some young man who was a police wanna-be, and wanted to stay on the amiable side of the Chief, which of course was the side the Chief showed to everyone, would quickly scurry out to the flagpole and raise the County flag - symbolizing the Chief's presence at headquarters. Whenever he departed, the PSA would dutifully sprint outside and lower the flag - signifying the Chief's absence.

The Chief loved it. He had gotten the idea during a trip to England to visit Scotland Yard. During a side trip to Windsor Castle where the Queen of England lived, he learned whenever the British flag was displayed, it signified the Queen was present in living her quarters. When she departed - the flag was lowered. As he remembered it, each occasion was a ceremonial event. But he thought that might be too ostentatious to require a formal event each time he arrived and departed. As he saw it, it was a matter of respect for his position - and of course the man holding the position.

His thoughts were suddenly interrupted by a light knock at the door. He turned toward the door as Celia Fletcher, his personal secretary, stepped into the office clutching an armful of papers and files to her chest.

"Excuse me, Chief," as she walked over toward his desk, leaned over and laid the paperwork down. "Major Simpson is waiting outside reference your planned meeting," she said. She straightened up, turned slightly toward him, waiting, expectant.

In a flash, his view took in her presence, and his thoughts

flipped backwards for a few moments, reveling in a tingle in his groin. She looked great as always. A small woman with a slender but full figure. She was wearing a short black skirt that hugged her thighs. She had shapely legs sheathed in black nylon and was wearing black patent leather three-inch heels. Her chestnut hair cascaded across her shoulders in curls and caressed large breasts that pushed against a yellow silk form fitting blouse tucked tightly into her skirt. She knew how much he loved the way she dressed. Sometimes when he admired her body, he couldn't believe she was fifty years old. Yet, the years were beginning to show around the eyes, and when she smiled, new lines appeared briefly which he hadn't noticed before. Maybe the makeup was a little heavier lately too. Still, it was difficult to guess her age accurately. It had been a long time since they had been lovers.

Seeing her every day, he couldn't help but remember the past. They had been lovers for four years. It started when he was a Lieutenant in Community Relations where she had been the secretary. She was the wife of a former police officer who had been retired on disability after he was shot in the hip during a robbery. When they started seeing each other, the husband was dying from prostate cancer. Even while the husband was upstairs in their home, incapacitated from disease, he was downstairs making love to a woman who ran bloody furrows up and down the length of his back. He remembered how he had to cover her mouth with his hand to keep her screams from being heard during their lovemaking. Sometimes he felt bad about those occasions, but he never felt bad about his time with her. He ended their affair himself, but only because he had found someone else more stimulating.

It was a long time ago. At the time, he didn't think anyone knew about the two of them. He later found out that he was wrong - everyone knew! He wasn't sure how everyone found out, but another cop told him later that everyone knew and that he and Celia had been seen getting it on one evening in his unmarked police car. He wasn't sure which night the cop meant, because there were plenty of nights the two of them were getting it on in his cruiser. He discreetly asked around, and although he wasn't sure, he finally believed that he knew which night he had been compromised and which cop had put the mouth on him.

He had been working part time at a church on bingo night. Celia came out to meet him, and like always they eventually gravitated out to his cruiser. The beat officer for that area stopped by to check on him and was told that he was out back. When the officer walked out to the parking lot, he stood there for a few seconds adjusting his eyes to the dark, searching for the cruiser. He finally located it back in a darkened corner of the lot – parked next to a bright orange Chevy Camaro with vanity license plates "READY", which every lust crazed police officer on the department, of which there were plenty, knew belonged to Celia Fletcher. The only light available to the night splattered from the Church's community room windows. But there was enough light reflecting off car windshields to see that the cruiser was rocking, and Celia's legs, in black nylon stockings and high heels, were planted firmly on the ceiling. The beat officer had wisely turned away and departed. After all, he wouldn't want to be interrupted if he were in a similar situation - which he had been on a number of previous occasions of his own.

Sometimes he wanted to start seeing her again. Even today, he knew, she was still thought of as the 'Chief's Girlfriend.' In his present position, with her as his secretary, that could be disastrous. It was dangerous enough screwing around with Betty - and she was plenty for right now.

"Chief...Chief?" Celia asked. "Are you alright."

The Chief shook his head. "Uh, sorry Celia. I was just thinking about how I'm going to handle Major Simpson." He strode quickly over to his desk, pulled his chair out and sat down, scooting himself up to the desk. "Look, uuummm, do this, give me five minutes, and then send him in. Okay?"

For a moment she stared at him. He could see some sort of a struggle going on in her eyes. Lately, she often looked at him like that. Then she responded quietly, "Okay Chief, in five minutes." She turned and started toward the door.

He watched her as she walked across the carpeted floor toward the door, exit, and turn around pulling the door shut behind her. He loved to watch her from behind. The way her hips undulated in the skirt, and the flexing of her calves as they squirmed in the nylons. The sight only intensified the surge of lust in his groin. He sighed. Looking down he started to examine the papers and folders she had left on his desk.

In a moment the feelings of lust dissipated and were quickly replaced with rising anger. A finalized internal affairs report lay before him, and a quick scan of the cover sheet showed a final conclusion of "Not Founded" for the investigation about the "rumors" he had ordered. Unconsciously, he started rubbing his forehead.

He had been Chief for about nine months now. When he assumed the position the new headquarters and academy were brand new; about six months old. Persistent rumors floated throughout the department that a police officer had been buried in the concrete foundation of the new police academy during construction (*). Ludicrous, he remembered thinking. Yet, the rumors survived and started taking on a life of their own. Stories began to emerge that crying and wailing sounds could be heard through the hallways during the night. Some mornings, police officers and civilian employees alike, complained that items were either missing or found out of place the next day. A local newspaper, The Prince George's Journal, published a front-page story with stories and quotes from various officers and civilian employees.

It wasn't the superstition or the stories that bothered the Chief so much - it was that bastard cop, George Munkelwitz! The one whose fellow officers call The Mad Munk! The Journal ran a front-page piece about the alleged haunted police academy, and splashed Munkelwitz's photograph alongside of the column. When interviewed, he told the reporter one night during his midnight tour of duty, he heard crying while he was doing a premise check of the headquarters. He further claimed in the story, that a few hours later into the morning, just before he got off at dawn as he was driving past the headquarters and academy - all of the red and blue emergency lights to approximately a hundred brand new cruisers waiting to be issued, which were stored at the west end of the academy - suddenly came on! Munkelwitz told the reporter the only occasion he, or any policeman for that matter, ever saw that many cruisers with their emergency lights on was during a policeman's funeral.

Goddamn that son-of-a-bitch! As he later found out, it was Munkelwitz who caught him and Celia in the parking lot that night behind the church. And there was no doubt in the Chief's mind that it was Munkelwitz who had spread the rumors around the department. Throughout the next eight years, while he was progressing through the ranks, he tried to make Munkelwitz's career miserable. Every opportunity that presented itself, he transferred him to another station, or misplaced his requests for a transfer when they passed across his desk. As far as he knew, Munkelwitz was the only police officer on the department who had served in all six districts in his career. Yet, try as hard as he could, there was always someone in the command staff who covered for him. It galled him beyond all imagination. But Munkelwitz was well liked on the department and worked beside a lot of officers throughout his twenty years on the department. Inevitably, some of those officers were promoted, and now were in positions to protect Munkelwitz from his wrath.

There was a knock at the door. Dazed, the Chief quickly looked up from the investigation he was clutching between both fists. He took a deep breath and willed his anger to subside, composed himself, and slowly laid the investigation down, pushing it aside. He wanted a clear head for the impending confrontation. He didn't want to anger the BPOA; just bloody their nose a little.

He grabbed a notepad with some remarks previously written down, snatched up a pen, assumed a position of concentration, and when he thought he looked deep in thought, tersely muttered, "Come in!"

He heard the door open, and in the corner of his eye, he could see the shiny black corfam shoes and uniform trouser legs of Major Jefferson Simpson stride into his view. The Major quickly commandeered a seat in front of the desk, sat back, laid a large envelope flat in his lap, folded his hands across the envelope, then swung one leg up perching his ankle on his knee, and waited expectantly for the Chief to acknowledge his presence.

Arrogant bastard, thought the Chief. He laid his pen aside, looked up at the Major, and quickly stood up. Feigning enthusiasm, he extended his hand across the desk - forcing the Major to jump up and lean forward across the desk to grasp the extended hand – and stated, "How are you, Jefferson? I haven't seen you in a few days."

"Fine, Sir. I appreciate you taking time out to see me. I know you're very busy."

"No problem," while starting to sit back down, gesturing for the Major to do the same. He leaned back a little in his chair, resting his elbows on the chair's armrests and entwining his hands across his stomach. "What can I do for you?"

The Major licked his lips, and imperceptible to him, leaned earnestly forward. "I wanted to discuss with you, if I may, the pending selection for the vacant lieutenant colonel's position."In his best contemplative voice, "Uuuhhh, well, I haven't made a decision as of yet," the Chief responded, watching the Major very closely.

The Major, in turn, watching the Chief very closely. "Sir, as you know, I'm also president of the BPOA. I'm basically here at the direction of the executive board. It is their feeling that the next selection for lieutenant colonel should be a black officer."

The Chief experienced a surge of satisfaction. This is what he was waiting for. The BPOA had been a pain in his ass since he assumed command. They were not an officially recognized organization within the department, but they had power which was strictly political within a racially polarized department, where management was terrified of accusations of racism, and within a county where the County Executive wanted to be governor. As a result, the BPOA was always bypassing the chain of command and standing at his door with some complaint or another. It was downright antagonizing. It interrupted the smooth operations of his department.

When he thought about it, he believed the BPOA probably significantly influenced the direction of the department in the last ten years. Or at least, certainly increased opportunities and promotions for many black police officers. Particularly the members of the BPOA's executive board, thought the Chief ruefully. Every one of them was at least a sergeant or above. There had been a sudden surge of black officers promoted within the past ten years. He remembered the rumors and accusations of privately proctored study sessions for black officers before promotional exams, and the suspicions of manipulated oral board scores conducted behind closed doors. Maybe true - maybe not. He didn't know. He tried not to think about it too much. It was all in the past now. The issues were complex and very emotional, and well beyond his range of comprehension. His complaint with the BPOA was not philosophical; he just didn't like it when anyone tried to impose their will upon him.

Major Simpson looked down at the envelope in his lap. He looked back up at the Chief. "I have something that I need to give you." He hesitated, laughed lightly to himself, then said,

"Actually, I'm not even sure what it is that I'm giving to you."

The Chief looked puzzled, "What do you mean?"

"Well, it's this envelope. It was given to me by Dolly Carter, who told me to give it to you" - he hesitated and began stammering, "...if...if, I should ever need to." He was obviously embarrassed. He leaned forward and laid it on the edge of the desk and slowly pushed it toward the Chief.

He stared incredulously at the Major. His eyes flicked down to the envelope. Dolly Carter - the Chief thought - Jesus, she died six months ago. Even as he was thinking about her, he felt a wave of icy cold fear flush through his body. She was the reason he was Chief today. Without her, he never would have been approved by the county council.

In a matter of a seconds, it all unfolded in his mind's eye. Eighteen long years ago when he was a young patrol officer, he and two other police officers apprehended three black suspects who just robbed a drug store. All three were spread-eagled on the ground and the officers were holding them at gunpoint. It was his job to search each of the suspects for weapons and evidence and handcuff each in turn. However, one of the suspects kept squirming around, and he kicked the suspect hard in the thigh and stated, "Boy, don't you know how they do it in Africa?" That was just the beginning of his miseries.

In a matter of days, a complaint was made to the department, not by the suspect, but by witnesses at the scene. He was on the front page of the all the newspapers, and became the lead story on the evening news. He was quickly disciplined by a nervous department for his racist statement, but ironically, he never got in any trouble for kicking the suspect.

But the repercussions from that night were felt by him for years. The incident affected him badly. Not because of the danger, but because he quickly realized what all police officers eventually learn - in the heat of the moment you could get in a lot of trouble while doing your job, and maybe find yourself unemployed. He promised himself he would get off the street as soon as possible. Within a few months, he transferred to the detective bureau and embarked on a program of intense study for the up-coming promotional exams. He wanted to get as far away from the operational side of the department as he possibly could.

It was while he was a lieutenant in Community Relations, where he started making contacts in the communities and with numerous political organizations, when he realized such efforts could conceivably propel him into the Chief's office. Yet, there was that unfortunate incident in his background, and in a coun-ty that was overly sensitive to racial matters, that past event could easily thwart any plans that he might have for the future.

So, he sought out and wooed Dolly Carter. At first it was a matter of political and career expediency. Yet, later he real-ized that he liked and admired the woman. She was a small black woman with a toffee colored complexion, imbued with a fiery zealous mission to enhance civil rights in Prince George's County, where she was an officeholder in every black organi-zation within the county. Wherever there was perceived racial injustice in the county, Dolly Carter was sure to appear on the scene shortly thereafter. As the police department's liaison of-ficer with the community, it was he who always responded to her complaints of brutality and racism within the department. As the years passed, he ensured that he maintained an ongo-ing relationship with her.

It all paid off. When his name was submitted as the next police chief, the newspapers dredged up his disciplinary ac-tion from the past. It was Dolly Carter who testified before the county council on his behalf. It was her testimony that suc-ceeded in swaying the council to approve his selection. It was very simple; without her testimony he wouldn't be chief to-day. About three months later she died of a stroke.

Was she reaching out to him from the grave? He stared at the envelope. He looked up at Simpson who gave a puzzled look in return. "What is it?" he asked.

Simpson shifted uncomfortably in his seat, shrugged and stated, "I don't know. Dolly carter gave it to me shortly after you were approved for the Chief's job and said I should give it to you if the need should ever arise."

The Chief slumped back in his chair and suspiciously eyed Simpson. His heart was pounding. What the hell was he up to? He didn't like the looks of this at all.

After a few more moments of studying Simpson, the Chief quickly sat up and casually placed his arms on his desk, determined not to display any agitation. Deliberately, and slowly, he said, "When I get time in the next few days, I'll examine the contents thoroughly and I'll get back to you."

Simpson stared at the Chief for a few seconds. Obviously disappointed that he wasn't going to see what was in the envelope, he stood up, thanked the Chief for his time, and departed from the office.

The Chief watched Simpson leave from his office. He quickly glanced down at the envelope. He was loathed to touch it. It was any standard size large manila envelope, addressed to him, with the flap taped closed with scotch tape. He could feel the hair on the back of his neck standing up. This was strange indeed.

He picked up the envelope and weighed it in one hand. Not heavy but there was certainly something in it. After another moment of hesitation, he tore it open at the top and dumped the contents out onto his desk. A one-page letter and a smaller envelope fell out. Quickly, he snatched up the letter and immediately knew that it was a letter from Dolly Carter. Her penmanship had always been neat with perfect spacing between words. A quick glance up in the corner of the letter revealed that the letter had been written the week she testified on his behalf at the county council meeting...a month before she died. He stared at the body of the letter and began reading:

Dear Darvan,

Although you have always cooperated with me every time, I made a request involving your police department, I knew there would come a day very soon when I would not be around to help the black police officers on the department. I passed this envelope onto Major Simpson in the foreseen event that someday he would need it in order to advance the cause of the BPOA. I'm fully aware of your political agenda and know full well that the day would come when I would no longer be around to exact payment for support- ing your nomination to be the chief of police. As a result, I'm hoping that the contents of this envelope will change your mind. In closing, I would add that I did not solicit the contents, but instead they were brought voluntarily to me by a person who also knows you very well. I apologize for any sadness that you may experience.

The Chief shook his head. The letter was simply signed 'Dolly.' He looked down at the second envelope, snatched it up and quickly opened it, dumping the contents - a folded one-page letter and another envelope - onto his desk.

His hand shaking, he grabbed the letter, unfolded it and quickly scanned the page. Jesus Christ! It was from his wife! He was breathing in short spurts and he could feel the heat in his face. He began reading the letter:

Dear Darvan,

I have no idea when you will receive this letter and the contents in the envelope. I only wish I could be there to see your face. For some time now, I have known about your relationships with various women - especially with Celia. Who knows who you will be seeing by the time you read this? I have remained quiet so far and I will continue to do so for the sake of our children and because I don't want my private life put on display. I wonder if you'll act any different after you view the contents of the envelope, or if you will continue to go on as if nothing ever happened?

The letter was signed in her easily recognizable writing with a smiley face alongside of her signature. There was no doubt about it, the smile seemed more like a smirk, he thought.

He slowly picked up the remaining envelope, shook it, and could hear something slipping around inside. Photos, he thought? He tore the envelope open, squeezed it open and peered fearfully into its gaping maw, thinking that something may leap out at him. He could partially see inside, that indeed the contents were color photographs - two to be exact. He reached in, pulled them out, in which one was atop of the other, twisting them up so he could see the top photo.

He leaped to his feet, violently shoving his chair back against the wall while holding the photos at arm's length. Incredulous! His face was contorted in ugly rage, his jaw working in fits spewing vicious damnation, "You no good worthless bitch! Munkelwtiz, you motherfucking bastard!"

He stared incredulously at the first photo, unable to pry his eyes away. His wife, naked, stood partially behind a complete and frontal view of a posing nude and grinning Mad Munk with his hands on his hips. One arm was draped over his shoulder and lay across his chest, her hand fully splayed where her wedding and engagement rings reflected a small starburst of light from the camera's flash. Her other arm extended from under his arm, where a breast was fully visible, her forearm pressed against his abdomen where her hand was fully visible fondling his erect penis.

He pulled the second photo out from under the first. He began making choking sounds and he felt as if he were going to pass out. His wife was kneeling down in front of the Mad Munk, her buttocks fully resting on her heels, slight indentations in each cheek, a position which caused her to tilt her heard up at a slight angle. Her left hand rested on his hip, while her right hand was hidden in front of her body. The Mad Munk, all the while grinning, had a handful of her long hair and was holding her head from behind. His other hand lay gently alongside of her face. There was no imagination required to know what she was doing.

The Chief flung the photos onto his desk - staring. He thought surely within the next few moments he would go mad. His anger pulsed behind his eyes and his breathing came in long wrenching gasps. His hands shook violently and he knew he was crying. Without thinking, he fumbled behind him trying to find his chair. Upon locating it, he pulled it toward him and slowly sat down – still staring at the photos.

He didn't know how long he had been sitting there. In a matter of moments, he tore up the letters and the photos, placing them in another envelope that he would discard somewhere outside of the headquarters. He knew there were other photos, possibly with more letters that would offer apologies for what had to be done. Sadly, he wondered when they would surface. He wasn't sure how he would deal with his wife, and as much as he would like to hang Munkelwitz, he knew there was nothing he could do there either.

He sat there fully spent. He sighed deeply, his gaze reluctantly searching out the intercom. He reached out and pushed a button, and noticed his hand was still trembling. Celia promptly answered, "Yes, Chief?"

He took a deep breath, wanting to ensure that he sounded alright, "Celia, get with Major Simpson - tell him reference our earlier meeting, that I'm sure that we can work something out in the near future. He'll know what you're talking about. Also, I don't wish to be disturbed for the remainder of the day." Without waiting for a response, he turned off the intercom, sat back and began quietly crying to himself again.

Readers may want to review the short story, Requiem for a Cop

A Face That Would Stop a Clock!

"I wish I could turn back the clock. I'd find you sooner and love you longer"

—**Anonymous**

POLICE OFFICER HEIDI Sharpe was in the lady's room of an Exxon gas station removing her ballistic vest from under her uniform shirt. The Maryland heat and humidity were stifling; a suffocating, smothering sensation that felt heavy on the skin. Even the most survival conscious minded police officer would remove their bulletproof vest on a day like today.

The feeling of relief was fleeting. At least now she was sweating under her uniform shirt, not under her vest, which always made her nipples itch when it got this uncomfortable. Days like this made her think of fat men in Southern style movies, sitting on porches in dirty, sleeveless, sweat streaked T-shirts, while rivulets of sweat oozed from unseen neck areas. Heidi involuntarily shivered at the picture in her mind.

She left the lady's room and started across the parking lot to where her marked Prince George's County police cruiser was sitting with the engine running. She could see her partner, his head laid back on the headrest vainly trying to absorb the vehicle's air conditioning.

She opened the driver's side of the cruiser, swung a leg in, flopped onto the seat, and in a sweeping motion of her hands up to her hair, she swept back thick black tresses into a ponytail trying to get some cool air to the back of her neck. Her partner, Bill Richards, was working his jaws viciously on a wad of bubble gum. The air conditioner was cranked up to the max, but only shuffled thick clammy air from the rear of the cruiser to the front.

Without moving, her partner said, "We've got a check on the welfare call on Keokee Street. Thirty-nine hundred block, apartment 101. The resident manager there wants us to check on an elderly female who hasn't been heard from in the last few days." Then he added, "Feeling any better?"

Heidi shifted the cruiser into gear, while responding, "Little bit, but I'll feel better when the shift is over."

Bill rolled his head toward Heidi, looking at her, and with a mischievous gleam in his eye, "We could always take a cool shower together."

Still holding her hair up, she looked at him from under her arm, "It isn't that hot, Bill!"

He just laughed and rolled his head back to where he was looking up at the cruiser roof. "This heat is making me sleepy. Wake me when we get there." He closed his eyes.

Yeah, I'll wake you all right, she thought. With a nightstick up alongside of your head!

It wasn't that she didn't like Bill. If the truth were to be known - quite the opposite. She wasn't about to let him know that. He was a great guy and a good cop. The best, in fact. Yet, true to his calling as a male police officer, he was always trying to get in her pants. These guys and their sex drives were unreal. Yeah, it was flattering - or had been for a while. She wouldn't even mind dating him - except that he was her partner. And that was a formula for big time personal problems. Besides, screwing one cop was the same as crawling into bed with all of them. She might as well stand up in rollcall and broadcast her sexual likes and dislikes.

She slipped the cruiser into gear and left the parking lot enroute to the call. She let her thoughts continue to wander.

She remembered a time when she was in the station on an arrest and had gone into a small office off from the rollcall room to finish some paperwork. There was a rollcall in progress, and while idly half listening, she had heard the all-male squad, who didn't now she was in the office, laughing at one of their fellow cops who was retelling his successful seduction of a female officer. She didn't know the officer. An officer named 'Elaine,' who was assigned to a specialty unit at the precinct. Great ass, small tits, but a good blow job. Yeah, how about those redeeming traits, she thought. She felt such a kinship and sorrow for her fellow female officer whom she had never met.

The men in this job could be such dicks! Yet, overlooking their inane sexual rituals of masculinity, they were some of the greatest guys she had ever met. She had never seen such people who were willing to discard their safety and wellbeing to protect others. Most of them were generous to a fault and would go to extremes to help a legitimate victim or a weeping child. They might be constantly stumbling over impetuous erections, but they were cops, and nobody, outside the job, was going to criticize them in her presence.

She glanced over at her partner. Lightly sleeping, and slack jawed. Every few seconds he would clamp down on his gum; then his jaw would sag open again. She wished she could get a picture for the rollcall bulletin board. On midnight shifts he would park the cruiser, fall asleep, and come awake just before a call came across the radio. He never missed a one. When she expressed amazement, he just laughed and said all veteran street cops develop the skill. She hadn't developed the skill yet, and she had three years on the street next to his twelve years. When she had mentioned those 'three years,' Bill had put his forefinger on the tip of her nose,

pushed gently, and said, "Trust me, you're a good female cop, but you got a long ways to go before you can call yourself a veteran."

Thinking about that "nose" incident made her bristle. Thinking back, she should have grabbed his finger, shoved about a half inch of that sexist finger up her nose, and smeared it around. He wouldn't be so quick again to apply that implied little girl crap on her.

A 'good female cop!' screamed her mind. It was a statement that always made her brain screech. It was the way the men described the women in law enforcement. That is, the ones they

liked. Weren't there any female officers who were ever referred to as just a 'good cop?' Which suggested that a 'good female cop' has, and will always have, by virtue of being a female, a slightly lesser ability than just a 'good cop.' She never heard any of the male police officers being called 'good male cops!' Six months ago, the detective lieutenant at the precinct took her aside and asked her to apply for the detective bureau. He said they needed a 'good female cop.' That term again. She just looked at him and said, "When you need a 'good cop,' ask me again!" A confused look spread across his face. She just smiled, and left him wallowing in his masculinity.

Heidi slowed at the light and turned right onto Keokee street. Bill was still laid back. Unbelievable. Once she stopped at the address, he would come alive again. When he got out of the cruiser, there would be the inevitable groan, attached to some sort of a complaint. These guys complained about everything. The citizens, the administration, internal affairs, their wives, and/or girlfriends. Yeah, well, the women did also, just not as much. Maybe when we're fully assimilated, we'll bitch just as much, she thought. Of course, if we women can add just enough input, maybe the men will come around. Ha! Fat chance!

If these guys wanted something to complain about - try working the midnight shift when you're on your period! Stepping into the middle of a domestic argument when you're feeling bloated, and your eyes are cross-eyed from cramps, is a brutality complaint waiting to happen. One hot flash too many, and you're talking right up alongside of someone's mug. Now that's restraint, she thought.

She slowed, turned left into the apartment parking lot, spied a parking space, accelerated smoothly, and expertly slid into the spot.

Bill immediately sat up. You'd never know he had been dozing. He grabbed his nightstick from beside his seat and flung his door open. Pivoting in his seat, he swung his legs out, grabbed the roof, and with a groan, pulled himself up and out of the cruiser.

Heidi rolled her eyes and smiled.

"Let's get this bullshit over with, and go somewhere cool to finish the shift off."

Well, she could agree with that.

As they started toward the address, Heidi could see a lady waiting at the entrance to the address. Probably the resident manager. The impatient look on her face was the first clue. It matched all the other irritated looks on complainant's faces when the police hadn't responded to their problem at warp speed.

As Bill walked a few steps in front of her, she knew that he could see the resident manager's impatience also. But he would have some silly disarming grin on his face that would totally melt any opposition. There was one thing about him that she knew she could always rely upon. He never took anything seriously. Always with a quick joke, a smart remark, or some sarcastic comment.

She remembered when she first started riding as his partner. He'd told her that if she wanted to keep her insanity intact, there were only two things that were important in this job. Even though she was the new cop, typically impressed with her senior partner, she caught the word 'insanity,' interrupted, and said, "You mean 'sanity,' don't you?" He laughed and said, "No, I meant 'insanity.' Believe me, if you try to make any sense out of everything you come across out here ('here,' like it was some kind of demilitarized zone), you'll never make the end of your career. It's easier just to look at everything from a skewed disproportionate view." Yeah, he really said, "skewed disproportionate view." Anyway, his two law enforcement career axioms were simple enough. First, never piss in a parking lot - always piss in the grass. That way you'll never spatter your shoes. And secondly, always, always go and get a milk shake after dealing with a corpse. The taste sort of gives you that alive feeling back again.

When she heard those simple rules, it was all she could do not to laugh in his face. Now after a few years of this job, she wasn't so sure that he didn't have it all figured out after all.

One thing for sure though - there wasn't any way he'd ever see her piss - anywhere, much less in the grass. It was difficult enough for a female cop to relieve themselves normally when they're on duty. Oh sure, the guys can stand over the toilet, unzip, pull it out, and piss - and, falling back on gender attributes, most likely miss! Not so the females. They have to take off the gunbelt, undo the pants belt, drop everything, and sit on the damned target. And then when they're through, go through the involved process of redoing everything. Talk about a major undertaking. Somewhere in the painstaking process of a woman just going to the bathroom, there was a valid premise for the penis envy theory.

Jesus, what aggravation!

And about those uniforms, she thought. She watched Bill as he casually sauntered up to the apartment building. His uniform fit perfectly. These uniforms were originally made with men in mind.

Bill stopped in front of the impatient lady. She was clutching a set of keys in her hand and look worried. She ignored Heidi, but offered a smile toward Bill. So much for being impatient with the police. Probably in her thirties, maybe, hard to tell with all of the makeup that was streaking in the humidity.

It was always the same, she thought glumly. On any call in which a woman was the complainant, she was sure to be ignored. Most women seemed to gravitate toward the male officers. Especially if that officer was her partner.

For a brief moment she thought about the uniforms again. On female officers, the uniform always had a sack like appearance. If the pants fit around your hips, they didn't fit around your waist. If they fit around your waist, you couldn't get them up over your hips. Every shirt had a couple of extra inches around the neck with a limp tie dangling from the throat area. If you were busty, a portion of the tie would extend over a precipice, with the remainder flapping in the breeze. If you're short, the end hangs down below the gunbelt buckle. And the colors. A light uniform with a black tie. No fashion-conscious women would ever consider purchasing clothing that was similar in color scheme to some gangster's wardrobe from an old James Cagney movie.

Heidi focused in on Bill's conversation with the resident manager.

She was close to tears. "Nobody has heard from Mrs. Moore in two days. She's seventy-eight years old and lives alone. There's no answer at the door and no answer when we call on the phone. She hasn't been well lately and has difficulty getting around."

"Okay, we'll check it out," Bill responded. "May I have the keys in case we have to go in?"

The resident manager handed him the keys, Bill motioned towards Heidi, and they turned toward the entrance with the resident manager bringing up the rear.

Just inside the apartment building, the resident manager pointed to the first apartment to the left at the end of the hall-way, saying that it was Mrs. Moore's apartment.

Heidi asked her to stay back in the hallway as she and Bill, without any conversation between them, assumed positions across from each other alongside of the apartment door.

Not a whole lot of danger here, thought Heidi. Yet, practicing tactical safety on every call was the way you survived out here. After working together for so long there wasn't any need for talk between them. Each knew what the other was going to do in almost any routine situation. One of the byproducts of working together for so long. A professional intimacy so to speak.

Of course, Bill would have it another 'intimate' way if he could, she mused.

When they first started riding together, he was always asking her out. Whenever she drove around corners in the cruiser, he would exaggerate then lean in the turn and end up half in her lap. One time they had arrested a drunk driver whose convertible car was filled to the dashboard with wadded napkins. Thousands of them. Napkins from every fast food restaurant in the area. While she had secured the prisoner in the back seat of the cruiser, Bill had disappeared. Probably into the 7-11 across the street for a coke. So, she thought. When she went back to retrieve the arrestee's registration from his vehicle's glove box, Bill suddenly emerged from within the wads of paper napkins, like some wraith, - and kissed her on her nose! It was pretty funny really - after she stopped screaming and apologized to him for the blackjack that she bounced off of his shoulder.

In any other environment, such antics would be called 'sexual harassment.' In law enforcement, make that style of complaint, and you have just developed a terminal case of ostracism. Anyway, she had grown to enjoy his shenanigans. Sometimes, anyway.

Bill leaned in toward the door and tapped lightly while calling out Mrs. Moore's name.

No response.

He tried again, but knocked harder this time. "Mrs. Moore, it's the police!"

Still no response.

Heidi said, "I guess we'll have to go inside." She looked over at the resident manager.

The resident manager, tightlipped, having dealt with these kinds of situations before, nodded her authorization to Heidi.

Bill looked at Heidi, then reached for the lock with the key. Mechanically, Heidi reached for her portable radio and notified the dispatcher they were going inside. Bill twisted the key in the lock, grabbed the doorknob and turned, and pushed the door open a few inches. A quick look over at Heidi to see if she was ready, he toed the door with a sharp push, and the door swung open the rest of the way.

Dull, warm air, fled out the door. It carried the stench of sour urine. The hair in Heidi's nose began twitching from the invasion.

The resident manager gasped. She knew what the smell might mean. She started snuffling, her face contorted signaling the onslaught of tears.

Jesus Christ! We've got a corpse, thought Heidi.

Jesus Christ! We've got a fucking corpse, thought Bill.

Bill edged his head around the door jamb and scanned the living room. He couldn't see Mrs. Moore. The room appeared orderly except for a large grandfather clock lying face down on the carpet.

Heidi couldn't see the living room. Her view allowed her to see down a small hallway past the kitchen, and partially into a bathroom and bedroom. No Mrs. Moore from her perspective. When Bill motioned for her to look, she leaned over and peered into the apartment where she could also see the fallen clock.

Bill looked over at the resident manager, and in a subdued voice, gently told her to remain outside until they had looked around. By this time, her hands covered her mouth, and tears were dribbling down her cheeks.

Bill stepped into the living room closely followed by Heidi. She closed the door behind them. Except for the clock, there wasn't any other signs of a disturbance. The smell of urine, coupled with the enclosed warm dank air in the apartment, rested lightly on their faces.

Bill started down the hallway, bypassing a neat and orderly kitchen. The stench was stronger. The bathroom was the next obstacle.

Heidi saw Bill glance into the bathroom, stop, and stare. He's found her, she thought. God, how I hate this. She came up behind him and peered over his shoulder into the bathroom. But it wasn't so. Bill pointed at a steel galvanized bucket, which was filled to the brim with the source of the smell in the apartment.

Heidi couldn't believe it. "Good God Bill, why does she have a bucket filled with urine?"

Bill stepped around the bucket, reached over and flushed the toilet. It worked. "I don't know. Maybe she had difficulty using the toilet, and instead, would just squat over the bucket. Probably easier for her at her age. Come on, let's check the bedroom."

Heidi, standing by the door, went out into the hallway and headed for the bedroom, a few steps away. At least there was now the hope that she was all right, since the source of the urine smell had been located. Maybe she was with friends. Most of the time there wasn't anything to these calls.

They entered the bedroom. Everything was in its place. It was neat and clean. It also proved to be empty of Mrs. Moore.

With a feeling of relief, Heidi started to feel like that maybe she might have some good news for the resident manager.

They both started back for the door. As they entered the living room, Bill said, "Might as well set the clock back upright. It would be too heavy for her to do it when she returns home. You take one side and I'll take the other. Okay?"

Heidi nodded and she walked across the thick plush style carpet to where the clock lay. It looked old. Probably a family heirloom. Hopefully not damaged. A shame if it was damaged. She leaned over to grab a side.

Odd! Sticking out from underneath - hair maybe?

Aw Jesus! She felt the back of her neck begin to tingle. She looked at Bill. He had seen it too.

His voice low, he said, "We're going to have to look Heidi. Just lift the clock up a few feet. Okay?"

With escalating dread, reaching down, she grabbed the clock and started to lift with Bill.

Something! On its back! Mrs. Moore? The clock had fallen on whatever it was, and the brunt of the impact had been to her face. Her head was crushed, and her face.... Well, there was no face! Heidi felt her legs become weak. Mrs Moore was clutching two of the clock's weights, one in each of her hands, both now firmly embedded into her bony chest.

Bill said, "Hold it steady for a moment." He got down on his knees to look closer and then looked up under the clock. "Goddamned! The time of her death is on the face of the clock. Ten thirty-three. I don't know if that's AM or PM though." He leaned back on his heels and stood up in one quick motion.

Bill was talking to her. "Heidi, you can set it back down now. Heidi!"

She looked at Bill and realized he had spoken to her. Without thinking she began to lower the clock back onto what was probably Mrs. Moore. Her face... if what was left could be called a face, was only a portion of something smeared above crooked shoulders that was supposed to be a head, but reminded Heidi of a peanut butter and jelly sandwich with the top piece of bread removed. As a former human being Mrs. Moore was unrecognizable. Heidi wanted to remove the clock from off of Mrs. Moore, but the detectives would piss red fits if the scene was disturbed any more than from what they had already discovered. The poor woman. She felt so helpless standing there. "God, what happened to her?" she croaked, to nobody in particular, barely hearing her own words.

Bill staring down at the clock, said, "I guess she was probably winding the clock when the thumper king struck."

The 'thumper king' statement drew a sharp look from Heidi. Couldn't he just say heart attack - like normal?

Bill didn't seem to notice. He continued, "She must have been holding the clock's weights when the pain struck, which caused her to fall and pull the clock down onto her. I would imagine she didn't even know what was happening."

"God, how tragic," said Heidi. I hope she died quickly with very little pain.

"Yeah, it really is," said Bill. "But you know what Heidi? There is a moral to all of this?"

She peered closely at Bill, examining him. Suspicious. "Like what?" she reluctantly asked.

He looked very solemn. Quite concerned. He leaned over

ED MORONEY

toward her, and in a low voice said, "You know of course - that she had a face that would stop a clock!"

She stared at him, shocked! Her mouth dropped open. He didn't really say that. No way! Nobody's that harsh. The words raced cold through her body. What an asshole! He kept looking at her, expectant, like she was going to agree with him or something.

Then it happened. It welled up from somewhere within her. She swung her hand up to her cover her mouth. It started as a low gurgling sound, then spasmodically began to spurt from her mouth. Small spitting sounds at first - then came little childlike giggles. My God! She was laughing. She felt so weak and helpless; as if her legs were going to give away. What he said - it WAS funny! It had to be. There was no other way. By now she was snickering, looking at Bill, who was smiling at her. She knew now. Either she washed away this tragedy with some sort of emotion now, any emotion, or she was doomed to wrap it around her heart for the rest of her life. There was enough hurt and sorrow lurking ahead in this job without additional burdens.

Bill spoke then. "You want me to call the detectives, or do you want to do it?"

"I'll do it." She looked around and saw a phone on a desk in the corner of the living room. An old black rotary phone. Still suppressing a few lingering giggles, she walked over and picked up the receiver. Dialing finger poised in midair, she looked over her shoulder, and asked Bill, "How 'bout we go and get a milkshake after we clear this call?"

The Widow's Walk

Please come to me in my night
Allow me to awaken
Refreshed and no memory
And once not feel forsaken

—Ed Moroney
Poem - Wide Eyed, First Time Death Is Still an Amateur

I **HAVE BEEN** diagnosed with Alzheimer's disease. I am only in the early stages where being routinely forgetful is more of a nuisance than it is a malady. I used to say in casual conversation that I would take my own life if I were ever to be diagnosed with such a terrible disease. Wanting to continue living seems to have altered my perspective somewhat in regards to such a dreadful deed. Now in casual conversation, to those who know of my condition, I just tell everyone that I have forgotten to take my life, and may yet be required to pen a post-it note reminding me to engage in such an act at some point. Always draws a laugh.

Yes, of course, I jest about such a thing...I think.

However, what I am writing about at this time is not about my condition, albeit the compelling impetus for the story that I am now writing about and which will be available to any curious reader. I must tell this story, to create some kind of a record, before it becomes lost in the hazy background of inevitable and innumerable frustrating efforts to recall what I saw that night so many years ago. I will tell the story of events, and of what I witnessed as they occurred on that fateful night and allow the reader to make their own determination; their own assessment as to my veracity and to the reality of what I saw.

I am sixty-six years old now, but in my youth, I grew up in a small seaside town in northern Maine in the sixties. The name of the town is not important although the discerning reader may be able to deduce which town I write of. It was a typical seaside town where the primary economy surrounded the fishing and lobster industry. The town was spread across green and steep hillsides with a pattern of winding roads, numerous intersections, and interspersed clapboard homes all weather worn to the same drab white color. The town's streets were not in the best condition due to enduring harsh winters that caused them to buckle and crack open. Dependent upon the wind or an evening breeze, most notably in the summer, the town consisted of a fresh smell of the sea that was sometimes combined with the added smell of the day's catch, which seemed to reside deep within a person's nostrils. Not an unpleasant sensation by any means.

The more expensive homes, mostly of Victorian architecture and seemingly constructed with innumerable rooms, were located on the hilltops overlooking the bay and ocean. They were something to see during the Christmas season. As one would progress down the hill toward the middle of the town and toward the harbor, the homes became less attractive and smaller, and those were the homes of the fishermen and their families. I lived in such a home. Mind you I am not complaining about where I grew up. I am not sure of my parent's finances at that time, but I never really wanted for anything. My father was a fisherman and my mother took care of the house. I had four brothers and five sisters, which made for crowded conditions, but they are not relevant to this story. I guess one could say I was relatively content at that time in my life.

I was a senior in high school when what I am writing about occurred. I was seventeen. I was not a good student and did not really care for high school, other than the social aspects and for the girls. My parents told me that if I wanted to have any money I would need to work. So, I had a job as a clerk at the local McIntire's Hardware store, which I and my friends always referred to as Mack and Myers. It was not a particularly difficult job, mostly customer service, some cashier duties, unloading trucks, and any other tasks the manager wanted done.

However, it was where I met Miss Ginny for the first time. Her last name was Cummings, but everyone in the town always referred to her as "Ginny," but not in her presence. I referred to her as Miss Ginny because my parents taught me that was the polite way to address an older woman who allowed you to use her first name. She often came into the store.

I knew some things about her. I had seen her walking the streets of the town before and the town's residents would laugh at her, or make snide remarks, although not as to where she would hear them. She was always barefoot and wore the same dress, which was black in color and had white polka dots, and fell just below her knees. She was of average height and had a slender figure, and as best as I could tell she might have been in her middle thirties in age. When I think back maybe she seemed a little bit underfed, but she had small breasts, which was something I noticed on all females at that time in my life. She had long black hair parted in the middle that touched her shoulders, but always looked like it needed brushing. Her complexion was pale, almost an unhealthy white color, which was set off by a full mouth, with eyes that might have been just a little bit close together that in later years I would describe as "Irish eyes." She appeared to me to possibly be an attractive woman that just needed to be cleaned up a bit. Regardless, nobody ever really took notice of her because she was considered daft and best left alone with her own thoughts. I really never took notice of her either...she was just there or around, like some feral cat roaming the streets that no one gave a second glance to. I did not know where she lived, but unbeknownst to me I would discover that information in a few months' time.

One afternoon at the hardware store I was in the garden center area of the store at the cashier's counter. I was alone and there had been no customers yet. I was idly staring out the window when I saw her walking across the parking lot toward the store. She came into the garden center, still dressed as I had previously described her, and turned down one of the aisles where she stopped to examine items on a shelf that I knew to be various types of insect sprays. She reached out and grabbed a yellow spray bottle and looking down studiously examined the label. It seemed to be what she was looking for and she approached me at the cashier's counter.

This was the first time I had ever seen her this close...

about two, maybe three feet away from me with only the counter separating the two of us. She placed the bottle of insect spray on the counter and looked at me...straight into my eyes. I know the total meeting and the transaction likely only took moments, but in my memory today I can recall vividly every aspect in detail of the occasion. I wasn't sure what to expect since all I had ever heard about her was rumors, not that I expected her to do anything irrational. I can still feel the raw emotion that arose from within me and how my breathing seemed to slow. I distinctly recall hearing my heart thumping in my ears and a sense of heat expanding around my neck and face. Her eyes were a grayish-green color, moist and large, overseen by thick arching eyebrows...and she was looking directly into my eyes. Later on in college I would learn that most people never really look into another person's eyes, instead unconsciously focusing on a person's face area just below the eyes, which most people just do not realize. All of this aside, I realized that entangled within her unkept appearance that she conveyed to the town, she was actually a very pretty woman.

When she spoke to me, she told me her name was Ginny Cummings and that she had an account at the store and wanted to charge the insect spray. In those days the store allowed town folks the convenience of purchasing items with a personal charge account in addition to paying in cash or with a credit card. I found her account and referred to her as Miss Cummings, which is when she told me to call her "Ginny." I never called her anything. After I rang up the sale and put her item in a bag and handed it to her...as she reached out to take a hold of the bag her fingers swiped lightly across my palm. I won't describe the sensation as electric, more of a fluttering gentle caress, of course likely meaning nothing to her. Yet, she never took her eyes away from mine, excepting during the charging part of her purchase, and they were again focused on me when I turned back to her. I watched her intently as she departed the store and as she walked across the parking lot and eventually out of my sight. I was hoping she would look back toward me. She did not.

I did not know much about girls...women, in those days (not saying I understand everything now). I did not quite understand the sensations I was experiencing during that initial meeting. I did not understand anything about sex, procreation, or the battle of the sexes. I was a seventeen-year-old kid from a Catholic family in which my parents were not too keen on educating their children about the mysteries associated with sex. A few months earlier my father had called me into his bedroom, where along with my mother they wanted to discuss something of importance with me. Apparently, my mother had found a note from a girl I went to high school with in the pocket of my jeans when they were going to be washed. Not that there was anything untoward in the note, as they explained it, they were concerned that the time had come for me to be made aware of certain issues that I might confront. My father grabbed a piece of paper on his dresser, and with a ball point pen put a dot down. He looked at me and pointing to the dot, said, "That is a sperm and you have millions of them and it only takes one to get a girl pregnant." He asked me if I understood what he was saying, which I acknowledged that I did and he told me I could leave.

I had not a clue what he was talking about! I had no idea what a sperm was, where it came from, much less what it could do. For some years I had been experiencing physiological manifestations, now best known as erections, which I then believed to be the result of some illness or another. I spent a considerable amount of time examining my malady and desperately hoping I would get well someday. Further mysterious experiences, such as nocturnal emissions, otherwise known as "wet dreams" was fears that I was occasionally wetting the bed. One day I was walking across a field on my way home school when I suddenly became all wobbly and flushed and had experienced what I now know was an orgasm. I did not have an erection at the time, it was just my hormonal reservoir had filled to maximum and had overflowed that day. My underwear was wet and sticky and I did not understand what had occurred. It would not be until the next summer after graduation before I would have a girlfriend aid me in discovering what turns all Catholic boys astray for many years. As an aside it is interesting to observe how Catholic parents who create large families so closely hold onto the secrets of the process. Regardless, all that was occurring to me then was not something I felt I could discuss with my parents, or anyone for that matter.

I have explained of my teenage angst because when I encountered Ginny for the first time, I did not understand yet how some women, by virtue of their persona, could affect the hapless male. For whatever ill-defined reasons that defy explanation I was quite attracted to Ginny. This while experiencing various sensations and not knowing why at the same time. When I think about her today, I recall the slender figure, thick dark hair, and her inquisitive eyes, small breasts and all of the curves, and maybe there was a slight fragrance about her too. If she had taken off all of her clothes and climbed up on the counter and lay back and invited me to attend to her, I would not have had the remotest idea what to do or where to begin. I am sure I would have experienced one of my mysterious raging penile events dismally unaware of the relationship between her naked body, my desire, and a belief I would need to take some aspirin to reduce the ache in my groin.

Once every few weeks she would come into the store and purchase some item or another. She always looked the same, wearing the same dress and always barefoot, even when it was cold and even sometimes in the rain. The store manager told me that she had grown up in the town and had married one of the local fishermen. They had been in high school together and were married within months of graduation and supposedly very much in love with each other. However, a few years after their marriage her husband and his boat he was working on were lost during a severe storm. Other members of the boat were rescued by the Coast Guard, but the husband's body was never found. To further compound the loss of her husband she had been pregnant at that time and ultimately lost the child. I don't know if it was a boy or a girl. After her husband's death she moved back in with her parents where she now lives and from where she originates her daily walks throughout the town. For the first few years after her husband's disappearance she would daily walk down to the harbor and stand motionless for hours with her arms folded across her breasts gazing out across the bay. People sympathetic to her sorrow would try and engage her in conversation, but she always politely declined their efforts. After a while nobody seemed to notice her anymore. After a few years passed she stopped lingering in the harbor area and would just conduct her walking trips throughout the expanse of the town. It occurred to me that maybe she was looking elsewhere for her husband.

I always hoped she would seek me out in the store whenever she came into to buy something. As soon as I saw her, I would approach her and offer to assist her. Each occasion she would look at me, her eyes focusing on mine, and maybe ask a question or otherwise politely declined my assistance. Every occasion was an emotional roller coaster because somehow, I wanted to know her better and to be her friend, and more, if I could and whatever that meant. Yes, I felt sorry for her suffering, but there was something more too. I am not saying I fell in love with her, like some tragic character in a Shakespeare play, but I am saying in my youthful heart I felt something that I was not familiar with in those days. Throughout my life I have tried to analyze and conclude some sense of this combined mysterious enchantment toward her that was likely an amalgam of attraction, empathy, hormones, and captivation. Even today I can see her eyes as she looked into mine. I always wondered if there was something she wanted from me, or did she respond like that with everyone? I was never to find out.

I did not do well academically while in high school. In fact, I was told a few months prior to graduation that if I did not pass my Problems in Democracy civics class I was not going to graduate. I had four close friends that I consistently hung out with who were actually better students than I was. I attended school because I had to and whereas I would not label myself a troublemaker, I was certainly involved in a lot of mischief of my friend's and my doing. In the Fall of my senior year, my friends and I would sneak out of our homes at night and meet at some predesignated location, and wander the town for a few hours. We were generally engaged in some minor acts of vandalism; silly stuff like painting our girlfriend's names on the water tower, or shooting out street lights, or toilet papering some good-looking popular girl's house. Cheerleaders were primary targets. We were quite accomplished at toilet papering someone's house. We would buy about forty rolls prior to a planned assault, and ideally before a rainfall, intricately interweave an artistic endeavor. We always left a sign in the front yard with the words "Wipe Out," which was a play on a popular guitar and drum record during that era. Oddly enough it became a status thing to have your yard toilet papered by us, although I am certain the parents did not feel that way. I often wondered why the police did not find out that it was us. All they had to do was go to the local supermarket and ask if there had been any persons of high school age buying a significant amount of toilet paper and spray paint.

Whenever my friends and I decided on a night to meet up and create havoc I had to walk through a heavily forested park area to get to the side of the town where my friends lived. Walking through the woods around midnight is a very spooky and scary endeavor. I used to carry a baseball bat with me at the ready, although nothing ever happened. When I emerged out of the woods, I would be overlooking a significant portion of the town and I could see all the way down to the harbor and across the bay. Those nights and the incredible views I witnessed are memories I cherish to this day. I would work my way through the streets keeping to the shadows in an effort to avoid any police patrols as I went to meet my friends.

On one scheduled night of mayhem while under a bright full moon, whose gleaming luminescence was splashed across the bay, being occasionally blanked out by clouds scudding across its face, I saw her...Ginny. I was cautiously working my way through the streets and happened to look up a side street preparing to jog to the other side if it was clear. About three houses up the street she was standing on a Widow's Walk, which essentially refers to a deck on top of a house. A lot of the homes had some form of a Widow's Walk which was really neat additions where one could overlook the town and view God's beauty all the way to the far horizon across the bay. All of the Victorian homes overlooking the town had a Widow's Walk. In the day time it really was something to be up on one and to be able to see all of the fishing boats leaving or coming back. In the town stories abounded of wives perched on Widow's Walks watching patiently for their husbands and loved ones to return safely from the sea, and of course waiting the many times for when no one returned.

I was stunned at seeing her. In the moonlight I easily recognized her form and the dress she always wore even though her back was to the bay and I was seeing her from her left side. Staying in the shadows I worked my way up the street to get closer to her. My heart was pounding and I could feel blood rushing to my head and I felt my breathing quicken. I thought maybe I could pitch a small stone up on the Widow's Walk and let her know I was below. My mind...my fantasies were running rampant. Clouds slipped across the gleaming shine of the moon snuffing out the light and giving me more latitude to maneuver closer to her house. I was eventually able to work my way to a fence that separated her home from a neighbor where I could look up and see her. I knew in a moment that the clouds would soon slip away from the moon and fully lighten the area again. I could already see the moonlight filtering through the outer edges of the covering clouds. Before the full exposure of the moonlight I saw that Ginny appeared to be holding her arms outward, where her head was slightly tilted backwards and cocked at an angle. As more moonlight began to emerge from behind the clouds, indeed, her arms were extended outward, but also partially upward and in such a position as to suggest she had her arms wrapped around something. I could only see a partial shadow of the left side of her face with her hair loose and dangling behind her. The full moon emerged from behind the clouds and waves of light sped across the town enveloping Ginny and the Widow's Walk in stark, cold, brilliant moonlight. I saw it! Something...someone...in her arms. I don't know what I saw, what I was seeing! It was a man for sure, of that I was certain, or seemed to be. Not a full image of a man, more like an outline of a man. The moonlight shone clear through the image of the man highlighting lines that appeared to have been drawn in place, like a pencil drawing. She was kissing this man and it was passionate and emotional, and in combination with trying to absorb what I had seen, was seeing, I felt the sting of jealousy and loss. In a moment clouds again obscured the light of the moon, my eyes now trying to adjust to the sudden gloom, the figure in her arms seemed to dissolve. Her position and stance did not change which I now knew her to be engaged in a passionate embrace with a man. I could not see this man now... anyone in her arms. Where was he? Who was he? I wasn't sure I was even seeing another person in her arms. Could it have been her husband? He was dead, wasn't he? My mind was whirling with sensations and fear about what I thought I was seeing. All I knew at the moment was whatever I saw was not something I could explain to someone else.

In a minute the moon was once again fully exposed

enveloping the town in its silver-gray light. I could see the man again, but this time she had her right cheek against his chest with his arms fully encircled about her. The left side of his face nestled in her hair and rested on her head. The moonlight literally passed through him. I could see the outline of a thick head of hair and a partial beard, and I could see that he was wearing a pea coat that local seamen often wore in the cold months and when at sea. When I say that I saw this or that, I am saying that I saw only outlines as if he had been traced from a copy of a photo where the moonlight was not inhibited by the bulk of his body. In the ensuing days I would recall his image as being crystalline but without any harsh angles or planed facets. It defies description...I know this.

I was spying on them both. I knew it. Then again, I may have been rooted in position by fear while trying to grasp any reality in what I was seeing. Honestly, I may also have been held in place by a complete sense of awe and fascination in what I was seeing. In some ways I thought maybe I was supposed to be there, that I had been invited unbeknownst to me. I wasn't really afraid anymore but I remember feeling that ecstatic tingling that occurs throughout your body when you are experiencing something exciting or dangerous. The same feeling, I would experience years later while in the Marines as I stood in the doorway of a perfectly good aircraft that I was getting ready to jump out of during a parachute training exercise. That feeling! I watched the two lovers in awe and I wondered if it were possible that a woman can love a man so much that she could summon some portion of his being back into her life after he had died?

Again, clouds had begun to smother the outer edges of the moon, and it was maybe ten seconds before it would be completely blotted out again. She saw me, and I think she knew I was there all along. She stared down at me while still in the arms of her lover. It was as if I were back in the hardware store talking to her as in the past. It seemed to me I could clearly see her gray-green eyes in the fading light looking down at me. The darkness fell again and she dissolved from my sight. When the moon came back into full brilliance she and her lover were gone. I waited in place for a while hoping that indeed they had not departed but they never reappeared.

I did not meet up with my friends that night, and instead I went back home. Somehow, I walked completely through the woods without realizing I had done so. The next day at school I told my friends I had been sick and I could not have gotten out anyway because my father had stayed up late prowling around the house. I didn't tell them about what I had witnessed because who would have believed me? I wouldn't have believed me. There was another full moon the following night and I slipped out of the house and went back to Ginny's house and watched the Widow's Walk for a few hours. I never saw again what I had seen the previous night. For about a week I would walk slowly by her house while trying to be inconspicuous. I would casually linger in the area and hoping beyond hope I would get a glimpse of her, or she would come out and talk to me. That never happened either.

Whereas the memory has always been a vivid ache in my life, after about a few days I accepted a sense that I had observed, or participated in something special, and that I should just consider myself fortunate, maybe unique.

Yet, it wasn't over for me. I first heard the rumors at school that the crazy lady had not been seen in a week. In that time the town folks had slowly realized no one had seen her walking throughout the town recently. It quickly became known that she was missing and the police were trying to find her. Within a few days, posters were circulated all over the town offering a reward for any information that would lead to her recovery. The posters included a large black and white photo which did not do her justice, I thought. Her gray-green eyes were hidden, withdrawn back into the pixels making up the photograph. The last time her parents had seen her was an evening when she had gone up onto the Widow's Walk to their home where they said she often went on moonlit nights. As best as I was able to determine that was the same night I saw her with her lover. How was I supposed to go to the police and tell them what I had seen that night? For about a week the Marine police swept the bottom of the harbor with no luck. I was certain they would not find her there although I could not tell you where I thought she might be found otherwise. As the months passed the posters were removed by both the weather and town cleaning crews.

The years have passed and rarely has a day passed that I have not reflected on what I saw that night. Until now I have never told anyone what it is I saw, or thought I saw. If I wasn't in love with her then as a moonstruck teenager trying to determine what physiological and adolescent manifestations was going on in my groin area, I surely came to love her over the years. Even now I can clearly see her face and gray-green eyes looking at me from within these sentences. I am stricken with fear in my present developing condition that soon I will not be able to remember her.

However, I also have faith that I might soon get to see her again.

To Right a Wrong

To bear with patience wrongs done to oneself is a mark of perfection, but to bear with patience wrongs done to someone else is a mark of imperfection and even of actual sin.

—**Thomas Aquinas**

Prologue

FOR THOSE OF you who read this story, my name is not important.

Although it is likely you will learn my name as my tale progresses, it is only important for you to know that I was a close friend of Jake's. We were both Chief Warrant Officers in the Marine Corps. I was a Chief Warrant Officer 3 and he was a Chief Warrant Officer 5. We were both counterintelligence officers and although we had often served together in different areas of the world, wherever the Corps had sent us, and Jake was always volunteering to go anywhere, and there were many different countries, we had last served together in Kuwait at the beginning of the Iraqi War.

It is important for the reader(s) to understand that Chief Warrant Officers are former enlisted Marines selected into the Warrant Officer corps based upon their proven performance and individual selection by a specially convened selection board. Everything in the Marine Corps is by a specially convened selection board. However, only a few warrant officers achieve the rank of Chief Warrant Officer 5. It was a mythical rank. As Jake once told me on that momentous occasion of his promotion to such august rank, he felt he could claim he was now "self actualized." Then he would laugh at himself. Chief Warrant Officers were always highly regarded throughout the Corps for their expertise in their field and for their wisdom as senior Marines. The saying was that Chief Warrant Officers were always admired by younger Marines for their advice and counsel and admired by older officers for their companionship and for somebody to look up to. I myself will never be promoted to Chief Warrant Officer 5. Especially after this story is revealed. The senior leadership in the Marine Corps never forgives blatant revelations of its inner workings, and like all massive complex structures nurtures its hypocrisy at its breast from those who would try to pry within.

Across the country the newspapers would leap on this story like snarling wolves and their carrion. It possessed all of the standard appeal of honor, integrity, scandal, drama, and death. Yet, like any story there was much the media did not print, although they certainly printed enough to destroy my friend. Indeed, there was lot they did not know of, or so I believe. A few newspaper reporters would call me repeatedly after having obtained my identity in some way I know not...but, I never spoke with any of them. Now, a year after events I feel it is incumbent upon me to at least present a side of the story no one else knew of, except for maybe one other person, other than myself that is.

What I will tell you of is comprised of what I observed first hand and of what Jake told me in confidence as a close friend and fellow Marine. It is for the reader to determine where honor and integrity and self sacrifice lay. Reader understand clearly this...that both I, and Jake, loved the Marine Corps, our country, and we had served both on many occasions under very arduous occasions. In Jake's case his career extended all the way back to Vietnam where he was assigned as a radio operator with an infantry battalion. He possessed an extended rack of ribbons the envy of enlisted and officers alike, which depth of decorations bespoke of his personal honors and great deeds and conveyed his participation in numerous campaigns.

I will begin my story on the initial occasion I first became aware of the depth of Jake's involvement...

- 1 -

I sat in the in the first row of church like pews in the smallest courtroom I had ever been in, or even had ever seen on

TV or in a movie. The courtroom was located in the Judge Advocate's General's (JAG) building at the Marine base in Quantico, Virginia. The pews were hard and uncomfortable and the heat in the courtroom had yet to surpass the cold morning of a February winter. I was in civilian clothes and I had not taken off an overcoat and I still felt cold. The courtroom was long and narrow. The occupants included a Marine major as the prosecuting attorney, a Marine captain as the defense attorney, and a Marine captain presiding as the Hearing Officer for this occasion for what is referred to within military legalese as an Article 32 hearing, within the Uniform Code of Military Justice, or "UMCJ" for short, in which the Hearing Officer determines if, after all of the facts and testimony have been compiled, whether or not to proceed with a court martial.

The Hearing Officer occupied an impressive position which was of an elaborate and enlarged fine wood construction at the far end of the courtroom. His seating was tactically poised so he (or she) could look down and over the length of the courtroom. The way he was presently seated he was actually poised looking at the opposite wall. He would have to make a conscious effort to turn his chair to his left where he could look down at the stand where witnesses testified, and looked even further down at the defense and prosecutor and anyone in the audience, which at that moment only consisted of me. In fact, I am not even sure he could see the defense table, if there was a witness seated in the witness stand...the room was that narrow.

The jury stand was situated across from the witness stand extending back up toward the Hearing Officer. Although there were not any jurors for this occasion and to the best of my knowledge there generally isn't any for an Article 32 hearing. Any person on the witness stand would be in reach of jurors if both witness and juror were to reach their hands out. I thought it would be disconcerting to be a witness and have jurors that close looking at you. Maybe that was the intent. I mean, if the accused were to take the stand, it would really be uncomfortable.

The courtroom was also occupied by the defendant, to wit, one Second Lieutenant Lacey Wilson, who was seated at the defense counsel's table.

And also occupied by my fellow Marine and close friend, Jake, who was seated in the witness stand, an elevated position that required interrogators, or interviewers, if the reader likes that term better, to look up at him.

The courtroom was quiet while the Hearing Officer was engrossed in reading some documents. As I had indicated earlier, he was a captain, but also a lawyer, and I already knew from the defense attorney he was someone who had achieved his present position from the enlisted ranks in the infantry. I thought that was interesting that a "grunt" enlisted Marine was smart enough to attend law school and then turn around and become a Marine officer. So he was older than your average Marine captain with some significant time already in the Marine Corps. Bottom line, no one was going to get anything by him. It was impressive if you thought about it. In this situation such a background could be a good thing or a bad thing. One had to know him in order to be able to determine advantage or not. I did not think he had a commanding presence like most Marine officers. He had short blonde thinning hair with fair features. Nothing stood out on his face. He was the human being who you could not find in a crowd. He was wearing the seasonal green winter camouflage uniform and his "railroad tracks," captains bars, silver and shiny, were brightly evident against the backdrop of the Corps' dark green and digital camouflage pattern design. I could not tell how tall he was; although I am guessing he looked to be of average height. The defense attorney said he was a good Marine JAG and a fair man. So, I held out hope for Second Lieutenant Wilson.

Second Lieutenant Lacey Wilson had been charged with Adultery and Conduct Unbecoming of an Officer.

I also knew she was guilty.

However, I also knew that there was not enough evidence to justify going to a court martial hearing. So I was hoping a "fair and impartial" Hearing Officer would find in her favor. I also knew that there was command influence from Wilson's command to send this to a court martial...but, more on that later.

- 2 -

Upon a nod by the Hearing Officer, Major Antonio Montague stood up from the prosecutor's table, walked around to the front, faced Jake in the witness stand, and instructed him to stand and raise his right hand.

Major Montague was a very tall man, maybe six foot eight inches, with a close buzz hair cut with slight gray at the temples. Like all such tall men he had a slight stoop that would likely plague him into his old age. He had an olive cast to his features with a rugged complexion, as if he had spent a lot of time outdoors in bad weather. Maybe he liked to hunt. Yet, his brown eyes were intelligent and he had a commanding voice in that small courtroom. When he instructed Jake to raise his right hand, I felt like raising mine too. He was also wearing the same uniform as the Hearing Officer.

Looking directly at Jake, he recited, "Chief Warrant Officer 5 Jake Griffin...do you promise to tell the whole truth and nothing but the truth, so help you God?"

Jake, right hand raised, looking directly at Major Montague...down, at Major Montague, responded, "Yes Sir."

"Take your seat!" Jake then sat down, with his left arm resting on the edge of the jury box.

Major Montague then turned aside and returned to his seat at his table.

My friend was also wearing civilian clothes. Although his gray hair was in need of a haircut it was neatly combed. He was wearing a black suit, light blue shirt, and light blue tie.

Jake did not wear suits well. He was of average height with a stocky body that was constructed with weights. If I had to be truthful with him, I would tell him that he needed to lose a few pounds. His facial features belied his age and, on that day, he was sixty-one years old and had just retired from the Marine Corps six months earlier after a career of forty-three years and five wars. Most people thought he did not look a day over 50 years of age. I am not sure that was a compliment, but then again, Jake laughed at just about everything when it came to himself. He had deep dark brown eyes that whenever he was looking at you, you could tell he was placing you into some index file in his mind. He was slow to anger and always asked lots of questions of people he met for the first time. Wherever he had been assigned in his career he was appreciated by his superiors, loved by his juniors, and well regarded for the concern of the Marines assigned to his care. On more than one occasion he had placed his career on the line bucking a senior officer who had not done the right thing when it came to taking care of Marines. Within our occupational field he was legendary. He was a brother to me and had assisted me throughout my whole career. That did not mean I was not aware of his shortcomings.

Capt Adam Hatfield rose from his seat at the defense table, stepped to his left and approached the witness stand. He was also a tall man but with a slender build. His face was long and narrow with freshly shaven pink cheeks. He displayed a close-cut high and tight haircut...brown hair and brown eyes. I guessed he was likely around thirty years of age. He was also wearing the same uniform as the others. I had spoken with him earlier and thought him to be capable and amiable. However, I was not sure that was sufficient to save the young lieutenant. He carried a notepad and was studying it intently.

After a few seconds he looked up at Jake on the stand, and said, "Chief Warrant Officer 5 Jake Griffin...are you acquainted with the accused, Second Lieutenant Lacey Wilson, who is presently seated at the defense table?"

Jake turned his head to the left to look down at the second lieutenant.

I knew Second Lieutenant Lacey Wilson. In fact, I had known her for the past 4 years. I met her when she was a corporal, at twenty years of age, and newly married to another Marine corporal, and the mother of young boy, pregnant out of wedlock, and, the reason she had gotten married at such a young age. At the moment I was looking at the back of her head. Now she was twenty-four years old and was a mother of second child, a daughter. Another unexpected pregnancy. Jake had had a profound influence on her career and was one of the defining Marines that encouraged her to pursue a commission. She had submitted a commissioning package to a selection board and was subsequently chosen for officer candidate school at Quantico, where she performed in an exemplary manner and graduated as the number one female second lieutenant in her class. In fact, she was one of the few remaining females in her class after over half of her female peers had been dropped due to injuries sustained during training.

She was impressive and everybody was quick to make that declaration. She was hot too! And no male, Marine or otherwise, failed to take notice of her beguiling beauty. I know I did. Jake and I had discussed her on many occasions. Oh, fuck the politically correct bullshit! We were men and she was a member of a male dominated organization. What the hell do people expect? In our admiration of her beauty we did not take away from her exemplary performance as a Marine. She is slightly taller than the average female, but with long legs and a muscular body. Likely acquired from Marine training through the years. I had seen her many times in her PT clothes. She had an olive complexion with gorgeous dark brown eyes slightly turned up at the corners. High cheekbones suggestive of a Native American heritage with a full mouth and white teeth. Her hair was a dark chestnut brown, long, thick, and absolutely luscious looking... like one of those models in those hair shampoo commercials on TV. At the moment it was pulled tight to the back of her head and done up in one of those buns with a dimple in the middle. It was always a mystery to me how they did that? When she wore civilian clothes, makeup, hair down to her shoulders, dress and heels, some men would be entranced to the point of embarrassment. I had seen this myself on a number of occasions when all of the Marines got together and went out on the town. She was the kind of woman Marine they put on recruiting posters. Today she was dressed in the uniform of the day as were the other Marines in the courtroom.

Her husband was extremely jealous of her and one of the reasons why she was here today. Maybe justifiably, I don't know. I know I did not have any right to pass such judgment. The reader will have to make that determination. However, more about that as my story unfolds.

All of this passed through my mind as Jake had turned to look at her. I wondered what he was thinking that moment as he was looking at her. I know he cared about her. In a matter of a few seconds he turned his attention back to Captain Hatfield.

"Yes Sir, I am acquainted with Second Lieutenant Wilson."

Captain Hatfield looked down at his notebook, looked back up at Jake, and said, "Chief Warrant Officer 5 Griffin, did you ever have a sexual relationship with Second Lieutenant Wilson?"

The only sound in that courtroom was my heart pounding in my ears. The Hearing Officer seemed to actually be leaning forward from his perch. Major Montague was seemingly immobilized. Hell, I was one of his best friends and I did not know what he was going to answer. I dare not move and just stared. I was frightened for my friend and for Second Lieutenant Wilson.

He stared at Captain Hatfield...I thought his eyes flicked over the Captain's shoulders to look at Major Montague... and back. After that second, maybe two...I saw Jake open his mouth to answer....

- 3 -

Major Montague stood in front of the witness stand. He was shuffling through some papers he was holding. Then looking up at Jake he handed the papers to him.

"Chief Warrant Officer Griffin, do you recognize the documents that I just passed to you?"

I watched Jake take the paperwork and lean back and start to read. I knew Jake well enough to know that he was stalling for time and was trying to compose his thoughts. He looked relaxed with the index finger tapping lightly against his upper lip. I knew he was as taut as a bowstring but I had to admire his composure. If the persons present thought this was going to be easy, they were sorely wrong in their analysis. Whether Jake would win out in the end remained to be seen. What follows in my story is as best as I can remember, although I am sure I have left some things out. Later Jake would tell me more about the contents of the paperwork.

I saw Jake look up from the paperwork and down at Major Montague, "Yes Sir, I do."

"Please identify then for the court."

"These are copies of e-mails...five to be exact...that I sent to Lieutenant Wilson."

Major Montague examining a copy of the e-mail, "I refer you to the highlighted sentences in the first e-mail, dated 9 September. Did you write those sentences?"

"Yes Sir."

"Please give a concise summary of the subject matter of those sentences."

"Sir...in this first e-mail I wrote to Lieutenant Wilson

telling her what an enjoyable time I had with her the night previously at a local restaurant in town. Reference the high-lighted areas, I am also telling her how impressive her body is, how smooth and silky her skin feels, and how it is she, or any woman for that matter, can wear thongs. Although of course, as you know, Sir, I am much more descriptive and intimate in my thoughts in this e-mail."

Those fucking e-mails! Jake told me later that Lacey's husband had hacked her Google account and found the e-mails from him. At first, he had confronted Jake over the phone about them...in a respectful manner, as Jake told the story to me. After all the aggrieved husband was only a ser-geant. Jake had shrugged them off telling the sergeant he was over reacting and that nothing had ever occurred be-tween them and that was the only communications that had ever occurred between he and Lacey. That his own wife had shut down any further communications between them. Jake said it seemed to mollify him. Until a few weeks later he sub-mitted his complaint through the chain of command to the Basic School, where Lacey was investigated, charged and suspended from training. As the sergeant knew the Marine Corps severely frowned upon extramarital affairs. The fact that Lacey's marriage was on the skids does not factor into the equation. Plus, Jake was not being completely truthful with me at the time.

To me Major Montague looked a little bit smug at that mo-ment. Within a second of Jake's answer he was all over him with an accusation. "Then it is correct to state that you were intimate and had sex with her on that occasion?"

Jake just looked at him, waiting a few seconds to answer. "No Sir, I was not...and I did not." I must tell you reader(s) disappointment in that answer was evident on the Major's face (in the Marine Corps it is Corps etiquette to refer to a more senior officer in the third person). To tell the truth, when I was later allowed to review those e-mails later that day after the hearing, I would also have believed something had occurred between them. Jake's own words within the e-mails seemed to confirm the investigating officer's conclusions and that aside from the prosecuting attorney's present allegations in this courtroom.

The Major looked incredulously at Jake, and I know he was thinking the "P" word. How could Jake deny an event that was evident in his own words in an e-mail to Lieutenant Wilson? I was wondering the same thing. Yet, I knew Jake well enough that he had something in mind, or he would not have been present that day. He had been asked to be here, and was not summonsed. Regardless of being summonsed or not, he was not about to abandon Lacey to the wolves. The Marine Corps had no jurisdiction over Jake because he was retired. I knew that thoroughly pissed off the senior officers involved in this alleged scandal, and a few others I did not know about. Especially the commanding officer of the Basic School, where young lieutenants who have graduated from the officer candidate course go for follow-on training. Captain Hatfield told Jake later that day that the JAG office had already looked into having him recalled from retirement in order to investigate him for the same allegations charged against Lieutenant Wilson, and possibly take him to a court martial also. However, it turns out that it is a very complex process and requires Secretary of the Navy authorization. Therefore, as Captain Hatfield stated, in these days of fiscal limitations it is highly unlikely they would bring back a retiree to face allegations of Adultery and Conduct Unbecoming. The expenditures and man hours did not justify the effort. Lucky for Jake. There was no doubt in my Marine Corps mind that if Jake had been on active duty, he would be facing a court martial. The Marine Corps wanted him badly, almost as badly as the commanding officer of the Basic School. I saw this situation as like being in combat. Some people get killed, and others get wounded, and most walk away unscathed. That is just the way it is. Regardless of the outcome of the hearing, Jake would walk away having missed that one bullet.

Major Montague took a step toward the witness stand and in a louder voice than previously, "It is your statement that you were not intimate with, or had engaged in sex with, Lieutenant Wilson? That is your statement? That is what you are telling this court today?"

I can tell you this, whereas Jake looked composed and in control of himself, I was practically squirming in my seat. It was no longer cold in that courtroom. I was very concerned for my friend and for Lacey too.

Jake looked up at the ceiling for a few seconds, then turned his attention back to Major Montague. "Sir, I am saying exactly that. It is common knowledge amongst my friends and peers that I am somewhat of a writer. When I was on active duty the command always gave me the awards to write up. I have a number of articles published in magazines to include our own Leatherneck magazine. I have written poetry that has been previously been published in magazines and in a book. In fact, a few of the poems from that book are included in subsequent e-mails to Lieutenant Wilson. However, I know you know this." He paused for a second. Everyone was hanging onto his words. "I am saying that I was indeed trying to seduce the young lieutenant. I admit it. However, she was not quite so receptive to my advances."

Major Montague didn't hesitate. "Chief Warrant Officer, your e-mails suggest otherwise."

"Yes Sir, I can see where you would draw that conclusion. Please note, Sir, I have known the young lieutenant for four years. Before she was commissioned and as a corporal. And I would add in my defense I was scrupulously behaved around her as an enlisted woman. I know much about her. I also know she likes romantic novels...bodice ripper style historical novels, if you will. Therefore, what you have extracted from those e-mails is nothing more than literary illustrations on my part to try and entice her curiosity via the only talent I have to employ on my behalf in my efforts to seduce her."

"You admit you were trying to seduce her then?"

"Again, I state such, Sir. I was trying to seduce her, and unfortunately, I failed. After that fifth e-mail, and as a young Marine officer exerting her leadership skills, she explained to me whereas she appreciated my attention toward her...I suspect she was being kind to me with that statement...my efforts had to cease. They did and we are still friends. Although I am guessing she might be somewhat peeved with me for having to endure what she is undergoing presently."

At this point Captain Hatfield stood up very quickly and requested to address the court.

Directing his remarks toward the Hearing Office, he stated, "Sir, the witness has made statements that can be readily used against him if charges were to be brought against him. Assuming of course if he were to be brought back on active duty. I am requesting that he be advised of his rights by this hearing. Not to mention that I would likely be the defending attorney on his behalf."

However, before the Hearing Officer could offer a ruling or even explain Jake his rights, Jake quickly stated directly to the Hearing Officer, "Sir, I fully understand my rights and waive all of these rights on this occasion. If there is an occasion, I do not wish to answer a question I will advise the hearing of this concern."

At this point, frustrated or pissed off, the prosecuting attorney stated to the Hearing Officer that he had no more questions of the witness, and returned to his seat. I didn't see any outward signs of frustration on the part of Major Montague. Of course, I am only passing onto you the reader that portion of the testimony that I thought was most important. There was actually much more, but mostly in the realm of follow up questions trying to pin Jake down even further after the culpable statements he made. Whereas I did not quite believe my friend Jake's explanation, I kind of wanted to believe him, mostly because he was my friend. I was certain that Jake knew the hearing likely did not quite believe him either, but I also suspected that was not his intent for the hearing to believe him. Yeah, I know, it doesn't make sense, but it all comes into play later.

Speaking directly to Captain Hatfield, "Does that meet your rights concerns, Captain?"

Still standing Captain Hatfield responded to the Hearing Officer that he was satisfied, which in return the Hearing Officer asked him if he had any questions of the witness? He replied that he did and stepped out from his table and positioned himself in front of the witness box.

It is interesting to note at this point that all throughout the hearing, I never once saw Jake look over at Lacey. When I later mentioned this to Jake, he just shrugged his shoulders and said he could not remember one way or the other. He guessed likely some subconscious response to a sense of guilt. He really did feel responsible for her being in her predicament. Later when the whole story came out, I thought she was also responsible too. Yet, whenever I thought about blaming her also, I always remember what Jake said that afternoon at the hearing while being questioned by Captain Hatfield.

Standing in front of the witness box and seemingly studying the witness, Captain Hatfield, peering up at Jake and in an even-tempered voice, asked, "Chief Warrant Officer 5 Griffin, why are you here today?"

Simple enough question I thought, but for what purpose? However, this was where Captain Hatfield demonstrated his skill in a courtroom. He knew what he was doing and told us so later that day. I would fully admire his tactic in that simple question.

I have to say Jake seemed taken aback...he just stared at Captain Hatfield. Yet, I knew his mind was working. One thing my friend could do was to allow his thoughts to wander and be in a different dimension from the rest of us.

Really, it seemed longer, but it was only about a dozen seconds passed before Jake responded.

"Sir, if I may offer" ...he hesitated, " I am here on behalf of Second Lieutenant Wilson, who is my friend and to whom I have done a grave injustice. For which I apologize profusely! First of all, and most importantly, there is the laughable distinction that anyone would believe, or I would even believe, that a woman of her quality and twenty-four years of age would have an interest in a man of my age of sixty-one years. Yet, in combination with the end of my career, transitioning from my acquired status as a senior chief warrant officer to a civilian life where no one knows of me...not to mention the added input of the stimulus of my aging and eroding supply of testosterone...who knows the specific and cumulative psychological reasons? Essentially, I ignorantly attempted to seduce the young lieutenant. I knew she was having marital problems but even that explanation does not come under the realm of mitigating circumstances." He hesitated...

"Please continue Chief Warrant Officer," urged Captain Hatfield.

I have to say, I was hanging on his every word. I realized I was leaning over and gripping the edge of the pew in front of me in an effort to hear his every word. He was sincere is only the best way I can describe his testimony at that moment. The courtroom was his.

"Sir, please consider these factors. Lieutenant Wilson is twenty-four years old. I have known her for four years. I have mentored her career up to this point, extensively encouraging her to pursue a commission. I have written letters on her behalf and I believe she wears one medal that I had written up and submitted for review. I gave her...her first salute as a newly graduated second lieutenant during ceremonies at the Marine Corps Museum. In conjunction with these considerations, I was a highly regarded and well-known chief warrant officer in my command prior to my retirement. I have participated in wars reaching all the way back to Vietnam and I am entitled to wear seven rows of ribbons by four across, to include gold jump wings and the Joint Chiefs of Staff service badge. If you can develop this image of my career and my status, then you can understand why Lieutenant Wilson did not stop my efforts early on. I believe she was trying consciously to confront her respect for me, and likely feelings of friendship and affection too. Or so I would hope. Yet, she did put a stop to my clumsy efforts and she was kind in her approach. For that I was grateful. I unconsciously, and maybe consciously...I would have to think about it more, but unconsciously for now, I took advantage of my position and relationship with Second Lieutenant Wilson. I was in violation of the standards of my Marine Corps. If the Marine Corps wishes to bring me back on active duty, I will sign any paperwork and accept any disciplinary action."

I think it took a minute or so for everyone to digest what he just said. Captain Hatfield just stood there, Major Montague was shuffling papers on his desk, and the Hearing Officer just stared at Jake. However, if I, or they, thought Jake was through with what he wanted to say, we were all mistaken.

"Captain Hatfield, I have a request, I would like to make one more statement, if I may?" At which point the captain turned toward the Hearing Officer and by his facial expression and raised eyebrows essentially inquired if it were permissible. All throughout this hearing the Hearing Officer never showed any emotions or reacted to any of Jake's testimony. He simply nodded to Captain Hatfield his acquiescence. I knew in this kind of legal hearing that there was greater flexibility as what is offered into evidence than in an actual court martial.

Captain Hatfield turned back to Jake, "Proceed Chief Warrant Officer."

I watched Jake collecting his thoughts. I was as curious as

everyone else but I also knew that Jake spoke his mind when he was angry, and I knew he was angry that this hearing was being undertaken. I did not have a good feeling about this.

"Please understand that what I am about say is with all due respect to the officers of the court. Upon completion of this hearing it is likely later today that you will all be in your offices talking about what an arrogant bastard I am. My arrogance I well earned as a United States Marine...on the other hand my sense of anger is recently acquired. Today I have confessed my sins. We are here today because Lieutenant Wilson's husband does not have the balls nor the moral courage to confront his failing marriage and alleged infidelity within the confines of his own home and his personal life. By his complaint he enlisted the juggernaut legal machine of the United States Marine Corps to achieve assassinations. Certainly, to intentionally humiliate his wife and gain some revenge. An old story we all know well. However, the more distressing concern is that there are three lawyers in this courtroom today, who know, based upon experience and training, that there is not sufficient probable cause for these allegations to be heard by any manner of hearing. Further, the investigation that preempted this hearing was poorly done and smacked of investigative incompetence. I suspect we are here today because of undue influence from external sources, and I further suspect that the commanding officer of the Basic School is primarily the impetus behind today's actions. Be assured gentleman I accuse no man in this courtroom today of improper or biased actions. I know well the politics of my Corps. I know that your marching orders come from way above the level of operations present in this courtroom today. I also know that the commanding officer of the Basic School is individually selected by the Commandant. I, therefore, understand the powers at play. I understand completely that this effort today is to purposely humiliate me as the target and to denigrate my career as a Marine officer. If you expect me to fall to my knees and start weeping while begging for forgiveness...it is not going to happen. I am as much a victim of my globe and anchor as are each of you. I accept what has been directed against me, but it is inappropriate to continue to bring charges against Second Lieutenant Wilson. Thank you!"

It was apparent that he had said all he was going to say. Yet, nobody moved. I am not saying everyone in the courtroom was stunned into silence. I just don't know really. A few moments later, from his position in front of the witness stand, Captain Hatfield addressed the Hearing Officer stating he had no more questions and returned to his seat. The Hearing Officer continued to write some notes for a few moments. The sound of his pen scratching across paper was the only sound in the courtroom. I confess I admired his sense of composure. I was also certain that his face appeared flushed, or at least as not as fair as his facial features appeared earlier in the hearing. It was warmer in the courtroom now. After a minute or so, he looked up, stated that he would have a decision sometime in the near future, and that the hearing was now adjourned. Yes, that abruptly!

- 4 -

Myself, Jake, Lacey and Captain Hatfield...we all went back to his office. Once seated behind his desk, an old military metal desk that confiscated what little room in the office that was available, he instructed me to close the door. I actually had to work my way around the edge of the door just to close it. That's how tight it was in there.

He said he was pleased with the way the hearing had progressed and he was fairly confident the charges would be dropped. He stated that no jury in a court martial would ever find Lacey guilty with that kind of testimony from Jake. I thought Captain Hatfield was a good guy. He never made any comments about Jake's final statement. Really, what could he say? He did tell Jake that he should not be too upset with himself. Everyone made mistakes, and as mistakes go, this one was not really one of the larger ones he confronted on a daily basis. You just don't erase forty-three years of distinguished service with one indiscretion. I wondered if Jake was thinking the same way. I wasn't so sure.

Although I felt pretty good for Jake and Lacey, it was the "however" that caught me unawares. Apparently both Jake and Lacey knew this. I did not. Lacey was on suspension from her training company and was basically passing the days confined to her dormitory room. Whereas Captain Hatfield thought the charges would be dropped, that would not be the end. Since she was a probationary second lieutenant, the commanding officer of the Basic School could force her to resign her commission for any reason he chose. Any reason...physical reasons, moral reasons, academic reasons, incompetent reasons...anything. I had not heard of that before. I guess it made sense, because the Basic School period of six months of training was where the Marine Corps watched its new and young leaders very closely. Rarely did the Marine Corps hesitate to discard someone they thought could not maintain the Corps' ideals. After all, America was watching.

When I departed from the JAG building that day, I saw Jake talking with Lacey at the end of the passageway. He told me later he apologized again. He said they were still friends. Yet, really, think about it. They were likely the kind of friends who would never see each other again. Small consequence to still being friends I remembered thinking.

I would not see Jake for about a month. On that occasion he called and asked me to meet him because he needed my help. From the time I left him in the parking lot at Quantico that day, up until the moment I heard from him when asked me for help...I had not received a phone call, nor e-mail. I had tried contacting him but he never responded back to me. I just assumed he was off brooding somewhere. I know I would have been. It is a humiliating experience to have your personal e-mails read out loud in a courtroom to strangers. Not to mention the overall professional embarrassment and damage to your reputation. I understood and I had left him alone during that time. That is what I would have wanted.

- 5 -

As I told you earlier, it would be about a month before I would hear from Jake again. He had called me and asked me to meet him at Murphy's, a bar in Old Towne Alexandria, which was well known as a watering hole for Marines. We had been there before many times over the years. Lots of Marine Corps birthday celebrated there. Good times. If I recalled correctly even Lacey was there on one Marine birthday occasion. This was when she was still enlisted. Of course, I asked him if there were any decisions from the hearing. He said he would talk about that when we hooked up.

Jake was already there when I arrived. He was seated in a corner and already had a beer ready for me. It was good to see him but he looked tired, but overall he seemed to appear to be well. He shook my hand and threw an arm around my shoulder and then pushed me into my chair. I took a quick swig of the beer and carefully put the mug down on the table, and then looked inquiringly at my friend and waited for him to bring me up to date.

"Ed, I guess I have some good news. All charges were dropped against Lacey a few days ago," he said.

"All right!" I mean, I was ecstatic for him. "That is great news." And ecstatic for Lacey too!

"It is...sort of. I have a lot to tell you because I have a request to make of you. I just want you to understand that I am only asking and will not be angry or resentful toward you if you decide you do not wish to get involved. You know me and you know that to be true. I think it only fair that you know everything before you give me your answer."

I did know him and did know that he was like that. Jake rarely carried a grudge against people who had injured him. I could never repay back to Jake everything that he had done for me in my career. See, Marines weren't just close friends; they were often brothers, comrades in arms, if you want to apply some trite explanation. Jake and I had been to war together and had been miserable together and had suffered together. With that kind of background, you could not help but become close and lifelong friends that you could rely upon. That is just the way it is with Marines. The way it is with all warriors in any service. However, I could not think of any reason I would not support him, short of burying a body somewhere, and truthfully, I would have thought hard about that one.

"Listen, Ed. I got stupid over Lacey. I mean, all men get stupid over women all of the time." He hesitated, "but I also got very lucky too."

I was confused, "What do you mean by...you got very lucky too?"

"I had an intimate and sexual relationship with Lacey... about a month long," he said, while watching me closely.

I wasn't sure what to say, although I confess "lucky bastard" came to mind. But I immediately saw the issues at play.

"You mean you lied?" I said.

He leaned back in his chair and he heaved a huge sigh. "Yes...I did. Everything that was in the e-mails was true. In some ways I regret what happened, but in other ways I do not. If that isn't a typical male response. I have to tell you, that first night together was incredible. Although we did not accomplish the deed that night, it would certainly come later. I don't want to go into great detail here. Suffice to say I fucked up!"

I laughed, "I agree with that analysis," I said. I had a hundred questions to ask him about Lacey but of course it would have been inappropriate. I mean, honestly, I would have fucked her if I could have. So, I certainly did not blame him for that. The hearing was a different matter though. I asked him, "Well does the Marine Corps know about this?

"No...of course not. Look, I am still stunned she ever allowed me such intimacy. I am still trying to figure out why? One thing I said at the hearing is true...I do believe that I took advantage of her as a former mentor combined with my senior officer status. Yeah, I know she is an adult and made her own decisions too. After all I didn't tie her up and force myself on her. How the fuck was I supposed to know such a young girl would actually allow me to get involved with her. I was certain she would just shoot me down, we would still be friends, and go about our lives. I mean...what the fuck?" I am an old guy by her standards...I mean a really old guy. And don't hand me that crap about 'father figures.' Hell, it was the end of my career, I would likely never see her again, I thought I would give it a shot. I think this falls under the category of being careful what you wish for." He laughed, but not in humor, more in irony I suppose.

He was looking right into my eyes. I could see anguish inside of him. His face was tight with a display of concern. Yet, what could I do? I asked him how was I supposed to help him.

"If I had any idea where it would have led to, I would never have unzipped my pants. Of course, I knew it could possibly have resulted in all that has happened, but I just never considered it would. I know her marital problems were not an excuse. Just because I am single does not mean she was available. Anyway, it happened, and I need your help to help me help Lacey."

I asked him, "I have to ask, how did it end?"

"You remember, I went off to Europe for two months? I knew it would end then, and while I was over there was when her husband made her complaint and an investigation was started against her. Of course, with all of that heat there was no chance anything else was ever going to occur between us again. I wasn't in love with her. Although I was certainly smitten. It really was an incredible experience." He laughed. "I had no fantasies of fidelity on her part or a serious relationship developing while I was in Europe. For Christ sakes, the woman trains every day with hundreds of men, who I am certain the larger portion of which would like to be where I have been. How long is an aging fool like myself going to be able to compete against that raging hormone pool?

"Yeah, I guess you're right? Well, what is you want from me, how am I going to be able to assist you?"

"I got a phone call from Captain Hatfield two days ago, which is when I learned all of the charges had been dropped against Lacey. Do you remember in his office that day when told us that the commanding officer of the Basic School can force Lacey to resign her commission, if he wants to?"

"Yes, but is he going to do that? I asked him.

"Do you remember in my statement at the hearing that I accused the system with an intention to humiliate me? That this really was not about Lacey?"

"Yeah," I offered cautiously. "How are they going to hurt you now?"

"Captain Hatfield, spoke with the commanding officer, Colonel Mitchell, whom he described as a guaranteed general awaiting his selection, and a hard charging, combat veteran, religious zealot. He sees this whole issue as some sort offense against God and by extension a religious calamity. Mitchell never actually used the "God" and "religious" words, but Hatfield said that was what he was referring to in essence. He told Hatfield that the only way Lacey would continue training and remain in the Marine Corps was if I were willing to stand up in front of an audience of his choosing and confess my sins to everyone."

I was stunned! "Holy Shit! Motherfuck!" I was practically coming out my chair.

"I am guessing the audience will be every second lieutenant at the Basic School. Sort of an object lesson how not abuse their authority in their careers. I am guessing Lacey will be present too."

"Are you going to do it? You know damn well something like this will run like wildfire throughout the Corps? Fuck... the Marine Times will hear of it...you will end up on the cover page likely. Jesus Christ!" I was some kind of fucking pissed at that moment. So much for religious forgiveness and compassion. This was straight out vindictiveness and revenge.

"I called Captain Hatfield earlier today and told him I would be willing to do it. Well...maybe not willing, but I would do it. I mean what else can I do? I guess I see it as atoning for my stupidity and helping Lacey. I am sure she would tell me that she did not want me to do it... but, you know and I know she does not want to lose her commission either. A Marine officer's commission is only conferred on the select few and she is one of the select few. We can say what we want but Lacey has potential to be a great Marine officer. I won't see it taken away from her."

"If you have already made up your mind to do this, then how do want for me to help you?"

"I need you to go with me that day. I guess I need someone in the audience who won't be antagonistic toward me and won't think I am an asshole. Maybe spiritual support, I don't know. You were at the hearing that day, and now you know everything. So, I am asking for you to take it to the end with me, and I want you to ensure that son of a bitch allows Lacey to graduate without any prejudice to her career."

I looked at him, "Me, what can I do, why can't you be sure of that, or maybe Captain Hatfield?"

"I am sure afterwards I will be a pariah and could not get anywhere close to the commanding officer's office to ensure compliance with the agreement that Captain Hatfield has worked out. Besides I am thinking about going away for while, somewhere, just not sure where I will go. Lacy has another four months of training and then when she clears the Basic School, she should be able to continue her career without any problems. "

"Yeah, but, everyone is going to know that Lacey is involved, right?"

"No. Captain Hatfield worked out in the agreement that Lacey was not to be identified. She may be there that day. I don't know. I am waiting for notification of time and date. Next week sometime, I think. Anyway, that is something good out of all of this. If I were still on active duty, I don't know that I could do it. Since I am retired who cares? I just basically disappear."

Who cared? I cared! There was a lot more that passed between us on that occasion. Yes, if you wish to know, he confided more intimate details to me about his time with Lacey. I will tell you I was envious of his time with her. She would be quite the conquest for any man. I am sorry I let my male lust overflow in this story. It is just that I promised myself I would be honest when this story was told. When we departed from the bar that afternoon, we shook hands and exchanged the usual arm around the shoulder hugs. I told him to call me with the date and time and I would meet him wherever. I would stand by him, and not to worry. I have to tell you reader; he held my hand firm in his handshake, with one hand on my shoulder and looked into my eyes. I could see resolution in his gaze and he held my look for about ten seconds before he let go of me and turned away and walked off. His hands were deep in his jacket pockets and his shoulders were hunched up against the winter wind. Later on I would recall that I had seen other things in his eyes too but I did not recognize what I was seeing at the time.

- 6 -

About a week went by, and again I did not talk to Jake during that time. I sure spent a lot of time thinking about everything that had happened, what he had told me, and what was going to happen. He called me late on a Tuesday evening at home and told me the 'confession,' and that is the word he used, 'confession,' was scheduled for 1000 the following morning. He asked if I were still willing to be present and again told me I could back out if I wanted to. Of course, that was not going to happen and I assured him I would be present. I have to admit there was a part of me that just had to see this. Please understand me I was greatly concerned for Jake, but still, this was going to be a very interesting situation. I wasn't, like, all upbeat or happy, or ecstatic, I just was very curious to see something like this. I mean how many of us could do what he was about to do? Plus, I was sure Jake would survive all of this. All of this would finally be over and he and Lacey could go back to their lives.

- 7 -

I met Jake in the theater parking lot at the Basic School at Quantico. It was the second week into March and it was still very cold and remnants of a recent snowfall still covered the ground. He had actually worn a dress shirt and tie for the occasion and was wearing a bulky waist length dark brown leather jacket against the cold. He seemed okay to me, but quiet, thoughtful maybe. I wasn't sure. He greeted me and I asked him if he was ready for this? He shook my hand and again threw an arm around my shoulder told me thanks for being here and that I was a good friend and great Marine. I later recalled he did not smile at me like he usually does whenever he meets a friend he has not seen in a while.

We both walked side by side up the sidewalk to the entrance of the school theater. There was a civilian, middle aged woman, secretary looking kind of woman waiting at the entrance. She had her arms folded across her chest attempting to ward of the cold. She was a small woman but very nicely dressed with long brown hair to her shoulders and fresh makeup. She asked which one of us was Chief Warrant Officer 5 Griffin. She said she was there to walk him to the aisle where he would walk down to the stage. Colonel Mitchell would make some initial comments to the audience and then introduce Jake. Jake would traverse the length of the aisle and then climb the steps to the stage, where she said that Colonel Mitchell wanted him to stand in the middle...where everyone could see him...his words she said. Jake seemed to be listening to her intently and would occasionally nod at something she was telling him. I wondered if she knows what was going on. I guess if she was the Colonel's secretary, administrative aide, whatever, she likely did know.

Meanwhile I was looking around. It was an old building constructed of cinder block that likely was painted on a bi-annual basis with paint that some government agency intended to discard. Upon entering the theater, you were located to the rear and had a choice of two entry points into the seating area, either on the far-left side or the far-right side. I stood at the entrance to the far-left side aisle and I could see that seating was at capacity. It was an amphitheater style half circle theater with seating descending toward an elevated stage. In fact, there were Marines and civilian employees standing alongside the walls. All of the Marines were in the uniform of the day, which was the winter camouflage utility uniform. The same uniforms worn by the courtroom staff during the hearing. A stenciled sign on the wall indicated that seating was limited to 210 persons. There were more people in there than that. That son of a bitch was ensuring everyone he could get was present for this.

The stage area was wide and well lighted and constructed of some sort of light-colored pine...I think. Whoever was up there would be well illuminated for sure. It was noisy as the audience conversed amongst themselves with the occasional laugh punctuating the din. I could tell that no one knew why they were in attendance that day. I did notice that all of the women Marines were in the first few rows in front of the stage. I could not tell if Lacey was present. Since I was looking at the back of everyone, I could see a large number of the women Marines had their hair pulled back into those buns, like Lacey had during the hearing. How do they do that?

It was at the moment that I saw a tall Colonel emerge from a side door to the left of the stage. In a few steps he was standing at the stairs to the stage. I assumed this was Colonel Mitchell, I could see his eagles on his collar but not his name tape on his utility uniform. Immediately when he first emerged, likely an aide, someone yelled ATTENHUT! The Marines in the theater in one smooth and quick maneuver as a group stood up and came to attention. There was the sound of one huge thump that reverberated throughout the theater.

He bounded up the steps and strode purposely across the stage and assumed a position in the center a few feet from the edge. From his position on the stage he was actually at the same level as the last row of seats and Marines in the theater. To look at the first row of seats and Marines required him to significantly bow his head downward.

I admit readers he was an impressive Marine officer to see. I am a Marine and this was a Marine's Marine. As I told you he was tall, he had steel colored hair with the requisite Marine haircut...very short. You could tell by the way he came across that stage he had been a superb athlete. It was hard to tell his age from his face but he was likely in his mid forties...since that is pretty much how old most colonels in the Marine Corps are. He had gray-blue eyes and they were not kind to his audience. He looked out over the Marines and civilians and it was clear he owned all of them. I remembered thinking this bastard would indeed likely end up being a general. Marine officers like him had many significant accomplishments in their career, but there was no doubt in my mind that this Marine officer understood the politics of the Corps and was plugged in.

This was one Marine colonel you did not want to cross swords with. I was very fearful for Jake. I admit I was glad I was not the one who had to do what Jake had to do.

When he spoke, his authority was evident. He did not yell as if he were on a parade field. He simply stated in a commanding voice, "At Ease! Take your seats!" In one combined rumble all of the young lieutenants took their seats. Then total quiet. Everyone's head was cocked toward this colonel...expectant, wondering why they had been instructed to be here outside of their training schedule.

"Good Morning Marines!" he said.

And in once combined voice they roared back, GOOD MORNING, SIR!" He smiled in appreciation.

"I will be quick. I want you to think of this morning and your presence here as an opportunity to engage in a unique training opportunity. I assure you that you will not experience something like this again in your careers." I remember that statement because if I had been in the audience and had no idea of what we were doing there, I am certain I would have thought we were going to get a lecture from some war hero, or maybe a Medal of Honor winner. In a way, I suppose that thinking would be partly correct. Jake was a combat veteran.

The Colonel continued with his remarks. "I will allow our guest speaker to introduce himself to you." With that final remark he turned to his left and strode off of the stage. I saw him take a position alongside the wall with a number of other officers, whom I guessed were staff or maybe instructors. He stood with his hands crossed in front of each other and was looking across the audience to where I was standing. I have to say I do recall a tremor of fear run down my spine. I, who had been to war, and in combat before, I was more scared now.

By this time Jake was standing beside me on my right side. I saw him looking down into the audience. He took a deep breath and then he clapped his hand on my shoulder, told me, "Thanks," and started slowly down the aisle. I mean he was certainly not running, or slowly examining every step...he was just walking down the aisle toward the stage. You would think a condemned man would be looking straight ahead and not take notice of what is going on around him. Not so. Jake was looking intently to his right and I could tell from the movement of his head he was scanning the audience. I knew he was looking for Lacey.

He reached the steps of the stage, hesitated for a second, like he was trying to find the first step. He then climbed upward reaching stage level, where he slowly strode across to the center of the stage to where the colonel had been previously standing. He stood there looking out and across the audience. I have to say he looked relaxed, feet slightly apart, both hands in his jacket. When he looked downward, directly to his front, he suddenly froze. I knew then that Lacey was likely sitting in the front row in the very middle. I am sure that was the intent for Jake to see her. How I cursed that colonel from my heart! Jake was smooth though. He gave no indication of a previous acquaintance, and I saw after a few seconds he had allowed his gaze to slide from Lacey's face to the other Marine's sitting beside her...other women Marines.

Jake was an excellent public speaker. I have seen him speak in front of hundreds of people at one time, both Marines and civilians alike. He had presence when he got up in front of people and he could charm an audience. He was often requested to be a guest speaker for many different occasions. I, on the other hand, despised getting up in front of an audience. Somehow, I did not think he was going to charm this audience today. I remember to this day, exactly, at that moment, I wondered how much of the story he was going to tell.

"Marines, my name is Jake Griffin, and I am a retired Chief Warrant Officer 5, having recently retired approximately six months ago. I am here today as a result of an agreement I have entered into with your commanding officer, Colonel Mitchell." He paused for a few moments. "It is not necessary for me to outline the specifics of that agreement, just important for me to tell you that you are about to observe something that you will likely never observe again in your careers...as the Colonel alluded to earlier. I would like for you to listen carefully to what I have to say and think of this complete exercise as an object lesson on Marine Corps ethics and leadership. I will be referring to specifically what you should not do. Please note that when I have concluded what I believe meets the Colonel's requirements as per our agreement, then I will depart this stage and I will not take questions from anyone."

Of course, from the rear of theater I could not see anyone's faces. The lights were low except for the glare of lights up on the stage, which brilliantly shone upon my friend. I thought it must be hot up there. Yet, I knew all eyes were on him. There was absolute quiet. I could see the Colonel across the theater and up front. Light from the stage splashed across his person and I could see what I thought was a slight smile on his face. It could have been the light playing tricks with my eyes. I don't know.

"Six months ago, I attempted to seduce a young second lieutenant. I am sixty-one years of age, for those who are wondering. This young lieutenant was married. She was in her early twenties." He looked out over the audience, and I knew he was thinking about what he was going to say next. "I suppose it sounds simple enough, but it is much more complicated." He looked down at the young woman Marines in the front row, and stated, "I fully understand there is a gross factor at play here." I actually heard a few giggles.

Jake went on to outline his career and accomplishments and told of his last command where he met this young lieutenant. Jake had told me earlier that he wanted to be careful what he said because he did not want to provide information that would aid people in determining who the young lieutenant was. So, he did not state which command he retired from. He did not mention that Lacey had two children within her marriage. He did not mention that she was now in the middle of a bitter divorce. He spoke about Lacey in generalities. He did make statements similar to those he made in the hearing. I would remind the reader he explained that he realized that he had applied prestige and rank and seniority and a long friendship with this lieutenant in an effort to engage her in a relationship. Again, basically, everything he said on the witness stand during the hearing.

With all of those Marines and civilians in the audience it was getting warm in there. I had to take my coat off. Jake still had his jacket on. I could see that he was beginning to perspire on his forehead and I wondered why he did not wipe his brow. In that thought he took his left hand out of his pocket and wiped his fingers across his brow. Then he looked down at his fingers for a few moments, and then looked back up at the audience.

"I am not doing this today for any altruistic reasons," he said. "I am not here to fall on my sword to protect anyone. I am here because I was wrong and I humiliated myself, besmirched my career, and damaged a friendship. It is possible all of you can learn from my dishonor and mistake."

He was perfectly still after that last sentence. His head was bowed to his chest. I do not know to this day if he was looking at Lacey, or he was somewhere else with his thoughts and was overcome with a sense of shame. I thought he well met the Colonel's expectations and was going to depart from that stage.

In one quick movement his right hand came out of his jacket. His arm was crooked at the elbow and his forearm was parallel with the stage floor. In his hand, palm up, he was holding a gun. Even from this distance I could see it was a Beretta 9-millimeter black in color...standard military issue today. He never hesitated. He put the gun in his mouth, stepped back, turned to his right and pulled the trigger. All in a matter of a few seconds, if it was even more than a second. The resulting damage to his head was seared into my mind and likely into the minds of all of those in the audience. There was a spray of blood and flesh at least ten feet across the stage. His body actually stood upright for a second afterwards before he tumbled to his right side onto the stage floor.

They told me later that I screamed, "NO!" Then I started running down the aisle to the stage. Before I got anywhere close to the stage there were lieutenants all over me holding me down. The most I can remember is being in someone's office...maybe that secretary's office. I don't know but I remember she was there and there were some other Marine officers in there too. I didn't know any of them. I could not tell you if people screamed when it happened or if there was havoc or how I got to that office.

Epilogue

I never saw Lacey again. She never tried to contact me, nor I her. What Jake did I believe was derived from a sense of sincere shame. In doing that, he ensured that Lacey would be allowed to pursue her career without prejudice. As I knew would happen Jake's photo was on the cover page of the Marine Times. Not to mention the coverage in the national media. Yet, surprisingly enough, a lot of people wrote to the Marine Times speaking well of Jake and saying they understood why he did what he did. I am telling you the truth, and it is easy enough to verify what I am saying. From his friends to people he worked with no one ever criticized what he did. Many expressed sorrows at his act, but nobody spoke ill of him.

Nobody ever knew Lacey was the young second lieutenant. Nobody ever knew they actually were lovers either, for the short time of a month. For a while her name occasionally surfaced as the involved woman. However, other young second lieutenant's names rose right alongside of hers when there was speculation. If there is one rank of which there is plenty of in the Marine Corps, it is second lieutenants. Eventually, I never heard her name again.

You as the reader may think you know her name now, since I have referred to her as Lacey Wilson throughout this story. Her real name is not Lacey Wilson. Only myself, Major Montague, Captain Hatfield, and the Hearing Officer know who she really is. The only person who could have ever provided testimony to convict "Lacey" is deceased by his own hand and by his own sense of honor.

Whenever I think about my friend and that day, there were two things I remember specifically that kept passing through my mind while I was in that secretary's office. The first thing was both he and Colonel Mitchell were correct in that those young lieutenants were going to observe something that day they would never see again in their careers. And the second thing – that colonel was never going to be a general.

The Lonely Policeman

*"Alcohol is good at disinfecting things,
it can clean a surface or erase memories."*

—Richard L. Ratliff – Author

THIS IS A love story. Spoiler alert, it even ends happily.

Kenny Harmony was the type of police officer that new police officers looked up to. I was assigned to his patrol squad as a rookie police officer fresh out of the police academy. Before recruit police officers graduate there are usually about a half of a dozen police officers that everyone knows about because of their legendary exploits and accomplishments as cops. Kenny was one of those cops.

As a rookie cop it is required that I ride with a number of different police officers on the squad to get a feel for the different personalities and styles of policing. Plus, to allow them to get to know me too. I well remember the first time I was assigned to ride with him. As a rookie there was a place in the pecking order that I am unofficially required to maintain. Once I was in the cruiser with Kenny, that all went out the window. He told me to relax and that the two of them would have fun that night. We did too. What most stood out for me that evening was learning about his photographic memory. We would park the cruiser in the vicinity of an intersection watching cars coming and going. At some point, he would point out to me that the car that just passed through the intersection, a 1976 red colored Ford F-150 pickup if I remember correctly, was a stolen vehicle. How the hell did he know that? "Let's go get 'em" he said. He was correct and we recovered the vehicle and made two arrests.

On the way to the station he confessed that he had a photographic memory and always reviewed the hot list of stolen cars before coming on the street. I don't have a photographic memory but I learned to keep a copy of the hot list with me. Of course, all of this happened before computers came into existence and revolutionized police work.

I would ride many times with Kenny in the future and he never treated me like a rookie. I knew I was not his equal, but in time, maybe I would be as good of a cop as he was. All new cops wanted to emulate some veteran or another. Kenny was the police officer I wanted to become. He had an easygoing personality that magically seemed to calm down the most antagonized disorderly subjects. People just seemed to gravitate to him. He had a sense of humor and ability to crack off-hand jokes that made me think he had missed his calling in life. He could have been a comedian. The career was all about ensuring your sense of humor remained in place and Kenny's sense of humor was rock solid. He didn't take anything seriously, and he thought everything was funny. I didn't know it at the time that his humorous approach to his job was the initial stages of depression and disorder. In those days the department did not have a psychologist monitoring the mental health status of its police officers. That would not occur for another ten years. Management's philosophy was simple enough; do your job and quit complaining. If you have a personal issue, then deal with it. There were plenty of other persons out there who wanted our jobs.

Kenny was a tall man, maybe six foot and two inches, a slender build with narrow shoulders, although his head seemed just a slightly bit large for his frame. I doubt anyone else noticed. He had brown eyes well protected by arching eyebrows and pronounced cheekbones. For some reason I thought his nose looked like a last-minute addition to his face, not that it detracted from his appearance, because he had a full mouth, with a full smile, that appeared as if it had been forcibly etched into his features. A good laugh, where he might throw his head back, loose an airy guffaw, revealed solid white teeth. He had a full head of light brown hair that he combed straight back, but without any kind of gel holding it in place. By the end of the day his hair tended to slip slightly forward over his forehead, poofed up an inch or two into a mini horn like a unicorn. He was always combing his hair back off of his forehead with his fingers.

I had been on the squad for almost three years when I and other members of the squad had begun to notice his deterioration. The sense of humor was still evident, but there was a bite to his efforts, self-deprecating, and a forced sense of humor. He had started running a lot of calls by himself, cancelling backups, telling the dispatcher he could handle it, and would request assistance if needed, which was not the smartest thing for any police officer to do, regardless of capabilities and time on the street.

I knew about his divorce at the time. Well, the whole station knew about his divorce. As a cop, it is very had to keep secrets about your personal life. It wasn't a particularly confrontational divorce, just a sort of odd divorce. One evening Kenny had cut out early, asking the sergeant if he could go home because he was feeling poorly. In doing so he would arrive home about four hours earlier than he would have been expected by his wife. He found his wife home, and in bed with another female, whom he knew as a next-door neighbor. As Kenny tells the story he wasn't upset because his wife was with another women, he was angry with her because she wouldn't let him jump into the middle and participate. I could actually see his point. Regardless, he knew he did not have a marriage anymore. He did argue that if he and his wife were to get back together, at least he did not have to worry about her stepping out on him with another man. I could see his point there also. Yet, I knew, I could tell he had been hurt. I knew that he loved her because he told me so one night while we were riding together. Always with the humor and the jokes. I think his divorce, combined with the ongoing demands and stresses of police work, was the point of origin for his eventual breakdown.

I think the second impetus for his breakdown occurred a few months after his divorce. One bright and hot afternoon, he received a call for an injured pedestrian struck by a truck. When he arrived on the scene, he found a seven-year-old black boy deceased, who had just been run over by a tractor trailer, towing a long bed trailer. As it turned out it was not the driver's fault. The child had lost control of his bicycle and had slid under the trailer in which the child's head had become pinned under the rear wheel. The truck driver had seen the child and bicycle slide under the trailer and had stopped immediately. Since he was approaching a traffic light he had already been coming to stop and had considerably reduced his speed. Once he was stopped the driver jumped out of his cab and ran to the back of trailer where he saw the child under the wheels. Extremely over wrought and in panic mode he ran back to the tractor, climbed into the cab, engaged the gears, and rolled the truck forward just enough to remove the rear wheels from atop the young boy's head. It was too late. The child's head had been crushed and the pavement was soaked with his blood and brain matter. His head appeared as if someone had laid a rubber mask on the ground, empty, crumpled and wrinkled.

The area was heavily congested with traffic and likely the young boy should not have been riding in the area. What mother would allow such a thing? An examination of the bicycle revealed that it had no brakes. This was a common practice to disable the brakes and use the bottom of one's shoes to slow down or to stop the bicycle. It really didn't make any sense but that is what the kids in the neighborhood liked to do.

I responded to that call also and I saw the same things that Kenny did. It was Kenny's call so he was responsible for the investigation and reporting. I basically helped with measurements and traffic control. I helped the rescue personnel put the young boy into the back of an ambulance. It was also Kenny's responsibility to notify the parents of the young boy's death.

Police officers see a lot of terrible things. Seeing children injured is right at the top of those events that can keep you awake at night. Yet, telling the parents that their child was not coming home because he had been run over by a tractor trailer supersedes anything a police officer can experience. So it was on that occasion. I was not present and I would not see Kenny until the next day during rollcall. He was very quiet and subdued on that occasion. I did find out later that the mother of the dead child, when notified of her son's death, collapsed onto the floor engulfed in her hysterics. This one time, Kenny's congeniality had failed him. For the very first time, while we were walking down the hallway toward the exit to the back-parking lot, I smelled alcohol about him. I would smell it many more times in the near future.

It became evident to me about a week later that Kenny was confronting personal demons. Not so much with the remainder of the squad, all experienced and hardened police officers, who accepted erratic behavior as a rite of passage. When I think back his psychological condition could not have been more evident.

The squad was on its last night of evening shifts. Our sergeant, John Letzker, had proposed a shift party up by the power lines. The evening shift went to 2AM. Our shift parties were held by the power lines, in which you had to drive a half mile off of a main road to a small parking lot next to a power station. It was isolated, quiet and away from the problems in the county. Usually everyone was there, and there was food and alcohol and occasionally some women would party with us. In other words, you could get stupid and drunk, have fun, and burn off tension accumulated throughout the past week. The famous police novelist, Joseph Wambaugh, a Los Angeles police detective, referred to such police social events as "choir practice."

During roll call before we went on the street, the sarge would assign everyone to bring certain items for the pending festive event. This included a reminder that women were welcome to party with us. We didn't have very many women police officers in those days, and we definitely didn't have one on the squad, which we were all happy about. Sergeant Letzker was one of the best sergeants I would ever work for. As I will attempt to illustrate later, he was well aware that Kenny was suffering to some level. The sarge was a very interesting person and a study in contrasts. Ironically, he did not look like a cop; he looked more like a member of a motorcycle gang. His graying hair was combed straight back with a left part, all held rigidly in place by some unknown brand of brilliantine. His face was worn and lined, all likely the result of his many years as a police officer. His faced appeared as if someone had pulled flesh from alongside of his face and tied it off under his chin. He had a full mustache that drooped down below the sides of his mouth. In short sleeve shirts his forearms bared tattoos that covered almost every available inch of skin. He had many others, but I never saw any of them. One of the guys on the squad said he had a large tattoo of a tiger across his back. He had killed two people in the line of duty. One of the persons he killed pointed a shotgun at him, which was later determined to have been unloaded. When he tells the story he always shrugs his shoulders and says, "How was I supposed to know it was unloaded." He was legendary and he cared about his police officers. He could have easily achieved higher rank, but he loved being a street sergeant and protecting his cops. Many of the persons he had come onto the department with were now in the higher ranks, including the chief. He told me one night he had dirt on all of them. He said it was always the same with the leadership in the department, who mostly forgot where they came from, and now damned those cops who got caught doing the same things they did when they were young cops on the street. Especially the vice cops in which he could convey some fascinating stories of misbehavior. However, such stories are for another time. I once asked him if he hadn't been a cop what other occupation would he have chosen. With a straight face, he answered, "An Assassin." I laughed, I thought he was kidding. Maybe he wasn't.

At rollcall Kenny volunteered to order the BBQ ribs from

Johnny Boys, and he would pick them up around midnight and meet us at the power lines. Johnny Boys was located in the southern part of the county and it would take Kenny at least 45 minutes, likely longer, to get down there and pick up the order. The BBQ was renown in the DC area for its flavor and heat, and it was very popular with police officers. Possibly the police discount contributed to its popularity. When we showed up at the power lines that night, Kenny was waiting for us and had all of the BBQ spread out on the hood of his cruiser. He already had a beer in his hand, and I could tell that he had a few already. Our cruisers were white in color with county seals on the doors, and the occasional "POLICE" decals front and back.

The prickly hot smell of the BBQ was tantalizing and permeated the air. When I went to get my share, I could see the BBQ sauce had leaked through the white paper bags and congealed in dark reddish-brown puddles underneath the food. We moved the food from the hood of the car and started wiping up the sauce with paper towels. It was too late. The sauce had eaten through the paint and exposed a large irregular circle of sheet metal. That incident should give the reader an idea of how hot the BBQ was, and some inkling of the type of spices and amount of hot sauce generously mixed in with the final product. The consumer would break out into a sweat within a few minutes of eating the ribs. Goddamn they were good! Kenny would keep this cruiser for another two years and the damaged paint would always be evident.

That night Kenny would drink to such excess that he fell asleep on the hood of one of the cruisers. He was curled up into a fetal position with his hands trapped in between both knees. Or maybe he had blacked out. I wasn't sure which. I took him home that night and carried him into his house and laid him down on the living room couch. I wasn't overly concerned, I had seen a number of my fellow officers drink themselves into insensibility. Yet, in retrospect I recall some tiny worm in my mind that suggested there was more to this. It passed; I locked up and went home.

Since I didn't drink, I often ferried one of my squadmates home after a late night of drinking and revelry from our party spot out by the power lines. I really didn't give it much thought, or felt inconvenienced. The way I saw it I was taking care of my brothers. Plus, I was the junior officer on the squad, and it was expected of me. Often times Kenny was the one I took home. He always apologized the next day and thanked me for looking out for him. He was definitely one wild card when he was drinking those nights. One night he was laid out on the pavement staring up into a starlit sky, or as much as you could see of a starlit sky considering the level of light pollution that blanketed the suburban area. A small toad, about the size of a large walnut, went hopping by Kenny's head seemingly determined to reach the edge of the blacktop, and off into the vegetation. It would stop in between leaps, survey the area, and then abruptly leap away again. This time though, Kenny turned over on his side, swept his hand outward, and snared the toad in his grip. Balancing the toad on his open palm, he brought his hand up close to his face, and stared intently at the toad. The toad stared intently back at Kenny. I would have thought he would have jumped from Kenny's hand, but I suppose maybe it realized it was up too high. Unfortunately, for the toad, that was its last chance to pursue a bid for freedom. While continuing to closely watch the toad, he declared, "Anyone want to see me swallow this toad?" This was certainly not an opportunity to miss. In seconds the whole squad had surrounded him, with statements like, "I have to see this," or "Oh, this ought to be good."

Kenny grinned at the toad, and not taking his eyes from his captive, stated, "Five bucks apiece to see me swallow this toad." Maybe due to the level of alcohol consumption by everyone, and maybe due to the erratic one-time nature of the claim, the squad ponied up five dollars apiece, including five dollars from me, and I had not even been drinking. The squad was enraptured. All was still. Everyone attentively watched Kenny. A few seconds passed. He opened his mouth wide, hesitated, and popped the toad into his gaping maw, quickly closing his mouth. There was a collective expulsion of giggles and groans. However, Kenny still had some showmanship in mind. He slowly opened his mouth revealing the toad sitting complacently on the end of his tongue. It sat there calmly staring out at all the police officers surrounding Kenny, quietly, resolutely, awaiting its demise. It had to know, and still it did not try to jump out of his mouth. I swear, to this day, and I remember my thoughts clearly, I had cartoon images flash in my mind, where I saw the skeleton of a toad doing a backstroke in sea of stomach acid. In seconds, Kenny closed his mouth, concentrated, and with one gulp, evident by his Adam's apple pulsating the length of his throat, he swallowed the poor hapless toad, and I lost five dollars. It wasn't long before that story made its rounds, throughout the station and well throughout the other precincts. For years afterwards, he would find toy toads and toads in his mailbox, sometimes even live ones.

By this time in my career, I was functioning on my own. Sometimes I would ride on a call where I would be dispatched to back up Kenny. Sometimes he would back me up, but since he was a senior officer, he had the run of the entire sector, where I was confined to a "beat," a geographically defined area of responsibility, my "beat" being one of six or seven other beats within a sector. As I had mentioned earlier it was during this time that he began cancelling his backups while enroute to calls, which was sometimes me or another member of the squad. This was a very perilous thing to do. A lot of what police officers do is routine and repetitive, like responding to burglar alarms, which ninety-nine percent of the time is not set off by burglars or robbers, but by electrical spikes, animals, and employees. Yet there can be that one time, which does occur occasionally, and then you have an injured or deceased police officer. I knew Kenny was playing the odds, assuming it was unlikely each occasion would be nothing more than routine.

One night the sarge took me aside before rollcall and told me that he believed Kenny had been drinking before he had come in to work that night. He wanted me to ride with Kenny that night and to keep an eye on him. Possibly go park somewhere, maybe behind a school, and let him doze off and let the alcohol run its course. If anybody asked, my cruiser was down and awaiting repairs, and I was doubling up with Kenny that night per the sergeant's directions.

Kenny let me drive his cruiser that night. I did smell some alcohol on him, but the odor was mixed with the clean smell of the mints he was constantly chewing on. In my estimation he did not seem drunk. Some years later I would arrest a woman for driving while intoxicated. She was a very attractive woman, about forty-five or so. She was dressed quite nicely, a colorful dress and heels, her makeup was in place, her speech was clear and distinct. She politely consented to a breathalyzer exam and her results would be the highest score I would ever record in my career. In fact, in review of the amount of alcohol that she had imbibed that night, she should have passed out. Early in my career, and while I was dealing with Kenny, I was not fully aware of the concept of a capably functioning drunk. I did park behind a school and he did fall asleep. We received a call for prowlers a few hours later, but by then he was alert, albeit somewhat subdued.

A few weeks later I was awakened by the phone ringing about 3AM. On the other end was a police friend of mine who had called me to assist him with Kenny. My friend told me that he had seen a police car coming down the road with its lights and siren on, running through intersections, barely slowing down to see if it was safe to do so. There were no calls in the area that required an emergency response, and he thought maybe the car was pursuing someone or trying to initiate a traffic stop. However, the cruiser just kept hauling down the road whipping around vehicles that were in its path. My friend followed the cruiser and pulled up alongside at the next intersection, seeing Kenny, who he knew, sitting on the passenger's side. There was some other man behind the wheel that he did not recognize. The man had long hair and a partial beard and was wearing sunglasses, at nighttime. He didn't look like a cop. He waived him over, which the driver readily complied. The man driving the cruiser was Kenny's brother, visiting from out of town, drunk but not as drunk as Kenny. Kenny told his fellow cop they were on the way home and he felt he was too drunk to drive. Kenny had surmised his brother was less intoxicated, and the better off of the two to drive them back home. However, as much he was intoxicated, it did not stop him from displaying his excitement at driving a police car down the road with its emergency equipment on, busting red lights and intersections, and forcing people to pull off to the side of the road. "It was fucking orgasmic," he said.

Kenny had dropped my name, and the officer called me to come and get him, and his brother. I did. I was pissed but I maintained my restraint. I lectured him all the way home about how stupid and dangerous that was, and what the hell was he thinking? "Think of the consequences if you had been involved in an accident?" I remember seeing him out of the corner of my eye; he was quiet, looking out the window. Then I heard him quietly say, "I don't care, I am tired of this shit." His brother was passed out in the back seat, having fallen over onto his side, gurgling, sounding like rushing water trying to bypass an obstruction in a water pipe. Once I got him home, he and his brother thanked me, staggered off, arms around each other's shoulders, laughing and giggling as drunks do, and entered the house, only after a couple of minutes of fumbling with the keys.

After I knew they were safely in the house I drove off shaking my head. I knew now Kenny had serious personal problems that could cost him his career. Tonight's event was about as reckless as it comes for a police officer. If he had been seen by a member of the command staff, the outcome could have been totally different. He was lucky that he was not involved in an accident. He knew his friend would not say anything, so Kenny's career was safe at the moment, at least until his next stunt. I felt frustrated and I just did not know what to do to help him. I was sure if I tried to help him, he would push me away.

It would not be long before Kenny brought further attention to himself and his ongoing struggle within. A fellow police officer, Mikey Janes, who he described as his best friend, and who was likely enabling Kenny with his own daily ritual consumption of alcohol, was in company with Kenny on a number of occasions where both were stupefied and numb. Mikey was assigned to a different station but worked the same rotating shift as we did. He lived in the same neighborhood as Kenny and he would often stop by on his way home after completing a shift. They seemed to be always drinking. Kenny liked beer and vodka. Mikey liked anything that could be described as hard liquor, but an established predilection to tequila, salt, lemon, and all. Mikey was of a slender built, about average height, and projected an image of quiet complacency, until he had been drinking. He had brown hair and fought with a cowlick of a few inches that stood straight up at the back of his head, consistently and nervously always pushing it down. Sometimes when I watched him try to comb it back or down, a cartoon sound of "boing" would pop into my head as the recalcitrant tuft of hair broke loose and sprung straight back up. He wore glasses that refused to sit comfortably on the bridge of his nose and were always offset by an inch or more. When on duty he tied his glasses to his head to keep them from sliding down his nose. On those occasion when his glasses slipped down his nose, he reminded me of a distressed high school teacher, staring over the top of his glasses, in combination with a sour look, was trying to convey a sense of disappointment toward his student's poor performance. His complexion was an Irish pallor sprayed with freckles. He had two different ears; one was pressed against the side of his head, and the other pushed outward sufficiently far enough to where I often wondered if he ever experienced any serious discomfort in a strong wind. When he was in uniform, he had additional loose width around the collar, which was typical for persons of his build, and his clip-on tie hung a few extra inches below a prominent adam's apple. He was a good cop and good guy and he and Kenny were like brothers.

One night while I was enroute home after an evening shift, I heard the dispatcher assign a call for disorderlies to an address that I knew was close to Kenny's house. He had called in sick earlier that night, and therefore was not present for work that evening. Could it possibly be? I decided to run on the call. The previous night there had been a significant snowfall, and although the streets had been cleared, everywhere else there were still deep inches of accumulation, not to mention the huge piles of snow that had been plowed from the streets into residential yards. The power had gone out earlier that evening, and although the residential street lights were not lit, a combination of the cold and a full moon illuminated the area with a dirty wash of lighting that partially obscured anything distant. As it turned out that was fortunate for Kenny and Mikey.

As I slowly drove down the street to Kenny's house, I splattered the cruiser's spotlight around the neighborhood looking for whatever events may have prompted a call by residents to the police. It didn't take long to discover the source of the complaint. My spotlight suddenly illuminated both Kenny and Mikey, who were standing in the front yard of Kenny's home, completely naked, both engaged in the oft referred to "pissing contest." Of course, I immediately snapped off the spotlight. Not before I acquired a full image of Kenny, a full stream of urine arcing through the stinging cold air, creating blooming transparent steamy clouds, his efforts noisily splattering into the snow, establishing newly formed pale-yellow miniature canyons. He was leaning backward, groin protruding upward, occasionally thrusting forward, trying to aid in the propulsion of his effort, his right arm windmilling by his side.

Mikey, on the other hand, was about three to four feet away and slightly set back from Kenny, in which position he was a danger to Kenny who could inadvertently be the recipient of "friendly fire." His feet planted deep into the snow were slightly apart, and he was jerking all about the yard in his urinary intentions, his stream looking like a lasso trying to catch a bawling calf. It took a few seconds, but it came to me that he was trying to write his name in the snow. I remember asking myself if he was going to include his last name in his efforts. He may have been naked but he did have his glasses on, which I noticed were a poised a few inches down the bridge of his noise. His cowlick seemed especially prevalent when I had the spotlight on him. Both of them were drunk. Haphazardly and giggly drunk. They were having a good time.

I notified the dispatcher that I had confronted a couple of intoxicated residents on the street, who had been singing a bit too loudly in the area, and who had since gone home and that she could clear the call with no report necessary. Then I turned my attention to Kenny and Mikey. I harangued both of them and grabbed them by the arms, and half pushed and pulled them back into Kenny's house. Their skin felt cold and dry and even in the stunted moonlight I could see their faces were crimson red from the cold, and each breath shot out a plume of moisture that dissipated in whirls and floating wisps. Each had their hands cupped around their genitals. I was certain each of their penises by now wanted to flee for cover and warmth. Once in the house I got them to put on clothes and wrap themselves in blankets. The power came back on in that instance; I heard the hollow thump of sheet metal expanding as the heating furnace came back into operation. I gave them both hell for their actions, and I kept asking them, "What do they think would have happened if some neighbors who hated the police had seen them cavorting about out front?" Hopefully, no one did see them, or at least did not know they were cops, or didn't care they were cops. There never was a complaint to the police department.

Mikey died a few weeks later. He experienced a sudden stroke when no one was around and died face down in his living room while watching a baseball game. The medical examiner's findings concluded alcohol was a contributing factor. I had already reached that conclusion. I knew this was going to make things even more difficult for Kenny. At the funeral I, and my fellow squad members, kept a close watch on Kenny. I am not sure what I expected from him, or what might occur. I thought for sure he would have been drinking, or be drunk. As it turned out nothing happened. That seemed ominous to me. It was deadly cold and there were still patches of snow about dotting the cemetery. Mourners were pressing the palms of their hands against their cheeks for warmth. Kenny appeared stiff, his hands crossed in front of him, his face drawn, his features immobilized. He did not seem to notice the cold. He showed no emotion, other than to bow his head when Mikey's wife led the gathering in a prayer. I suspected he would be prone and passed out before the night was concluded. After the gravesite activities were concluded I offered to hang out with him for the evening, if he wanted some company. He declined my offer, and I knew he would. If it had been me, I wouldn't have wanted any company either. I told him I would call him later. I did call but there was no answer. I left a message.

I did not think Kenny was suicidal, although most times people, friends, and family never actually realize the symptoms for such a dire act were present all of the time. He was different, but not different at the same time, if that makes any sense. He still joked and laughed and was always present for work. Still, I noticed a distance about him, moments where I would see him lost in thought, eyes unfocused, but seemingly concentrating on some image no one else could see. In his detached moments, I swear I thought I could see a dark cloud hovering over his head. Something in my eye I guess, or just poor station lighting. The smell of alcohol was often present with him and he constantly chewed on breath mints. I know I often use the term "smell of alcohol," but for clarification purposes, it is not the alcohol itself that is the cause of the odor, but the alcoholic beverage that creates the smell. When an intoxicated person pukes on themselves, or into the street, it is the alcoholic beverage the unfortunate bystander smells, in addition to any stomach contents assisting the effort, as opposed to the alcohol by itself. Some his dawning days and his hangovers must have been hellish. Still it must be working for him, possibly relieves the suffering, or he wouldn't do it, or so I surmised. I did wonder how much more he could take before he broke.

Yet, he often displayed a sense of endurance. Some members of the squad used to get together on one of the days off and do some boxing. Nothing really harsh, just with an intent to mix it up a little bit and get some exercise in. Every once in a while, one of us would get a good shot in. That was fun, unless of course you were the hapless recipient. The day before one of our scheduled workouts I invited Kenny to join us, thinking for sure he would decline the invitation. He did show up the next day, and it was glaringly evident he was suffering from a hangover. He had not shaved for a couple of days, his hair was askew, eyes bloodshot, a face resembling an unhappy bulldog, with facial features swollen and sagging. Every few moments he would burp spraying his breath about. Holding a beer in his hand was a further clue that he had been drinking. However, his appearance was hardly the consequence related to the one beer he was drinking while waiting his turn to box. In keeping with his often-skewed sense of humor he had arrived wearing only a pair of shorts and a bathrobe conveying his readiness to enter the ring. Of course, it was funny, the jokes and humor were hysterical, and of course we wore him out for his appearance and pending asswhipping. The sarge was also present, who had previously boxed when he was in the Coast Guard so many years ago, and he kept repeating to everyone to avoid full blows to the "ganglias," whatever they hell they were. He said they were located in the area above the cheekbone and alongside the head. I remember thinking if the "ganglias" were that prevalent and vulnerable about the head, how come more boxers were not knocked out. So, there were plenty of jokes about "ganglias."

When Kenny's turn came to box, he was matched up against me. He had about five inches in height on me, which translated to a longer reach. Although I was shorter than he was, I was bulkier from years of weightlifting. I knew I could take the punches, but did he have the endurance to box with me that day? As it turns out, yes, he did. When the sarge blew the whistle, I moved in quickly and pummeled him about the chest and torso. Kenny told me later he could feel the power in my strikes and they hurt. He warded off my blows, using his gloves to protect his face, and his elbows pressed into his chest to protect his upper body. Then suddenly he came around with a quick right hand that landed smack dab in my "ganglias." I never saw it, and right down I went, passed out.

I wasn't out for very long. A few seconds, maybe. When I awoke the sarge was slapping my face calling my name. Other members of the squad were looking over his shoulder and I could see sunlight streaking toward me from in between the various faces. To a man each had a shit eating grin on his face. As my sense of presence returned an inch at a time I looked around for Kenny. I saw him over by the fence, fully bent over at the waist, both hands pressed against the front of his thighs, heaving up the contents of his stomach. He was quite noisy in his efforts. The air was still but the alcoholic smell of his stomach's previous contents spread across the yard like soldiers in World War I undergoing a gas attack. I swear in my dazed condition I could see a yellow cloud quickly forming, expanding into billowing fumes that carried the stench of vomitus to our vulnerable noses. When Kenny completed his puking exercise, he washed out his mouth with the beer he had brought with him, then drank the remaining amount in one sustained guzzle. One had to admire the man. However, festivities were done for the day, although we continued to meet every few weeks for the next couple of years, until the squad was broken up due to transfers and promotions. Sometimes Kenny would come and he always looked as if he had a rough time the night before.

A few weeks after the boxing affair, the squad had rotated to evening shifts, which started at 4:30 PM. Most of the officers had already arrived for rollcall and were waiting for the sarge to pass information and convey any other police business required for police officers to do their job. Rollcalls generally lasted from fifteen minutes to a half-hour and was an occasion for officers to socialize and joke around, in addition to addressing administrative requirements. Kenny Harmony walked in during that last minute, where a minute later he would have been technically considered late.

"Holy shit!" exclaimed one police officer. Everyone looked toward where he was staring. Kenny was sporting a new look, a new hairstyle, which could only be described as an afro hairdo. A perfect globe about his head, the hair was curly and looked abrasive. The texture reminded me of brillo pads. He must have gone to some women's hairstylist where they laboriously put rollers in his hair intending to create tight curls, and also probably put some of those small pieces of tinfoil in his hair, one always sees in movies when a woman is having her hair done. I had no idea what those pieces of tinfoil were intended for. The images I had of him in a hair salon, maybe getting a shampoo and rinse, curlers protruding all over his head, and the tinfoil, and maybe a hair dryer over his new do, did not sit well with me. Well, it was a prevalent style at that time and a lot of actors and musicians were displaying the new look. It was an extreme look on him. His fellow police officers rode him mercilessly, but he took it all in stride with a huge grin and claimed he was just trying something new. I thought maybe he was drunk when he had it done. I teased him too. I told him he could work in restaurant washing pots and pans with his hairstyle. He looked at me quizzically. I said, "Put the pots or pans on your head, spin them around a few times, and surely they would be quickly and thoroughly cleaned." He didn't think that was very funny. The squad did though.

I found out a few days later, along with his new look he had gotten himself a dog. He had purchased a St. Bernard puppy, which was about two months old. I came to visit him on one of our days off and was introduced to "Brandy." It was a fun puppy to play with and very gentle. Very round with mottled brown and white fur. Kenny said he got the dog for some company, plus St. Bernard dogs were known as rescue dogs in the Alps, and always carried a small cask of brandy around their necks. I think that was more legend then reality. He thought it was a pretty good idea, and had a barrel and collar made up for when Brandy was older. However, he filled the barrel up with vodka instead of brandy. Maybe he should have named the dog "Vodka."

The puppy grew up very fast. Within a year it had become a very large dog. When Kenny bought the dog, I don't think he realized how large the dog could eventually grow up to be. When it would try to run it was like watching a snow plow push through snow drifts. A "lumbering stride" might be a more applicable description of Brandy's mobile ability. Whenever Kenny left the house, he would put her in the laundry room with bedding, water, and food. One night when he came home after a ten-hour evening shift, he discovered that Brandy had chewed her way through the laundry room wall into the kitchen area. She was probably looking for Kenny. Dogs get lonely too. That cost him five-hundred dollars for repairs.

Brandy liked everyone. A watchdog she was not. One night while I was visiting and sitting on a couch in the living room, Brandy sauntered over to me, whom she knew well, and began rubbing her face and head against my legs. Not a bad thing unless the dog has lengthy strands of dog slob flowing from its mouth. Some portions of which had broken off and lay as small glutinous miniature ponds irrationally placed here and there across the carpet. The carpet looked as if some rambunctious and overly testosterone laden snails had sped across the carpet, posting shiny and slick mile markers every few feet, with intent to provide navigational aids to other visiting snails. Kenny was always chasing after the dog with a towel to wipe its face. Within a half hour Brandy was again adorned with sliver-slob, extending from both sides of her face, in swinging tempo in sync with her pondering walk.

One night while waiting for roll call to start for a midnight shift, I noted that Kenny had not arrived yet, although there were a few minutes remaining before he would be considered late. I did not learn until later that night the sarge had called Kenny at home a few hours earlier and had told him he was working the desk that night. Kenny had gotten into an argument with the sarge because he did not want to work the desk and was downright emotional over being assigned the task. All of us on the squad despised working the desk. One had to sit with maybe one, or two, civilian clerks all throughout the shift answering phones and dealing with walk-ins who wanted to report crimes. It was especially difficult to work because of the down time and trying to stay awake, and confronting the sheer boredom, and especially trying for a young officer who wanted to be out on the street looking for the bad man. The desk was often used as an informal instrument of punishment. However, on this occasion Kenny wasn't being punished, it was just his turn.

At exactly the required minute that Kenny was required to be present for rollcall, or he would be considered late, he walked into the rollcall room. He was wearing a woman's dress over his uniform, with his gunbelt on over the dress and his badge pinned to the dress' upper left breast. The dress didn't fit very well and wasn't buttoned in the back. It was a dreary and faded cloth speckled with worn out flowers. It didn't take more than a few seconds for the squad to understand what was happening. Kenny had often been vocal in his dislike of desk duty and railed against a system that assigned a police officer to work the desk supporting civilian employees making a third of his salary. I think the sarge was experiencing cramps from laughing so hard as he was bent over the podium and clutching one side of his body. Equally, the squad was laughing so hard together, with the number of persons in the room, it must have sounded as if there was an ongoing rally. However, Kenny was not done yet. When the rollcall room return to some semblance of order, and after the sarge wiped the tears from his eyes, he proceeded with passing required information to the squad and making assignments for the night.

When Kenny was assigned desk duty for the night, he leaped up out his chair, "Motherfucker!" he exclaimed. "You know I hate that fucking desk!" With that statement he unbuckled his gunbelt, threw it into the trashcan, handgun included, and declared, "If I have to work the desk then I am going to do it as a civilian. As a civilian clerk, I will answer the phone tonight as "Mister Harmony," and not as "Officer Harmony." He then yanked his badge from the dress, tearing a few inches of cloth in the process, tossed it also into the trashcan, and went storming out of the rollcall room toward the clerk's office. By this time the squad, me included, were laughing so hard there was some question as to how long it would be before we recovered and were able to get on the street.

Once we had all regained our composures, we had to pass the clerk's office to the building's side door that led to the parking lot. Almost to a man we all waived at Kenny and wished "Mister Harmony" to have a good night. That night, I and my fellow officers, we would call the station throughout the night just to hear Kenny answer the phone putting forth his name as "Mister Harmony, how can I help you?" We would pretend we were citizens, who wanted to make a complaint that required a police response, such as, "There is a woman taking a shit in my rose bed," or "There are two dogs having sex in my front yard and my three-year-old son keeps asking me what it is they are doing," or "My ten-year old brother keeps cheating while we are playing Monopoly." People actually do call the police for such unrealistic and trivial reasons, and have called the police for the calls I have just mentioned. When he realized who it was, he would respond, "Fuck you!" and hang up.

We had so much fun with him that night. If there was one redeeming trait that Kenny possessed it was his vast sense of humor. I didn't get close enough to him that night to see if he had been drinking, although such behavior might suggest that he had. Of course, there was the issue of challenging the sarge and his authority in all of this. Somehow, though, I think the sarge just left it alone and let it be seen as what it was, just clowning around within the squad. Oddly enough one can argue it actually enhanced the morale within the squad.

As scheduled, our squad would be working the midnight shift on Christmas Eve. That evening at rollcall, I could tell Kenny had been drinking. He looked tired, his eyes were red rimmed, and he kept staring off into the distance. By now I knew some of his habits well enough to know he was not likely incapable of locomotion, but probably should not be pushing a cruiser around into the early hours of the night, especially on Christmas Even when we would likely get a lot of calls for service. The sarge noticed it too. After rollcall the sarge called Kenny and I into his office. He told Kenny he wanted to put him on the breathalyzer and get a read-out on his level of sobriety, or level of intoxication, however he wished to view it. The sarge stared at him from across his desk, his look firm and resting directly onto Kenny's person, daring him to argue with him. Kenny laughing, nervously, I heard just a little bit of a high note in his giggles, acquiesced and followed the sarge into the processing room. The test is relatively simple, blow into a tube and the machine magically registers a reading. In Kenny's case he had indeed been drinking and registered a reading below the legal limit. He looked triumphantly at the sarge, who was grinning back at him in return. I knew some-how, I was about to become involved. The sarge told Kenny, "You beat it this time, but guess what, you are riding with your buddy tonight," and he pointed at me. Then said, "At least un-til the legal amount of alcohol in you has ebbed." He really did say "Ebbed."

The sarge made it clear I was to do the driving for the night. Maybe Kenny could come back to the station about mid-morning and drive his own cruiser around the remainder of the night. I preferred to be by myself when I was on duty, I liked the solitude, but I didn't have a problem with Kenny being in the cruiser with me. It would give me time to talk to him.

Police officers have a brother-to-brother intimacy that does not exist elsewhere in other professions, including within their own families. This kinship does not supersede the fam-ily, but instead supplements it as some potentially lifesaving force. A cop spends a minimum of ten hours daily with fellow police officers, and there is much down time, where police of-ficers talk about everything from family to politics. In some ways they are worse than gossiping old ladies in a knitting circle. It stands to reason this situation would exist since each police officer relies upon the other for their personal safety, indeed their very life, when doing their job. It is a brother-hood joined in defense against an unappreciative populace. Probably the closest parallel is being a member of the military, except everyone appreciates the military presently. Police officers are easy targets for a community's resentment, and a ready-made story line for the media, who rarely get it right, but generally, probably intentionally, lean a story in such a way as to suggest a police officer had alternatives, or didn't need to handle the situation the way he did. It doesn't help any when police managers quickly discard a police officer involved in a controversial incident for political reasons in effort to protect their own posteriors. All of the critics never had to do the job, and never had to confront violence, and in essence do not know what they are talking about. One wonders why any sane person would want to be a police officer in our society today?

Yet, all of that aside, such philosophic topics were not present in my cruiser that Christmas Eve. We started out the night with relatively minor calls, mostly reporting requirements without any confrontations. One man had his car stolen while he was in a liquor store making a purchase. It was cold out tonight, but he should not have left his car running with the keys in the ignition, just to keep the car warmed up.

So, I finally got the nerve to offhandedly ask Kenny why he was drinking so much this past year. I added that it always seemed like he had a beer in his hand, or there was some evidence about him that he had been drinking, like an ever-present odor due to the consumption of alcoholic beverages. I expected him to go into defensive mode. Instead, he laughed, he seemingly wasn't offended at all by my question.

"I don't know, really," he said. "I mostly drink because I am bored and if truth be known I miss my wife too. Not so much her personally, but just having someone around, I think." He laughed again, but with a sarcastic tinge to it, as if his laughs were more about him then any irony in missing his ex-wife.

"And, I like the part where I get to see angels when I am really fucked up," he said.

"What? Angels? Seriously?" Now I was laughing.

"I doubt I am really seeing angels. I long ago concluded they were alcohol induced. Although it would really be cool if they were real. Maybe they are just figments from my alcohol induced dreams, now that I think about it. Seem very real at times though," he said, his gaze drifting off through the passenger door window, becoming very quiet.

"What do these angels do in your dreams?" I asked, knowing I sounded skeptical.

He looked thoughtful, staring up at the ceiling of the cruiser, the index finger of his right hand rubbing across his bottom lip. "There are usually two angels, your standardized images of what angels look like, large sets of wings though. Oddly enough each one is wearing a gunbelt and each has a badge. I kind of wondered if they were maybe guardian angels for police officers? I don't recognize any of the faces. I also thought maybe they were a couple of the police officers from the department who were killed in the line of duty."

Not really a believer, I asked, how often he saw these angels? Were there clouds in the background, were they hovering over his head, wings flapping?

He appeared thoughtful, and actually quite relaxed in his expression. "Quite often, really," he said. "I can't answer about the background, a lot of clean white color, and I seem to recall them as kind of hovering, but no wings flapping. They just look at me, not an uncomfortable feeling, but more like how your conscience feels when it bothers you. That feeling." He went on to say, "I think they are trying to convey a message, or tell me something." Then he added, "Of course if they are real, that is." He laughed, and this time I knew he was making fun of himself. "Who sees angels?"

It was at that moment when the dispatcher came across the radio and assigned us a loud party call. Usually the disorderly level of the loud party call is determined by the amount of complaints made about the party to the police department. A query to the dispatcher returned a response there had only been the one call so far. Therefore, likely a low-level Christmas Eve party that was offending the one person in the neighborhood who had not been invited. Generally, a routine call for the police, which was usually resolved by asking the homeowners to dial it back a little, turn down the music, and remind the guests coming and going to be considerate of the homeowner's neighbors. Except this night was different.

When we received the call, we weren't very far away, maybe five minutes or so. We had already driven through the neighborhood earlier that night as a matter of routine, so we had an idea of where the party was located. Lots of colorful lights adorned most of the homes, and most homes had interior lights on suggesting the residents were up and enjoying the holiday evening. There had been a snowfall a few days earlier, and it was cold this evening, but some of the snow had partially melted in areas as a result of a couple of sunny days, revealing irregular patches of frozen grass and dirt. Although we were responding to a specific address, when we arrived in the area of the address, it was readily apparent which house was hosting the party. Cars were tightly parked on both sides of the street extending into the next block. The target home was festooned with colorful red and green lights, running across the roof and down the sides of the house. Every light in the house must have been on. In the front of the house spread across the expanse of the front lawn, there were lit up life-size religious Christmas figures, alongside of a large sled with a Santa, and reindeer "bounding" across the extent of the yard. Rudolph's extra-large red nose was blinking on and off. Overall, the house was quite festive in appearance and oozed Christmas. It was also very noisy with Christmas music streaming from the house and pulsating rhythmically louder into the night every time someone came and went through the front door. Through the windows we could see there were a lot of guests present.

We double parked in the street about one house down from

the party. No sense in being blatant about our arrival. There was no room to park elsewhere because of the large number of parked cars taking up all of the room. Kenny told me to pop the trunk because he wanted to get something out of the back. From the trunk he took out a gas mask and put it on.

I was incredulous. "Why do you want that?" I asked.

His voice distorted within the gas mask was deep and muffled, and he answered, "You will see, we are going to have some fun with this call."

He started laughing maniacally, head flung back, the movie madness kind of laugh that sounded like survivor in a cave-in screaming for help. I knew he was just playing with the mask.

He continued to rummage about and yanked out a riot flak vest, which he quickly donned, grabbed a riot helmet with a clear plexiglass face shield, which he set on his head, wiggling it around to ensure it was seated tight, and tightened the chin strap. Then he pulled the face mask down, a quick snapping sound, and it was locked into position. The helmet displayed "POLICE" decals on both sides, just over the ear holes, and the department's seal decal in the front middle, just above the upper edge of the face mask.

He stood tall, a position of triumph, legs apart, shoulders pulled back, head partially looking upwards, and beat the front of the flak vest with his fists, while spewing that play maniacal laugh of his, reverberating off of the inside of the face mask.

What the hell was he thinking, I wondered.

Once again fishing about in the trunk, although I guessed what it was he was looking for, he came up with a standard riot baton, in which he gleefully announced, "Found it!" This particular piece of issued equipment was rarely used by police officers, most notoriously during riot and crowd conditions. The riot baton is three-feet in length and designed for prodding and poking challengers, and not so much for striking an opponent, although it has been used extensively in that capacity.

Once having obtained the riot baton he slammed the trunk lid shut, looked at me, and stated, "Let's go!"

I had no idea what he was doing or what he was planning, but I took the lead and we crossed the street and started down the sidewalk to the party house. I kept thinking that if anyone saw us, or at least Kenny, with all of his riot gear on, they would surely think all hell was about to break loose. I wondered how much trouble I would be in before the night was out.

When we finally got to the front door, only a glass-front storm door between the revelers and outside in the cold, through the glass I could see a lot of people inside having a good time. I thought we would probably not receive any trouble from anyone. Then again there was Kenny standing a few feet behind me off to my left.

I knocked on the door. A woman standing close looked back over her shoulder, and seeing me, she just stared, surprised to see a policeman at the door. In a few moments she regained her composure, came over and opened the door, and nicely asked me if she could help me. I asked to speak to the owner of the house. She wandered off looking for him, or her.

A few minutes later, I saw a tall, black male of medium complexion, emerge from within the revelers and approach the door. He was wearing what can only be described as an ugly sweater. It was mostly of white wool, that depicted a Santa upside down with Rudolph biting him in the ass, which portion of the sweater was in color. As best as I could tell, Santa had a surprised look on his face. The man's hair was close cut to his skull and he had large brown eyes that seemed to be tinged in yellow. He had a large diamond stud earring in his left ear. He reached to push open the door and I noticed his hands, which were not large, but the fingers were slender, long and artistic like, ideal for playing a piano, I thought.

He opened the door and stepped out onto the porch. "Yes, can I help you officer?" His voice was deep, bass like, and seemed to me to match his presence. However, before I could answer I saw Kenny abruptly assume a prepatory stance, one leg back behind him for balance, crouched into a defensive position, the riot baton extended straight out before him, prepared to thrust upward if the owner made any aggressive move. Kenny then screamed, "READY!" The image was of an anonymous police officer behind a gas mask and face mask, outfitted with riot equipment, a menacing riot baton, verbally and aggressively announcing his intent, who now appeared frozen in place, waiting for the next move.

The man stared at Kenny, taken aback. I could see his mind working behind his wide eyes, the yellow tinge more evident against the background white of his eyes under the porch light. Or maybe it was just the incandescent porch lights smearing the subtler aspects of his appearance.

His eyes shifted back toward me. I was just as surprised as he was. I shrugged my shoulders, then I tried to explain why we were there. "You have a complaint from someone in the neighborhood that the music is too loud." In my best diplomatic manner, I asked," Sir, do you think you could turn it down somewhat?" I watched the man's gaze turn back to Kenny, who had not moved a bit during the exchange. I was expecting the man's mouth to fall open at any second, further defining his dismay. He turned back toward me, nodded his head yes, and said, "No problem, I will take care of it."

Then he asked if we would like something to eat. Well, hell, it was Christmas Eve and some cookies would have been nice. At the same time, I was hoping he would not invite us into his home. I had these terrifying images of Kenny sauntering across the living room, fully encased in his riot equipment, and preparing himself a plate of food in front of all of the guests, riot baton casually being held in place under his arm. I knew he would do it too. So, I politely declined his generous offer.

He thanked us for our presence, turned away, and entered back into his home. We stepped off of the porch but hung around for a few minutes to ensure he had complied with our request, which he did.

Once back at the cruiser Kenny dumped all of the riot gear back into the trunk. I thought to myself my fellow police officers weren't going to believe this story. I was hoping we would not get a complaint. It was that moment when it occurred to me, I realized that Kenny could not have cared less about a complaint, probably not caring at all if he were to lose his job. Nevertheless, that was how legends were made.

During his period of personal travail, Kenny had two girlfriends who were interesting character studies to say the least. I would guess he had other short relationships. It was not uncommon for police officers to further expand their contacts with a female complainant.

One girl he met at the scene of an accident, where she was the victim, having been struck by a turning vehicle while crossing the street, after departing from a local bar. The girl was a college student attending the local university and the bar was a college hangout. One of those local bars where there was usually standing room only, loud music, a musty smell you could feel on your skin, and standing in place on the carpet was like walking across a squeegee that had soaked up years of spilled beers, and who knows what else. She was slightly drunk, and only received a glancing blow from the striking vehicle, driven by a woman who was in hysterics, thinking she had run over a pedestrian. As Kenny told me the story a few days later, after he had written the accident report, he sent the alleged offending woman home, whom after calming her down, explained she was not at fault for the accident. With the alleged victim in his front seat, whom he described as really hot, wearing shorts and a tight blouse, blonde hair, and a recent summer tan, he pulled off into a parking lot to complete the accident report. She was very chatty, and impulsively, she leaned over and kissed him on the mouth.

Kenny admits he was taken by surprise, and looking at her,

explained that they could not be doing that here. She looked disappointed.

He looked at her, saw the hunger in her eyes, as he tells the story, paused, then he responded, "We will have to go somewhere else."

Somewhere else is where they went and she wore him out. Wanted it all and did it all. Kenny said it was likely she was fulfilling some sort of fantasy. This all occurred on duty. As a thought, the reader may recall, my statement where I explained how legends were made?

He said they went out a few times, but after a few weeks she wandered off and he didn't see her anymore. It was a fun time with her, but he thought she was just a little bit too young for him.

When I and other members of the squad went over to his house one Sunday afternoon to watch a football game, that is when he introduced me, us, the squad, to Amy. If the previous girlfriend was too wild for him, as far as I had observed, she was a neophyte compared to Amy.

Amy was one good looking woman. I would "encounter" her a number of occasions over the ensuing months, to include having her show up at my front door late one night wearing only a raincoat, stockings and heels. She had glistening brown eyes in whose sight seemed to envelop you when you were looking at her. Her hair was a brownish red color that was styled at about chin level and curled inward. She had a slender body with great legs and all the gentle lines and curves a good-looking woman should have. She was funny, liked laughing, and was touchy feely with everyone. She apparently liked me a lot. Too much.

After I had known her for a few weeks, whenever I was at Kenny's house, she would try to tease me. She would play footsies with me under the table, or brush up against me when passing me in the hallway. One time I went to the bathroom, and when I opened the door, she was standing there, and suddenly pressed up against me and started kissing me, her hand rubbing my groin. I can't remember if I responded back, but I knew I was terrified Kenny would come around the corner any second. One time she was at the top of the stairs and had pulled her dress up, no panties, and there it was, the golden fleece (unshaved). Of course, I wouldn't do anything with her, she was Kenny's girlfriend! However, I confess the temptation was a terrific whirlwind of surging testosterone.

I tried to stay away, but Kenny would ask me why I had not been around lately. What was I to say? I really was caught smack in the middle of a dilemma. The last thing I wanted to do to my friend was create further problems for him with his girlfriend. The night she came to my house scantily dressed beneath the raincoat, required me to exert all of my will power, and whatever I had available in the future, to send her on her way. I watched her walk down the sidewalk to her car, hands in her pockets, her high heels tapping rhythmically on the concrete, the back side of her raincoat flipping to and fro in sync with her walk. I practically had tears in my eyes.

Like other women in his life he stopped seeing her too. He never really gave me a reason, just said he sent her on her way. When he told me that, I swear there was a sensation of something floating up and away from my body. A feeling like being constipated and the dam finally breaks. I actually ran into her a few months later in a WalMart, of all places. She barely spoke with me, quite abrupt in her attitude, and made an excuse about an appointment and walked away. I was probably no longer a challenge, I guess, no longer an opportunity for a dangerous and titillating liaison.

Then he met Susie.

Susie lived in the sector, in an apartment. She had called the police one night because her car had been broken into. There was nothing to steal, other than some college textbooks, but the thief had broken out the window to the driver's door. Hence, she required a report for her insurance company. I actually caught the call. Kenny was in the area and had wan-' dered over to the location just to see what was going on. There had been a number of car break-ins over the past few weeks and Kenny wanted to see if this was related to previous incidents, which it likely was.

She came out to meet me in the parking lot. She was quite attractive and very pleasing to the eye. I would not describe her as beautiful, nor pretty, but somewhere in between those two descriptors. She possessed unique, and separate facial features, that set her aside from other women. She became prettier and prettier every time you looked at her. Her hair was a light brown shade that touched her shoulders and abounded in curls. Locks of her hair would fall across her face, and watching her routinely brush it back, seemed as natural as breathing. Her eyes were a dark brown and slightly almond shaped. Thick eyebrows carefully attended to. She had a pale, light complexion that was flawless, where one would have enjoyed stroking her cheeks with the back of a hand. She was tall for a woman, by only a few inches, which was enhanced by a slim form that a man would desire to envelop in his arms. A body that you knew would mold to your own. She wore a loose and light-colored cotton blue blouse that failed to hide what were hopefully perfect breasts, which was tucked into a pair of faded jeans that were a perfect fit. Not skin tight but comfortably ensconced about the turns and curls of a woman's hips and posterior.

When she smiled, even white teeth, were visible behind a small full mouth. At the moment, when I first met her, she was not smiling so much because her car had been damaged. She spoke clearly, her voice decidedly feminine in lilt and pitch, her enunciation of every word was perfect, avoiding contractions. Kenny arrived on the scene while I was conversing with her, gaining the information I needed to complete the police report. At first, he walked up to me and asked me what I had. He smiled at Susie and said hello. While I was gathering the information, he made a big show of examining the crime scene, bending down and sorting through the shattered glass, open and closing the door, which only caused more broken glass to break away and fall onto the pavement. He walked back toward me, and looking directly at Susie, he announced, "Looks like a break-in to your vehicle." He smiled again. She stared back at him, eyes focused on his grin, seemingly taken aback, as if to say, pretty obvious, don't you think? Then spontaneously she burst out a laughing. "You must be a detective," she said. Then he burst out laughing. As for me, I was nonplussed, accepting the evident ongoing male/female mating ritual as standard behavior for Kenny.

It didn't take me long to complete the report, and further explain there wasn't a whole lot we could do, other than step up patrol activity in the area, in hopes an apprehension could be made, but her property was likely never to be recovered. That was the standard line every policeman explained to victims of such crimes. Kenny chimed in at this moment, "However, I will make every effort to be in the area more often." Susie smiled in response, and suddenly she seemed shy, her head turned sideways and slightly downward, and she said "Thank you." I just rolled my eyes, said goodbye and headed back to the cruiser.

As I was driving away, in my review mirror I could see the two of them still conversing. Susie was looking at him with a huge smile, and Kenny was talking to her about any possible subject I was unaware of. He was quite animated with his hands, and he had a smile on his face that easily matched hers, his body and features slightly leaning in toward her person. Police officers learn very quickly to interpret body language in their careers, and it did not take a lot experience to analyze what was occurring between those two. All the better for him, I thought.

A few weeks later, Kenny invited the squad over on a Sunday to watch a football game. When I showed up at the front door, and knocked, it was Susie who opened the door. Seeing it was me she immediately squealed a hello and hugged me and told me welcome. To say I was caught off guard is an understatement, although after the surprise it did not take but a few seconds for me to be happy to see her. She tugged on my elbow and directed into the house, sat me down on the couch and said she would get me a coke. How did she know that?

It was a few moments later when Brandy came out of the kitchen, and seeing me, started to come over where I was sitting. Her tongue was floppily pushed to one side and the pink voluminous tip kept flipping up and down. She had the usual streamers of combined dog snot and rivulets of dog saliva, flipping back and forth across her huge gentle-faced maw in rhythm with her ponderous gait. Oh God! Recognizing me, I knew she was about to shove her snout and sticky bodily fluids into my crotch. Suddenly, Susie came running out of the kitchen, calling Brandy to stop, who dutifully complied, sat back on her haunches, tail thumping a cadence on the wooden floor. Susie, carrying a towel, knelt down in front of Brandy, all the while cooing to her for being a good girl, and stroking her head. Using the towel, gently wiped Brandy's face cleaning her muzzle of drool and nasal excretions. I swear Brandy looked at Susie with love in her face. In a second that huge blanket of a tongue swished across Susie's cheeks, which aroused a collective groan from everyone present. Susie just smiled and patted Brandy on the head, then Brandy got up and came over to say hello to me. I was really appreciative for Susie running interference before Brandy could get to me. Yet, I thought to myself, it has only been a few weeks since Susie and Kenny met each other, and already she had a connection to his dog, and willingly, and lovingly, tended to her. This was something I had not seen before with Kenny and previous girlfriends. As the afternoon progressed, between the snuggling and the long yearning looks from across the living room toward each other, it was evident that there was more going on with Susie and

Kenny then just a casual relationship. Certainly, more than the policeman to the rescue and how about dinner later tonight after I get off duty, practice of hooking up, which was probably the way it started for those two.

Over the next few months it was easy to see changes abounding with Kenny. He was always on time for rollcall, never again smelling of alcoholic beverages, his appearance neater and well kept. He no longer conveyed a dull and distant look to his eyes. Although he continued to participate in the squad's parties at the power lines, he did not get intoxicated anymore, a few beers and no hard stuff, and he often departed much earlier than he used to. At least I was not taking him home anymore and pouring him into his bed. The superior wit was still evident but not as biting or as bitter.

One Saturday evening shift he brought Susie to our rollcall, and that night she was to ride-a-long with Kenny while on duty. The ride-a-long program was the department's effort to interact with the community, allowing just about anyone who wanted to, to ride-a-long with a police officer during a shift. Kenny told me later that Susie had been pleading with him about bringing her along with him one night whole on duty. Finally, he had relented. She was warmly received by the squad, when she entered into the rollcall room and squealed with delight when she saw everyone, warm hugs going around for all of Kenny's fellow officers, and a kiss on the check for me because I was credited with bringing them together. If ever I were to doubt the depth of their relationship and where it was going, I would forever have it laid to rest that evening.

It was a late Spring evening and the night was clear and comfortably warm. There was a steady dispatch of a variety of different calls, but nothing that was overwhelming the level of available manpower on the street. As I remember, it was about 8 o'clock when Kenny called out with a traffic stop. As a matter of routine and police officer safety I started toward his location to provide backup. I was about a good ten minutes away coming from the northern area of the sector. I wasn't that far away, but to get there required traveling on streets that zig-zagged in defiance of originally projected route intentions, and highways that led away before they turned back toward his location.

It was about five minutes into Kenny's traffic stop when the dispatcher advised there was a warrant for theft for the driver of the vehicle. Kenny acknowledged the notification, and further related the driver had a friend in the car with him who was acting disorderly, interfering and arguing with him. I quickly told the dispatcher that I was already enroute to provide backup and I was about two to three minutes out. I immediately applied haste to my intentions and began hauling ass to his location.

As I came around the corner, I could see Kenny's cruiser, with the roof top emergency lights flashing, stopped in a convenience store parking lot. Along the left side of the cruiser, he had his subject handcuffed pushed over onto the hood. It looked like to me that he had the situation under control. He yelled at me to take the prisoner, and as I came up alongside of the cruiser, and grabbed a hold of the prisoner, Kenny sprinted around to the front right side of his cruiser. Where I was standing with the prisoner, I could see that another subject was on the ground, presumably the disorderly subject that Kenny had indicated over the radio, curled up into a fetal position with his hands covering the sides of his head. I know my mouth was hanging open in total shock. Susie was whacking him with a nightstick about his ass and thighs and yelling at him. The unfortunate recipient, a white male in need of a haircut and a cleansing, was screaming for her to stop, and with every stroke, the sound like a heavy muted slap, he would howl in pain. Kenny ran up to her and put his arms around her and lifted her up, turning her toward the side, and away from the soon to be arrested subject. All the while she was still swinging the nightstick at the now subdued subject. I need to mention accompanying her effort was language that I can only describe as non-lady like. I would have never guessed such vernacular could be spewed from her mouth.

I was laughing so hard; my prisoner could have gotten away if he had tried. Susie had finally calmed down, while leaning up against Kenny, her face pushed into his chest. He grinned back at me. Susie looked over at me and she had a sheepish grin on her face. She did not know it at the time, but she had entered the annals and lore of county police legendary stories that would be repeated at shift parties and social events for years to come. As for the previously argumentative subject, amidst his groans and now cooperative manner, he was quickly handcuffed and secured in my cruiser for the trip down to the station. He didn't say very much. I guess, while Susie was around, for him it was the better part of decorum.

Kenny told me later, when he tried to arrest the driver based upon the warrant, the subject's friend got angry. He came up to Kenny while he was handcuffing the driver and tried to push him away from his friend. Susie, seeing all of this, grabbed his nightstick, got out of the cruiser, ran around to the front and laid the nightstick across the subject's back, the sound a solid thud, and definitely the sound of a successful blow. The subject shocked by the sudden impact, fell to the ground accompanied by his piercing scream. Then Susie began to go to work on him. She later said that she purposely avoided hitting him in the head, remembering the stories of the many cops who struck resisting subjects in the head, and all of the blood flow that followed.

The really funny part came about four months later, when Susie's hapless victim appeared in court. He pleaded not guilty to the charge of assault and battery on Kenny, which required Susie to testify. When Susie testified to all that occurred that night, in company with Kenny's testimony, persons attending court practically fell on the floor they were laughing so hard. Susie was red-faced during the testimony and seemed a little bit embarrassed. She projected an image of innocence that seemed to charm the judge and the onlookers. When she stepped down there was a smattering of applause, which was quickly squelched by the judge and his gavel. Her victim was found guilty, but the judge was lenient with him, arguing he had received additional justice at the scene of the arrest. That statement evinced some giggles and guffaws from the audience.

About a month later Susie received a citation from the Chief of Police for her display of courage and unhesitating response in providing assistance to a police officer in extremis. The photograph of her from that night, holding up her citation, while standing with myself, Kenny and the Chief of Police, hangs on the wall right over the area where Brandy's bedding is located.

Six months later Kenny and Susie were married. He would study for sergeant, get promoted, and be awarded his own squad. By that time, I had transferred to the station's investigative section. I was one of the groomsmen during the ceremony, along with some other members of the squad. Mike Janes was the best man. A life size cardboard cutout of a photograph of Mikey was placed alongside of Kenny during the vow ceremony. It was a huge hit.

All police officers have a story to tell. Some of great pain and suffering. Some are able to put large portions aside as their life progresses. Others cannot. No one police officer ever puts everything aside. Many can laugh about much of what they encountered, applying a form of "gallows humor," a psychological device explained as warding off horror and stress, often only temporarily. As my career progressed, I would encounter other police officers such as Kenny. Some I was close to, as I was with Kenny, many others not so much. There are many other stories I could have included in my tale about Kenny and Susie. There was the night we were on duty during a blizzard and all movement came to a halt. Since Suzie resided in the sector, he was at her apartment, and warm and cozy, and whatever else. I, on the other hand, was buried in snow so deep it was cresting over the top of the hood to my cruiser, where I was cold and stranded on a highway all by myself. An eerie feeling, I might add. Of course, there are many other tales, but for another story someday. Oddly, as I have observed many times, the eccentric police officer always made for a superior performer. Kenny survived his personal ordeal and a blind man could see that it was Susie who arrested his freefall. Possibly, one could argue, maybe there was something to the love of a good woman that trumps all. Regardless, however the reader comes to their conclusion, Kenny was a great police officer and I am appreciative for having known him.

The Lady or the Tiger?

"It is often said that a wrong decision taken at the right time is better than a right decision taken at the wrong time."

—Pearl Zhu
Decision Master: The Art and Science of Decision Making

IT HAD BEEN a long shift. Day-work. From rollcall at 0700 to check off time at 1700.

Master Patrolman John Haines was sitting in his police cruiser parked way back into an isolated corner of the parking lot at the local WalMart in Langley Park. He had about another 45 minutes of duty time before he could call it a day and go home. The engine to the cruiser was on and idling because the air conditioner was a must today. It was hot outside, July, stifling heat combined with Maryland humidity that subdued the senses. He knew patrons of the store could see him, from far across the parking lot, but generally nobody really took note of his presence. Likely they would think he was providing security to WalMart, which he kind of was due to his presence, but in reality, he was on duty, waiting for his shift to end.

In his lengthy career he despised day-work the most. On evenings or midnight shifts there was always activity, and action and arrests to be made. On day-work a police officer spent most of the time responding to calls or writing reports about what happened in the nighttime. A lot of officers would be in court during day-work shifts, which meant double duty for the few police officers on the street. In essence a day-work police officer was just an armed report taker, often running from call to call. Of course, there were occasions when a police officer got involved in situations and had to make arrests, but generally day-work was slow and boring. Bad guys generally do not commit crimes in the daylight where everyone can see who they are.

Regardless, at the moment there were only four cars on the street staffing the entire sector. Three of them were busy on calls, writing reports. Even though his duty day was close to an end, he knew it was likely he would be assigned another call before the evening shift completed rollcall and came onto the street. He groaned inwardly thinking about the prospect of writing another report that day.

He was slumped back in the driver's seat, arms folded across his chest, his head back and resting comfortably on the head-rest. He had to be careful he did not doze off. The last thing he needed, and embarrassingly so, was to be aroused by some citizen tapping on his driver's side door window in an effort to gain his attention. Lazily he watched the bustling customers coming and going, his eyes partially hidden behind half-closed eye lids.

How many day-work shifts had he worked in his career of some twenty-five years? His thoughts wandered, and just like he had asked himself countless times before, he asked himself again how much longer was he going to do this? It was getting close to the time where he had to make some life decisions and truly contemplate putting his police career behind him. One of these days, he thought.

It was that moment, about twenty minutes remaining in his shift; the radio came to life, the dispatcher designating him to respond to an accident with possible injuries at the intersection of Riggs Rd and East West Highway, about a mile away from his position. The dispatcher followed up with more information stating they were receiving additional calls from citizens who said one of the occupants in the vehicle was pinned in. The dispatcher concluded the assignment indicating fireboard and rescue personnel were notified.

Even before the dispatcher had completed assigning the call to him, he had already turned on his emergency lights and siren and was speeding across the parking lot. Slowing down as he approached the exit, seeing no vehicles in his path, he shot across two lanes, swung the cruiser hard to his left, accelerated and sped up the hill toward the location of the accident. Amused, he thought to himself, he must have put on a pretty good show for the local citizens who watched him hauling ass across the parking lot.

Moments later as he crested the hill he could immediately see what had happened. Cars were stopped everywhere, in all four directions approaching the below intersection, and a number of onlookers had gathered on the sidewalk, in the roadway, and alongside a light blue Toyota Rav 4. Two men were yanking on the Toyota's driver's side door trying to force it open. A dump truck positioned about five feet from the Toyota apparently had t-boned the Toyota, crumpling the driver's side inward, pushing the driver of the vehicle into the middle of the car. Now the driver was trapped inside the car.

He brought his cruiser to a stop about three car lengths behind the Toyota. So far fireboard and rescue personnel were not on the scene. He would learn later that the closest fire station with rescue personnel had been previously dispatched to another call, and that fire and rescue personnel assigned to his accident were coming from another station. What previously would have taken only a few minutes to arrive at the scene now had an extra ten to fifteen minutes, or more, added to the response time.

The dump truck had obviously struck the Toyota, but that did not necessarily mean the driver of the dump truck was at fault for the accident. Whereas the Toyota was a crumpled tin can, the dump truck displayed minor damage to the front bumper and grill area. One or the other had likely run the red light. He wondered if the driver of the Toyota had even seen the truck before it struck him. It was going to be his job to determine who was at fault. There were certainly a lot of potential witnesses around. He was praying the evening shift would come on duty quickly and take this report for him. That was normally the practice, to relieve day-work police officers from calls they had received close to check-off time. At the moment it was his accident scene and his report.

Advising the dispatcher that he was on the scene, while simultaneously conveying that the driver was indeed trapped inside his vehicle, he noted in the rear-view mirror that more cars were coming over the hill and stopping in the roadway. This was going to be a major cluster, he thought. He needed more cars to assist him, but there weren't any other assets available to support him.

Quickly exiting from the vehicle, he started back toward his trunk to get some flares to close off the road. Immediately he smelled gasoline and knew he would not be able to use flares in this situation. He turned back toward the damaged car, and by now the two men originally trying to get the door open had given up and were bent over and talking with the driver through the smashed window and the punched in door. As he approached the vehicle there was the sound of shattered safety glass being ground into the pavement beneath his shoes. The smell of gasoline was much stronger now. When he leaned over and peered into the vehicle through the damaged driver's door, he observed a man, his face entirely covered in blood, two eyes within staring back at him. Seeing the policeman, a gap opened in the bloody face, and a frightened voice spilled out, "I am stuck and I can't get my legs out from under the dashboard, I don't know what is holding them back." Looking down at the man's legs he could see that his jean trousers were ripped down the side and blood was dripping onto the floorboards from an unknown source. His right knee had been peeled back by the dashboard providing any onlooker with a view of the anatomical makeup of the human knee. An airbag, initiated from within the steering wheel, hung limp and seemingly useless, and partially covered the man's lap. It was easy to see why the driver was in his present predicament. The Toyota was definitely totaled and had basically been compressed into a ball of wrinkled metal. It would take a lot of different pieces of extrication equipment to get him out. Where the hell were the rescue personnel?

He was helpless to aid the driver. Until fireboard arrived on the scene, all he could do was try to preserve and protect the accident scene and try to keep the injured driver calm. Realizing that the gasoline smell was stronger now, he got down on his hands and knees and looked under the vehicle.

He could see it now, gas dripping from the area of the engine, which had been partially dislodged from its mounts, and violently shoved into the vehicle's firewall that separated the engine compartment from the driver and passenger area. Possibly the damaged engine was aiding in keeping the driver pinned in the vehicle. It appeared to be protruding partially into the same area of the firewall where the driver's legs were positioned.

However, the primary concern was the gas dripping from the engine onto the pavement. Underneath the Toyota gas had puddled vehicle-wide, which further extended beyond the passenger's side in slender rivulets that snaked away from the vehicle adhering to the slight downward slope of the side of the roadway. Standing up, facing onlookers, his arms outstretched, he flapped slow sweeping gestures, back and forth, trying to push people back without actually touching anyone, while simultaneously announcing to persons close to the vehicle and watching from the sidewalks, to back up due to additional danger. Some persons quickly obeyed him, while others reluctantly started to back up, but required additional commands and emphasis from him.

Satisfied he had pushed everyone back out of the danger zone; he quickly went to his cruiser, opened the trunk and retrieved a small fire extinguisher. Slamming the trunk shut he started back toward the Toyota and the hapless victim of the accident. As he passed the driver's door to his cruiser, he heard a popping sound. He saw the explosion before he heard it. The shock wave knocked him down to the ground, thrumming his senses. Lying on the ground he knew what likely had happened. In the span of a few thoughts he realized there must have been an open flame somewhere around the engine block, concealed under the hood of the vehicle. It had likely been isolated to a small area of the engine, if it had been viewed by an observer, it would have seemed like a tiny and seemingly harmless flame flickering about. This time it spread those few inches necessary to ignite the gas dripping out from under the displaced engine. In the movies someone, or something, lights a gas trail and the camera dramatically follows the trail of flames to some ignition point, which results in a large and impressive explosion. In reality all of the gas explodes as one element and it all occurs well before the sound reaches the human ear.

Aside from what he thought may have occurred, the Toyota was now a blazing inferno and flames had consumed the leaking gas across the pavement. He ran up to the vehicle's driver's door and began spraying the contents of the fire extinguisher into the passenger compartment, attempting to hold back any flames that might reach the pinned in driver. In the direction he sprayed, fire suppressant chemicals released from the extinguisher were expelled in a mighty and noisy and sharp whooshing sound. The interior of the vehicle disappeared in an off-white cloud that leaked from the interior of the vehicle into the air.

For a few brief seconds, it appeared he could hold the flames back. Then he realized quickly the moment was lost. As the chemical cloud began to disperse and settle to the floor of the burning vehicle, he could see the driver's face and head had been scorched, and the blood that had previously covered his face had been seared from his features. His hair was gone and the surface of his now bald pate was multicolored in hues of red and purple highlighting the suddenness of the enshrouding fire.

The man was screaming! Screaming like nothing he had ever heard before. His clothing was on fire and the flames were licking upward toward his neck and face. He convulsed in agony, his torso violently rocking back and forth, mouth wide open, head flung backward, and screaming hysterically. **"HELP ME...PLEASE GOD HELP ME!!"** The man's suffering was so intense the vehicle was rocking back and forth.

All occurring in a matter of seconds, Haines watched

helplessly as the man's inhuman screams, steady and accelerated, pleaded for salvation. What was he to do? He would not hesitate to reach in and pull him from the fire if he were not pinned under the dashboard. All he could conceivably do was watch the man burn to death. He realized the crowd of onlookers was yelling at him to do something. Looking at the people he could not hear the voices, he was so stunned by what the tragedy unfolding before his eyes. He could see their anger and demands etched into the contorted expressions on their faces, their fists pumping the air, leaning aggressively forward from the safety of the area where he had pushed them back not five minutes ago.

In an instant his mind reeled backwards to a class at the police academy where an accident instructor had lectured on this exact type of event. At that time, he said, "You may have to watch someone burn to death." The driver, passenger, even children, not to mention the family pet. You are going to want to aid them, and on their behalf, you will likely do everything you can in your power. It could include being injured, just short of giving up your own life in an effort to put them out of their agony. The instructor hesitated for a moment, and then said, "Whatever you do, don't shoot them." Looking down at the class from the podium, he said, "I am required to tell you that, but in ending the class, I would say to you, if you should ever confront such horror, what would you want if you were the person pinned inside of a vehicle that was on fire?"

Even now after some seconds the man was still screaming, the onlookers were demanding action. Somewhere in the back of his thoughts he could hear sirens in the distance, but they would be too late. The man continued to scream, earth shattering shrieks that penetrated him as if needles had been plunged into his eyes. The complete vehicle was engulfed in flames. The victim was pleading for someone to kill him. His hand impulsively grabbed the butt of his holstered Beretta 9-millimeter handgun.

Within the space of time prior to even giving existence to a thought, his mind was awhirl with indecision. Fear, horror, pleas! The handgun was now in his hand. The man's screams, the onlookers, and witnesses, he had to do something. But what! What would be the repercussions if he did shoot him? Termination, criminal charges, civil charges? His conscience one way or the other? These images would stay with him daily for the remainder of his life. How is it he is standing here watching this man die under the most unimaginable of horrific circumstances, and he was helpless to do anything. There was only the one option available to him.

It flashed in his mind, what would he want done if he were the victim in this situation? Or would he selfishly demand death to relieve his agony at the expense of another human being's spirit?

A block of memory emerged from his college days. A story he had once read for an English assignment. A man had been confined to an arena facing possible death for the amusement of others. He was offered an ability to choose his fate by selecting and opening one of two doors. Behind one door was a tiger, that would likely kill him in a violent manner. Behind the other door was a beautiful lady, his life would be saved, and with whom he could choose to spend the remainder of his life with. The protagonist was immobilized with fear and indecision.

He had to do it; every second for the man was raw agony. Yet, could he do it? Should he do it? His hand subconsciously squeezed the grip...then the weapon was unholstered and in his hand. Oh God, help me make a decision, he prayed.

The lady or the tiger?